THE PHARM HOUSE

Frontispiece

THE PHARM HOUSE

A Novel
By

Bill Powers

Hope You Enjoy!

All The Best

Bill Powers

The Pharm House

Donnalnk Publications, L.L.C. 2014
Registered offices: 12750 Sophiamarie Loop, Orlando, FL 32828, United States
www.donnaink.org | (888) 564-7741

First Edition Digital | First Edition Print – Revised 2014.

For more information: bulk orders and/or marketing and promotions contact the Special Markets Division at special_markets@donnaink.org
12750 Sophiamarie Loop, Orlando, FL 32828

Library of Congress Cataloging-in-Publication Data: 2013936105

Powers, Bill–Author, 2014.
The Pharm House / Bill Powers.
440 p. cm.
ISBN – 13 – 978-0-9885388-8-7 (alk. paper)
ISBN – 13 - 978-0-9885388-9-4 (alk. digital)
1-Literature-fiction, 2-Medical Mystery-fiction, 3-Men's Adventure-fiction, 4-Suspense-fiction, 54-Thriller-fiction, 6-Pharmceuticals-fiction, 7-Medicine-fiction, 8-Corporations-fiction, 9-United States-fiction, 10-African American-fiction.
First Edition 10 9 8 7 6 5 4 3 2 1; May 2014

Contents

Dedication

To my parents, William and Annie Powers.

To Dad, for showing me the real meaning of, and how, to be a man.

To Mom, for schooling me in the love of books and stories and for teaching me words are my friends and toys.

All I am I owe each of you.

Epigraph

"If injury has to be done to a man, it should be so severe that his vengeance need not be feared."

Niccolò Machiavelli

Prelude

On a cold rainy Saturday night in Manhattan, now an early Sunday morning in January, the $2,000.00 a night suite at the Peninsula Hotel looked like a room whose occupants had gotten more than their money's worth. Remnants of gourmet meals, short-charred cigars and cigarette butts shared a well-used bar. Ornate Sake cups were scattered throughout the room, large windows looked out over mid-town and it was as close to being a city at sleep as it could ever be.

The meeting was finally ending, business concluded. The participants (most, but not all, middle-aged men) hoped their host had arranged post-meeting entertainment "party girls," who were routinely scheduled to provide needed relief, but they were severely disappointed. Not that the host didn't enjoy the company of young women. He just didn't want to attract any unnecessary attention to his business group.

At last, the men were able to gather their belongings, say their good-byes, put on their heavy overcoats and leave.

The business operations called for the participants to stay at four or five differing hotels around mid-town.

As they departed, some were picked up by limos, others by taxis and a few walked. Large sheets of icy rain continued blowing across the almost empty streets. The wind and rain had slacked, but an umbrella was still required.

One guest had been living in France with his wife and children for nearly five years. While there he acquired a taste for all things French, especially young French women.

He stayed at the Parker Meridian where he had an expensive arrangement with the assistant manager. After he placed a call, he could expect a girl who only spoke French and would be waiting in his suite for his return.

The eager businessman, consumed in his thoughts of the prize awaiting him, envisioned the young woman's small breasts and firm curved hips. He imagined the musky aroma of a sexually aroused young woman and succeeded in producing a rather large erection.

A bump came from a passerby. It wasn't so hard as to knock him off balance and there was no verbal "excuse me." He considered the contact yet another example of American rudeness. It was only after the stranger was several steps away that a noticeable stinging sensation began. At first it seemed to be just a dull pulsation – then more discomfort arose, which quickly transformed into a piercing pain.

Yoshi Mikasi stopped and leaned against a storefront window displaying a springtime picnic scene. The slim razor sharp knife, which had made contact with him, severed a major artery. Yoshi's hand, now pressed against his abdomen, was covered in blood.

As he slid to the cold and damp pavement, Yoshi's last conscious sight on Earth was of his own blood running in rivulets down a deserted Manhattan street.

A block away a car started. It drove toward Yoshi while slowing so the driver could see him clearly. By this time, Yoshi's pupils had started dilating as he rasped his last gulps of air. The driver, now satisfied, accelerated and quickly drove further into the city.

A high-priced French whore waiting in the Chairman of Takada Pharmaceuticals' suite would only be paid for silence on this night.

Acknowledgements

At DonnaInk Publications, I wish to thank my publisher Ms. Donna L. Quesinberry (CEO-President and Founder) for helping me to make this dream of being a thriller writer come true.

Thanks to my biggest fan, supporter and best friend, my brother Styron; my daughter Cyrene, who is my muse; and my wife, Vina. A special heart-felt thank you to my favorite uncle, Nathaniel, who opened my eyes to the world of science; and a special shout-out to Mycroft, Daryl and T.C.

It took several years to get *The Pharm House* to come to life and I wish to thank all who have helped me along the way.

Just to be clear, *The Pharm House* is a work of fiction. All persons, places, locales, corporations or government institutions are either fictitious or used fictitiously.

1

The Flight Home

"Dr. Harding, Dr. Harding." He could hear a voice calling him in the distance. Perhaps they could help him. He could feel he was losing control of the car; there was a pull of gravity as he swerved into the curve. *If only he could regain control and get back into his lane.* He saw the blinding lights and felt himself falling. Slowly, he realized it was the dream again. He tried to recall where he was.

"Dr. Harding, you must have been having a bad dream. We just hit a little turbulence." Harding looked up at the stewardess. Correction: flight manager. He wouldn't want the politically correct grammar police to seize him in his slumber.

"Thank you," he muttered, reading her nameplate, Lisa. "I hope I didn't wake anyone, Lisa."

"Oh, no," she responded. "They're all sound asleep, or drunk, or both. Are you okay?"

"Yeah, I'm fine thanks."

The expanded United Airlines Boeing 747-E was somewhere over the polar icecap. Even with four movies, countless meals, snacks and drinks and first class service, this is a grueling flight.

It was fourteen toilsome hours long to be exact, and the trip from Osaka, Tokyo to Newark, New Jersey just wasn't Harding's idea of fun.

After a week in Japan his round-trip door-to-door excursion, from limousine pickup at his home in Florham Park to the debarking at the Osaka Royal Hotel in Tokyo, including layovers and plane changes, had taken him 24 toilsome hours. Even traveling first-class couldn't lighten that fact.

As part of a six-member team from the Morristown, New Jersey-based Marshall Pharmaceutical Company this was Harding's second trip to Japan, both to Osaka. For this event, Dr. Nicholas Harding served as team leader for a new development program.

Nicholas had gotten up from his seat to venture to another part of the plane and stretch. A stranger sat, slept rather, in the seat next to him. Not one for idle chitchat, Nicholas neither knew nor cared who the seatmate was.

He returned to the first class cabin and looked out the window. He saw nothing. There was just the vast white expanse of the polar cap. It was obvious if the plane were to go down their survival would not be desirable.

Briefly he wondered, *what would happen if the large opening handle on the door were activated?* He had no desire to open the door; he was just curious what would happen if it were opened.

Would the mechanism work in flight? Would alarms go off? Would the plane depressurize, killing all aboard in seconds? The travel was getting to him and mind-games passed the time.

These types of morbid mind games he played were something almost everyone he knew had indulged in for most of his life. His wife, Paula, and a few other friends of theirs had indicated otherwise when they discussed the matter once over cocktails.

Nicholas now kept his mental diversions to himself while admitting to something bordering on psychopathic. *As long as they are only thoughts they are harmless.*

Nicholas wasn't quite sure of the time; it had been late afternoon leaving Osaka and he'd been in the air about seven hours.

Changing time zones always complicated matters. It's about 2 AM in Osaka, so in Jersey it's about noon yesterday.

No longer sleepy, Harding contemplated the meetings held in Japan.

There were some strange vibes coming from some of the Tanaka reps, but those men are always hard to read.

Not knowing what to make of their unexpected decision to terminate the meeting regarding Tanaka's development of MR-548 had been disconcerting. They claimed MR-548, an anti-viral agent, would cannibalize their current product line. *A fine time to share the news, but overall, the meetings went well.* His bias showed.

While there, Harding managed to corner the Sr. Vice President of Research & Development who was also on the trip, Mr. Jack O' Connor; feedback from Marshall's head of R&D, remained very favorable towards Harding's endeavors.

As Marshall Pharmaceuticals' newly pronounced team lead for the MR-548 project (licensed through Tanaka Pharmaceuticals six months earlier), Nicholas's past year was a serious roller-coaster ride.

Some days I just couldn't tell whether I was up or down or just holding on. Leadership isn't the easy ticket; I'd thought it could be. The last few months, however, have grown stable. Perhaps things are back to normal. Nicholas knew he'd strayed off the bell-shaped curve for a while. He still wasn't totally back on track or anywhere near his 'A-game.' When he'd joined Marshall twelve years earlier as a bench level scientist with a new Ph.D. in toxicology, he had been predominantly associated with extremely visible, yet complex, but successful projects. No one ever made a desirable reputation by being associated with unsuccessful projects.

Just one year earlier, at the youthful age of 37, Harding was promoted to Director of Toxicology. He headed a group of 75 people. Now he was only one step (one long step) from a vice-presidency.

Now, he coveted some degree of normalcy in his life again.

Success: it sucks sometimes.

Lisa returned to check on him. "Can't sleep?" She quietly approached from the right.

"I have slept for a while. I guess I'm up for the remainder of the flight now, but the first movie didn't interest me much.

"Don't you guys get to sleep? Fourteen hours is a long haul to remain awake on a plane."

"We take turns napping. Do you go to Japan often?"

It was hard to see facial features clearly in the darkened cabin, but Harding could see Lisa was an attractive woman. Her voice had a slight lisp, the kind that's sexy on a woman.

"Only my second trip. But I'll be making it more frequently for a while."

"You seem to be the quiet one. I saw your group get on board – pretty rowdy bunch. How many of you are they?"

"Six."

"The others were rather boisterous. Things must have gone well for them. What do you do?"

"We're drug dealers from New Jersey," he stated without a trace of humor.

After an uncomfortable amount of silence, while watching the questioning confusion on the stewardess's face, Nicholas added with a smile, "pharmaceuticals. We're with Marshall Pharmaceuticals. We have a joint development project with a Japanese pharmaceutical house –Tanaka.

We're developing one of their anti-viral drugs for North America and Europe. Tanaka handles the remainder of the world."

"How do you know I'm not a spy for one of your competitors and won't sell trade secret information you just shared with me?" she queried him with a slight smile and her sexy lisp.

"Well," Nicholas responded in his best flirty tone, "don't give up your day job. If you are a spy for one of our competitors, you're not a very good one. You could have read what I just told you in the trade papers months ago.

"So, since we've established what you don't do for a living ,how long have you been doing this, flying?" asked Nicholas.

"Two years. This is what four years at an overpriced liberal arts college will get you. But, I get to see parts of the world I'd otherwise never get to see. Plus I've met some fascinating people and collected some interesting stories. Can I collect you?"

"Pardon me."

"Can I collect you?" Lisa repeated her question with more deliberateness. "When I collect someone, I take their picture on my iPhone, draw a sketch and write a note in my journal. Then I have them forever. So, what do you say?"

"I doubt you'd find me very interesting."

"Oh, I don't know, you look like someone with a lot on his mind – very intense, serious. You seem very different, Dr. Harding."

"You mean anal-retentive?" he inquired, feeling the barb of her observations.

"Well, I was trying to be polite," she retorted in a chuckle. "Are you? Anal-retentive, that is?"

"Just a little," Nicholas replied. "Okay – a lot."

"Family?" asked Lisa.

"I have a daughter, Andrea. She's eleven. She's currently obsessed with turning 17 and getting her driver's license. She even conned her uncle into getting her a driver's manual for the test, which she's now studying."

"You sound like a proud father."

"I am. Andrea's the center of my universe. Here's her picture." He pulled out his iPhone and shared Andrea's recent photo taken just before he departed for Osaka.

"She's quite a little princess. Her mother must be very lovely."

"Yeah," his tone softened.

"Well, I've got to get some supplies readied. I enjoyed talking to you. You're a good guy, Dr. Harding."

"How can you tell?"

"Just trust me – I've collected a lot of people. I know one when I see one."

"Um, thanks."

Their discussion took the edge off the remainder of his flight.

2

New Jersey

The group from Marshall gathered their baggage and proceeded to their respective limos to head home. All the men were anxious to return to their families.

A tall, barrel-chested gun-metal gray crew-cut haired gent, Jack was one of those over-testosterone manly men who thought regardless of whose company he was in he was of superior intellect and by default was always the leader.

He took a home moment to give his boys a pep talk on what he felt was a successful trip. "I know you boys are tired and want to get home, but I just wanted to thank you. You all put in a lot of hard work and it showed. I was proud of you. The Japs are always bitching about how goddamn superior they are to us. Bullshit! You boys put on a class act. You're every bit the equal of those bastards. And Nicky..." O'Connor went on talking losing Harding's attention at 'Nicky'.

Nicholas allowed, even enjoyed it, when his mother or even his grandmother, who died when he was 19, called him Nicky. He despised it when others became overly familiar and called him Nicky – and O'Connor knew it.

Jack droned on, "I'll be honest with you Nicky. I wasn't sure you were the right man to be team leader on this project. I thought you were too picky and too quiet. But Kronan stood up for you and I'm man enough to admit I was wrong."

Arthur Kronan was Nicholas' immediate superior, the Vice-President of Preclinical Safety & Metabolism. He was also Nicholas' mentor, friend and corporate 'Godfather'.

O'Connor went on. "God-damn it, Nick – you out-Japped the Japs!"

Jack laughed hard at his own humor. Nicholas and the others fervently hoped no one was listening to this bullshit, but in a corporate setting O'Connor served as the epitome of political correctness. When he let his guard down, as he was doing on the departure platform, Nicholas figured he was one of the most bigoted bastards he'd ever met.

Jack continued, "You detailed and nit-picked those bastards to death. Drove them crazy. I loved it! But enough of this. Good job, boys. I'll expect to see a trip report with action items by Monday afternoon. Nicky – you coordinate. Have a great weekend boys!"

And, with a flourish, he turned and walked away to his personal limo driver, leaving Nicholas and his four associates. Drs. Dennis Cordova, Matt Anderson, Gary DeSontes, and Jeff Callahan were directors or senior directors in each of their respective R&D departments. Dennis, considered by far the biggest suck-up and snake in the company, asked, "So Nicholas, what did Jack mean by all that 'too picky and too quiet stuff'?"

"I assume it means I don't have a spittoon in my office like you, Dennis," Nicholas responded in a half joking manner. "Let's call it a night," he remained fluid while continuing, "I'd appreciate it if all you guys could have your trip reports to me by 10:00 AM Monday, so I can get them to O'Connor in the early afternoon. Have a nice weekend."

Nicholas walked toward his limo driver, having forgotten his name. He recognized him from the service he used and knew the driver was one of the quieter ones, which was just what he wanted. He hated it when a driver became a Chatty Cathy the whole drive back home to Florham Park.

Jack was correct on that score, he surmised privately.

Nicholas was quiet. He said what he had to say and that was it. But he missed nothing. He was very sharp and there was much more going on inside his head than most anyone else suspected.

"Good evening, Dr. Harding," the driver said. "Let me help you with your bags."

The drive home from the airport was relaxing for Harding.

Newark, a classic early 21st century American inner city cesspool, continued the thread of that concept to surrounding airport suburbs. It wasn't safe, but it was a far more accessible airport and featured fewer constraints for travel than JFK or LaGuardia.

On the drive west from Newark, Nicholas noted New Jersey morphed into a sprawling green suburban landscape. The neighborhoods appeared clean and safe, with numerous pockets of affluence. Morristown, of course, was one of these pockets of wealth even though it had a large, stable, lower economic Black and rapidly growing Hispanic ghetto population.

Marshall Pharmaceutical was located in the middle of Marshall Farms, a sprawling industrial park with few tenants (only those controlled by Marshall).

Nicholas lived in Florham Park, one township east of Morristown and only six miles from their Headquarters. His home was a large modernized Victorian.

It was after 11:30 pm by the time the limo dropped him at his house. Everyone was asleep, but they'd left a light on for him. He was anxious to return and wanted to be back, but coming home was different now. He entered through the back door and quickly deactivated the central alarm.

As Nicholas walked through the kitchen, he noticed a shadowed figure sitting in the faint moonlight coming through the window. He could tell it was female and was at first startled. "I didn't mean to frighten you," said the dark figure. "How was Japan?"

"Okay," he bent down to kiss his mother.

"I didn't get to see much, too many meetings, you know. But I did get you something, if you can wait until tomorrow. How's Andrea?"

"Fine. She missed you. I can make you something to eat if you want."

"No thanks, Mom. I'm fine."

Nicholas' mother Dorothy lived with him and his daughter, Andrea, as did their nanny/housekeeper Anna Stevens from St. Lucia.

Dorothy had been widowed for ten years. A retired high school English teacher, she now wrote children's books with six published thus far.

Her home was in a small town near Raleigh, North Carolina, but when Nicholas' wife, Paula, died in an auto accident a year earlier, Dorothy stepped in. She knew that with his job and family demands her son would need her help.

While Anna was good with Andrea, she was still an employee; she wasn't family. So Dorothy moved in without hesitation.

It remained an unspoken communication between an adult child in need and a mother's understanding. Harding needed his mother's assistance and she pulled up roots and came to his aid.

Dorothy Harding tried not to interfere in the lives of either of her sons. Nicholas's younger brother, Michael, lived in Princeton. So they were close – the three Hardings.

Not the hugging, kissing kind or as Nicholas said in reference to Paula's family, "We don't lick all over each other, but if you go after one, you'd better take out all three." His satire always shared a loving tone.

"I'll be back," Nicholas stated. "I want to see Andrea." He went upstairs to her room, opened the door and saw his daughter asleep under her *Star Trek* covers. She was a lovely child and looked more like her mother every day. She was sharp as a tack and as an only child was quite comfortable interacting with adults. She definitely kept Nicholas on his toes. He looked forward to their weekend get-togethers.

He tucked Andrea into the covers and noticed the green eyes of Andrea's cat watching him from across the room. He'd been reading about the Mad Monk of the Russian Revolution to Andrea when she'd gotten her cat, hence the name 'Rasputin'. He left her room and went back downstairs to the kitchen.

On the way down, he thought of Paula. A picture hung on the wall in the stairway as a reminder from their honeymoon in Hawaii. Little had changed in the house since her death. In fact, the only substantive change had been his mother moving in and the loss of his wife. He'd told himself he'd avoid change for Andrea, wanting to provide her with a stable, familiar environment after her mother's death.

But it was just as much for him as a creature of habit, he didn't want to upset the status quo. Plus he felt guilty for not being able to grieve.

Nicholas and Paula were married for 13 years. They'd met shortly after he joined Marshall. A mutual friend introduced them at a party, referred to frequently as 'the single young scientist and the single young attorney.'

Paula had just joined a prestigious Morristown law firm as an associate. She was a New Jersey girl; spent most of her life in the Princeton area, including undergraduate school. You couldn't call their first meeting love at first sight by any definition. No sparks flew.

But then Nicholas rarely exuded sparks.

They did share mutual interests and enjoyed one another's company. On reflection, Nicholas noted that they were both professionally ambitious and devoted to their careers, so neither of them had desired a smothering relationship, yet they still desired companionship. So, as a couple, they fit one another's needs – they complimented each other.

Their relationship remained more of a partnership than a traditional marriage. But perhaps that was what early 21st century American two-career marriages had become: small impersonal businesses.

Nicholas returned to the kitchen where his mother had moved to sip tea in her favorite tattered old robe.

"I'm a little old to have my mom wait up for me, you know," he said.

"I've never waited up for you," she replied with a warm smile. "Well, not often. That was your Dad. When you were a teenager and out on a date or with your friends he'd toss and turn until I'd throw him out of bed. I'd tell him, 'If you can't sleep, just sit up and wait for him.' But he was embarrassed to let you know. So he'd lie awake until he heard you come in and then he was out like a light."

Nicholas's dad had died of a massive coronary. They were close, but again in the quiet and reserved Harding sort of way. So, when he died unexpectedly there was much left unsaid between the two men.

"You'll see what it's like when Andrea is older," Dorothy cautioned.

"Can't wait," he replied, joining his mother at the table in the breakfast nook.

"So, how did the boys treat you on your trip? What's that term you and Michael have for them?" she asked.

"Snake boys," Nicholas chided. "They'd knife their mothers in the back and sell their souls for the next promotion. They treat me fine. They know I'm not one of them and I know I'm not one of them. Although, I'm sure we have different reasons for knowing it."

"And you're not capable of being like them?" his mother asked, looking into her son's eyes.

"No, actually I'm quite capable of being like them, but for different reasons. To take is the only way they know. Whereas with me, it's more of a method of last resort."

"You always were the complicated one," his mother said.

"Yeah, sometimes a little too complicated for my own good," Nicholas replied. "Andrea behaved the past few days?"

"She was perfect as usual."

Nicholas worried about how he was raising his daughter, much more so now after Paula's death. *Am I spending enough time with her? Am I spending too much time on my job?*

He did tend to be a workaholic. *How is she adjusting to her mother's death? To being an only child?* The questions were endless and Nicholas was afraid he didn't have the right answers, or any answers, in too many instances.

Andrea seemed normal to Nicholas, but what was normal these days? Is there something going on under the surface I'm missing? There is always something under the surface with everyone, am I missing something important? Am I doing enough? Nicholas' mom assured him he was doing a good job and Andrea was doing okay. The counselor he and Andrea had started to see after Paula's death thought they were right on track, but, but, but…

Why do I always have to find a 'but'? Nicholas thought to himself. Maybe it's not Andrea. Maybe Andrea is fine. Maybe it's me.

The dream wouldn't go away.

Nicholas was in a room with no doors or windows and someone was calling him. He didn't recognize the room, but the voice was familiar and it wasn't using his name. But he could see no means of exiting the room.

"Dad."

"Dad."

"Dad," the gentle voice continued. "He's still asleep."

Nicholas was beginning to realize that he may be in a dream; that foggy in-between state. Was the voice part of the dream?

"Rasputin! *Yong Qong lan!*"

Nicholas realized he'd been dreaming and was in his own bed. However, as often occurs with frequent travelers, he wasn't initially sure what bed or exactly where he was.

As his dream state subsided, he was uncomfortably, perhaps frighteningly, aware of something or someone else in the bed. He saw two greenish-yellow-orange lights near whatever was in the bed with him. Just before pure fear started to rise in his chest reality came into play and Nicholas realized what was happening.

"Hi Daddy!" said Andrea, who was on the foot of Nicholas' bed.

"Did you see that? I'm teaching Rasputin to respond to commands in Klingon! I just told him to get on the bed. Cool, huh?"

Nicholas noticed the two greenish-yellow-orange lights belonged in the head of Rasputin, Andrea's 22 pound Maine Coon Tabby cat. Rasputin's large furry head was now about two inches from his face emitting a rather loud purr.

"Hi Andrea. Hi Rasputin," Nicholas said. "Miss me?"

"You bet Dad!" Andrea almost shouted. "Isn't it neat, Rasputin and I are learning Klingon!"

"I'm impressed," he answered while suppressing a yawn.

"What did you bring me?" Andrea began scouring the room for goodies. "You haven't unpacked yet. Need any help?"

"Sure, but what you're looking for is in that bag over by the closet door."

Andrea saw a large bag with a box inside and ran towards it.

"Be careful. It'll break," her father warned. Meanwhile, Rasputin had curled into a nest on the other pillow preparing to indulge in his favorite past time: sleeping. "Bring it here; I'll help you open it." Andrea's father motioned to her.

Andrea brought the package over to the bed and began to open it with her father. Nicholas restrained her from being too rough.

When she finally got the box open, a delicate porcelain oriental Geisha doll was wrapped in layers of soft green tissue paper.

"Daddy, she's beautiful! I'll add her to my collection. Rasputin, *ghoS*"

Although he appeared to be asleep, the cat's ears perked up and he bounded off the bed following Andrea out of the room as she carefully carried her new doll away.

Hmmm, maybe that pile of fur does understand Klingon.

Andrea, currently a semi-Tomboy, rarely admitted playing with dolls, but she did say she liked to collect them.

"Just to look at sometimes, Daddy," she'd stated while claiming to be too mature for them.

In their many father-daughter projects, Nicholas worked with Andrea to construct a series of shelves in her large walk-in closet in her room. So she had a neat place for her doll collection. Nicholas always tried to find a doll while on business travel, always something unusual.

Maybe she is okay, he sat up in bed, *maybe it's me that's not.* His thoughts trailed off.

3

Marshall Farms

"This is the AT&T International Teleconference Operator. All parties are on line in New Jersey, London, United Kingdom, Basel, Switzerland, and Japan. Would you like a roll call of participants?" a polished male voice served as help desk central command.

"No, thank you Operator. We're old hands at this and we know how to get you back if there's a problem. If you don't mind, we'd like to get started."

"Thank you for using AT&T," the Operator chimed off the call.

"Is he off the line? I can never tell," one of the callers got pensive.

"Yes, he's gone. Let's get started."

"Isn't this dangerous? These teleconference calls leave a record; a trail," another nervous sounding participant queried.

"Of course, they leave a trail and what's someone going to find? A record of a teleconference meeting of a group of pharmaceutical executives with legitimate business concerns. So what?!"

"I'm just trying to be careful, that's what. This isn't a game and I don't have a desire to see the inside of a fucking federal prison, although you'd probably be more at home there!"

"God damn it! I've had enough of your bitching and moaning!"

"That's enough, all of you!" said the calm, female voice from London. "What the hell's wrong with you? We've worked on this for three years now. The end is in sight and it's the end we planned and controlled. That's the key: control! We've always been in control and we still are. Just a few more months. By the end of the year the first stage is over; that's the big hurdle. The second stage is a piece of cake, just waiting. And then, my friends, we'll own a major pharmaceutical house."

"Do you have any idea what it's going to be like around here when Stage I is over? The Food and Drug Administration is going to come down on us like the wrath of God. It's going to be a state of siege here. The stock will bottom out."

"Good!" the calm voice from the United Kingdom continued. "And then we'll buy the controlling interest."

"We're cutting a fine line."

"I know. We know. We've always known."

"What's the status of MR-548?"

"The Project Team just got back from Japan. I haven't seen their report yet. It should be out soon."

"Does Harding suspect anything?"

"No. He's a follower. He'll do as he's told. The team's getting ready for an FDA Advisory Committee meeting."

"Can he hurt us when this goes down?"

"No. It'll look like he was in it up to his neck. He'll be too busy trying to stay out of Leavenworth!"

"I have an 11:00 meeting. Do you need me for anything else?" said an older, more distinguished voice.

"No. Just stick to the plan, okay?"

"Sure. You can brief me later on anything else you cover."

It was a cloudy, overcast, and cold spring morning in New Jersey. It matched the way he felt as he exited the executive offices building, where most of the Sales and

Marketing bigwigs were housed and started to walk towards the main Research and Development building.

"Good morning Dr. Kronan," said a young technician whose name he couldn't remember.

"Good morning," he replied absently. Arthur Kronan felt the tinge from his ulcer. *What have I done?*

4

Nick and Karen

"Dr. Harding, you have an 11:00 appointment with Dr. Kronan."

"What's the topic, Karen? You know I hate meetings right after I get back from a trip."

"You hate meetings all the time. Dr. Kronan's secretary said it was a short, direct reports meeting to go over last month's FDA audit. It's only an hour and a half and I've made sure you're free the remainder of the day. Did you get last week's mail at home on Saturday?"

"Yes."

"Did the Tanaka delegation like the gifts I selected?"

"Yes."

"Small, light, compact – yet delicate and tasteful?"

"Yes."

"Perhaps in the future I can be more efficient, yes?" she said with a barely detectable German accent, very seriously.

"I doubt it, Karen. You're perfect and I'm one of the luckiest people alive to have you working with me." Nicholas complimented Karen as often as possible to keep her spirits inflated as she performed better when happy.

"You are so full of it, Dr. Harding," Karen turned to leave his office. "And thank you for the scarf from Japan. It is lovely. My favorite color."

"You're welcome Karen," he watched her leave his office. *Nice view*. Harding made this amusing self-commentary every time Karen left the room.

Harding hired Karen Stemmer after he had to fire the secretary he inherited as Director of Toxicology. Karen had no industry experience and she had trained in her home country of Germany. She'd recently moved to America with her parents. At 28 years she stood 5'8" with shoulder length blond hair and eyes so blue anyone could drown in them. She was all Aryan in looks as well as demeanor. And, she was also knockdown, drag out, drop dead beautiful.

Ms. Stemmer kept to herself and in two years had managed to intimidate all the other R&D secretaries into giving her a wide berth. She was also fiercely loyal and protective of her Dr. Harding.

Rumor among half the company was she was a lesbian. The young gorgeous woman was single, unattached and living with 'family' no one ever saw. And the remaining half of the company believed she and Harding were in the midst of a torrid love affair.

Nicholas didn't know about the lesbian part but he seriously doubted it. But there had never been anything physical between the two of them. Occasional flirtations,no more than that. He recalled the first time Paula had seen Karen. Like most women, Paula took one look and immediately disliked her based on looks alone.

Intimidatingly beautiful, Karen had a difficult time with the jealousy of women in the office and visiting wives. One of the few open and real fights Nicholas and Paula shared had taken place due to Karen. Harding's wife insisted he, "Get rid of her! I don't give a shit if you transfer, fire or drown her as long as she's gone!"

In recollecting the argument, Nicholas realized he'd love to share another moment like that together, but at the time he asked her, "exactly what is the basis for your loathing of Karen? You just met her. Is it just because she's attractive? You afraid I'm going to sleep with her, Paula?"

"Are you?"

"Do you really give a shit or are you just concerned someone might take one of your toys?"

"Go to hell Nicky!" Paula had yelled, which was rare. As an attorney her emotions usually remained balanced and their fight had died down as quickly as it had flared up.

Over time, Karen managed to carve out a sort of respectful, though distanced, relationship with Paula. But then all of Paula's relationships, including the one with her husband, had been distanced.

The two women seemingly respected but quietly disliked each other. Nicholas never really knew the source of Paula's feelings towards Karen.

Since Paula's death, he'd wanted to ask Karen why she'd disliked Paula, but the right time never occurred. *The right time*, he thought. *I'm always missing the right time for something or other.*

Enough daydreaming. Harding turned to his computer on his credenza next to his executive desk and called up his corporate email account. He'd reviewed last week's messages from his laptop at home over the weekend. Already another 18 messages were waiting for him.

He clicked on his New Messages icon and it listed the titles and authors of his 18 new messages. He quickly scanned down the listing to see if there was anything requiring urgent attention.

Meeting notifications from Karen. A message from two of Nicholas' senior managers complaining about what a bunch of pricks Quality Assurance were being. Messages from the Director of Quality Assurance complaining about what a bunch of pricks Nicholas' managers were being. A corporate March of Dimes announcement. An excuse from one of his study directors for why she'd be late with a critical report. Nicholas made a mental note to see her later. The usual assortment of boring stuff, with one exception. One message stood out. It was from Don Marshall. The topic was simply "Lunch."

Nicholas knew Don occasionally invited senior managers to lunch. Nicholas had met him briefly in passing, but mostly knew of him by reputation and rumor. The message had been sent at 3:15 AM Monday morning.

Supposedly, he was an eccentric. The one word that came to Nicholas' mind when he thought of Don, and that admittedly wasn't often, was 'pity.' Here was a guy whose grandfather had built one of the top ten pharmaceutical houses in the United States from nothing and now after only two generations, it'd essentially been taken away from the family by a bunch of back stabbers, the snake boys, who'd do anything they thought they could get away with to make a buck.

Yes, thought Nicholas as he typed a quick, brief response to Don Marshall agreeing to have lunch with him.

I'll collect him.

"You're going to be late if you don't leave soon, Dr. Harding," he heard Karen say from her desk in the outer office.

Nicholas hit the return key to send the reply off to Don and got up from his desk. "Okay. I'm going," he shouted out to Karen.

As Nicholas was heading out of his office, he ran into Mark Stevens. Mark was Director of Drug Metabolism and also reported to Arthur Kronan. Nicholas and Mark were semi-close. They were about the same age and temperament.

"Hey Nicholas, let's head over across the street to Graves for lunch after Art's meeting. I want to hear the scoop on the Japan trip," Mark engaged him.

"Isn't Art serving lunch?" asked Nicholas

"Are you kidding? You know how cheap Art is."

"Yeah, sure, let's grab a quick lunch."

5

Arthur

In addition to Nicholas and Mark Stevens, Kronan's department heads included the heads of Operations & Administration, Computer Support & Technology, Lab Animal Medicine, and Pharmacokinetics and Statistics.

Nicholas was clearly Arthur's right hand and first among equals.

Rumor had it Nicholas would succeed Arthur when he retired in a few years. It was obvious to everyone Arthur was grooming him for his position. Of course, in the pharmaceutical industry these days, a few years could be an eternity and much could happen.

The last ten years in big pharma had not been pretty. The industry seemed to be in a stampede. But a stampede to where? No one knew.

In the 1980s and early 1990s the pharmaceutical industry had been a stable old boys' club. Now in the early 2010s, it joined the rest of America's dog-eat-dog corporate world.

"Nicholas, how was Japan?" Kronan asked when everyone was seated around his conference room table.

"Good Art," Nicholas replied. "We got a detailed overview of the MR-548 Pharmacology, Toxicology, Metabolism, Manufacturing and Clinical programs. I've arranged for our department to receive a copy of all the Pharm-Tox-ADME reports within two months – all 314 of them."

"Did you say 314?" Mark asked with seeming shock.

"That does include all nonclinical Pharm, Tox/Path, and Drug Metabolism. But you're right. That's an incredible number of studies, even for a Japanese company. What makes it even more incredible is that Tanaka has dropped plans to submit MR-548 in Japan," Nicholas said.

Art joined in, "Why is that so incredible? I understood Tanaka has something better in the pipeline and they don't want to cannibalize an existing product."

"Just seems strange, Art," Nicholas said. "Tanaka has billed MR-548 as the next Zovirax broad-spectrum antiviral. Only ten times more potent, with a longer half-life and essentially no significant side-effects. A blockbuster.

"Projected peak year sales are north of $3 billion. Marshall outbid the big boys, Merck and Glaxo-Wellcome, to get this. If it's that hot, why wait for something behind it in the pipeline that might fall out? It just doesn't play for me."

"That's for the marketing team and bean counters to know," Arthur retorted. "We're just egghead scientists," He changed the subject. "How are plans for the FDA Advisory meeting?"

"Good. The meeting is set for six months from now, which gives us time to review the full data package from Tanaka and line up our outside consultant big guns who'll testify to the FDA that MR-548 is the greatest new drug since penicillin. Further, life will end on planet Earth if it's not immediately approved. If the Advisory meeting goes well and FDA accepts our submission plans the New Drug Application will go in two years from now on an accelerated approval path of less than one year."

Mark toned in, "after which the good Dr. Harding will be crowned Emperor of Marshall and we'll all have to stand in line to kiss his ass."

"I like that. I think I'll add it to the development plan," Nicholas said, smiling.

The meeting continued with discussions on activities involving other projects, new computer systems, maintaining old systems, QA issues, and a myriad of never-ending problems.

As the meeting broke up and people were heading out, Arthur approached Nicholas. "Helen and I would like to have you over for dinner on Saturday. Are you free?"

"What did you have in mind, Art?"

"There are some things you and I need to talk about – the future – and we may as well do it in a relaxed atmosphere over a nice meal."

"None of Helen's unattached friends or relatives?" asked Nicholas.

"None, I promise."

"Good. I accept. You okay Art? You look tired."

"Just working too hard. We'll talk Saturday."

Graves

"Hey Karen, is the good Dr. Harding ready? I'll just pop in if you don't mind," Mark said as he walked into Nicholas' outer office.

"I do mind. He's on the phone. He'll be out shortly, Dr. Stevens," Karen said in her usual no-nonsense tone that stopped Mark in his tracks. "Why don't you have a seat?"

Karen showed not the least interest in Mark as he fidgeted with a copy of *Toxicology and Applied Pharmacology*. Like every other heterosexual male at Marshall, Mark thought Karen was a knock out and he would have eaten out of her shoes if she had shown the slightest interest in him. Of course, Karen had shown just as much interest in Mark as she had in every other heterosexual male at Marshall – none. The exception to this of course was her relationship with Nicholas.

"I thought I heard you out here," Nicholas postured as he came out of his office.

"Yeah, I would have come in, but I didn't know today's password," said Mark, giving Karen a mischievous look.

"Have a nice lunch, Dr. Harding," she answered without looking up from the spreadsheet she was working on.

"We're going over to Graves. Can I bring you something Karen? That Chef's salad you like?"

"If it's no trouble, yes that would be nice. Thank you," Karen replied with an almost smile.

Out in the parking lot Mark turned to Nicholas, "you're doing her, aren't you?"

"What are you talking about?"

"You and Karen. I can tell from the way you two talk to each other."

"You mean the way I offered to buy her a salad? You know that act has been known to drive some women insane with passion!"

"Funny. So are you?"

"No."

"If you were, would you admit it?"

"No."

"So, you must be!"

"Whatever makes you happy, Mark."

On the way to the car Nicholas and Mark met several people.

"Good morning, Dr. Harding."

"Hello, Dr. Harding."

"Nicholas, good morning."

"Nicholas, how was Japan?"

A lot of folks on the Marshall campus knew Mark, but *everyone* knew Dr. Nicholas Harding.

Nicholas didn't really stand out physically; average height and weight at 5'10", 165 pounds. He did dress exceptionally well. Most scientists weren't known for their fashion sense. Nicholas favored Italian suites and shoes. The marketing boys who welded the real power in most pharmaceutical houses liked him for his reputation as Arthur Kronan's hand-picked successor and the exception to make Vice President before he hit forty.

All that made Nicholas known and recognizable to most of Marshall. But to add to that, the fact that Nicholas was the highest ranking of the few black executives at Marshall made him stand out. Like many U.S. pharmaceutical houses, Marshall was still an old boys club, i.e., middle-aged wealthy white men. Although the last few years had seen a large infusion of Asians. Nicholas walked their walk, talked their talk and played their game – well. He clearly wasn't one of the boys, but he fit in and he didn't threaten them.

Graves was owned by a former Marshall employee, Sheila Casterini, an M.D. clinician with a different sense of humor and a lot of capital. Marshall Management wasn't amused by the choice of name, but their opposition only strengthened Sheila's resolve not to change it.

A couple of years earlier Sheila had come into a sizable inheritance. Her first act had been to submit a brief letter of resignation that expressed her true feelings towards the business world.

The text of the letter read, "I resign. Kiss my ass. Respectfully, Sheila."

The interior of Graves could be politely described as "unusual." It could more bluntly be described as "sick and twisted." People either loved it or hated it. The food was average. The décor was, well, not. There were posters of various medical/surgical scenes from movies, including several from the horror movie genre. Nicholas liked Graves. He found it relaxing. Mark loved it!

"So Nicky, old man, when you're my boss will you remember the little people or become a pompous, inflated, self-absorbed ass?"

"You mean I'm not already?" replied Nicholas.

"Depends on who you ask, pal. For someone at your level, you've managed to make surprisingly few enemies. But, I'd watch my back if I were you, Nick."

"What do you mean, Mark?"

A waiter dressed as a mortician arrived with menus shaped as tombstones.

Mark asked Nicholas, "Do you think I'm sick to love this place as much as I do?"

"Yes. Now, who's out to insert sharp instruments into my back?" Mark caught Harding's attention.

Mark put down his menu and answered. "No names – yet. Just word out that you're likely to make VP soon and you know how people are. Some are jealous."

"Specifics, Mark. I'm a big boy. I can take it."

"Okay. Some say it's because you're black. It's an affirmative action thing. Some say it's because you're Art Kronan's personal pet. Most don't feel this way Nicholas, but some do. It's human nature. Don't forget Karen's salad."

"I won't. And where do you stand on all this Mark – honest?" he asked, trying to gauge Mark's level of loyalty.

"Alright. Here goes," Mark said before taking a sip of water. "You and I are about the same age, professional experience and background. So, do I feel a twinge of jealousy? Yes. But that's all. In my mind, if you get Art's VP slot you deserve it. You've run the largest part of his group and run it well. It's by far the most productive. You've run project teams, special projects and taskforces. Everything they've thrown at you, you've handled exceptionally well. You've walked on water, pal. You've had ample opportunity to fall on your ass and you haven't, at least so far. And honestly, I'm not as ambitious as you are. I don't want to get any deeper into the snake pit. Bottom-line, do I wish it was me? Sure. But I'll be happy for you. And honored to work for you, unless, you're planning to fire me. How's that for kissing up to my future boss?"

"I've always thought you kissed up with the best, Mark," Nicholas replied with a smile. "Let's order."

Service at Graves, designed to cater to the mostly Marshall lunch crowd, was quick and good.

"Guess what I got on email?" Nicholas asked after their food had arrived.

"An obscene message from Karen saying how she secretly desired to tie you up and lick you to death as only an Aryan goddess can do?"

"You know, you're even sicker than I thought. No, an invitation from Don Marshall. What do you make of that?"

"Go on! Rumor has it those invites only go out to the chosen few."

"Chosen for what? Don's got about as much clout around here as a lab rat, or at least a wealthy one."

"No, tell me how you really feel about Don Marshall, Nicky."

"You don't want to get me started on Don Marshall, Mark," Nicholas said as their drinks arrived. Mark had a glass of merlot. Nicholas avoided drinking during lunch unless he was with senior executives who wanted to drink and then he limited himself to one glass of wine.

Nicholas went on, "Don Marshall's grandfather, Don Senior, built this company from the ground up, starting with a little one-room pharmacy. No inheritance, no government assistance program, no rich wife, just good old-fashioned American hard work. He made Marshall Pharmacy the largest pharmacy group in the New York-New Jersey-Connecticut tri-state area.

"The acorn didn't fall far from the tree," he continued. "And Don Junior, through some shrewd buy-outs and a rarely mentioned venture with J.D. Rockefeller's New Jersey-based Esso, took Marshall nationwide as a true pharmaceutical company. Then he moved into Canada, the Central and South Americas, and Europe. In two generations they took Marshall Pharmaceuticals to the top. Poised for nothing, but more growth.

"And what's the future?" Nicholas went on. "Why Don J. Marshall, III. West Point graduate -lower third of his class, by the way- and Harvard, M.B.A. Everyone thought he was going to set the pharmaceutical world on fire. When Don Jr. died the Marshall family controlled 78% of Marshall stock and held the majority of board seats."

"How do you know all this? Are you stalking him?" Mark asked.

"Because Mark, studying successful people is a hobby of mine. I admire them. So I've studied the Marshall family. And they were a very successful family until the latest generation when some stray idiot gene managed to express itself."

"Well, don't just leave me here , go on," Mark said.

"Okay. So, what brilliant West Point, Harvard strategy does Donny-boy implement? Well, first he sets off to spend every dime he can get his hands on, screw every good looking woman in the Western hemisphere and to top it off take a one year cruise around the world. When he got back ten years ago he'd been ousted as chairman of the board, the family now had only one seat, his. His assorted cousins, uncles, aunts, family sycophants, etc., had sold out on him."

"But he still controls 40% of Marshall stock."

"Might as well be four percent, Mark, as long as the current pack of snake boys controls the other 60%."This didn't just happen. The guys in charge, some of whom are now on our board and some behind the scene, went after the Marshall family with a vengeance and Donny-boy never knew what hit him," Nicholas said as the waiter delivered his food.

"So why are you so hard on him, Nick?"

"Mark, when my father died the only material thing he left me was a pocket watch. He told me his grandfather had taken it off a Confederate captain he killed during the Civil War. I polish it, wear it occasionally, but I cherish it and take care of it. Far better care than Don Marshall took of his legacy. Don's father and grandfather entrusted him with $12 billion of family sweat, toil and pain and he just pissed it away. I just can't respect someone like that. But I am curious, so I'll have lunch with him and see firsthand what the weirdo is like. You can learn something from everyone, even assholes."

"Here's your salad with that honey mustard dressing you like and a bottle of ice tea, Karen," Harding handed off the Chef's salad to his secretary.

"Thank you. Sometimes working for you is not so bad, Dr. Harding," Karen said with her slightest trace of a smile, which was about as close as she ever came to a compliment.

7

Michael

"Lunch is on you, big brother, since I won this round of golf." Nicholas and Michael were at the Birchwood Country Club in Florham Park. Nicholas was a member, as were most Marshall Pharmaceutical executives.

"You know my game's off due to jet lag, Michael."

"Jet lag my ass. You've been back a week."

"Oh."

Michael lived in Princeton, New Jersey with his wife. He was an attorney specializing in environmental law. Five years younger than Nicholas, he admired his older brother but chided him a lot. Through no pre-planning, the two North Carolina boys had ended up in suburban New Jersey.

They were close, with always a degree of friendly competition between them. Lately Michael had been urging Nicholas to leave Marshall and the two of them set up an environmental/pharmaceutical-consulting firm.

"So, how's the snake pit, Nicky?" asked Michael, sitting in the club luncheon restaurant.

"Mike, I tell you, the snakes are bigger, meaner, and hungrier than ever."

"Then why do it, Negro!"

In private, the two Southern-raised brothers often slipped into a pattern of talk that most Whites wouldn't understand, but the brothers and friends took comfort in.

"The challenge, you know how they are. It drives them crazy to see one of us do something as well as they do or, Heaven forbid, *better* than they do."

"Be careful, boy. You also know they'll just keep trying to knock you down."

"I know. But I want that V.P. slot – a lot!"

"Do you have a chance?" Mike asked.

"I think so. In fact, I'm having dinner with Art tonight at his house. I've earned it, Mike. I've walked on water for these people. Every crummy assignment I've handled and I've made Art and O'Connor look damn good. So I'm going for it. After I get it we'll see. I don't envision many more years of having to carry around a snake-bite kit everywhere I go – you know what I mean?"

"I hear you, bro. Now, let me see how much of that inflated Marshall salary of yours I can consume during lunch," Mike said with a hearty laugh.

"Don't hold back on my account."

"Don't worry, I won't!"

"But on to a more interesting topic, you get laid yet?" Mike asked as Nicholas almost choked on his diet coke.

"Pardon?" Nicholas asked his little brother while looking around to make sure no one was in ear shot.

"My God, it's worse than I thought! You've even forgotten what it's called! You know laid, screwed, sex– any of this rings a bell? At least tell me you're dating, Nick."

"I've been busy and it has only been a year since Paula died."

"I see," said Mike.

"You see. Tell me what you see Michael."

"Forget it. Let's talk about your pathetic golf game instead of your pathetic love life."

"No. You didn't like Paula, did you?"

"I didn't have to, bro. She was your wife. The big question is, did you?"

"Alright – let's talk about golf."

"Nicky it'll be okay. You'll meet someone and live happily ever after. You always were the romantic one. Me..."

"Yeah, I know – wet the stick, do the nasty, etc., etc., etc. Does Linda know about your sickness?"

"She encourages it. With her at least."

"I promise, tomorrow, I'm all yours Andrea. But tonight, I have to go to Dr. Kronan's for dinner," Nicholas was trying to explain to Andrea.

"But why can't I go?" she asked.

"Because it's a grownup dinner."

"I'm mature for my age."

"I know, but you're still not a grownup."

"Are you taking a date?"

"What?" Nicholas was a little shocked. Andrea had never mentioned his dating before.

"No."

"Good. Then I can be your date," she declared, triumphantly sure she'd won the argument.

"Not this time, honey. But tomorrow, you can be my date. Okay?"

"Okay, Daddy," she said while searching her 11-year-old mind for other options to the argument. Finally giving up she said, "Rasputin! *GhoS*!" and she, followed by the giant tabby Nicholas didn't even know was in his study, scampered out to play.

8

Arthur's House

"So Nicholas, how was your trip to Japan with Jack? Did he manage to offend everyone, including the Emperor?"

Helen and Arthur Kronan and Nicholas had just started dinner at the Kronan house, a rather large old turn-of-the-century Queen Anne-style Morristown mansion. Arthur's position as Vice President of Drug Safety and Pharmacokinetics paid quite well and Helen was from old Morristown money. Nicholas had always thought it a little strange that they maintained the old mansion as their primary residence since they had no children.

"Actually, Jack can be quite charming when he wants to be."

"I know, God knows he's come on to me enough times when he's gotten a few drinks in him," Helen responded pensively.

"And who can blame him, dear?" Arthur said smiling at Helen. "After all, you are a very lovely woman."

Nicholas knew Helen was in her early 50s, but she took excellent care of herself and could easily pass for early 40s. And Arthur was right; she was a beautiful woman. She and Arthur had been married for more than 25 years and appeared to be a happy couple that had survived those rough middle years. They'd seemingly settled into the comfortable latter life marriage years. Theirs was the type of relationship Nicholas had wanted with Paula, but certainly wasn't the direction in which they had been heading.

"You know, Helen, I'm pleasantly surprised no prospective dates, friends, cousins, etc., have jumped out tonight. My thanks," Harding raised his wine glass to toast her.

"Don't thank me, Nicholas. I had the perfect young lady lined up for dinner tonight – not a date, just dinner – but Arthur read me the riot act. But don't worry. This is only a minor setback. I haven't given up," she replied with a mischievous grin.

"And, I'd be disappointed if you did." *I hope she doesn't.*

After dinner Arthur quietly moved Nicholas into his study. "Time for some shop talk, dear," he motioned to Helen to occupy herself elsewhere.

"Helen. Thanks for a lovely dinner," Nicholas said as he kissed her cheek.

"My pleasure, as always Nicholas, good night. Should I wait up for you Arthur?" she asked.

"No. Good night, dear. I love you."

Arthur's study was a combination study/library, with a large selection of books. Nicholas had always liked this room. It felt both powerful and comfortable

"A brandy, Nicky?"

"Yes, a small one. Thanks."

Once the two men settled into the soft leather chairs Arthur raised his brandy glass in a toast. "To your future, Nicky," he said.

"To *our* future, Art," replied Nicholas.

"You want the vice-presidency, don't you?"

"Am I that transparent?"

"No. But I can tell. And you're right to want it. You've earned it. And it's yours. Grant Michner, our CEO, and Jack O'Connor have agreed and signed off on the succession plan. You're the next Division Vice President of Drug Safety and Pharmacokinetics. It's just a matter of when. But you know, Nicky, sometimes wanting is far better than having? Yes?"

Arthur asked. But he was looking out a tall dark window. It was as if he were talking to himself.

"I know it'll be hard, but I think I'm up to it," Nicholas answered.

Arthur's study was a smaller version of the Main Reading Room of the Library of Congress. A large circular desk took up the center of the room. The walls were lined with bookshelves from floor to ceiling. The books ranged from medical to historical to classical to current fiction. On some shelves there were small busts of Jefferson, Lincoln, and Paracelsus, a 16th century German physician often referred to as the Father of Toxicology.

"You're up to the part you're aware of, Nicholas. But what of that of which you're unaware?" Arthur inquired with a far off look.

"We all deal with that of which we're unaware every day, Art. You just do the best you can based on your knowledge, experience and your heart."

"You always say just the right thing, Nicky." After a rather long silence Arthur said, "it won't be two years." He'd moved away from the window and was now touching – caressing – an old text book.

"I don't understand," Harding answered questionably.

"Until I retire, Nicholas, it won't be two years. It'll be much sooner."

"What are you and Helen going to do? Will you stay here?" asked Nicholas.

"No. I won't stay here. We'll leave." Abruptly changing the subject, Arthur asked, "do you know what this is?" He referred to the book he was fingering.

"Looks like an old text; biology." Nicky responded.

"It's what put me where I am today," Art declared. "I'd planned on going to law school when I went to college.

That's what my family wanted, so that was it. But then I took First Year Biology and fell in love with science. Events all strung together. Some good, some bad. But I'm rambling, aren't I Nicky? You'll make a good V.P.," said Art.

"Art, are you okay? Are you ill?"

"Ill? No. Okay? Who knows, it's late, Nicky."

"I know. I'll see you later. I can let myself out."

"Take care of yourself, Nicky," Art said and then turned back to the window he'd been looking out.

Nicholas let himself out and went to the foyer closet to get his coat. He heard a soft rustle behind him and turned to see Helen.

"Oh, Helen, you startled me."

"I know. Large old and quiet, creaky house," she said.

"Is Art all right, Helen?" Nicholas felt he was going out on a limb, he wasn't actually that close to Helen, but he needed to know.

"He doesn't sleep much. He told you he plans to retire early?"

"Yes."

"But he won't discuss what he wants to do after he retires. Are things bad at work?" she asked.

"No more than usual," Nicholas answered.

"Is he seeing someone else?" she asked looking directly into Nicholas' eyes.

"No. He worships you, Helen. Maybe the two of you need to get away for a while."

"He always wanted children. But I couldn't carry a pregnancy. He'd be better if he had children," she said suddenly, looking like a lost child herself. "Thanks for coming Nicky. He loves you, you know."

"And, I him and you too, Helen. I'll keep an eye on him at work."

"Thank you, Nicky."

"Good night."

Nicholas stepped out into the cool spring night knowing something was certainly taking its toll on Arthur. He'd never seen him like this. But he had heard good news. Not only was the vice presidency his, but even sooner than he'd thought. But something didn't feel right.

It was about a 20 minute drive from Arthur and Helen's back to his home, so Harding had a little time to think. *Things are out of balance. The Tanaka deal on MR-548 was going exceptionally well, but Tanaka itself stopped development, why? My move into the V.P. slot was guaranteed and even accelerated, but Art's behavior is erratic and at best troublesome. The bizarre message from Don Marshall – I'm curious. At least things at home are relatively normal, considering. Andrea still has the occasional nightmare, but fewer these days and Mom has been a godsend. I couldn't have managed without her.*

Balance, he thought. *I just need more balance in my life.*

9

Nicholas & Drea

"'Drea. Wake up," Nicholas said to his still-sleeping daughter under the watchful eyes of Rasputin.

"What time is it, Dad?" a small voice asked from under a mountain of bed covers.

"It's 8:00, get up. I'm yours today, remember?"

"I'm sleepy."

"Come on, get up. We've got stuff to do."

"Like what?" Andrea asked, still buried under the covers.

"Well, how about you get up and we watch all the Sunday news shows. You know, *Meet the Press*, *Fox News Sunday*, and then *CNN* all afternoon?" said Nicholas.

"Yuk! No thanks. I'll stay in bed."

"Okay, then how about Liberty Science Center?"

A head now deemed it worthwhile to emerge from the covers. "Liberty Science Center?"

"Yep."

"Cool."

"You know the routine. Eat your breakfast, brush your teeth, wash up, and clean your room. Let me see your homework. Then we can go."

"Okay, Dad," Andrea bounded out of bed.

The Liberty Science Center was a New Jersey State business-sponsored science museum and learning center. A lot of interactive exhibits were featured, mostly for kids, but some grown-up stuff too. Andrea loved it and Nicholas enjoyed taking here there. It was near the ferry docks for the Ellis Island and Statue of Liberty ferries. Sometimes Nicholas and Andrea would ride the ferries around and just be together; a father and daughter enjoying each other's company.

Nicholas came into the kitchen and saw Andrea having cereal. Rasputin was having his breakfast and Nicholas' mom was sitting at the table.

"So, I hear you two are going to Liberty Science today," Dorothy looked at Nicholas.

"Yeah, I thought we'd spend the day there. We both like it," he answered, looking for something quick and portable to eat.

"It wouldn't hurt to take her to church too you know," his mom said quietly as she left the room.

Having been raised in a Southern Baptist family, Nicholas knew all about religion and had made a conscious decision to ignore it. It just didn't stick with him. No matter how much time he spent in church, how many sermons he heard, stories read, he'd only had one religious feeling – pure unadulterated boredom! As a little boy, he'd felt that the only good thing about church was getting out, with the possible exception of looking up the skirts of the girls. So it was one of those areas where he and his mother agreed to disagree.

Dorothy Harding went to church every Sunday and was involved in numerous church activities. Nicholas' attitude was that he worked 50-60 hours each week. He usually had Saturdays and Sundays relatively free. So he wasn't about to give up one of those days. Especially to something he felt was excruciatingly boring and a general waste of his time.

By 10:00 Andrea was ready and they were off to Liberty Science Center. Nicholas' favorite part of LSC was the

Omni-Max theatre. Andrea found most of the I-MAX movies boring, but they were only about 20 minutes, so she put up with them. She loved the interactive exhibits. Her favorite was the dark tunnel. A winding, twisting tunnel with sharp turns, rises, and drops about 100 feet in length. You had to crawl through it. The difficulty and challenge was that the tunnel was enclosed and in the absolute dark.

On this particular excursion LSC was having a special "Bugs of the World" exhibit. Nicholas had found a South American Hissing Cockroach part of the exhibit to be fascinating. The bugs nested in groups of hundreds or thousands. Each bug was about four inches long and two inches wide. He'd thought Andrea would get a kick out of holding one. However, bugs tend to clasp with their feet. It doesn't hurt, but Andrea didn't take to the bug and shook her hand and sent the bug into sub-orbit across the room.

Harding guessed they could scratch entomology off the list of career potentials. But they had a great day. After about three hours at LSC they went to the docks, boarded a ferry, got hotdogs and sodas and rode the ferry to Ellis Island and the Statue of Liberty. It was a warm sunny day and they sat on the open top deck. They'd visited Ellis and the Statue before so they didn't get off. They just enjoyed each other's company. A father and daughter. Nicholas wondered *how long will this last? How long will it be until she reaches the phase where she thinks Dad is the biggest asshole on Earth?*

All his friends said it would come. *Oh, well. For now this is good. It can't get any better.*

10

The Feds

Driving home late after work, Nicholas had allowed his mind to wander. Everything was starting to turn a dark, lush, spring-time green and suburban Morris County began to resemble an enchanted forest. As he turned into his long drive, he noticed an unfamiliar car with U.S. Government license tags parked in front of his house. After pulling into the garage he entered the house through the kitchen, heard voices in the living room and went in. He saw his mother, Andrea, and two strangers.

The first was a white male; mid-thirties, athletic, tall, good looking, self-confident, Southern accent – Nicholas knew the type. The other stranger was a young white woman, slim, on the short side, with short brunette hair. She was sort of attractive, but had striking, cold, gray, and bird-like eyes.

"Good evening, Dr. Harding." The gray eyes were slightly warmer now. "I'm Dr. Beverly Coston, Food and Drug Administration Field Investigator," she said, showing him her badge. "And this is Agent Barry Kenan, U.S. Marshal's office."

A chill went through Nicholas, giving him goose bumps. He tried not to show his fear. "And I'm very disappointed in both of you." He said without a smile. "Mom, can you please take Andrea upstairs?"

Dorothy and Andrea left the room. As soon as she was around the corner and out of sight 'Drea issued one of her guttural Klingon commands. "Rasputin! *GhoS DaH!*" (Come now).

Nicholas smiled when the U.S. Marshal jumped with a start when 'Drea gave the command and Rasputin, who had been sitting behind Kenan on a bookshelf, jumped down with a large *thud* and followed his daughter out of the room.

"Jesus Christ! What the hell was that? And, where'd it come from," he cried, looking as stupid as Nicholas had surmised he was. Nicholas' low opinion of Kenan was sinking rapidly.

"Calm down. It's just a cat. A Main Coon, I believe? About 20ish pounds?" Apparently, Dr. Beverly Coston didn't have a particularly high opinion of Barry Kenan either.

Nicholas nodded 'yes' to her question.

"And it's been sitting behind you, watching you since we got here. It's obviously his daughter's cat and probably would have tried to rip your head off if you'd gone near her. How's that?" She looked at Nicholas. "Although, I don't know what your daughter just said."

"Right again," Nicholas said, his opinion of Coston rising slightly.

"I don't mean to be rude, but I want the two of you out of my house – now!" Nicholas said, leaving no uncertainty in his tone.

"You can't talk to us that way!" Kenan shouted, almost letting the b-word (boy) slip out.

"The hell he can't!" Coston said emphatically to Kenan. "So Agent Kenan, since I'm the lead investigator and you're just here because the regs say you have to be, kindly sit down and be quiet."

"You know, I'm happy to see the federal government live up,pardon me, *down* to my expectations of incompetence, and I'd like nothing better than to watch your two-Stooge's routine, but I want you out of my house. You want to talk to me about company business? You do it at Marshall, not my home. And by the way, Special Agent Kenan, so there's no misunderstanding: if I ever see you in the same room as my daughter, you either will have a warrant or I'll have that shiny little badge of yours. We clear?" The two men glared at one another. When Nicholas spoke to Agent Kenan he did so quietly, slowly and coldly. You could see Kenan unconsciously take a step back.

"You can address your comments to me. I'm in charge and I think you'll want to hear what I have to say," said Beverly Coston. "Barry, wait in the car," she said to her partner.

"You know it's against the regs, Beverly," he replied in an official tone.

"My discretion, Barry. Wait outside," she replied in an equally official tone.

Nicholas was watching this, his mind trying to absorb the seriousness and ridiculousness of the moment. Here he had an FDA investigator and a U.S. Marshal in his living room. That meant only one thing: something major was going down in Washington and Marshall was the target. Question was what the angle was involving him. Was he under investigation, about to be indicted? Talk about being dropped in the middle of an ocean without a boat.

Special Agent Kenan followed, "I'll be right outside if you need me."

Coston replied, "Good. I'll call you if the cat comes back."

Nicholas was almost about to like Beverly Coston, but realized she represented a clear and very present danger to him and his career, perhaps even more.

As soon as Barry Kenan closed the door behind him, she turned to Nicholas. "Look, I know the drill. All you company executives are under orders not to talk to federal investigators away from the company or without house counsel present. Listen to me, something the likes of which the pharmaceutical industry hasn't seen in years, maybe never, is about to go down. The Watergate of your industry and you're right in the middle of it.

"Here's the deal: I won't ask you any questions. I'll just talk for five minutes and then I'll leave. After that, it's your move. Officially, this meeting ended when you told us to get the hell out of your house. It's just you and me – off the record. If I claim we had a conversation, I have no proof. It's your word against mine; no collaboration."

"And, how do I know you're not wired?" he asked.

Beverly stood up and extended her arms straight out by her side. "Pat me down."

Nicholas stared at her for a minute before saying anything. "No thanks. Five minutes, use them wisely."

"You have a lovely home," she said as she sat down.

"Clock's ticking."

"The Japanese Pharmaceutical industry has done a good job of keeping you guys, the U.S. pharmaceutical houses, out of Japan. But it' been trying for years to get major footholds in the U.S. and Europe and for the most part not been very successful. Yes, there are a lot of licensing and joint venture deals, but no Japanese-owned pharmaceutical house has made it big in the U.S. or Europe and therefore has yet to break into the top ten worldwide.

"We received a tip about six months ago," she continued. "It made reference to a possibly illegal collusion between top executives at a U.S. and Japanese pharmaceutical house which may result in Japanese part ownership as a major stakeholder of a big U.S. Pharm house."

"A tip?" Nicholas asked. "You have an informant or informants?"

"I forgot to tell you. You don't get to ask any questions," she answered. "But maybe I'll answer the obvious. Yes, Marshall is the U.S. pharm house. That's all the specifics I can give you."

"What the hell do you want?" Nicholas asked. "You sneak in here and tell me some tale of a plot to conduct illegal business between Marshall and some unnamed Japanese company. I'm supposed to buy all this? Am I a target of the investigation?"

"If you were an individual target, I wouldn't be here. We, I, need your help. I need a contact I can trust in Marshall," Beverly said to Nicholas.

At that point, Nicholas started to laugh. "This is all some sort of joke, isn't it? Mark put you up to this, right?"

"Think about everything I've said. And, before you contact anyone at Marshall ask yourself who you can trust."

"I suppose I should trust you and Special Agent Barry out there?" Nicholas said coldly.

"You'll interact with me. You agree and I'll have Foghorn Leghorn Jr. out there transferred off the case. It's my case and I'll fly solo," she stood to leave. "I'll give you a couple of days to think and I'll call you. Goodnight, Dr. Harding. I know I've dropped a lot on you tonight, but something evil -I really can't think of a better word- is going on at Marshall. Evil and illegal. Because, not only is it illegal, it could hurt a lot of people. And with or without you, I'm going to find it and kill it." She then paused, frowned and said, "figuratively speaking. Sometimes I get overly dramatic. But I'm no less serious."

She opened the door to leave and stuck her head back in. "Oh, tell your daughter she has a pretty neat cat."

Nicholas's mind was racing at warp drive. He'd had a gut feeling something strange was up with some of the Tanaka executives during his last visit, but he had passed it off as being paranoid.

And at Marshall there were always various plots and intrigues boiling, just as at any large international business. Company politics as usual. Or, was this something more?

And, what of the FDA investigation? Most Americans saw the FDA as an efficient government agency; the protector of citizens from the evil and greedy pharmaceutical industry who would sell anything for a buck.

As a pharmaceutical executive who interacted with and was regulated by the FDA, Nicholas had a far different opinion. One-on-one, Nicholas had an excellent relationship with several FDA scientists. However, he found the FDA to be a bloated, inefficient monument to government bureaucratic incompetence. And, they played political hardball with the best of them.

"Where's 'Drea?" Nicholas asked his mother. He was sitting in his study in the dark where he had moved to think. Sitting in his large, overstuffed leather chair similar to an old Englishmen's club chair, Nicholas' eyes closed. He needed to think. He heard, no, rather sensed, his mother's presence as she entered the room. Dorothy rarely entered his study.

It was obvious she unconsciously viewed it as his private sanctuary, like the clubhouse he'd built in the back yard when he was a boy.

The room fed Nicholas's true bibliophile pastime as it contained a large library. Two full walls were covered with floor to ceiling ten foot high shelving where books and oddities Nicholas had collected were stored. This included the real human skull Paula had given him as a birthday gift. A third wall held his various degrees and awards along with a few pictures and more books. The fourth wall was floor to ceiling length windows that lead outside to a porch, which wrapped around the entire house. Thick black drapes allowed for light to open the room up or shut out any exterior illumination, plunging the room into absolute darkness.

Dorothy expected to go in and find Nicholas with the drapes closed, engulfed in a lightless room. Instead, she found him sitting with the lights out, but the drapes open. The effect, once one's eyes adapted to the light was to show a room bathed in soft moon and starlight with darkened shadows. The appearance of the room appeared to fit his mood exactly.

"She's getting ready for bed. Not much homework tonight. She's ready to be tucked in."

"Okay. I'll be there soon."

"Trouble?"

"I don't know. Something's not right. The FDA and U.S. Marshal's office are investigating Marshall. Humn, there's a play on words."

"What are you going to do?" Dorothy asked.

"I don't know."

Dorothy was worried; her son was usually very self-assured.

"I don't know what's going on and I don't know who to turn to or who to trust," he said softly.

"Is there anyone at Marshall you can talk to – trust?" she asked.

"Maybe Arthur. But, I just don't know."

Dorothy asked, "what about that Investigator from the FDA?"

"Trust an FDA investigator? I don't think so. I'll take my chances at Marshall. I may need a lawyer. Not a company lawyer, but my own lawyer. The company legal will look out for the company."

"What about Paula's firm? Can't someone there represent you?" his mother asked.

Nicholas now opened his eyes as a thought dawned on him. How shallow his depth of trust lay. "Paula's firm gets about a third of its billings from Marshall. I'm not sure I'd trust anyone there."

"Maybe I can help," Dorothy said.

"How?" Nicholas asked, curious.

"Give me a couple of days," she said. "Go tuck in Andrea and you get some rest."

11

Brothers

Nicholas hadn't gotten much sleep that Friday night. His mind had been a blur of images and thoughts. Is this how his career would end, caught in some political game? He had been extremely careful over the years to avoid the pitfalls of company politics. As he'd moved up the management ladder, to do so had been harder and harder.

Being naturally quiet and unpretentious and, more importantly, being a black man in a middle-aged white man's world, he was often overlooked or underestimated. In a way he preferred that. People didn't take someone they underestimated or didn't consider an equal seriously. And they certainly didn't consider him a threat, which gave Nicholas an advantage. Extremely ambitious, he was, in his own way, ruthless.

Many an adversary over the years had looked at Nicholas and ignored the quiet black guy, only a few months or years later to find themselves reporting to or, in a few cases, being fired by that guy. Nicholas took full advantage of a rule most knew, but never verbalized, "a white male never considered a black man as his equal." He'd once explained it to his brother Michael like this.

"A white guy is like a rooster. Another rooster comes into the yard and the two roosters square off. They ruffle their feathers and strut around each other. Why? Because they see each other as equals and therefore a threat. That's how white men see each other – as threats. Now a black man, that's like a baby turkey coming in the chicken yard. The rooster's curious, but he doesn't see the turkey as a threat; it's not another rooster.

"So the rooster ignores the turkey. But you know what? If the baby turkey keeps to himself and stays out of the way he grows up. Eventually, he's bigger and stronger than the rooster. And, then the turkey can take over the chicken yard.

"Same for women. When a new hen comes in the yard the rooster doesn't see her as a threat. That's why white women are moving up in management so quickly."

Michael had stopped over to see Andrea and Nicholas on Saturday, but Andrea was visiting a friend. "So let me get this straight," he said as the two brothers sat on the wraparound porch outside Nicholas' study. It was an unusually warm spring afternoon. A few trees had started to bud, but there was still more brown than green. From their view on the deck the brothers could see more than a mile through the naked tree branches. In a few weeks, their view would be limited to a few hundred feet due to the heavy foliage.

"You come home and there's a deputy U.S. Marshal and a FDA field investigator sitting in your living room? You're in deep shit, boy!"

"Tell me about it," Nicholas said. He poured them each another glass of Conti Formentini Pinot Grigio. Nicholas fancied himself a minor wine connoisseur. Michael emphasized the 'minor' and indulged his older brother in his skill. Often the two brothers would sit on the deck starring out into the well-to-do New Jersey countryside and discuss the latest topic of interest: politics, business, the stock market, or just sit and enjoy each one another's company.

No need for conversation if they didn't want to. They were supremely comfortable in each other's company.

"There's something I've wanted to ask you since Paula's death, Nicky. Now seems to be the right time," Michael looked over at Nicholas. " Why still work at Marshall?"

"I don't know. I've asked myself the same question, but I honestly don't know," Nicholas answered, looking over to the next town.

He recollected at the time of the Paula's fatal auto accident she had been a partner at Donalds, Coombs and Cooper (DCC), one of the top legal firms in Northern Jersey, based in Morristown. The accident involved an 18-wheeler from a large nationwide trucking firm, who, to their misfortune, had a driver who fell to sleep because he logged over his time limit. His vehicle had failed its last inspection due to brake problems.

Nicholas and Paula both carried rather heavy life insurance, what with Andrea's education and all. So Nicholas and Andrea received a life insurance payment of $2.5 million, which couldn't compensate for his wife.

The topper was DCC. Having lost a young partner with rainmaker potential, they went after the trucking company with a vengeance. It was like a piranha feeding frenzy. The last thing the trucking company had wanted was a trial.

Attractive, young wife and mother leaves her husband and 10-year-old daughter behind. Also a talented attorney with a brilliant legal future.

The trucking company saw the 'zeros' adding up and tried to settle for about $7 million. DCC wanted blood and so, to some degree, did Nicholas. After DCC threatened a long, bloody very public fight the trucking company finally agreed to a settlement that gave DCC alone $10 million and Nicholas and Andrea $20 million, even after legal fees and taxes the $20 million settlement left them in a financial position where Nicholas would never have to work again if he chose not to. He certainly didn't need any financial incentive from his position at Marshall. But he told himself he had a goal – the vice presidency – and he wanted to see it through.

That, plus he just couldn't deal with any more major change right now. So he'd convinced himself and he stayed at Marshall. See it through to the vice presidency, then walk away and set up a consulting company with Michael. As Nicholas now tried to explain this to Michael, it was the first time he'd verbalized his thoughts or feelings on this topic to any other than Dr. Coleman, his and Andrea's therapist.

"So that's it?" Michael asked when Nicholas finished. "You're putting up with all this horseshit at Marshall, so you maybe, might possibly get a chance to be a vice president and then walk away from it?"

"That's the essence of it – yeah!" Nicholas replied.

"You're nuts. Abso-fucking-lutely nuts! You don't owe those white boys at Marshall a goddamn thing. They don't give a shit about you, which should be obvious now that someone's trying to shove a telephone pole up your butt with this investigation. If it were me, I'd hire one of those planes that pulls the sky banners to pull a big banner over the Headquarters site and say 'Marshall – screw you, love Nicholas!'" Michael was laughing when he said this, but Nicholas knew he was serious.

"That's what I love about you Michael, always the subtle touch. But it's not about them. It's about me. Whether I can cut it. Whether I can compete in their world."

"*If* they let you compete, Nicky, *if* they let you," Michael said. "Remember what Dad used to say when we were kids?"

And the two now slightly inebriated brothers together chanted words that held meaning to them that most wouldn't understand: "The only good one is a dead one!"

And they laughed.

"Do you believe it?" Nicholas asked.

Michael answered, growing serious. "When I first heard Dad say that, we were driving by a white cemetery and he said, 'look over there. There're a lot of good white people over there. Cause the only good one is a dead one!' I didn't quite know what to think. At first, I thought how sad to have lived a life so you believe something like that. Over the years, I've gone back and forth. And now I don't think they're all evil, but when it comes to dealing with us, I think Dad was on to something. Maybe all the good ones aren't six feet under but I can guarantee you one thing, Nicky, there aren't that many good ones at someplace like Marshall. You watch your back, bro."

"I intend to," Nicholas said, staring into the twilight. "Speaking of nuts, I'm having lunch with Don Marshall on Monday," he said for no reason.

"Why? Is he as nuts as everyone says?" Michael asked.

"Don't know. All I know about Don Marshall is the rumors. I plan to collect him though," said Nicholas.

"You still into that? Why collect someone you dislike and don't respect?

"Curious. Besides, you can learn something from everyone."

"You're weird, big brother," Michael said.

"I know," Nicholas replied softly.

12

Don Marshall

"Karen. What time is my meeting with Don Marshall and where am I meeting him?" Nicholas called out to Karen from his office.

It had been a typical flurry of Monday morning activity, reviewing problems which had occurred on various studies over the weekend with directors; refereeing a fight between a toxicologist and pathologist, both of whom could have used an ego reduction procedure; approving timesheets; reading emails and more. The normal routine.

There had been a confirmatory note about lunch from Don Marshall, but he'd left out all specifics regarding time and location. Karen had everything under control and obtained the necessary information for their luncheon.

"Karen, can you see if Arthur has a brief opening in his schedule today? Just 10-15 minutes, I don't need much time." Nicholas's request was delivered while walking by her desk.

"Sorry, Dr. Harding, Dr. Kronan's not in today. He took a vacation day," Karen answered.

How does she know everything happening in the office, she rarely talks to the other secretaries, they don't seem to like her much, but she talks with someone. She always knows everything.

"Okay, call down to Glen Morgan and tell him I need to see him ASAP," Nicholas returned after getting a bottle of water, went back into his office and began to review draft study protocols. It seemed like only a few minutes had passed when he heard a soft knock and looked up to find Glen Morgan at his office door.

Glen was one of the senior toxicologists on Nicholas' staff. He was somewhat unusual in that most of the senior toxicologists in the group were Ph.D.'s. Glen was as good as most and better than some of the Ph.D.'s in the department, but the rumor was he had walked out of an Ivy League Ph.D. program.

Nicholas didn't care. Glen's skills as a pharmaceutical industry toxicologist were not matched by his interpersonal skills. Nicholas tended to allow Glen to work alone or directly with him.

"Come on in, Glen. Have a seat," Nicholas answered as Glen slid into a chair and curled his legs under him.

"Hi Nick. You wanted to see me?"

Glen always looked angry, so most people stayed out of his way. Nicholas had asked him once if he was angry and the response was, "no,this is just how I look, always has been."

"Glen, are you familiar with the MR-548 project from Tanaka Pharmaceuticals?"

"Yeah, antiviral, right? You're the team leader," Glen peered at Dr. Harding quizzically.

"That's the one," he answered, giving Morgan a focused stare. Harding played with a silly stress toy as he talked. For their meeting he was fondling a little bag filled with a hard putty-like material.

"I hear there's a shit-load of toxicology reports from Japan," Glen cut in, while appearing to look out the window.

"Right and that's why you're here."

Glen Morgan was not a corporate type; he was one of those people who didn't thrive in American industry or corporate settings. He appeared to be too opinionated and stubborn to only express politically-coached discourses.

Contrary to what everyone says or desires, being honest and forthright in corporate America is not usually the best course of action in big business and Morgan never failed to be both. He was considered a smart-ass and was often referred to as a loudmouth by most of the other R&D managers. However, a hands-off policy surrounded him as Nicholas' pet.

"I need a favor, Glen," Nicholas sat behind his moderately cluttered desk and looked squarely at his subordinate.

"Oh, so the big Dr. Director needs a favor from little me? And what might that be?"

"I need you to do a quick review of the MR-548 tox, metabolism and clinical studies," Nick responded.

Glen laughed out loud, "Oh, I get it. You want me to do your work for you. It is your project, Nick. That's why you make the big bucks, you know?"

"Speaking of big bucks Glen, what was your annual compensation package last year?"

"Since I work for you, you probably have a pretty good idea of my comp package," feeling backed into a corner, Glen's words were cutting.

"Humor me, Glen," Nicholas responded. "What was your comp package last year?"

"I don't know, I guess it was kind of respectable," Glen shrugged.

"Try very respectable, Glen. Most folks at your level don't receive stock options or grants such as those you receive."

"Okay, if you say so, but aren't we off the subject of me doing your work for you?"

"We'll get back to that," Nicholas kept to the line of discussion. "You know most of the directors around here don't make what you do, Glen, and without a Ph.D. or any management responsibility; and why is that?"

"Because I'm good," Morgan held his ground.

"That's true, you are. But let's be realistic. Being good isn't enough. It's because you report directly to me and I protect you from all the assholes that think you're just another weird fuck who should be tossed out. Without me, you'd be just another mid-level bench scientist making half what you make now. So, what does that mean, Glen? That's a rhetorical question. Don't answer.

"It means you owe me and I'm calling in my mark. Are we clear?" Nicholas' eyes bore into Glen's.

"Okay. We're clear. What do you need, Nick?"

"Good.

"It won't be easy Glen, but I do need a quick review of all the tox, metabolism and clinical studies on MR-548 in the Tanaka package. We don't have copies of all the reports in-house, but I have a direct online tie-in to Tanaka's data acquisition/report generation system. I'll have the IT folks tie you in too."

"Alright, when do you want this done?"

"I want it done in two weeks," Nicholas answered Glen Morgan's hopeful question.

"Two weeks, sure. You want me to make pigs fly too while I'm at it?"

"Look Glen, I know you can't do a detailed review of everything in two weeks, but I need an overview. I'm looking for anything that stands out. If it's there, you'll see it. Most people will not, but you will. I'm counting on you Glen, okay?"

"Okay Dr. Harding. For you I'll put arm back in joint and get right on it," Morgan had a one-sided smile as he chidingly spoke.

"Thanks, Glen." Nicholas stood up to walk Morgan out the door.

"Dr. Harding," Karen walked into Nicholas' office. "Mr. Marshall's car is picking you up at the main entrance at 11:30. You'll have lunch in his private dining room at the Marshall mansion."

"Thanks, Karen. Please close the door when you leave. I have some calls to make."

"Of course, Dr. Harding."

Nicholas dialed an international number to London. After several short double toned rings a male voice answered in a proper British accent. "Ms. Sullivan's office."

"Hello, this is Dr. Nicholas Harding U.S. R&D, is Ms. Sullivan in?"

"A moment please, Dr. Harding." While holding, Nicholas created a visual image of the owner of the voice, which was rather boring because he sounded very British.

Visualizing Catherine Sullivan was much more enjoyable. Catherine was Marshall's Senior Vice President who headed European Marketing. She was in her early forties, looked late twenties and resembled a *Vogue* fashion model. She'd clawed her way up the Marshall Sales and Marketing ladder to her current Board of Director level position and she was by no means satisfied with her current position.

Nicholas and Catherine had met years ago when she'd been a U.S. Sales Rep and had kept in contact, helping each other when possible. White males in power tended not to take most women seriously, especially attractive women, much like they considered Blacks. A few made that mistake with Catherine and survived to tell the tale. She had a natural instinct to know when to go for the jugular and she rarely missed. Cathy Sullivan looked fairly harmless, in addition to being beautiful, which threw most men off balance. She was short, petite and visually about as threatening as a junior high school cheerleader. But under her façade was one of the most ruthless business minds Nicholas had ever encountered.

Catherine also had exquisite tastes and immediately after taking the head position in European Marketing had nested herself in a sprawling Mayfair apartment in London. There were numerous rumors as to how she'd pulled that off, ranging from embezzling company funds to sleeping with the right people (although there weren't too many people left higher than Catherine in Marshall). Nicholas just chalked it up to Catherine's wheeling and dealing.

He definitely admired and liked her, but he wasn't so sure about trust. He'd always wanted to be as self-assured as Catherine, but could never quite pull it off. He'd asked her once how she did it and she'd surprised him with her answer.

"Most of the time I fake it. No one knows but you. Half the time, I'm bluffing about something or other and scared to death someone will see that. But I just fake confidence. 'Fake it till you make it.' That's my motto. Inside, I'm still a scared little girl hiding under the covers."

Catherine answered the phone, "Nick, you scoundrel, I haven't heard from you in weeks. How are things?" Catherine asked. "You are coming to the European Investigators Conference next week?"

"Wouldn't miss it, Cath. Can you recommend a good hotel?"

"I'll have my staff take care of it for you."

"Thanks. Catherine, have you been involved with MR-548?"

"Peripherally. I thought you were driving that one," she replied.

"I am. I just need to bounce some things off you when I see you."

"Sure. Look, Nick, you know I'd love to chat, but I'm heading out to a meeting."

"That's okay, how about dinner or something next week?"

"Dinner's boring. I'll take you up on the 'or something' though," she said in a wicked tone.

"Can't wait. See you next week."

"Okay, bye Nick."

Nicholas sat and looked at the phone after he'd hung up. Could he talk to Catherine about what was going on? Could he trust her? He and Cath went way back, but he hated this feeling of being vulnerable. He'd have to talk to Arthur, but first Don Marshall. He'd collect Don Marshall.

Nicholas had one more phone call to make before he left to have lunch with Don. He looked up Gerry Michael's number in his online phone directory and clicked on his line information for his computer to dial the number. Gerry was Marshall's Chief Legal Counselor. For having been married to a lawyer and having a brother who was one, Nicholas was surprisingly untrusting of them as a whole. Or maybe he was just untrusting as a whole.

"Gerry Michael," He heard in his phone receiver.

"Gerry. It's Nicholas Harding in R&D."

"Hi Nicholas. Haven't seen you in a while. What's up? Is this about that new project you're heading MR-548? It and you are quite the buzz in the Executive Office Building."

"I'm not quite sure what it's about, Gerry. I need to report a contact with an FDA field agent and deputy U.S. Marshal at my house," Nicholas said. He'd expected to hear questions from Gerry, but heard only silence.

"When and what happened? I need details, names, etc." Gerry said calmly.

"It was last Friday. I left you a voice mail."

"I was out yesterday and haven't picked up my voice mail. Go on."

Nicholas went on to describe what had happened with FDA agent Dr. Beverly Coston and agent Barry Kenan. "Basically, they, no, she. She was in charge. She said there's some sort of investigation involving Marshall. I told them it was inappropriate for them to contact me at home and to leave."

"And?" Michael asked.

"And they left. What the hell's going on here Gerry? You guys in legal have to know something about this. FDA investigators and U.S. Marshals don't drop by to chat. Something big is going down and I want to know what, since I seem to be stuck in the middle."

"Nicholas. You report to Dr. Kronan, right?" Gerry asked.

"Yeah, why?"

"Have you told him or anyone else in your organization about this?"

"Art's out sick and no, I haven't told anyone else."

"Okay, you need to inform Jack O'Connor and I'll get on it from my end."

"Alright."

"Now, Nicholas. The rest of this is off the record. Do you have a good personal attorney?"

"No. I haven't really needed one."

"You do now. Just at face value. You're right. This is major league bad news. Protect yourself. I'll be in touch."

Nicholas sat at his desk looking out his window. What the hell was happening? Maybe Michael was right. Maybe he should just leave. He didn't need to put up with this crap.

"Dr. Harding," Karen said softly, standing at his doorway. "Mr. Marshall's car is waiting out front."

"Thanks Karen," Nicholas said as he rose to go out to meet and collect Don Marshall.

13

Collecting Don

When Nicholas entered the large open lobby of the main R&D building, he could see a long black limousine through the front wall, which was all plate glass. He said hello to the receptionist who had been on the job since before he joined the company and went through an open arch that was actually a well-disguised metal detector/security scanner. As soon as he exited the building the driver's door opened and he exited the car and moved around to open the right rear passenger door.

"Good morning, Dr. Harding," the driver said as Harding entered the car.

The drive from the Marshall Farm Business Complex to the Marshall family estate and mansion was only about ten minutes. The Marshall estate was situated well off the main roads of Florham Park, so none of the buildings on the estate could be seen from any public street.

As the car turned into the gated driveway of the estate, it appeared to be entering a heavily wooded forest, but after about half a mile opened up into wide manicured lawns. The tree-lined drive led to a stone wall with another large gate. Beyond the stonewall gate the driveway became cobblestone and much wider. Once through the last gate and onto the cobblestone drive, the main mansion became visible.

The Marshall mansion and the surrounding grounds exuded the concept of money and power.

The mansion was a classical early 20th century style estate with sweeping copper roofs, turreted towers and gables, four floors visible, expansive gardens and fountains. This was the result of two generations toiling at Marshall.

Nicholas had read the mansion had seventeen bedrooms and Donald Marshall, the founder, had built it to intimidate the locals. *Must have worked.*

The limousine pulled up through an arched cover by the front door and stopped. The front door of the house opened and a uniformed servant stepped forward and opened the car door.

"Good morning, Dr. Harding. This way please," Marshall's butler led Nicholas into their home. He was middle aged, maybe early 50s, obviously British and black.

"If you'll be so kind as to wait here," the butler gestured to a large library. "Mr. Marshall will join you shortly."

When the butler left Nicholas took an opportunity to explore the library, which intrigued him. There were two levels with a mezzanine on the upper level. A large fireplace was on the wall to the right as he entered the room.

Across the room, positioned so the fireplace could be seen was the largest roll-top desk Harding had ever laid his eyes on. Nicholas had a fondness for roll-top desks. This one was dark heavy wood with dozens of small drawers and compartments. It was a beautiful piece of furniture.

On the wall over the fireplace were two portraits of two middle-aged gentlemen who clearly resembled one another. Harding recognized the two men as the founder of Marshall Pharmaceutical, Donald Marshall I and the II, Don's father. There was no sign of the current Don's portrait anywhere, but there were literally thousands of books organized neatly and efficiently as in any private library. Some appeared to be rare collector's items.

The outer walls had large eight-foot tall windows with a beautiful view of the manicured lawns. From the mezzanine windows a faint outline of the New York skyline was visible.

The windows had heavy velvet drapes of a rich dark blue, which could be pulled to shield the books from sunlight.

Lustfully admiring the desk, imagining the minor fortune it must have cost, Dr. Harding was slightly startled hearing a voice behind him.

"It's ironwood from Jamaica. One of the densest woods known to man, extremely difficult to work with. My father hired a Jamaican wood worker and his son to make it. He brought them and two tons of ironwood here. It took them three years to make the desk. It weighs almost a half-ton. Of course, we also have all kinds of ironwood knickknacks all over the house they made from the scraps.

"The wood carver, his son and family stayed in New Jersey. My father set them up with a shop in Morristown. They're doing well. That desk was probably my father's favorite thing in the house. He polished it himself every Saturday morning. I'm sorry; I didn't introduce myself Dr. Harding. I'm Don Marshall," extending a hand toward Nicholas, Marshall smiled courteously. He had walked to the desk and begun gently stroking it while he spoke. "Thank you for agreeing to lunch with me, Dr. Harding."

Harding took note of Don Marshall, the heir of all things Marshall Pharmaceuticals. He's a little older than I'd expected – late forties or early fifties. His resemblance to his family's portraits is obvious though. Looks about six feet tall, good physical shape, graying hair, firm handshake. But those cold, steel-gray eyes. Looks like a West Point graduate, but not a rich playboy. There was a serious, yet somewhat detached air about him. Nicholas couldn't read him clearly, something he usually did well with others, but not Don Marshall. Harding was perplexed.

"I understand you are a lover of books, Dr. Harding. It's a passion we share. Let me show you my latest toy."

Marshall went over to the massive roll-top desk and rolled the top back. The open desktop of heavily varnished and polished wood gleamed.

Nicholas saw there was only one item on the desktop, a large leather portfolio, which was closed. The portfolio was about 11 x 14 inches with rich dark tan leather. As Nicholas moved closer he noticed the seal of the President of the United States. Don caressed the portfolio as he had the desk.

Curiosity spiked on multiple levels for Dr. Harding. First, he wanted to see what was contained inside the portfolio, but he was more curious as to how Don Marshall knew of his love of books. Nicholas considered it to be his only real vice because he obsessively acquired books. He couldn't travel anywhere without going to a bookstore and buying a book. He began researching hard to find books and collector's editions; he also roamed Amazon.com like a cat stalking prey for newer titles. Consequently, books were piled all over his house, which led him to own a smaller library in his own home. Paula had been on his case about buying so many books and asked why he didn't check them out of the library. He always replied, "a book had a soul and to capture its soul, he had to possess the book." He often purchased sought after books and carried and caressed them for days before he read them. When his wife inquired what he was up to, Harding told her, "when a man meets a beautiful woman he has longed for and they agree to make love, he doesn't throw her on the floor and ravish her as soon as he sees her. That would be barbaric. He takes time to gently caress her, know her, and love her before making love to her."

He'd tried to explain to Paula that reading a good book was like two lovers – the reader and the book – making love to each other. Paula had always responded with laughter suggesting Nicholas was an odd duck, ending the discussion.

Don moved to open the portfolio. "I also understand, Dr. Harding, you enjoy reading Civil War era titles, so you should appreciate this." Carefully Don Marshall opened the folder to reveal an obviously old handwritten letter on the left side of the page with printed text on the right.

"A collection of twelve original letters from Abraham Lincoln to his generals during the Civil War; including some to Sherman and Grant and one to McClellan, telling him to get off his ass and attack Lee." Don went on, fascinated with his own story, "of course, he (McClellan) didn't move his ass and Lincoln fired him."

"Only to bring him back after Hooker lost at Antietam," Nicholas added.

"Very good, Dr. Harding. But alas, it was a short-lived return engagement. Lincoln was forced to re-fire Little Mac when he returned to passive form and refused to move his Army. Tell me, Dr. Harding, what do you think of General McClellan?"

"I've always thought him one of the most fascinating characters of the Civil War, yet relatively little has been written about him. After all, at the age of 35, he gained command of the most powerful army on Earth and then proceeded to do absolutely nothing with it," Nicholas expounded.

"And, went on to become?" Don inquired gleefully knowing he had an equal playmate on the topic.

"A losing presidential Democratic candidate against Lincoln in 1864 and then elected Governor of New Jersey in 1877," Nicholas replied. "Though few know that. In fact few probably remember who McClellan was."

"Potential unachieved. Such a waste," Don Marshall responded while looking out the large window at the acres of Marshall lawn.

"Is that what they say of me, Dr. Harding?" Don's steel gray eyes fixated on Harding.

"Yes, it is. Perhaps without the McClellan analogy, but yes, that's the general gist of it Mr. Marshall," Harding replied without breaking eye contact.

"And, your assessment, Dr. Harding? Am I the McClellan of my family?" Don asked.

"No sir." What the hell is the guy is asking? He doesn't appear to be in the mood for someone to give him a butt-kissing politically correct answer. "Wrong as he was, McClellan believed he was right and stood up for those beliefs. With all due respect sir, at least from what I've heard, you didn't do that. You chose to walk away."

"Fair enough, Dr. Harding," Don said as he walked towards a far wall. The wall had a sliding door, which appeared to be part of the wall, but was visible only when standing near the wall.

Don slid the door open to reveal an annex to the library; perhaps a reading room with a large oval table (of the same wood as the desk). Nicholas noticed the table was set with a service.

"Since we both are lovers of books I've taken the liberty of having our lunch here in the library, if that's acceptable to you."

"I'd like that, Mr. Marshall," Harding took in the room as he made his way towards the table.

"By the way, please call me Don or Donald. I'm not Mr. Marshall, at least not yet," he said.

This room is much smaller. Nicholas noticed a state of the art desktop computer terminal at a desk on a side wall.

"Please be seated, Dr. Harding," Don gestured toward a chair while taking his own seat. "May I call you Nicholas?"

"Yes, of course, Don," Nicholas replied.

Another uniformed servant appeared out of nowhere and began to serve lunch. Nicholas thought it must be something they teach at servant school or wherever these people were trained;how to silently appear and disappear like ghosts. *They have that down to a fine art; make themselves unobtrusive and unnoticed as possible.*

"I am curious though about lunch. Why? And, why me?" Nicholas asked.

"I recently started doing this on occasion with some of the more interesting senior managers and scientists. I want to know what is going on, *really* going on. After all, the company does still carry my family name and I am the largest shareholder," Don explained.

"But still a minority shareholder," Nicholas interjected.

"Correct for now," Don stated. "As for why you Nicholas, I've heard much about you, you interest me. I think you're going places in Marshall. Most of the executives at your level are professional butt kissers. I get the distinct impression, especially after your response to the McClellan question, you're different."

"And, how do you know so much about me – books, Civil War, etc., ?" Harding's look was again inquisitive.

"I have my ways. I can't divulge all my secrets. Suffice it to say, I'm better connected into Marshall than most people think. Anyway, I admire a man who has real interests outside of work."

"As long as there's a balance," Nicholas ventured, again being brutally honest.

"Touché," replied Don.

Nicholas noticed a lack of any feminine influence in any areas of the house he'd seen.

"Is there a Mrs. Marshall?" he ventured to ask.

"My mother died some time ago. As for me, my one foray into matrimonial bliss was, unsurprisingly, an abysmal, but brief failure. As I recall, her departing words were something to the tune of, 'I should have married the only person I was capable of loving – myself.' To which I replied, 'I considered that option, but couldn't get around the legality.' You get the essence of the type of relationship we had."

"Fascinating," Nicholas replied.

"And you Nicholas are a widower. My condolences. I also understand you and your daughter are very close. That's good. Hold onto that relationship."

Nicholas detected a trace of sadness in Don's voice when he spoke of the parent-child relationship. They finished their elegant lobster bisque and were almost finished with the warm salad with duck breast, when Nicholas asked. "Do you do this much research on your every Marshall lunch guest?"

"No."

"So to what do I owe the honor of such intense scrutiny? Just out of curiosity, is this anything to do with the fact I'm the highest ranking black man in the company?"

"Ah! One hour and forty five minutes!" Don exclaimed.

"Pardon?" Nicholas asked.

"Nicholas, you and I have been conversing, intelligent man to intelligent man, for almost two hours now, without any mention of race. Which is not bad, mind you, but still you had to spoil it."

"Sorry, I tend to get a little paranoid sometimes," Nicholas answered with a significant degree of sarcasm. "After all, race really isn't an issue at Marshall. There aren't enough of us to be an issue."

"No argument here. That's another subject. But one that has no bearing on my interest in you. Suffice it to say for now I find you interesting and predict a long relationship." Don furthered, "there's a sea of change about to sweep over Marshall and I see you in that sea, Nicholas."

"Am I in a boat, a life raft, or just overboard?"

"I don't know, Nicholas," he said with a sly smile.

Another servant appeared to serve coffee, after which Don insisted on giving Nicholas a tour of the house. After the tour, Nicholas had to agree that the library was the most interesting part of the house, although it did have several non-standard features, such as a small movie theatre, full gymnasium, indoor pool, three-lane bowling alley, billiards room, etc. and, of course, neat toys.

By now it was well after 3:00 PM when Don walked Nicholas to the front entrance. "I hope lunch was all you expected, Nicholas."

"Actually, I had no expectations, so it exceeded them."

"Excellent. Now, how about you, your daughter Andrea and a guest come over in a couple of weekends? I get first run movies in my screening room. I'm sure I can find something suitable for all. What do you say?"

Nicholas felt his antenna go up; not sure what was going on here. But saw no immediate harm. He could always cancel if he thought of a good reason.

"Okay. Andrea would like that."

"Good. Till then," Don Marshall turned and disappeared into the recesses of his mansion and left Nicholas by the door with another servant, who opened it to reveal the limousine driver waiting outside.

On the ride back to his office Nicholas tried to sort things out. Don wasn't what he'd expected. He had expected a flake, but eccentric though he may be, Don had all his oars in the water. Something didn't compute here. Nicholas had planned to collect Don and it appeared Don collected Nicholas.

Too many bizarre things are going on in my life.

14

Jack's Lair

It was about 3:45 when Nicholas returned to his office on the fourth floor of the R&D office complex.

"You've returned," Karen said looking up from the spreadsheet she had on her computer screen. Nicholas recognized it as his department budget spreadsheet, which he allowed her to manage. "I thought perhaps you had been adopted by the Marshall family, yes?" Karen intoned with her odd syntax.

"Not yet, but I'm working on it," he replied while quickly scanning the inbox to see if anything urgent had come in. It all appeared to be junk. Nicholas had learned many years earlier most paperwork generated in corporate America was C.Y.A. bullshit. Very little useful information was conveyed. And, as for a decision being made; forget it. The secret to success in a large corporation was to never be tagged with making a decision. Always involve a group – a committee or taskforce. That way, when things go wrong, there's a lot of room to spread the blame. If things go well, you can always take credit as the leader of the successful effort.

Nicholas hated the political crap and usually did the opposite of what was expected. Through a combination of luck and skill he'd managed to have a more successful track record than many of his back-stabbing peers.

"Any word from Arthur?" He asked.

"No. He's still out sick."

"Odd. Is Jack O'Connor in today?"

"Yes, and by the way, he called earlier looking for you, Dr. Harding."

"Okay. I'm going up to his office, Karen."

O'Connor's office was on the R&D fifth floor executive building executive. As head of all Marshall R&D, both clinical and non-clinical, Jack ruled his global empire with an iron fist. Nicholas had read an article on James Baker, Secretary of State under George H. W. Bush. Baker was described as 'the velvet hammer', someone who welded extreme power, but with finesse and class. Given that, O'Connor's style could be described as 'the rusty spiked hammer'. When Jack was in the room, there was space for only one opinion – his.

With some degree of technical respect for O'Connor, Nicholas felt his bullying; micromanaging style was about 30 years outdated. As a member of the Marshall Board of Directors, Jack carried considerable clout. He'd long ago wiped out all potential enemies and competition and the rumor was he lusted after the company CEO position.

O'Connor's lair was spacious and designed to intimidate; a large open anteroom with chairs for waiting victims far away from the workspace of his secretary, Roberta. That way if you're waiting for Jack, you can't see what she's working on. And, Roberta was a piece of work. She ruled over all the R&D secretaries like the Wicked Witch of the East ruled her flying monkeys, with the exception of Karen, whom she despised but left alone. Roberta was one of those secretaries who took glee from using her bosses' power to terrorize everyone else in the organization.

Nicholas learned two people you absolutely never want to piss off are the bosses' secretary and spouse, in that order. So every Secretary's Day or Administrative Assistant's Day or whatever the current politically correct term was - even though he hated it as a holiday created by and for Hallmark and the florist industry - Roberta received flowers and candy from Nicholas. The same was true for Christmas and her birthday. Consequently, Roberta, Queen of the Vampires, had a soft spot in her cold, atrophied heart for Nicholas.

"Hi Roberta, how are things?" Nicholas walked in and went over to her desk. Most people had learned to keep a respectful distance from Roberta's desk, but Nicholas was one of the few allowed to approach.

"Just fine, Nicholas." She appeared busy. Of course, she rarely had much to do, since she worked for only one highly placed person.

"Is the chief in?" Harding asked, referring to O'Connor.

"Yes, in fact, he was looking for you earlier today. He said for you to come in if you came by. So just knock."

"Thanks Roberta. Pretty scarf."

Roberta smiled a thank you and went back to work.

Nicholas went beyond Roberta's desk and turned a corner to reach O'Connor's door, which he always kept closed.

Another control thing. O'Connor keeps the damn door closed so he has to give permission to enter. He just loves to remain dominant by making everyone receive permission to enter his office.

It was amazing people fell for these O'Connor's head games. Nicholas knocked and heard Jack say, "enter."

O'Connor's interior office was also designed to exude power and intimidate visitors. Rich leather furniture, a wide desk in front of a floor to ceiling window. If you were facing O'Connor as he sat behind his desk, the glare from the window caused you to squint and not be able to see what he was doing. The impression was one of talking to a disembodied voice.

Nicholas usually avoided this little trick by stepping to the side and conversing with Jack from an angle, but today was different. There was Jack bathed in light from his window giving him what he probably thought to be an angelic glow. Nicholas always thought it was more like the Devil in the glow from the fires of Hell. But today, seated to the Devil's right was Gerry Michael, from Marshall Legal Department. Nicholas had come to inform Jack about the FDA visit to his home, but didn't expect to see Gerry or anyone from Legal. It was obvious they had been in deep conversation.

"Nicholas, come in. I hear you had visitors the other night. Tell me about it," Jack got directly to the point.

Nicholas, without being invited, took a seat. "That's why I came here. Arthur's out and I informed Gerry this morning. When I got home Friday night an FDA field investigator and deputy U.S. Marshal were in my home. I told them they'd have to see me at work if they have questions. They made mention of an ongoing investigation involving Marshall. Then I told them to leave."

"And?" O'Connor asked with a freezing gaze.

"And, they left," Nicholas said, leaving out his one-on-one conversation with FDA agent Beverly Cost

"That's it?" O'Connor asked.

"That's it," replied Nicholas. "Have they contacted Marshall?"

"No, and as far as we can tell, no else has been contacted," Gerry stated matter-of-factly.

"So, Dr. Harding," O'Connor said slowly. "Why does the FDA and U.S. Marshal's office have such an interest in you?"

"I wouldn't know, Jack. In fact, I came here to ask you why the FDA and U.S. Marshal's office is investigating Marshall Pharm."

"I don't care much for the tone of that question. Now, I want to know why the hell the FDA's on your ass, Nick?" O'Connor was becoming increasingly steamed.

"And I don't care to be accused of something when I don't even know what it is. Now, if someone in Marshall is doing something they shouldn't be, no, let me re-phrase that, Jack. Because in a company this size there's always someone doing something they shouldn't be. If someone at Marshall has gotten *caught* doing something they shouldn't be doing and has caused the feds to look at me, then I don't care for that, Jack! And, I also want to know what the hell is going on!"

Nicholas and Jack were now glaring at each other when Gerry decided to speak up.

"Okay guys. Right now, we don't know what's going on, so I will call the FDA Investigative Division tomorrow and ask. In the meantime, we sit tight. This all may be nothing. Okay?"

"Yeah, sure," O'Connor retorted with a hiss.

"Okay Nicholas?" Gerry asked.

"Okay, but I'm getting legal counsel."

Jack stood up. "What the hell for? You just told us you're Dr. Clean. We don't need any outsiders involved. Gerry will look out for us."

"Gerry will look out for Marshall," said Nicholas. "I'll look out for myself, Jack."

"Suit yourself," O'Connor mumbled. "Where's Arthur?"

"Home sick," said Nicholas.

"Find him and brief him on this."

"Sure. Anything else?" Nicholas asked of Jack and Gerry.

"No," they both said.

Then Jack said, "wait. Nicholas, if you insist on legal counsel, go to DCC. They'll take care of you."

"Sure. Good night," Nicholas said and he walked out of the office.

Nicholas went back to his office. It was after 5:00 PM now and Karen was packing to leave.

"You need anything before I leave, Dr. Harding?"

"No thanks, Karen."

"Your daughter's school called. A Mrs. Carter said Andrea's okay and it's not an emergency, but can you please call."

"Okay, thank you, Karen. Good night."

Nicholas took the call note from Karen with the message from Mrs. Carter.

When it rains…

15

Charring Cross

Mrs. Carter was vice-principal of Charring Cross School, an independent and private elementary school in Madison. It was a bit snobby for Nicholas, but its educational program was rated one of the best in New Jersey; actually the entire Northeast. The children of congressmen, legislators, the rich and powerful went there. Nicholas and Paula had been in total agreement when it came to Andrea's education. But they were concerned that Charring Cross was, to be frank, 'whiter than white'.

Charring Cross had an all-white administration, faculty, and board of trustees. And, about a 94% white student population. The school was over 100 years old and the old-money Morristown-area families ran it with a heavy, but well cultured hand.

If Mrs. Carter was calling, it was probably a discipline issue. It wouldn't be the first time, Nicholas thought as he dialed the number.

"Charring Cross School," a pleasant voice answered.

"Mrs. Carter please, this is Dr. Harding returning her call."

"Just a minute, Dr. Harding."

"Hello, Nicholas? Pam Carter here. Not to worry, Andrea is fine, but we do have just a bit of a discipline problem. Anna is here to pick up Andrea, but perhaps you could come over and we can resolve this now, if it's not too much trouble," she said.

Translation: It's important. Get over here now!

"I'll be there in about 15 minutes, Pam. You can tell Anna to go home. I'll take Andrea. Can you tell me briefly what this is about?"

"Well it's sort of a fight, but it's complicated. I'll see you soon, Nicholas."

Harding quickly packed his organizer and a couple of files to work on at home and dashed out. Karen had already left while he was on the phone. Nicholas went out the back to the executive parking lot where he kept his car; it was his latest automotive toy, a Lexus IS 350 convertible.

Even though he lived only about 15 minutes from his office, he did frequently visit other Marshall facilities in New Jersey and Pennsylvania, so his rationale was if he had to spend a lot of time in his car and he hated to drive, he may as well be comfortable.

After all, what many considered luxuries, like theMark Levinson® Premium Audio System, HD Navigation System with voice command, heated leather seats, and the ability to reach 160 m.p.h. should the need ever arise, Nicholas now viewed as necessities. Since the accident when Paula was killed, one would think Nicholas would have some baggage around driving, but he didn't. He thought it was part of his inability to feel anything about Paula's death.

He and Dr. Coleman, their psychologist, Andrea had discussed this seemingly endlessly and so far to no avail. Nicholas had admitted he considered most mental health professionals about a half step above palm readers and voodoo queens, but he had developed a respect for Coleman. It was all related somehow, Paula's death and a noticeable shift in Andrea's behavior at school. Academics remained strong, but she had become quicker to lose her temper with her peers and remained more of a loner.

Nicholas left the grounds of Marshall Farms and maneuvered the less crowded back roads that lead to Charring Cross located off Route 24 in Madison. The school was started in one of the old mansions that were so numerous in the area at the end of the 19th century. The Morristown-Madison area had been a summer haven for the New York money magnates.

He drove slowly onto the old estate, now school, grounds. School was out so there were few cars around. Nicholas parked near the building housing the administration and went inside. He knew where to find Mrs. Carter's office, as he entered the old mansion he noted the foyer, which opened into a large sitting room with a grand staircase and a large marble fireplace. Over the fireplace was a portrait of the founder of Charring Cross. Nicholas had never really cared who he was. Mrs. Carter's office was on the second floor of the building, so he took the stairs up.

When he opened the door to the outer office area, he looked towards the waiting area on the right and saw Andrea sitting on one side of the room reading. Nicholas went over to her.

"Hi kid."

"Hi Dad."

"We're going to have a lot to talk about tonight."

"I know," she said looking up at him.

"You okay?"

"I'm okay now, Dad. You're here," she said and smiled.

"Okay. You wait here. I have to talk to Mrs. Carter. Alright?"

"Dad," Andrea said as he started to walk away.

"Yeah."

"I didn't have a choice. I did what I had to."

"Okay, 'Drea."

Nicholas knocked and entered Mrs. Carter's office. She was seated at her desk and rose to greet Nicholas.

"Good afternoon Nicholas. I'm so pleased you were able to join us." Pamela Carter had been teaching for more than twenty-five years and spoke in the slow deliberate cadence of someone used to speaking to young children. Nicholas found it extremely annoying and had once made the mistake of telling his mother, a former teacher. As Mrs. Carter came around her desk, Nicholas noticed someone sitting in one of the two chairs in front of her desk.

"Dr. Harding, I don't know if you know Mr. Kent. His son Charles is in the fifth grade."

"I believe we may have met at some function or other," Nicholas said.

The two men shook hands but Kent came across as aloof, as with a lot of Charring Cross parents. In Nicholas' opinion the man had his head up his ass.

Mrs. Carter took her seat, steepled her fingers and resumed her cadence, which was oriented towards 8-10 year olds. "Unfortunately, Dr. Harding, Mrs. Castine, Andrea's teacher, can't join us, but we seem to have all the details and Andrea agrees with them."

"Okay, so what happened?" Nicholas asked, growing increasingly impatient with the pace of things.

"Well, it appears that Andrea and Charles have had several arguments over the past few weeks. She says Charles pushed her. In fact, she told Mrs. Castine that last week. Did she mention any of this to you?"

"I recall her mentioning that someone names Charles bothered her at recess. I told her to tell her teacher," Nicholas said.

"Well she did. But frankly here at Charring Cross we encourage our students to resolve their own differences rather than running to the teachers," Mrs. Carter said with obvious and rather smug pride.

Nicholas started laughing. "I'm sorry, Mrs. Carter. I don't mean to laugh at you. No. No. Actually, I do. You'll have to excuse me; it's been a long, long day. But that's about the dumbest thing I've heard in quite a while. Resolve their own differences? You've got to be kidding. I work with Ph.D.'s, M.D.'s, D.V.M.'s and M.B.A.'s who can't resolve their own differences. And, you actually expect ten and eleven-year-olds to resolve their own difference?"

Nicholas could tell from her expression that Pamela Carter didn't like to be laughed at and have her well thought out idea called stupid. And, she most certainly wasn't used to being spoken to in this manner.

"I see," she said rather coldly. "Well, it seems Andrea took a rather creative approach to solving her problem. After several altercations with Charles, she apparently hired two seventh grade boys to beat up Charles. She paid them $10.00 each. Fortunately, Charles was not seriously injured."

"I see," Nicholas said. "In other words, she resolved her problem?"

"Is that what you teach your daughter, Harding? To hire thugs to beat up my son?" Kent asked with a self-important air.

"Thugs? I would hope that we don't have any thugs here at Charring Cross, not for the tuition I'm paying. And oh, by the way Kent, did young Chuck learn to beat up on women at home?"

Apparently, that was enough to light Kent's obviously short fuse. "How dare you! You son of a bitch! I don't have to listen to this crap. Your daughter put a contract on my son! I won't stand for this!" Kent's face had shifted to a bright crimson and veins bulged out on his neck.

"Gentlemen," Mrs. Carter intervened. "There's enough blame for all. Mr. Kent, Charles must learn that hitting other people is not acceptable. And, Dr. Harding, I hope you'll agree Andrea's solution was not acceptable, either. Both students will be withheld from recess for one week to work on a paper on conflict resolution."

"Look, Pamela, I agree what Andrea did was wrong. I agree with your punishment, and she'll be punished at home as well. But I hope you'll take the time to look at the problem from her viewpoint. I'm sure she felt she had no choice. Expecting kids to behave like adults, when most adults can't behave like adults, is noble but not very realistic. Right, Chuck?"

Kent mumbled agreement, but was clearly still furious. Nicholas could tell the 'N-word' was rambling around Kent's little brain right about now.

Mrs. Carter seemed to realize this was the best she could do with a bad situation and made an excuse about seeing the Headmaster before he left. This left Kent and Nicholas to leave Mrs. Carter's office together.

Kent, not too happy with how things had gone, decided to get in one last shot. "Make sure this doesn't happen again, Harding," he said in his best snobby, inherited wealth tone.

"Okay," replied Nicholas. "Tell you what, if Chuck Jr. pushes Andrea around again, I'm going to 'resolve the conflict' directly with you and I can afford a lot better than the seventh grade bully. How's that, Kent?"

"Is that a threat?" Kent demanded.

"Yes."

Kent, not knowing what to say and half-afraid, decided to make as graceful an exit as possible.

16

'Drea's Punishment

Nicholas went into the outer office waiting area where Andrea was still waiting and sat down next to her.

"I finished all my homework, Dad," she said, hoping it would distract her Dad.

"Good job, hon. Let's go home. We have a lot to talk about, like how to handle bullies and punishment."

"Punishment? Dad, I was defending myself!"

"Save it for when we get home, counselor," Nicholas said as he put his arm around his daughter.

Wrong though her method may have been, Nicholas was proud she'd stood up for herself and done what she'd had to do. *She'll go far in this world.* Nicholas was definitely not a proponent of the turn-the-other-cheek school of human interactions.

On the drive home, Andrea gave a lengthy review of the days academic activities, obviously hoping to distract her father from the Charles incident. She knew it was a long shot, but maybe she could make him forget it. Next, she covered the fact she'd completed all her today's homework assignments.

"'Drea, I'm very pleased with how you're doing with your class work and homework, but honey, you put a hit on one of your classmates! Don't you see the problem with this?"

When Nicholas and Andrea pulled into the garage, it was past her dinnertime. Andrea jumped out of the car and went into the house through the rear entrance near the kitchen. Anna and Dorothy were both in the kitchen waiting. They knew something was wrong at Charring Cross and by now, as people who loved and cared for a child are wont to do, had imagined the worst.

"Andrea, your dinner is ready," Anna said to the blur as Andrea hurried past the kitchen. "Your grandmother and I waited for you."

"I just have to change out of my uniform. I'll be down in five minutes," she yelled back as she ran up the back stairs, "Where's Rasputin?"

"He's in your room, dear," her grandmother answered.

Nicholas had stayed behind in his car when Andrea had quickly scurried off into the house. He certainly understood her hurry. Knowing she'd done something wrong, she thought the longer she put off any serious discussion, the less serious the punishment may be. Nicholas certainly recalled trying the same thing when he was a kid. Never worked, but he sure had tried it. *Of course the stakes had been higher in those days when parents addressed their kid's misdeeds, especially in Southern black families, with a good old-fashioned 'whupping'.* The worst Andrea had to look forward to was grounding or withdrawal of TV privileges. *Different world.*

Nicholas turned on the CD player, searched for and found a sad mournful dirge-like saxophone instrumental, closed his eyes and leaned back against his headrest. He forced his mind to go blank; reaching for nothingness. He stayed there floating for a while, and then tried to view the events of the past few weeks.

In the months after Paula's death, he had worked hard to try and impose a sense of stability and normalcy to his and Andrea's lives, and he'd thought that he had succeeded. He and Andrea had entered therapy with Dr. Coleman. He'd tried to get into a more routine work cycle at Marshall. Taking on the MR-548 team leader role was his first big new assignment since Paula's death. Dorothy had come up to add stability to their home life. And, for a while, it all seemed to be working – at home, at Marshall, school, things seemed to be about as close to normal as they could hope. Hectic, yes, after all it was the "you can do everything" 21st century, but not bad. They'd gotten back to a routine. 'Drea's nightmares were fewer. Dr. Coleman felt that Andrea was dealing with Paula's death better than her father, since Nicholas had shown no emotion. But, overall, they were coping.

The past few weeks had shown a fragile state. The thing with the feds, a weird lunch with Don Marshall, the strange talk with Arthur, and 'Drea's incident at Charring Cross today. Nicholas felt he was losing control and worse yet, more was to come, and there was nothing he could do to make it better or normal.

The sad, depressing saxophone solo wound to its dismal end. Nicholas turned the car off and got out and went inside his home.

Andrea had managed to avoid her father after having her dinner. Usually, pretty good about doing her homework without too much encouragement, after a quick dinner, she and Rasputin had scurried off to her room where she'd buried herself in books at her desk, even though she'd completed her assignments for the night.

Nicholas gave Andrea her space and went into his study to work on one of the files he'd brought home. It was a small no-brainer type project. Something he had to do, which wouldn't take too much time or cerebral horsepower, but would briefly take his mind off his woes.

When he'd finished the work file, he checked his company email. Nothing much important. Although since he'd left the office he'd received 55 new email messages. In the last few years, email had become the primary communication vehicle at Marshall. No one actually talked to one another anymore in the office.

There were the assorted messages from IT about whatever computer system was not working as it should. Every major company had its jokes about the IT group; the morons who couldn't spell 'computer'. There was the usual whining, bitching and moaning from the one or two whiners, bitchers and moaners Nicholas had left in his group. He couldn't abide whiners and had managed to get rid of most of the ones he'd inherited with the group.

And, there was one strange message from Arthur. It was time stamped 8:15 PM. He'd obviously sent it from home. The subject was 'succession planning', but the message template was entirely blank. Nicholas assumed it was just a mistake or Arthur having problems with the email system.

Arthur wasn't a technophobe, but he was very close to being one. Nicholas had received similar blank messages from Arthur in the past. They'd completed the annual round of corporate succession planning a few months ago and maybe Arthur had a question. The company Board of Directors mandated that each department have a formal succession plan, the who-steps-in-if-you're-hit-by-a-bus routine, although it was mostly for show and succession was driven by internal politics.

Nicholas finished reading and replying to emails and packed his briefcase for the next day.

He knocked before entering Andrea's room. She was becoming, in her words, "a woman now, Dad," and needed her privacy, which he respected.

No answer.

"'Drea, I know you're not asleep. I just saw you come in here," Nicholas said through the door.

He heard Rasputin meow in his small voice for such a large, muscular cat and then a soft, faint, "come in."

Nicholas opened the door to 'Drea's large bedroom – described by realtors as a, "Princess Suite, no less." It was a little neater than one would expect for an eleven-year-old, but still moderately junky. Directly across from 'Drea's bed were two posters.

On the left a Space Shuttle take off, with the shuttle rising out of a massive white plume spewing tons of flame. On the right was the shuttle in earth orbit with the bay doors open, looking into the work bay with the blue and white ball of earth in the background. In between, there was an autographed photograph of Eileen Collins, a shuttle commander. Andrea and Nicholas had spent a long weekend a year ago at Space Camp, in Huntsville, Alabama.

'Drea had loved it and fallen in love with the idea of being an astronaut. Nicholas had been an old space-nut from way back – the Mercury, Gemini and Apollo days.

In the middle of 'Drea's full size bed, there was a large lump under the comforter with Rasputin standing, rather sitting, guard. Nicholas sat on the edge of the bed. "You know, when I was your age I went to the school where my mom, your grandmother, was a teacher and my Dad was the principal. So when I did something bad, or rather got caught doing something bad, I got the crap beat out of me at school and I knew that when I got home, I'd get the crap beat out of me again." This elicited a small giggle from under the covers. "So, on one of those days when I'd gotten the you-know-what beat out of me, you know what I dreaded most?"

"Getting home and getting the crap beat out of you!" 'Drea added, still out of sight.

"Nope. Actually, it was the ride home."

"The ride home, why?" This coming from one eye and a nose peering out from the covers.

"Because, I'd sit in the back of the car on the ride home and my parents were up front and they didn't say a word about what happened. So, here I'd sit thinking, 'maybe, if I'm very, very quiet, they'll forget about it and I won't get' – what?"

"The crap beat out of you!" answered an entire head now out with glee.

"Right. So I sat back there, not making a peep and do you think it ever worked?"

"Of course not, Grandma's not stupid!"

"You're right, it didn't work. So I went home and got what?"

"The crap beat out of you!" 'Drea now shouted loud enough for Rasputin to leave with a startle.

"Right. So do you think you're going to get the crap beat out of you?" Nicholas asked.

"No. But I'm going to get punished, right?"

"Yeah. But I want you to know why, 'Drea."

Andrea emerged fully from the covers, sat up and looked Nicholas in the eyes. "I didn't have a choice, Dad. He kept pushing me and I told the teachers and they didn't do anything."

This was one of the many things Nicholas loved about 'Drea. She stood her ground. She wasn't going to let anyone push her around. He let her go on and give all the reasons she'd hired the seventh graders to beat up Charles. At last, she finally exhausted her reasons, and Nicholas had to admit that some were pretty good.

"'Drea, I understand why you did what you did and it didn't turn out too bad, except for the getting caught part. But what if Charles had been badly hurt or what if he'd hired someone to hurt you, to get back at you? Did you think of that?"

"They wouldn't have hurt him too much. That would have cost $20.00 each. He wasn't worth it. And Charles is way too stupid to hire someone to come after me. He only got into Charring Cross because his family is rich and bought him in. But I'm sorry, Dad. I didn't mean to bother you or cause you problems."

Nicholas was touched by Andrea's concern for bothering him, but was starting to see 'Drea as some sort of miniature *Godfather* – Michael Corleone– of the fifth grade. "Okay honey. Now here's the deal, a week without TV and no movie next weekend. That's your punishment."

"Okay, Dad."

"Any questions."

"Nope. That's fair."

Sometimes 'Drea could be surprisingly mature.

"Goodnight, honey," Nicholas said as he kissed her goodnight. "I love you."

"Love you too, Dad."

17

Dorothy's Friend

Nicholas left 'Drea's room and went down to the kitchen to look for something to eat. He had terrible eating habits and often ate late dinners. He'd found a diet coke and was heating some leftovers in the microwave when Dorothy came in and sat at the kitchen table. It was a large spacious kitchen, because Nicholas actually enjoyed cooking, but rarely found the time.

"Is she okay?" Dorothy asked while nibbling on a cookie. "I overheard you two talking."

"You mean you eavesdropped, Mom."

"Whatever. So, is she okay?"

"Yes. Not quite the appropriate action on her part, but she's going to be okay. She can take care of herself."

"And I suppose reminding you of what the Bible says about turning the other cheek would be a waste of time?"

"A complete waste. So let's change the subject."

"Okay, remember after that Agent was here and I said maybe I could help?"

"I remember," Nicholas had thought the offer unusual, but let his mother continue. Meanwhile, he was making a sandwich and trying to decide on the ingredients.

"Well," Dorothy continued, "I think I've found you some help. A friend of mine is an attorney in Raleigh. I called her and told her about what happened. She agrees you need someone you can trust, but you most definitely need your own lawyer. She says she's willing to make some calls, but it may take a while to find someone."

"Who is this lawyer friend?" Nicholas asked. "I didn't know any of your friends were lawyers."

"Her name is Beth Cowlings. It's sort of a strange story how we met. I'll get back to that. Anyway, Beth says you need a lawyer now and she's willing to come here and represent you until you can find someone local to work with."

"She's licensed in New Jersey?"

"Yep. She's an extraordinary person."

"And, she's willing to drop everything and come here?"

"If I ask her. We're that close."

"And you trust her?"

"With my life and with yours and Andrea's."

Nicholas looked at his mom, whose eyes said *Trust me, Son.* And said, "Okay, there's plenty of room here, so she can stay with us. We'll try it and see how it works. How soon can she get here?"

"She'll be here in two days."

"You'd already arranged this, hadn't you?"

"Well, yes," she answered sheepishly.

"Okay, so tell me how you met the extraordinary Beth Cowlings? Wait a minute," he said. "Cowlings." Dorothy's maiden name was Cowlings.

"Is she related to you?" Nicholas asked. Which he doubted, since he'd never heard of Beth.

"Not really – well, maybe," she replied. "Remember that little run-in I had with the Board of Education in Cranston County?"

"The lawsuit? Sort of hard to forget, but I don't recall anyone named Beth. Your lawyer was some guy named Ron," said Nicholas.

"Beth was advising me sort of behind the scenes. It's kind of a long story."

"You have my attention now – you can't stop."

"Okay," Dorothy said with a mischievous smile. "It was the summer you were ten. There wasn't a whole lot to do in Carrington."

"Tell me about it," Nicholas said as he opened a bottle of Chardonnay. He and Michael often joked over how boring their small town North Carolina childhood had been. Dorothy had been a sixth grade teacher in the segregated elementary school. The teachers had the three months of summer off along with the kids. Their father, who was the principal of the Black high school, worked through the summer. Carrington was a small rural tobacco-farming town in southeastern North Carolina. In the '60s and '70s, it was a typical small Southern town – totally segregated. Whites and Blacks both knew their place. The Whites' place was wherever they wanted it to be and Black's place was wherever the Whites allowed them to be.

The Ku Klux Klan met and marched openly and proudly. The pre-Senate version of Jesse Helms owned a TV station in Raleigh, North Carolina and gave a nightly editorial opining the world as God meant it to be would come to a calamitous ending if his little white children were forced to go to school with little 'nigra' children. Doctors and dentists offices had two entrances and waiting rooms. People of two races who fervently worshipped the same God did so in separate churches in separate parts of a town with a total population of 1000, because their parents, grand- and great-grandparents before them had.

And before that, it had been the way they'd wanted it and many still did. Slavery may have ended 100 years earlier, but in the mid to late 20th century in thousands of towns like Carrington across this great land every moment of every day of every week of every month, every year, Blacks were reminded,no, *bombarded* with the fact they were not wanted or respected and were, in fact, despised. Nicholas had hated the South with a passion and gotten away as soon as the opportunity arose.

Though black and white schools were segregated, they were controlled by one county school board of education – of course all white males. Besides all the blatant inequities in funding and benefits to white vs. black schools, there were different rules for Blacks and Whites. The one, which created the problem in this case, was a mandatory maternity leave rule. White teachers were required to take one-year maternity leave after having a child. After all, it was the '50s and '60s in the conservative South. The Board of Education, in their wisdom, felt that a white mother should be home with her child to nourish and nurture them for the first year.

If the Board of Education had let it go at that, you could chalk it up to the times and being conservative. But no, in their little racists minds, the Board of Education decided if a white teacher had to take a one year leave of absence after having a child, then a black (or as they preferred 'colored' or 'negra') teacher would have to take a five year leave of absence. Their rationale was they didn't want to force a mother to leave her child. In fact, the real reason was a blatant punishment to any black teacher who had a child. Why? Because they could get away with it.

Dorothy, after sitting out five years with Nicholas and three (the rule had been modified from five to three) with Michael, had had just about enough. She hired a NAACP lawyer and sued the Board for lost pay and benefits on behalf of herself and other black women teachers.

Things quickly went downhill and got pretty nasty after that. Whites in power in the rural South were not used to being challenged by Blacks. The concept of right and wrong meant nothing when it came to Blacks. Whites were always right – that's the way their white God and his white son Jesus meant it to be! There had been threats, calls, and Klan meetings. But when these didn't work, they'd reached a settlement. Dorothy got her back pay and benefits and a small damages claim and the rule was abolished. But Dorothy had been harassed until she'd retired to write children's books. Nicholas' father never received another promotion afterward.

"So, I recall your NAACP lawyer, Ron, but what was Beth's role?" Nicholas asked.

"Beth and her people go way back in that part of North Carolina," Dorothy said.

"Is Beth black or white?" Nicholas asked, now figuring out where this was going.

"White," Dorothy answered quietly.

"Cowling? Did her ancestors own us as slaves?"

"Yes."

"And you're friends? How'd that happen?" Nicholas was now enthralled.

"Things weren't going well with the lawsuit. The Whites in Cranston County weren't about to be intimidated by the NAACP and certainly not by me. The threats were getting bad. They threatened to burn us out. Your father and I were worried about you and Michael. We thought of sending you away to stay with relatives. But when they directly threatened the two of you, we'd decided to call off the lawsuit and move away," Dorothy stopped to make herself a cup of tea, knowing she was at a critical point of her story.

"You're doing this on purpose, the suspense, aren't you?"

"I am a story teller, you know."

"Okay, okay, obviously, we didn't move, so what happened?"

"Well, the morning we'd decided to tell our lawyer to call it off, Beth showed up on my doorstep.

"She looked like she was about ten years younger than me and scared to death, but so was I. I'd never seen her before. She lived in the western part of the county. She introduced herself and asked if she could come in and talk to me. With all that was going on, I was more than a little concerned when a white woman knocked on the door. She told me her name was Beth. She didn't mention her last name," Dorothy's tea ritual now complete, she joined Nicholas at the table.

"Back then Whites didn't go to black folks homes, so honestly I was afraid when she asked to come in. For all I knew, she was the wife of the Grand Dragon of the Klan. Actually," Dorothy said tilting her head to the side as if to recall a distant thought, "that wasn't true. We all knew who the Grand Dragon was. So, Beth came in. You and Michael were playing at one of your cousins' houses, so it was just the two of us."

"How come Michael and I never heard about any of this?" Nicholas asked.

"Your father and I tried to shelter you boys from this as much as possible. As the two of you grew older, we knew how you felt about Carrington and wondered how we could stay there. It was our home," She said with that far off look. "But we saw it for what it was just as clearly as you and Michael did. So, we tried to shelter you from that side of it as much as possible."

"So," she said, going back to her story. "It was awkward at first. She looked around at everything like she was in a museum.

"'You've never been in a colored person's home before, have you?' I asked her.

"'No,' she said. "She looked flustered, and scared herself. She was very different then from the way she is now. She seemed almost childlike.

"'I'm sorry,' she said. 'I don't mean to stare.'

"'You were expecting something different?' I asked.

"'I guess. You're not poor,' she said, as if surprised.

"'No, we're average. We're blessed. I'm sorry Beth; I didn't catch your last name.'

"'I'm sorry. It's Russell. My husband is John Russell. He's a lawyer over in the county seat. He's represented a lot of colored people.'

"'I see.' I replied, looking at her. My God, it's coming back like it was yesterday. We were in our living room. I was on the sofa and she sat in the side chair all straight, hands in her lap – like a proper lady. I think she was about 29 then. She had long light brown, not quite blond hair. She looked like a frightened little mouse. But those eyes. You'll see when you meet her. She has steel-gray, cold eyes. I always remembered that her eyes didn't match her face. At first glance, she looked like fluff, but the eyes said there's something substantial there."

"'This probably seems very presumptive of me, Mrs. Harding and I don't mean to intrude. I've been reading about your lawsuit against the Board of Education.'

"'Oh really?' I said. The hair on the back of my neck was probably standing up by now.

"'Yes, it must take a lot of courage for you to sue the Board.'

"'Because I'm colored?'

"'Yes, it's just not the way things are done here,' she said smilingly.

"'I see,' was all I said. 'Why are you here Mrs. Russell?'

"'Yes, well like I said, I've read about your case. The law has always fascinated me.' She had easily side-tracked off the main topic. 'Maybe because my husband is a lawyer, but I don't think so.'

""I was starting to lose patience now." Dorothy recalled. "I told her I already had a lawyer."

"'Oh, that's not why I'm here. My husband wouldn't represent you anyway.' She said with no embarrassment. 'He couldn't risk getting into a fight with the Board of Education. But I have talked to my husband about your case and he agrees with my assessment. Remember, I said the law is sort of a hobby of mine. You have a strong case against the Board. The only problem is you're colored and your lawyer is colored.'

"I was really starting to lose patience with this chirpy little white girl telling me that my problem was that I was colored! So I said to Beth, 'I'd appreciate it if you'd get to your point, please.'

"'I'm sorry she said, sometimes I don't put things very tactfully. I didn't mean that the way it came out. But the fact is you don't stand a chance even though legally, you're right – you're going to lose. But you shouldn't give up.'

"That was a little disconcerting, since giving up was exactly what I planned to do."

"'They want you to give up,' she said. 'Expect you to give up. No colored person has ever stood up to them.'

"'And when the Klan comes to burn down my house?' I asked looking into those cold eyes. She looked pained – actually pained.

"'Can I call you Dorothy? I'd like for you to call me Beth.'

"'Okay, Beth.'

"'I'm not going to insult you by saying I know what you're going through – what you and your people go through every day here. But I do see what you go through or some of it and I couldn't do it. I'd rather be dead than live like the colored people do here.'

"'You've said a lot, Beth. But you still haven't said anything. What do you want?'

"'To help you.'

"'How?'

"'Later.'

"'Okay, why?'

"'My family name before I married was Cowling. My ancestors once owned yours,' she said as if discussing the purchase of Kleenex.

"'So, you're feeling a little guilty and want to help the poor little colored woman?'

"'If that's what you want to think. What difference is it to you why?'

"Now I lost it. I'd had enough!

"'What difference? What difference! How dare you come in my house and talk down to me. You want to know what difference? The difference is the Klan can burn down my home. They can hurt or kill my children, my husband or me and what would happen to them – nothing. Because that's the kind of world I live in where your people can still do whatever they want to my people. So, if you have some problem with guilt because your ancestors owned other human beings, you need to deal with it somewhere else. Now, Mrs. Russell, get out of my house!'

"I'd expected her to scurry out when I yelled at her," Dorothy said as she got up to refill her tea. "But she didn't budge. She just stared at me with those icy eyes."

"'I'll leave and again I apologize if I've upset you. But if you're thinking of quitting, you shouldn't.'

"I was curious," said Dorothy. "First about how she knew I was thinking about quitting and more so about what she was really up to."

"I'd forgotten how tense things had gotten about this," Nicholas said.

"Well, I hadn't," his mother said. "For a while, your Dad and I were actually afraid the Klan would come after us."

"So I said to her, 'why should I listen to you Beth?'

"'Because I can tell you how to win, Dorothy,' she said. "'Actually, even more importantly, because beating them may just make them mad, I can tell you how to win and get them to leave you alone. Only I can't right now,' she said finally getting up and looking at her watch.

"'I have to get home and make supper for my husband,' she said as she hurried towards the back door she came in. 'I promise you I'll contact you in a couple of days with the information you need.'

"She turned back to look at me with those cold eyes as she got to the door.

"'Why should I trust you, Beth?' I asked.

"'Because you have no one else to turn to, you can quit and give them the pleasure of seeing you beaten down or you can strike back. And by the way Dorothy, the fact my ancestors owned slaves – I'm not one of those people who carry guilt over the past. Right or wrong, the past is past and I sleep just fine at night. I'll be in touch.' And she left.

"Talk about confused and scared. I didn't know what to do. Your Dad and I talked about it that night. And we decided to wait a couple of days to see what happened. We kept the two of you close to the house, not wanting to take any chances. A couple of days later, it was about 9:00 at night and there's a knock on the door. It's Beth. She'd come back and alone. Now a white woman coming to a black person's home during the day was unheard of back then. But one was coming to a black person's home at night, alone – that was unthought-of of! She came in and looked a little more composed and mature than she had before."

"'Good evening Dorothy,' she said. 'Mr. Harding,' she said to your father. You two were somewhere in front of a TV set. We went into the living room again and she got right to the point.

"'I'm sorry I left so abruptly the other day, but John's a bit picky about his supper.'

"'You said you could tell me how to win my case and keep them off my back,' I said to her.

"'The Board of Education's lawyer has told them legally having separate maternity leave rules for Whites and Coloreds is not only stupid, it's illegal. He thinks if it goes to trial, a fair and impartial jury would rule in your favor. But we all know there's no such jury around here. There's no way a white jury, and it would be white, would rule in your favor over the Board.'

"'So what's their worry?' your father asked.

"'The worry is it makes them look bad. So they want it to end – now with you withdrawing your case.'

"'So where does that leave us, Beth?' your Dad asked.

"Beth got a wicked look in her eyes that you'll see later. She said, 'here's where it gets real interesting. The Board has not changed its makeup for the last 12 years. Every one of them is taking kickbacks.'

"'From whom?'

"'From themselves! A percentage of their state and Federal supplements ends up in their pockets.'

"'I don't understand,' I said. 'What does this have to do with me?'

"Beth went on, 'they left a trail. Figuring, who's going to do anything? Local – no problem. Just like they know you'd never get a ruling against them, they know they'd never be convicted of a crime here. State – a little dicier, but basically the same argument. Federal – now that's something these old boys didn't count on. They go up on Federal embezzlement charges and someone or ones is going to see the inside of a Federal prison.

"'Like I said, they left a trail a blind man could follow. All you have to do is have your lawyer draw up subpoenas for all school Board funding expenses, including Federal and they'll back off. Here's what you do – let them think it's a fishing expedition, but your lawyer lets them know he can add. He'll drop everything in exchange for a settlement (they'll insist on it being sealed). And/or letters to state Attorney General and Federal Prosecutors outlining details of the Boards activities to be submitted if anyone so much as sneezes on you.

"'It all sounds so simple,' I said. Beth's only request was her name stay out of it. She said she'd stay in touch from time to time to see how things were going and she did.

"She was right. They huffed and puffed, but caved in when they realized what I was up to. Everything was sealed. They didn't want any other uppity Negroes getting any ideas.

"Beth and I stayed in contact and became friends. She invited me over to her house and showed me old papers and pictures from her great-grandparents who had owned a small plantation in Southern North Carolina just before the Civil War. She even had some pictures of slaves. Some sort of bond grew between us."

"That's weird," Nicholas said, refilling his wine glass.

"Don't knock it, smarty," his mom said. "Her husband died in a car accident and she moved to Raleigh and went to law school. She finished and set up a solo practice. We write a lot. None of that email or texting stuff that your age is into. That's what pen and paper is for. We usually see each other about once a year. Brag about our kids. She has a daughter who's also a lawyer. But I gather there's some friction between the two. So, that's Beth Cowlings."

"When will she be here?" Nicholas asked.

"Early Saturday. She had some things to finish up in Raleigh."

"Can't wait," Nicholas said without much enthusiasm.

"You don't sound excited."

"I don't know what to sound like. Too much is going on. But Beth certainly sounds interesting enough. Let's see what happens. I'm going up to bed. I'll see you tomorrow."

"Good night, Nicky."

"Night, Mom."

On the way to his room, Nicholas looked in on 'Drea, who was asleep with the ever-vigilant Rasputin sleeping at the foot of her bed. The little, or rather large, beast was certainly loyal to 'Drea. Nicholas liked the cat. Dorothy and Anna both felt people should live indoors and animals outdoors, but 'Drea had final say. Rasputin was her buddy, and therefore had free run of the house. After all, just because he was a cat didn't mean he wasn't a person. As long as he kept off eating surfaces, most of the time, everyone got along reasonably well.

Nicholas went into his bedroom and turned on *Fox News*. He was a news junky. He got out clothes for tomorrow, showered, changed and went to bed, the images of the day's news stories blending in with his own bizarre recent events.

18

Arthur

Nicholas tossed and turned and heard a distant ringing. He slowly recognized it as his telephone, as he gazed in the direction of his iPhone alarm clock. He was not accustomed to receiving telephone calls at 2:30 in the morning and his first thought was that it was something wrong at the lab.

"Hello," he said groggily.

"Nick?" Nicholas was now sitting straight up, as were the hairs on the back of his neck. Nicholas recognized Jack O'Connor's deep voice. The only time Jack had called Nicholas at home had been after Paula's death.

"Jack. What's up?" Nicholas still thinking something had gone wrong at the lab.

"Nick," Jack said, followed by silence. "Nick, I'm at Arthur's. Jesus, Nick," O'Connor was clearly shaken up.

"Jack, what the hell's going on?"

"It's Arthur, Nick," he said again. "He's dead."

Nicholas thought his heart was going to explode out of his chest. "What?! What happened, Jack?"

"I got a call from the Morristown police to get over to Arthur's house. God, Nick, it looks like a suicide. He shot himself."

"Helen – where's Helen, Jack?" Nicholas asked, sitting up on the side of his bed. "Is she okay?"

"She's upstairs with a friend and some cops, including a Detective. Markus was the name"

"I'm coming over Jack," Nicholas said.

"The cops – they said they don't want a lot of people here, Nick. Maybe it's not such a good idea."

"Fuck the cops," Nicholas said. "I'm on my way. Jack?"

"Yeah?"

"Do you have any idea why Arthur would do something like this?"

"I was about to ask you the same thing. You were closer to him than I was, Nick."

"I'll be there in a few minutes," Nicholas quickly brushed his teeth and threw on some jeans, sweater and sneakers.

On his way out, he quickly woke Dorothy to let her know he was out and why.

"If his wife needs someplace to stay, you bring her back here, Nicky. She shouldn't be alone," she said slowly getting out of bed.

"Okay, Mom."

"I'll make some tea, can't get back to sleep now anyway."

On his way down to his car, Nicholas reflected on how good it was to have his mom here. It just felt right.

The streets of affluent, suburban New Jersey were desolate at 3:00 in the morning. The wealthy, no doubt needing their rest so they can go out the next day and do, in their minds, the important things that keep them wealthy.

Before Nicholas could see the house, he could see the glare of flashing emergency vehicle lights. This suburban street was anything but desolate. It looked loud, but there was little sound. Neighbors had come out to stand on the streets. Nicholas couldn't get close with all the police cars. He parked and started walking towards Arthur's and Helen's house, passing almost dozen flashing red police lights, two EMS vehicles from Morristown Memorial Hospital (The Minute Men as they were called), four or five unmarked police cars, Jack's Jag and the Marshall Security car.

The police had cordoned off Arthur's house with barricades and that insipid yellow crime scene tape that is seen on the evening news every day. Nicholas approached a uniformed officer, half expecting to get a hard time.

"I'm Dr. Harding with Marshall Pharmaceutical. I'm a close friend of the family. I need to get in to see Helen Kronan."

Nicholas was surprised when the young cop said, "yes sir. Dr. O'Connor said to expect you. You can go right in, sir."

Strange, thought Nicholas, it's almost as if Jack was in charge of the crime scene.

Nicholas stepped under the yellow tape and walked towards the house. The police had also erected a battery of flood lights that made the night around the house look like a synthetic day, with the chirping of crickets in the surrounding night.

At the door he was directed by another uniformed officer to a plainclothes detective in a front sitting room. She was talking to another uniformed officer and Ken Joseph, head of Marshall Pharmaceutical Security. Nicholas approached the three.

"Excuse me, I'm Nicholas Harding. I'm looking for Detective Markus."

Nicholas, knowing Joseph by sight only and eliminating the uniform, directed his comments to the most likely candidate.

"I'm Kerry Markus," she said breaking off her conversation with the uniform. Nicholas could now observe that Ken Joseph wasn't really doing anything other than trying to look important. Joseph's presence made Nicholas uncomfortable.

"Detective Markus," he said shaking the hand she extended to Nicholas.

"I'm very sorry about your friend, Dr. Kronan."

"What happened here?" Nicholas asked, directing his question to Detective Markus.

Ken Joseph piped up, "looks like old Arthur blew his brains out," and then gave everyone a smug look.

There were several moments of silence as everyone in the small group, the uniforms, Detective Markus and Nicholas all looked at Ken Joseph like the complete imbecile he obviously was.

This was Nicholas' first face-to-face with Ken Joseph, but he knew him by his reputation at Marshall. He was rumored to be an ex-cop who'd cashed out when he 'accidentally' beat a suspect to death. He was loyal to O'Connor and was thought to have helped him climb up the Marshall ladder by digging up dirt on competition. He'd also been reported for hassling low ranking women and minorities at Marshall. He wasn't stupid enough to mess with an executive as high ranking as Nicholas, so the two had never met. But each had obviously heard of the other and it was apparent there was no love lost.

Ken Joseph looked the part of a thug ex-cop. Barrel-chested, turning to beer belly, late 40s, crew-cut, about 6'2"; he was used to intimidating people with his size.

"It's too early to tell what happened. All we know now is we have Dr. Kronan dead in his study with a bullet wound to the head," Kerry Markus said in a matter-of-fact, but respectful tone.

Nicholas was so far impressed with her.

"His wife," here Detective Markus had to briefly refer to notes, "Helen, says she was upstairs reading. Heard the shot, called out to her husband. When she didn't get a response, she came downstairs where she found him in the study. She says she checked for a pulse, couldn't find one and dialed 9-1-1."

Ken decided to try and butt-in again at this point.

"I don't think we've ever met, Dr. Harding. I'm Ken Joseph, Marshall Security Head," he announced as if that was the equivalent of being Secretary of State of the United States of America.

"Yes, I know, Ken," Nicholas said rather hurriedly. "Do you mind my asking why you're here?"

"Jack, Dr. O'Connor, got the call from the Morristown P.D. and he gave me a call and asked me to meet him here. What with me being an ex-cop and all, thought maybe I could help out. After all, we're just one big Marshall family, aren't we?" he said with that smug fake smile.

"Yeah, sure," Nicholas said as he turned his back to Joseph, effectively ending that conversation. "Detective Markus. Is Helen okay? I'd like to see her."

"In a moment, Dr. Harding," the detective answered.

Kerry Markus had the look more of a schoolteacher than a detective. She appeared in age to be in that late thirties-early forties neutral zone and had just missed being attractive. The term handsome would be used to describe her.

"Mrs. Kronan is still being questioned right now," the detective informed Nicholas. "And if you don't mind, Dr. Harding, I have a few questions for you now."

Does she have her lawyer present?"

"Pardon?"

"Does Helen have her lawyer present? If she's being questioned by the police, isn't she entitled to have her lawyer present?"

"Absolutely," the detective replied as she fixed Nicholas with a stare. "Do you think she has something to hide?"

"No. I just tend to be overly cautious."

"Well, I just have a few questions for you, and then you can see Mrs. Kronan. Unless, of course, you need your attorney present before you can answer any questions, Dr. Harding. I wouldn't want to be accused of taking unfair advantage of you."

Nicholas was thinking the lawyer question had only served to piss-off the detective. He breezed through the few questions Detective Markus had for him. *Routine stuff about how I know Arthur and Helen, how long, my opinion of their relationship, etc.* More than anything else, it appeared to be a sizing up of Nicholas by the detective and with her neutral demeanor. *Wonder how I faired.* He gave her his home and office telephone numbers and she said she'd contact him in a few days for follow-up questions. She then directed a uniformed officer to take him upstairs to Helen.

She was in a sitting area adjacent to hers and Arthur's master bedroom. She was standing to the side of a window looking out at the many lights. In the glare of police floodlights and flashing red lights, Helen looked every bit her age. She hadn't seen him enter.

"Helen," he said. "Helen," he said again gently.

There was no one else in the room, so the questioning must have ended, at least for now. And, there was no sign of the friend Jack had mentioned. Come to think of it, Nicholas hadn't seen Jack – just the gold Jag.

"Nicky," Helen said softly as she saw him enter the room. She broke her gaze out the window and looked up to Nicholas. The two slowly embraced and Helen began to cry. "I don't know what to do, Nicky."

"Helen, let's pack some things and you can come to my place. Then you can decide what you have to do later. Okay?"

Nicholas got Helen to start to pack and went downstairs to inform detective Markus and to find Jack. He found Kerry

Markus and she was okay with Helen leaving as long as she knew where to find her.

He found Jack and Ken Joseph outside. Ken walked off when Nicholas approached.

"Nicholas. What a goddamn mess! Did you see any of this coming?"

"Of course not, Arthur had been out sick a couple of days, maybe it was serious, who knows. Anyway, I'm taking Helen back to my house. She can stay there until she decides what she wants to do. I may be in late tomorrow."

"No can do, Nicholas. There are some things we have to straighten out on the business-side. I need you in my office at 7:00 AM."

With that, Jack got into his gold Jag and drove off. Nicholas looked at his watch. It was now almost 5:00 AM. He pulled out his cell and called home. Dorothy answered on the second ring. He brought her up to speed on what had happened and let her know he was bringing Helen home.

After he hung up, he checked his cell for his staff telephone numbers, and selected Karen's home number. She also answered on the second ring and didn't sound sleepy, which he found odd, but certainly not the oddest event of the evening – no – morning.

He told Karen everything that had happened and asked her to get in early and schedule two meetings. The first at 7:30 with Arthur's staff and then at 7:45 with Nicholas' staff.

Nicholas figured that the 7:00 AM meeting with Jack was to ask him to step in for Arthur. But full time? Temp? Acting? Who knew? Maybe Jack would bring in someone else and toss Nicholas out. Who the hell knew?

Nicholas looked back at the old mansion. There were only two or three flashing red lights now. The ghastly glare of the spotlights was fading into the faint dawn light.

"Arthur," Nicholas said to no one in particular. "What the hell have you done? What could have been so fucked up for you to do something like this? What the hell have you done?" He continued to mutter to himself as he headed back in the house to get Helen and take her away from this little hell Arthur – one of the most stable people Nicholas knew – had created!

Arthur's staff sat stunned at the conference table down the hall from Arthur's office. Karen sat at Nicholas' side. He finished by saying, "there's not a lot we know right now. The police are investigating, but it looks like an apparent suicide – a gunshot to the head."

"It just doesn't figure," said Mark. "Besides it being Arthur, which makes no sense, Arthur was a toxicologist just like you, Nicholas. No way one of you poison docs is going to splatter their brains all over a room when you can do it with a toxin – no fuss, no muss, no mess. It doesn't compute."

"Look Mark, suicide is not a rational act, so who's to say what was going on in Arthur's mind," Nicholas checked his watch. "Sorry to rush guys, but I'm meeting with my senior staff in a few minutes. Each of you should do the same. For now, until Jack figures out how he wants to handle this long term, I'm acting VP. As soon as I hear any details about the funeral, I'll pass them on."

Mark stayed behind as the others filed out of the room and Karen prepared for a repeat performance with Nicholas' staff.

"Nick, so what's with the acting VP stuff? Everyone knows you're Arthur's successor. Why not just give you the job now?" Mark asked.

"Ask Jack," Nicholas said as he scribbled a reminder note to himself. "This is the way he wants it."

"How long?"

"Who knows – maybe with Arthur out of the picture, Jack will want his own boy."

"Fucking weird!"

"This place has gone way beyond fucking weird, pal," said Nicholas. "Way, way beyond."

Nicholas met with his department heads and gave them the same run down and then went back to his office. He sat at his desk looking out his window with a view of the springtime rolling hills of New Jersey, just starting to turn a lively green, before the lush thick green foliage kicked in. He felt tired from lack of sleep, but wired. Wired and off balance. And for one as used to control and balance as Nicholas, it was a most uncomfortable feeling.

He casually glanced towards his computer screen, remembering that he hadn't checked his emails yet. They were starting to stack up already, so he sorted by sender and was startled.

"Jesus Christ!" he muttered to himself as he saw two messages from Arthur, with today's date. The first was time stamped 12:35 AM, which was technically possible, since he recalled detective Markus saying she thought the time of death was around 1:00 AM

But it was the second email message from Arthur that gave Nicholas a cold dark feeling. It was also from this morning, but the time stamp was 3:25 AM Not possible, since by 3:25 this morning, Arthur was dead and Nicholas along with Jack and half of the Morristown PD was in his house.

Nicholas got up and closed his office door. He double clicked on Arthur's first message.

From:	*Kronan, Arthur [MPC]*
Sent:	*12:35 AM*
To:	*Harding, Nicholas [MPC]*
Subject:	*I'm sorry Nicholas. I'll explain later.*

No subject, which was not unusual for Arthur. 'I'm sorry Nicholas. I'll explain later.' Then thirty minutes later he blows his brains out. What the hell did this mean?

All Marshall Pharm staff had double password-protected system accounts. Executives at Nicholas' level and higher had a tertiary security level, which meant, in theory; anyone trying to access their files would have to crack through three security levels. Nicholas rarely bothered with the third security level, knowing that anyone good enough to get past the first two could easily handle a third.

But today he made use of his highest security level. After printing Arthur's message, he transferred it to a tertiary secure level and locked it.

He then double clicked on the second Arthur message – the one sent after Arthur was dead and this one made his skin crawl.

From:	*Kronan, Arthur [MPC]*
Sent:	*3:25 AM*
To:	*Harding, Nicholas [MPC]*
Subject:	*Who can you trust Nicholas?*

Nicholas was about to print the second message when without even thinking, he clicked 'Reply' and typed 'I don't like games. Who are you?' and hit the send key.

Great, now I'm communicating with a dead guy. Next I'll be calling the psychic hotline. He thought to himself.

Nicholas printed the second email from Arthur and moved it to the secure file also. He then folded the two printed pages and put them in his jacket pocket and opened his office door. Karen was on the phone.

"Yes, I understand. We can discuss this later," she said, and then hung up.

"Do you have minute, Dr. Harding?" she asked as she stood up, implying it was important.

"Sure, come on in, Karen," he said. "Karen, we've worked together, what two years now? Why don't you call me Nicholas or Nick?"

"Dr. Harding works best for me, if that's all right with you," she said as she took a seat at Nicholas' small conference table with her notepad, long, lean, tanned legs in a mini-skirt, which stopped just short of 'Oh my God!'"

"That's fine, Karen – whatever works for you. I guess we have a lot to go over, don't we? What's first?"

"Dr. Harding, I just want to say that I am very, very sorry about Dr. Kronan. He seemed like a good man, but more important, he seemed like a friend to you. First, your wife a few months ago and now this. You deserve better."

Nicholas thought Karen's last sentence odd – it could be interpreted a couple of different ways. Maybe it was just her weird syntax or maybe he was becoming paranoid.

"Thanks, Karen," he replied. "Yes, Arthur was a friend, so that makes this even harder. So, what's on your list?"

"I spoke with Donna, Dr. Kronan's secretary. She's packing all his personal belongings to be stored until Mrs. Kronan decides what to do with them. Will you move into Dr. Kronan's office?" Karen asked. Her question could have two meanings, so Nicholas decided to answer both.

"No. I'm only acting VP, until Jack decides what he wants to do. Until then, I'll have to do Arthur's job and continue to run my department. So, I won't move into Arthur's office, unless I officially get his job. And if I do get his job, I want you to come with me – if you want."

"I want – yes. I enjoy working with you, Dr. Harding. But do not let the flattery go to your head, no?" she said with a minimalist smile.

"What about Donna?"

"We'd find something elsewhere for Donna, but we'll cross that bridge when we get to it."

"Very well, is your London trip next week still on? The preview of MR-548 with the European Marketing Heads?"

"Yes, I need to go and I have some things to discuss with Catherine Sullivan."

"Hum, I see," Karen said with a slight tone of disapproval.

"Call her office and she'll have them handle my London arrangements."

"I see," Karen replied again with slightly more ice in her tone.

"Is there a problem, Karen?"

"Absolutely not," she replied.

"Good, also I need to meet with Glen Morgan late next week before I go to London, also Jack and Gerry Michael early next week. Okay?"

"I shall make it happen, Dr. Harding," she replied.

Nicholas frowned. "Karen. Are you a *Star Trek* fan?"

"The space people television show? No, I rarely watch TV, Dr. Harding. Why do you ask?"

"Nothing," Nicholas was dying to ask Karen how she occupied her time in lieu of television, but figured now wasn't the time.

"Is there anything else critical on my calendar, Karen?"

"Not for now, Dr. Harding. Since you are doing two jobs now, I shall be vigilant in protecting your valuable time. Also, your mother called just before I came in and she said to tell you that her friend will be here tomorrow morning."

"Great. Karen, I left a file I need at home, so I'm going to run home and get it. Can I grab you something for lunch while I'm out?"

"No thank you, Dr. Harding. I'll get something from the cafeteria."

Nicholas grabbed his car keys and on the way out, at the door to his outer office, he stopped.

"Karen. Don Marshall invited Andrea and me to his house next weekend to see a first run movie. Apparently he has his own movie theatre. I wasn't planning to go, but I've changed my mind. I need a distraction. He said I could bring a guest, but I'm not seeing anyone. Would you like to go with us?"

Nicholas had decided to be less passive and more active and this was one planned step.

"Would this be a date?"

"No."

"Work?"

"No."

"Then what?"

"Just a movie with me, 'Drea and Don Marshall."

"Just a movie. Hum, I think I will like that – just a movie. Yes, I will go."

"Good. Can you call his house to confirm and find out when we should arrive and if we should bring anything? I'll be back in a little while."

Nicholas got in his car and drove in the opposite direction than his house to a mid-sized mall. He went inside and after looking around to make sure there were no familiar faces, he used a pay phone to make a call.

"Mike Harding."

"Good. You're in." When one of the brothers called the other, they just started the conversation with no warm-up.

"Hey Nick. What the hell's going on over there? Mom called and told me about Arthur."

"It's the fucking *Twilight Zone* over here. Looks like Arthur blew his brains out and last week, I come home to find an FDA Investigative Agent and a Deputy U.S. Marshal in my living room. Marshall Pharm is a target of some sort of big investigation out of Washington and for some reason unknown to me I'm in the middle of it.

How's that for a typical day in the snake pit?"

"You want some advice?" he asked. "Hell, I'm going to give it to you anyway. Get out. Resign, quit, tell them to kiss your ass, walk – no run out and don't look back."

"No."

"I knew you were going to say that," Michael responded.

"It's too late for that. I've got to ride it out."

"No you don't, big brother! You don't have to fix everything."

"This isn't why I called. Can you come by the house tomorrow night?"

"Sure, why?"

"Mom's friend, my apparent new lawyer, gets in tomorrow morning and I want to have a strategy session with her tomorrow night. I'd like you there."

"I'm environmental law, remember?"

"Not as a lawyer. As my brother."

"I'm there. You will feed me won't you?"

"Funny."

"You know if things are as bad as you seem to think, you shouldn't make calls like this from your office."

"I'm not in my office. I'm in the Livingston Mall on a payphone. See you tomorrow. I haven't even told you the weird stuff yet."

The silence emphasized the seriousness.

"See you tomorrow night, bro."

Nicholas hung up and said to himself, "I'm tired of being the fuckee. Now I just have to find out who the fucker is." He made one more phone call to Bethesda, Maryland.

"Beverly Coston's office," a receptionist who sounded like she was about to drop dead of terminal boredom answered.

"May I speak with Ms. Coston, please?" Nicholas said.

"Who's calling?"

"Her brother," Nicholas didn't want to leave his name and came up with a quick, but pretty lame lie.

"Hello, this is Beverly Coston."

"It's Nicholas Harding, Ms. Coston."

"Oh, I see, next time try something better, I'm an only child. I heard about Dr. Kronan. I'm very sorry."

Beverly knew the value of complete silence in a conversation and said nothing else.

"I think we should talk, but I need a couple of days," Harding felt uncomfortable as if he was in a bad mystery movie.

"Okay, call me in two days and we can arrange something. What made you decide to trust me?"

"Let me be very clear Ms. Coston. I don't trust you any more than I trust anyone else right now, which is to say none. Let's just say I'm spreading my risk around. And one other thing, I will deal with you and you only. I don't want that redneck asshole from last week anywhere near me."

"Agreed. See? That wasn't so bad. I'll be expecting your call in two days, Dr. Harding. And for what it's worth, you can trust me. I don't lie."

"Yeah, sure," Nicholas hung up.

Nicholas looked around the mall and observed the middle-to-older exercise walkers finishing up their rounds and the first wave of suburban soccer moms with their strollers and toddlers moving in, Harding realized he wasn't used to being out in the real world at mid-day.

He stopped by his house on the way back to his office. He hadn't forgotten a file, but wanted to check up on Helen.

Nicholas entered from the garage into the kitchen where his mother was sitting at a small desk. He smiled when she looked up and said, "and, what's so amusing to you?"

"Seeing you using a laptop, Mom. You've taken to it like a fish to water."

"I'm still kicking myself for waiting so long," she stated peering over her reading glasses perched on her nose.

Dorothy was in her early 60s, but because she refused to dye her hair, she looked a little older than her actual age. Harding thought she resembled a black Barbara Bush.

"How's our guest?" Nicholas asked.

"She's fine," Helen's voice came from the dining room, where she was doing a crossword puzzle and having tea.

"Helen, I thought you'd still be resting," he responded.

"You mean lying in bed sobbing into my pillow? Well, I did that for a while, but all that gets you is a soggy pillow. So I came down and had tea with Dorothy. Nicholas." She looked up at him with her warm brown eyes. "You and Dorothy and Andrea have been so nice to me. Thank you so much dear, I don't want to impose, I have to get back to the real world. As painful as it may be."

"There's no rush Helen. The real world's not going anyplace. Do you need help with any arrangements?"

"I think I can handle everything. Someone from the funeral parlor is coming by today." Helen went on down her list of mourning activities. "We weren't very religious. It will be a small service in a couple of days. Would you say something at the service, please, Nicky? Arthur talked about you a lot. He was so proud of you. Like a father would be of a son. He loved you, Nicky," she said looking down as a tear dropped on her puzzle.

"Yes, I'd be proud to Helen."

"Good. That detective lady..."

"Detective Markus?" said Nicholas.

"Yes, she's also coming later today. She says they'll be finished at the house today. And Dorothy arranged for cleaners to clean the house tomorrow. The study, you know?" she said softly.

"Then I can go back home, Nicky. I'm not sure what I'll do yet, but I'll be home. The only home we had in the twenty-five years we were married. But I'll be okay," she said.

"Yes, you will dear," Dorothy stood behind Helen. "You'll be fine. It'll take a lot of time and a lot of tears, but we learn how to move on when our men are gone." The hurt Nicholas' mother still felt for his father was evident.

"Well, I have to get back to the office. I'll see you tonight Helen," he said heading back into the kitchen followed by Dorothy.

"Beth will be here tomorrow morning," she said as Nicholas opened the garage door.

"I got the message. I asked Michael to come by tomorrow night when I talk to Beth."

"I'm not surprised. You two always were like peas in a pod."

"Well, I figure I need all the help I can get right now."

"Good. Maybe I'll sit in on this brainstorming session with you boys."

"Okay Mom," Nicholas smiled while leaving for Marshall Pharmaceutical.

Nicholas got back to his office after 1:00 PM and noticed Karen had cleared his calendar. He had turned off his computer before he left. Normally he left his desktop on all day, but now that he was receiving email from the beyond, he didn't want anyone to walk in and see his mail.

He quickly re-booted and went to his inbox, scanned the usual crap, but there it was: an email from Arthur. No, he reminded himself, from someone using Arthur's system account.

From:	*Kronan, Arthur [MPC]*
Sent:	*11:45 AM*
To:	*Harding, Nicholas [MPC]*
Subject:	*Trust*

You had best start liking games or rather doing well in them because you are part of a game now Nicholas. A deadly serious game. And your doing well in this game is far more important than who I am. Whom can you trust Nicholas?

Nicholas hit the reply button and typed, "I need specifics, not riddles. Why should I trust you?"

He then printed this message to add to the first two in his pocket and moved the electronic file into the secure file site.

19

Jack, Don and Grant

By the next day things were slightly less chaotic at Marshall. Word had spread throughout the entire company of Arthur's suicide. Nicholas received calls from executives from various Marshall sites throughout the world.

Fortunately, since he and Arthur were close and Arthur had relied on Nicholas as his backup, Nicholas was aware of just about everything on Arthur's plate. He was getting ready for a meeting with Jack O'Connor to discuss said plate.

Nicholas had become more than attentive to his email, but hadn't received any further cryptic messages from the great beyond.

At the previous day's brief meeting with Jack, he asked Nicholas to take over as acting VP and then abruptly ended their discussion. Now a day later, Jack wanted to continue the dialog. *To what end?* Harding figured, *who could tell?* With Jack, people never quite knew what he was up to, but always knew he was up to something. He seemed to have several plots brewing simultaneously.

At the 7:00 AM meeting, it was far too early for Roberta and Nicholas managed to avoid her anticipated gush of fake sympathy. No such luck today; however. As Nicholas entered Jack's outer office, Roberta shooed away a secretarial underling. She stood and walked around her mini-fortress of a desk to hug Harding while sobbing profusely.

She muttered how sorry she, or the imperial 'We,' was about Arthur.

Nicholas was not one to enjoy being touched by anyone not personally close, which eliminated just about everyone except his daughter, mother and brother. Harding had as much desire to hug Roberta as to hug a Komodo dragon, but he bit the bullet putting his arms around Roberta. It was no mean feat and he returned her hug. After the appropriate time, far too long in his estimation, he disentangled himself from Roberta, leaving her standing, still sobbing in the middle of the office while walking into Jack's office. Harding was so flustered, he forgot to knock.

Entering Jack's office, Harding was surprised to see Grant Michner, Chief Executive Officer and Chairman of the Marshall Board, there. If a producer were casting the role of a CEO, Grant would fit the bill. A tall, lean, thick gray haired man in his early 60s; Grant was very tan. He had a commanding voice. His name, Grant, was perfect for being a CEO.

Unfortunately, that's as far as it went. Grant was an over-the-hill pretty-boy marketing guy who started out carrying the bag (i.e., as a sales representative, who was now only lacking the leash that O'Connor kept him on - in other words, a figure head).

But Nicholas was even more surprised to see Don Marshall. The trio had been sitting at Jack's spacious conference table that overlooked a hideous portrait of a bull goring a matador.

"Nicholas. Come in, join us," Don said. "Isn't this a fabulous office?"

"Nicholas," Jack said, wanting to be in control. "Good to see you, son, come on in. Have a seat. Do you know everyone here? I know you've met Grant, but probably not Don. This is Don Marshall."

"Actually, Jack, Nicholas and I have met. He came over for lunch a few weeks ago and we conversed about our mutual interests."

"Oh, I didn't know. You didn't mention it," Jack said.

"Must have slipped my mind," Don replied.

The only remaining seat was at one end of the oval table, facing Jack with Grant and Don each to one side. Before being seated, Harding shook hands around the table. Grant was obviously bored with the entire scenario and gave an air of someone who'd rather be working on their tan or better yet, nailing one of his secretaries; probably the 22-year-old with the IQ of a cabbage, but with certain other more obvious attributes.

Don had an amused look, having only met him once; Nicholas couldn't tell if that was a permanent condition. Jack seemed a tad uncomfortable.

"So, Nicholas, when we met yesterday, I asked you to take over for Arthur as Acting VP. I didn't want to make any hasty decisions, what with all that's going on. Thought I'd let it ride for a while. You understand?"

Nicholas chose not to answer and to see what Jack was up to. If he had to venture a guess, Jack desperately wanted to find a way out of making him a VP, but was having trouble coming up with excuses.

"I'll be honest, I think it's a big step and I have some reservations, but," he said slowly looking at Marshall, "as Don pointed out to Grant and me and a couple of other board members, if there is a good fit for the company's sake, we should get this behind us."

"In other words, as Jack so elegantly rounds that bush he's beating, what's the point of all this succession planning we do if we don't use it? Right guys?" Don seemed to have somehow managed to get under both Jack's and Grant's skin and was taking extreme glee in the moment.

"Of course," he continued, "we all wish the circumstances were different, but heck, you make the best out of what you got!"

Everyone had a quizzical look on their face after that statement.

"Anyway, may I, Grant, Jack?" Don asked like a kid asking to play with a long-lusted-for toy.

"Yeah, sure," Jack murmured.

Grant, who had yet to say a word, just nodded agreement.

"Well, Nicholas, obviously we're all sorry about Arthur, but congratulations, you're officially Vice President of Drug Metabolism and Safety," Don said with a far too big smile on his face.

Nicholas hadn't expected this; he thought Jack called him to explain why he hadn't got the job – not this. And, from the looks of things, reading between the lines that may have been Jack's original plan, but Don Marshall had gotten involved and interfered.

"Thank you. I didn't expect this so soon," Nicholas said.

Grant finally woke up long enough to look at his $8000 Rolex and managed a mumble. "Well son, as Mr. Marshall here said, we need closure and to move on. Congratulations. I'm sure you'll do well and have Jack's full support and mine. Now, you'll have to excuse me, I have an early luncheon engagement. Gentlemen."

Grant's closing statement was a stirring contribution, ensured he'd performed his role and excused him so he could get to something he liked doing more. So, with his confirmation of Harding's role came Grant's departure.

Nicholas could imagine his luncheon engagement, probably at the suite he was rumored to maintain at the local Hilton, in 'deep' consultation with his 22-year-old Executive Assistant.

"Well, I guess that about wraps it up for now. Nicholas, I'm sure there's hell of a lot on your plate now, including picking your own successor for your old job, but I think Arthur kept you up to speed, so the transition should be easy. Just remember, I'm always here."

Harding found Jack's statement less than comforting.

"Arthur and I," Jack droned on trying to sound more in charge again, "had a breakfast meeting at 7:00 to 8:00 AM every other Tuesday, let's keep it up, okay? Roberta will call your girl, what's her name?"

"Karen," Harding responded.

"Yeah, Karen, she's a USDA piece of ass if I recall," Jack laughed and having amused himself settled back into supreme slime mode, which was a normal position.

"You going to keep her or use Arthur's girl?"

"I'll stay with Karen. She's very good and knows all my quirks."

"Well, certainly can't hurt having something that good looking around, can it?" Jack continued.

"I'd love to stay here and listen to your locker room chat Jack, but you boys have to get back to work – keeping Marshall stock going up. And, I have to get back to, let me see, what was on my schedule for today?" Don asked more to himself, looking up as if in search of a thought. "The polo pony was yesterday. Oh, yes, now I remember – nothing!"

There must have been bad joke laughing gas in the room.

Nicholas and Don walked out together, but Roberta trapped Nicholas on the way out.

"Nicholas honey, first congratulations. We all knew you'd make it one day. Terrible it had to be like this, but what's one to do?" Roberta had obviously exhausted her day's supply of crocodile tears. "Now Nicholas, you're a Vice President and that's a dignified status position. And the people around you must also be dignified."

Nicholas thought he knew where this was going.

"As a Vice President, your secretary – oops, Executive Assistant, as we're called, is an extension of you," Roberta prattled on.

Hum, Nicholas thought. Thinking of Roberta as an extension of Jack was an easy connection to make.

"Now to be frank, dear," she continued.

He could also envision Roberta being 'Frank,' but chose not to take his mind down that warped path.

"Nothing personal, of course, but I just don't think your Karen is, well – Executive material."

By now Nicholas was starting to think Roberta was some distant dim witted descendent of the Borgia family.

"Now Arthur's Donna – she's first class all the way. None of those tight mini-skirts – no sir, just business and professional."

"Why thank you for the advice, Roberta. I'll take that under consideration," he said as he exited her outer office and discarded the entire conversation into his mental trash bin.

Nicholas opened the door to the staircase to go down to his fourth floor office and almost ran into Don Marshall.

"We must stop meeting like this Dr. Harding, again, my congratulations."

"I get the feeling you had more than meets the eye to do with this. Would that be a correct feeling?" Nicholas asked.

"Perhaps. Or perhaps Jack and that fossil Michner would have eventually seen the light," he said. "Who's to know? The important thing is that in this time of something bad – your friend's death – something good (I think and hope you do as well) your vice presidency has come about."

"Well," said Nicholas. "If you did have something to do with making this happen – thank you."

"You are most welcome Nicholas, if I did anything of course," he still took some glee in something not shared with Harding.

"I understand you and your daughter, Andrea have accepted my movie invitation for Saturday. This is excellent news! And, your assistant Ms Stemmer will accompany you. How interesting. Tell me Nicholas, are you and Ms. Stemmer…"

"No," Nicholas answered before Don had an opportunity to finish.

"You didn't let me finish," Marshall retorted.

"Doesn't matter," Harding was growing tired of the underlying conversation regarding Executive Assistants. "Karen and I are simply … Karen and I."

"Enough said, I thought I'd stop by your office and personally give her information – directions, time – you know that type of stuff. Shall we walk?"

"I'll catch up. I have to stop by the library," Harding went down to the first floor.

The Marshall Pharm library was in a major state of renovation. It was being converted to a cyber-library so the staff could access anything in the library electronically from their desk. They'd never have to set foot in the physical library if they didn't want to once it was completed. Harding went to the far back reaches of the library where the individual private reading rooms were located. Each reading room had a medium sized desk in the middle of the room with two chairs and credenza-like shelving on the walls for storing text temporarily.

On a window ledge overlooking a spectacular view of the rural Morris County New Jersey landscape, was a bronze bust of Alfred Tucker, the first head of R&D at Marshall. He was credited with convincing the Marshall family that Marshall Pharmaceuticals should convert from a pharmacy distribution company to a R&D driven house. They'd then asked him to lead the new R&D unit. Tucker ran it for 30 years and lead Marshall to the Top Ten of U.S. big Pharma houses.

Harding sat at the desk in the reading room and gazed out at the tranquil scenery. Years earlier, when Nicholas originally interviewed with Marshall, it had been a long and grueling day he recollected. His last interview of the day was with Arthur as the last person on the list. Exhausted from a day of appearing sharp, interested and brilliant to a group of strangers all asking the same boring questions over and over again had taken its toll.

With Arthur's office under construction at that time, they'd met for their interview in this same reading room; "You look tired Nicholas," Arthur noted when their discussion began. From that point onward, Arthur called Harding Nicholas and nothing else.

"Tell you what," Arthur had continued getting up from the small table, "you sit here, look out the window, enjoy the view, and relax for a bit. I'll go and get us some sodas. We're not supposed to eat in here, but what's the point of being a VP if you can't break some rules?" Harding recollected Arthur always shared a mischievous smile.

"That's really not necessary, Dr. Kronan." Harding had answered at the time.

"Just tell me what kind of soda you want Nicholas; I'm certain my staff has asked you every question relevant to this position and several irrelevant ones as well."

When Arthur returned with two diet Cokes he and Nicholas talked about just about everything but the position he was interviewing for.

"This is my favorite room in this whole place," Arthur had shared. "Few people use the reading rooms any longer, so it's quiet. I can think here. I do a lot of writing and talk preparation here. That bust – he's one of my heroes," Arthur had shared.

"Alfred Tucker – first head of R&D at Marshall. In the 1920s and 1930s, most of the pharmaceutical houses were just big drug stores. They mass marketed known remedies. There was little D and almost no R. Tucker, at Marshall and a few other visionaries at the Merck's, Pfizer's, Squibb's, etc., realized that to take the industry to the next level, the big Pharma companies would have to industrialize R&D – otherwise, they'd just be big snake-oil salesmen. They convinced their companies to invest millions of sales dollars in creating massive research and development centers. That forever changed the industry – due to the vision and conviction of a few."

As Nicholas recalled, he and Arthur had talked for almost two hours – never discussing anything relevant to the actual job. But they had immediately hit it off. Nicholas now sat where Arthur had during their first meeting and looked out the window and at the bust of Tucker. The quiet of the library was filled with the buzz of construction.

On a whim, Nicholas rose and picked up the bust, it was just heavy enough to discourage it from being moved around. He carried the bust to the head librarian's office, "what do you plan to do with this after the construction?"

"Probably storage. I don't even know who it is," the librarian sounded uninformed for her role.

"In that case, I'll keep it in my office," Harding headed out the library door before any objection could be aired.

Entering his office, Karen noticed the bust. "So, we are to be joined by Dr. Tucker?"

Harding peered at his assistant. "You know who he was?"

"First head of R&D at Marshall."

"Karen, you never fail to amaze me."

"But of course, Dr. Harding."

"Actually, he's going to join us in our new offices. They gave me Arthur's job."

"Yes, I know. Mr. Marshall was just here and he shared the news. Congratulations, Dr. Harding. Will I still be with you?"

"Absolutely. Wouldn't have it any other way."

"Thank you, Dr. Harding," Karen shared a big grin.

"You can work out the details of the move with Donna."

Entering his office, Harding checked his email and saw what he was looking for – another email from Arthur's account.

From: Kronan, Arthur [MPC]
Sent: 4:00 PM
To: Harding, Nicholas [MPC]
Subject: Riddle

Can you see what I see?

Can you know what I know?

Can you think what I think?

Can you go where I go?

This time, he decided not to reply. He printed a copy and filed it away with the others.

He picked up his phone and dialed Information Management & Technology services, the computer support group.

"Yes, this is Nick Harding. I want to check on the status of Dr. Kronan's system account. He had high level access."

"Hold on Dr. Harding, I'll check."

After a few minutes pause, the nameless voice returned.

"Dr. Harding?"

"Yes."

"Dr. Kronan's entire system account was deactivated at 9:15 this morning."

"Would that include any remote access?"

"Everything. His account's dead," the technician paused, realizing what he'd just said.

"Thanks," Nicholas said and hung up.

20

Beth

On his way home later in the week, Nicholas wasn't sure whether he was excited, apprehensive or what about Beth's visit. He had been just a little concerned about having this session with Helen in the house, but his mom told him as soon as Helen found out everything was straightened out at her house, she wanted to return there and plan Arthur's funeral. So he made a mental note to call her.

When Nicholas entered his driveway, he saw Michael's Audi and an unfamiliar car, which must have been a rental. He entered the house and heard voices coming out of the living room. Then he saw 'Drea setting the dinner table in the dining room. Always glad to see her Dad, she carefully put down the china plate she'd been holding and ran to her Dad.

"Hey Dad!" Andrea gave him a big hug.

"Hey back, kiddo," Harding returned the hug. "What's this? We're eating in the dining room?" knowing they rarely did so.

"Yep," 'Drea answered going back to meticulously setting the table. "Grandma said we could eat in here tonight. So, I'm setting the table."

"Did you cook too?" he asked.

"No silly!" she answered seriously. "Grandma cooked. I just set the table. But I can cook," she announced proudly.

"I bet you can, sweetie pie."

"Guess what, Dad?" she said, eyes shining. "I know something you don't know."

"Bet I can guess," he answered.

"What do you want to bet?" asked 'Drea, sounding a little too mature for Nicholas. "Hum, how about access to the

Sony Play Station for one hour tonight? Homework's all done," she said.

"Okay, and if I win, I get?"

"I take it the Play Station doesn't interest you?" she said with a straight face.

"No."

"Okay, let me think. I've got it," she said after a pause. "I'll clean up after dinner if you guess. So guess!"

"Your Grandma's friend, Beth, is here," Nicholas said.

"Ha! Wrong," she answered almost dropping a crystal goblet. "The Play Station is mine!" A celebratory dance followed.

"What do you mean wrong? If that's not it, what?"

"Uncle Michael is here!" Andrea yelled excitedly. "I gotcha Dad!"

Nicholas should have known. 'Drea worshipped her Uncle Michael.

"Okay, but I want to see that homework," he said.

"Don't be a sore loser," she said as she finished setting the table. *"Rasputin, re ghaj Quj loDHom! (We have the Play Station!)"* She went to tell her Grandmother she had finished setting the table accompanied by Rasputin.

Nicholas went up the staircase for a quick shower and changed before dinner. He was stalling before meeting his new lawyer.

Beth Cowling was the type of person who became the center of attention no matter where she was. A tad on the short side, compensated for by heels, her favorite color was white. And today she was a vision of flowing white from her shoes to her white pantsuit with long floor-length vest. She had piercing grey wolf-like eyes, but the most striking aspect was her hair – snow white and shoulder length. Somehow the white hair actually made her look younger than her mid-50s.

Nicholas quietly entered the living room where Beth was holding court with Dorothy, Michael and Andrea accompanied by the ever-faithful Rasputin.

With a slow melodious swaying Southern accent – the kind used by refined Southern ladies, Beth could lull listeners into a false sense of superiority. Nicholas had remained fascinated by the fact that average Americans hearing Southern accents automatically deducted about 15 IQ points and the same person hearing a refined British accent would add 15 IQ points. He suspected Beth made ample use of this trick and had been underestimated by many a foe – most likely to their serious detriment.

"I hope you don't go skiing in that outfit," Harding stated across the room.

"Not to worry. Why I'd just melt the snow with my charm," Beth retorted while walking towards Nicholas and extending her hand.

"Mr. Nicholas Harding, I presume?"

"And you must be my attorney, Ms. Beth Cowlings?"

"Well, you're half correct. We'll just see about the other half," She gave him a firm handshake and looked directly into his eyes with her steel gray eyes. *Those eyes go well with the white outfit, that outfit is no accident. She doesn't seem to be one to leave anything to chance.*

"You have a lovely home, Nicholas," she said.

Nicholas loved the way his name rolled off her tongue.

"And your daughter Andrea and her associate, Mr. Rasputin, are just darling," she said looking at 'Drea and her cat.

"Thank you, and watch out for him," Nicholas said, pointing to Michael.

"Michael has been flirting with me all evening. Why, if I didn't know better," she purred slowly, "I'd think he was trying to seduce me and if he's not careful, I just might let him."

"Okay everyone, before I have to get the hose out, let's have dinner," Dorothy said from the kitchen. "I made us a good old fashioned Southern dinner: fried chicken, rice with gravy, collards, peas and sweet potato pie. Beth, you should see the East Coast New York swill these boys eat – but none of that tonight – no sir. We Southern girls are in charge tonight."

Nicholas could see that if nothing else having Beth here had made Dorothy happy.

"Nicholas, old boy," Michael said with a fake British accent. "I say, what wine does one have with fried chicken and collard greens?"

"So glad you asked, old chap," Nicholas replied, picking up on the gag. "Actually, fried fowl and collards call for a mild Merlot or an oaky Chardonnay – everyone knows that."

Dorothy, not one to let the boys get one over on her said, shaking her head to Beth, "I just don't know where I went wrong, Beth. I tried to raise them like two good Southern boys and look at 'em, two of the biggest East Coast snobs you wouldn't want to meet. And, that one," she pointed to Nicholas. "That one likes – what's that raw fish you eat?"

"Sashimi, Mom. It's a delicacy in Japan."

"Um huh - it's sad, just sad," she said, shaking her head.

And, so the meal went on with much laughing and joking. Beth sat next to Andrea and even joined in feeding Rasputin fried chicken under the table, which was a no-no at Dorothy's table.

After the meal and clean up, 'Drea received the coveted Play Station and she and Rasputin adjourned to her bedroom. Nicholas briefly wondered if somehow she'd taught the cat to play.

Beth chimed in, "why don't we all move to the big ol' wraparound porch you have and Nicholas, be a dear and bring me a brandy."

It was a little cool on the late spring night, but still comfortable. Nicholas and Michael, living up to their reputations as East Coast snobs, each had an after dinner sipping sherry. Dorothy had tea and Beth her brandy, now accompanied by a small slim cigar.

Waiting for the others to arrive, Nicholas stared at Beth as she sat slowly smoking her cigar and drinking her brandy.

"Why what is it Nicholas, dear?" she purred.

Nicholas laughed, "I'll bet you have six inch fangs."

"I've never heard it put quite that way, but very perceptive dear, very perceptive."

As soon as everyone returned, Beth became more serious and said, "now Nicholas, I want you to reach in your pocket, pull out that huge wad of hard earned money and give me $1.00 and then give Michael $1.00 also."

Nicholas did as requested.

"Good," Beth said, folding the dollar and to Nicholas' amusement, stuffing it down her top. "Now, Nicholas, I'm your attorney. If you don't like my advice, you can fire me at any time. In fact, I consider this temporary until you can find someone up here you're more comfortable with. But more importantly, now we're protected by client-attorney privilege. Everything we discuss is protected. And, since Michael is licensed in New Jersey – even if he is environmental law – your conversation with him is protected as well.

"Now Dorothy, we can't extend client privileges to you, so I'd suggest you not sit in on this meeting or others," Beth said. "You can be subpoenaed. Michael and I can't."

"No!" said Dorothy firmly. "I might be able to help, so I'm staying, unless Nicholas wants me to leave. And they can subpoena me until the cows come home. I'd never say or do anything to hurt my boys," she finished and looked at Nicholas.

"She stays," he said.

"Okay. Let's get started," Beth said after taking another sip of brandy.

Beth sat back in her rocking chair, eyes half closed, looking up at the half moon. "Beautiful night, isn't it?" They were sitting outside of Nicholas' library on the porch. "Nicholas, do you have music in your library?"

"Sure," he answered, thinking the question strange.

"Good. Can you put some on please and point the speakers at these beautiful tall windows? Keep the windows closed." Then she put her head back and closed her eyes completely.

"Any requests?" Nicholas asked with a sarcastic tone.

"Since you ask, Mozart would be nice. Stimulates the neurons, you know."

Nicholas put on the Mozart and directed the wall-mounted speakers towards the floor to ceiling windows.

"Anything else, while I'm up?" he asked returning to the porch.

"Since you asked, if you could freshen up my brandy and then all of you move your chairs closer to mine. I won't bite."

"Yeah, might explode," Nicholas mumbled to himself as he went to refill her brandy.

"I heard that," she said, head back, eyes shut.

When Nicholas returned with the brandy and they'd all pulled their chairs around Beth's, she sat up; slate gray eyes open and stone sober. "The music will keep anyone from picking up our voices off the window vibrations. We should all assume until proven otherwise, our conversations are being monitored. I've arranged for a detective agency in New York I use on occasion to come out tomorrow. Nicholas, I'd like for them to electronically sweep your house and car. Can you get them into your office to sweep there and your phones?"

"I can, but is all this necessary? It's a bit cloak and dagger, isn't it?" he asked.

"Well, let's see what we've got here. There's an active federal investigation of something going on between Marshall and probably Tanaka – correct?"

"Yes," Nicholas replied.

"A federal investigation in which somehow you're involved, explaining your visit last week. And believe me, when the feds have their sights on you, they don't pull any punches. And, on top of that, we have two dead executives on our hands."

"Wait, wait – two?" Michael asked. "How do you come with two? Arthur and who else?"

"Nicholas?" Beth said turning towards him.

"Oh my God," he said. "I'd forgotten. That was six months ago and I didn't connect the two."

"What Nicky?" Dorothy asked.

"Last January, the CEO of Tanaka, Yoshi Mikasi, was stabbed to death in New York. But it was chalked up to another robbery. His wallet, watch, and coat were taken. I hadn't thought of it as being related to this."

"I'm not saying it is," Beth continued. "It may well be what it appears to be – a New York mugging gone wrong. It just seems a little strange to me that two companies caught up in a Federal investigation each have a senior executive turn up dead. What it means is we don't know who or what we're up against – hence the bug sweeps. Now, Nicholas – any further contact with the Feds?"

Nicholas hesitated before saying. "I called the FDA agent, Beverly Coston, a couple of days ago from a pay phone. I'm to meet her in Washington later in the week."

"You think that's a good idea? Can you trust her?" Michael asked.

"No. I don't trust her, but she's my only access to the Fed's information."

"Hum, I'll have her checked out and see what I can find out about this investigation," Beth said. "What about the company – Marshall lawyers? They must have an army of litigators ready to fight this."

"They're aware of it," Nicholas said. "I informed them of the first contact. They didn't seem as concerned as I thought they would be. And as for the army – actually the internal legal staff is rather small. They farm out most of the big stuff. To DCC actually, Paula's firm."

"Any contacts there?" Beth asked.

"No. I was never that chummy with any of Paula's work friends or associates, or her with mine."

"So," Dorothy said, reaching over to take a sip of Beth's brandy. "We have the dead Japanese guy – definitely murdered. Maybe mugging, maybe something else. We've got Arthur – a suicide."

"We're assuming a suicide," Michael said. "Sometimes, it can be awfully hard to tell a suicide from a homicide."

"Or things could be what they appear to be and we're just paranoid," said Beth. "But if they're not, then whoever is involved in this is playing for keeps and Nicholas, you need to be careful.

"Now, Nicholas," she went on slowly. "Do you own a gun?"

"No!" Michael and Dorothy said as one.

"Actually, I keep a handgun for target shooting at a gun club," Nicholas admitted.

"I see. Hard to believe you people are from the South. Hell, when I was growing up everyone in the house had at least one gun; my dog even had a gun. Okay, at the least, you need to upgrade your security system. I can have my detective friends take care of it, alright?" Beth asked.

"Okay," Nicholas said. "Jesus, what the hell have I gotten into?"

"That's easy, son," Beth drawled. "Money. You've got two multi-billion dollar, multinational companies with someone up to no good. The only thing companies this big give a rat's ass about is their money."

She took another sip of brandy and went on. "Now, your friend Arthur, Dorothy tells me he was as solid as they come. So, either he was involved with the wrong people who killed him or he knew of something so horrible it made him killing himself. Either way's pretty bad."

"Oh, yeah, I almost forgot, since Arthur died, I've been receiving emails from his work account. It's like they're trying to tell me something, but they don't make any sense," Nicholas added.

"Hot damn, Dorothy! Emails from the dead. Honey, I'm so glad you called me. If I had to deal with one more frigid pea-brained housewife whining about her cheating husband. You know what I told the last one? 'You're more boring than spinach, no wonder he's cheating on you. Hell! I'd cheat on you if I was married to you!' Needless to say, she sought counsel elsewhere, but emails from the great beyond – now this is a case!"

Beth was on her third brandy, occasionally assisted by Dorothy, but didn't appear drunk.

"Did you keep a copy of these electronic messages from the other realm?"

"I have them up stairs," Nicholas replied. "I'll get them."

He came back and handed Beth the printed copies of the four emails.

"Hum," she said reading them over and over. "Could Arthur have actually sent any of these?"

"He was still alive when the first one was sent. 'I'm sorry Nicholas. I'll explain later.'

"The time stamp is 12:35 am. What was time of death?" Michael asked.

"The police think it was around 1:00 am," Nicholas answered. "By the way, I have a meeting with the detective on the case tomorrow night. Do you want to sit in on it, Beth?"

"No. You having an attorney present at this stage of the game would just make him suspicious."

"Her," Dorothy corrected.

"The detective is a her? Hum…" Beth closed her eyes in thought.

"So," Dorothy piped in. "Sounds like Arthur had a case of the guilts about something. Must have a big case and then finds himself dead half an hour after he sent this message either by his own or someone else's hand."

"Then," Michael joined in. "Someone using Arthur's email account to hide their identity starts sending you mysterious vague messages. But to help you or screw you – that's the million dollar question."

"With a family of detectives why do you need me?"

"Who could access Arthur's account?" Michael asked.

"Anyone with the IT skills," Nicholas replied. "I checked and officially his account has been deactivated."

"So two – actually three – questions, Nicholas honey," Beth spoke with her eyes still closed. "If something evil and bad is going on at Marshall – and it looks like a good bet it is – who are the top candidates for the bad boys or girls to be behind it?"

Harding looked at his brother, who was smiling and laughed. "That's an easy one. Jack O'Connor, Senior Vice President of Research and Development – the Devil Incarnate! Anything evil at Marshall, I guarantee, he's involved. Anything evil on this planet … it wouldn't surprise me if he would be involved. He's the Saddam Hussein of Marshall."

"Anyone else?"

"There a few other minor players and sycophants, but Jack's the man. There's his head of security, Ken Joseph, who's the muscle behind Jack's putrid brain. Then there's the CEO, Grant Michner, but the running joke is Jack's got pictures of Grant in bed with a live boy or a dead girl. Jack says jump and Grant says 'how high?' He's just a figure head until Jack figures out how to take over entirely."

"Maybe he has," Dorothy said.

"Maybe," Nicholas went on. "But these other guys are all followers."

"So, if there's something rotten in the Marshall apple," Dorothy said. "Old Jack is at the core?"

"You've got it," Nicholas answered.

"Okay, we've got numero uno bandito – Jack O'Connor. What about good guys, other than yourself of course."

"Not too many of those at the upper level either," Nicholas replied. "Maybe Catherine Sullivan, VP of

European Marketing. We've always been close. Mark Stevens, head of Drug Metabolism, he reports to me now. Karen Stemmer, my administrative assistant."

"You mean secretary?"

"Yeah."

"You may have noticed, I'm not too politically correct. Hell, you screwing any of these women for that matter? Oh, never mind. I'll ask you later when your mother's not around."

"Thank you," Dorothy said.

"Now, neutral parties?" Beth asked.

"Right now there's one big question mark at Marshall, at least for me. Don Marshall," Nicholas went on to explain his brief, but interesting, relationship with Don.

"So probably O'Connor would have figured out a way to keep me out of the vice-presidency, but Don interfered. Pissed Jack off good. But I can't read what, if anything, he's up to. For all I know, I could just be entertainment for a bored rich guy."

"And our mysterious emailer?"

"I don't have a clue who it is," Nicholas said. "I mean this could be someone trying to guide me over a cliff, but I'm inclined to believe they want to help."

"Hum, so am I for now – gut instinct," Beth said. "Well folks," she said, rising. "This is quite a little mess we have here. Oh, by the way, I accept the case. And, it's past my bedtime. I'll be in the city tomorrow to spend the night. See you kids in a couple of days. Remember what I said: be careful."

"I'll make sure you have everything you need, Beth," Dorothy said, going with her, leaving the two brothers alone.

"Is this some kind of nightmare or what? You can say it now," Nicholas said.

"Say what?"

"I told you so."

"It's too late for that now," Michael retorted.

"We've figured out who's trying to fuck me, probably. Now we just have to figure out why, how and who else is involved."

"Nick – I just thought of something."

"What?"

"If this is all going on at Marshall, it probably means the same thing is going on at Tanaka. You know what you have to do?"

"What? You've lost me," Nicholas said.

Michael spoke slowly and softly. "If a group of baddies from Marshall and Tanaka are in cahoots and you're the squeeze play here, a.k.a. 'the fuckee', chances are there's a Japanese version of you at Tanaka. If you can find out whom the fuckee is at Tanaka and join forces – that's something the bad guys probably never planned on."

"Not bad for an environmental lawyer, bro," Nicholas stood and stretched. "Let's go to bed."

"That Beth's a pistol, isn't she?"

"Yep. Glad she's on our side. I'd hate to have her after me."

21

Detective Kerry Markus

The next day at work was fairly predictable, given the circumstances. People were still calling to say how sorry they were about Arthur and congratulations. Nicholas felt strange; he'd wanted the vice presidency, but never dreamed it would happen like this. Karen was handling their move to the large office suite down the hall – Arthur's old office – with her usual efficient perfection.

Nicholas had been concerned with just moving into Arthur's office, but Karen had arranged to have everything moved out, the office repainted a completely different color and brand new furniture delivered, even new art work. Karen could be scarily efficient sometimes.

There had been no further emails from Arthur, but there was a reminder from Don about Saturday.

Arthur's memorial was the following day and Nicholas spent most of the morning working on his short eulogy. He left early at 3:30 to meet Detective Markus, who had said she'd rather meet him at home. He took advantage of leaving early to pick up 'Drea at Charring Cross on the way home. The two teased each other mercilessly and she always put him in a good mood.

When he got home, he saw the unmarked police car and looked at his watch, seeing that detective Markus was early.

"You going to do your homework now?" Nicholas asked as they entered through the garage. 'Drea was lugging her 20-plus pound back pack.

"Yep," Rasputin waited for 'Drea by the door and began purring while rubbing against her leg in his typical welcoming ceremony. Nicholas didn't warrant the cat's attention and the duo were off to study.

"Hi Mom," Harding motioned to his mother. "Is that Detective Markus' car?"

"Yes. I asked her to wait in the study; thought you might be more comfortable in there." Dorothy was sitting at the kitchen desk putting the finishing touches on her latest book. "She seems nice."

"I bet you wouldn't say that if she dragged me out of here in handcuffs."

"Now, why would she do that?" Dorothy asked.

"She's a cop, Mom. I'm a black male. Cops give me the creeps."

"Excuse me; I'm sorry, I just wanted to return this cup. Good afternoon, Dr. Harding." Kerry Markus had entered through the door behind Nicholas while he was talking.

"Good afternoon," Harding managed to mumble, completely embarrassed.

"Can I get you more tea, Kerry?" Dorothy asked.

"If you don't mind, it's very good," Detective Markus replied.

Dorothy rose to take the cup from Kerry. "No problem at all; it's mango you know. You just go right back in the study and I'll bring it to you."

"Oh, thank you. I'm sorry I'm early, Dr. Harding. I was just in the area and thought I'd stop now. I can wait if you want," Kerry Markus said.

"Oh, no problem, Detective Markus."

"Kerry, please, Dr. Harding."

"Okay – and please call me Nicholas, I'll be back down in a few minutes."

"Great, I'll just wait," the detective returned to the library.

Nicholas noticed Detective Markus's appearance in the daylight had taken a decided shift to more attractive. He turned toward his mother when the detective left the room. "A first name basis, huh?"

"She's single and she's very nice."

"You've got to be kidding!" he said as he went upstairs to wash off before his interview by Detective Markus. Checking his watch Harding thought, *she's twenty minutes early*. He quickly brushed his teeth, took a shower, and changed before going back down to the library – he took his twenty minutes.

As he walked down the front stairs towards his library – Nicholas thought, *what the hell am I doing – she's a cop!*

He entered his library through the glass-paned double French doors. Detective Markus was reading a Civil War surgical text he owned.

"Sorry to make you wait, detective."

"Kerry."

"Sorry to have kept you waiting … Kerry."

"Not a problem. I could wait in here forever. Your library is lovely.

"Thank you." Harding hesitated and then asked, "just how much did you hear of my conversation with my mom?"

"Ah, let me see – 'She's a cop. I'm a black male. Cops give the creeps.' Was there more?"

"Look Detective,, I mean, Kerry, I didn't mean it the way it sounded."

"Yes you did. Look, I know where you're coming from. I know the crap black men have to put up with from cops. So you don't owe me an apology," Markus shared a warm smile. "And, I promise not to throw the cuffs on you and drag you out unless absolutely necessary."

She's definitely attractive, but not in a flashy, fashion model kind of way. Very nice legs, skirt just over the knees, flash of thighs when she crosses her legs. Jacket concealing her gun … Am I nuts? What am I thinking? Harding cleared his throat while adjusting his thoughts.

"Again, Nicholas. I'm very sorry about Dr. Kronan. From what I hear, he was more a friend than your boss. I just have a few things from the investigation to go over."

"Sure." *She sure has a soothing pattern of speech*, Nicholas thought as he began to relax.

Detective Kerry Markus pulled a small notebook out of her pocket. Nicholas noticed she didn't have a purse, having never been around a woman cop, he wasn't sure if this was the norm or not.

After flipping through notes Kerry reached the page she wanted.

"Now, you've known Dr. Kronan how long?" she asked

"Twelve years. I met Arthur when I interviewed with Marshall. We sort of hit it off right away. I was low man on the totem pole at that time and didn't report to Arthur, but he took me under his wing. He became my unofficial mentor. I don't believe anyone told Arthur to mentor me, he just did."

"And, when did you meet Mrs. Kronan?"

"About a month or so after joining Marshall. Arthur invited me over for dinner. I met Helen for the first time at their home."

"And, your impression of their relationship then and over the years?"

Nicholas felt himself relaxing more and more under Kerry's disarming style of questioning.

"In my opinion, during the time I knew them as a couple, they were completely devoted to one another. It sounds corny, but they seemed to be in love with each other. When

Arthur and I traveled, he talked about Helen, always found time to call her and buy her little gifts. I thought they had the type of marriage I would want."

"I see," the detective tapped her pen against her lower lip. "Were you aware of any friction in the marriage?"

"I never saw any, but I'm sure they had the normal amount," Nicholas replied.

"What about the lack of children? Do you know if this caused any problems?"

"Not that I'm aware of. It didn't seem to be an issue with Arthur. Helen mentioned it a few times. In fact, I recall her saying she was the one who couldn't have children and she felt bad for Arthur because they had no children.

"May I ask you a question, Kerry?"

"You may ask," she replied with that little smile he was beginning to enjoy. "But I can't guarantee an answer."

"Is Helen a suspect in Arthur's death?"

"I think I can answer that," she said. "When a spouse is found dead and the only other person in the house is the other spouse then, regardless of the apparent manner of death, the surviving spouse is suspect until we can eliminate all possibilities. That's the point of my questioning."

"So," Nicholas retorted, "Helen is a suspect?"

"Officially, yes, but only because we haven't closed out our investigation. So," she responded, easily shifting the subject, "Arthur and Helen, to your best knowledge had an unusually strong marriage. The only apparent issue was lack of children, which was more of an issue for her than him. Hum," she paused doing that little trick with the pen on her lower lip, which for some reason unknown to Nicholas, he found extremely enchanting.

"What about religion? Were they very religious?"

"Helen was moderately. I believe Arthur – no Arthur wasn't religious. But I don't recall it being an issue between them."

"Hum. Was it because he was a scientist?"

"I don't think so. Actually, most scientists, at least the ones I know, are religious. I think it was just Arthur's choice."

"And you, Nicholas. Are you – no let me guess. You're an atheist – no, an agnostic. You're not religious because you can't put blind faith in something with no proof. But an atheist puts blind faith in the opposite view. So, I'd wager you're an agnostic. How'd I do?"

"I'm impressed. You're some detective," he replied.

"Actually, I cheated and pulled your Marshall psych profile. Now that's a subject for a whole separate discussion, Dr. Harding," she said with a delicious smile while continuing to tap her firm lower lip with her pen.

Nicholas was considering asking her to stop with the pen, but figured having to explain that her tapping her lower lip with her pen was making him terribly aroused probably would not help matters.

"Now, Nicholas," she looked into his eyes and Harding noticed hers were a tan-ebony with flecks of green.

Good lord man, he thought to himself, get a grip on yourself. You're behaving, or at least thinking, like a 16-year-old.

She continued, "you've described your relationship with Arthur as more than a supervisor-subordinate relationship. Can you tell me more? Did it cause any problems at work?" she asked.

"Well," he started, "as I said, when I started at Marshall, it was as a bench level scientist. I was about four levels below Arthur."

"Had he held the same position for the last twelve years?"

"Yes."

She took more notes, and then said, "Okay – go on."

"As I said, we just enjoyed each other's company. Helen said she thought he thought of me as a son"

"Hum."

Tap, tap, tap, tap on her lip…focus Harding. "Arthur assigned me to key projects. He advised me. Some people thought he played favorites and a few thought I was his pet. But that's how the industry works: people use their connections to their advantage. What was important was that I performed well, so I moved up quickly. Then, when Arthur saw my capabilities, he began to groom me as his successor. It happens all the time. But I could see how someone who had the same ambitions, but didn't have that type of relationship with Arthur, would be jealous and think it inappropriate."

"But you don't?" she asked.

Nicholas noticed the green flecks in her eyes moved around, depending upon the lighting.

"Nope! Arthur helped me, yes, but I performed. I could just as easily have fallen flat on my face."

"So you now have Arthur's position. You're the new Vice President of Drug Metabolism and Drug Safety?" Kerry referred to her notes to get the title correct.

"Yes. Does that make me a suspect?"

"No. As I understand, you were home in bed when this happened. Alone?"

Tap, tap, tap. Harding sighed, "Uh, yeah."

"Oh, my God, I'm sorry Nicholas. I just remembered you are a widow. Your wife died in a car accident several months ago, correct?"

"Yes."

"That 'alone' comment was completely inappropriate and I apologize," Detective Markus blushed, which only served to make her even more attractive to Nicholas.

"It's not a problem, really," he said.

"It must be very hard for you and Andrea."

Harding noted the detective hadn't referred to her notes in recalling Andrea's name.

"Sometimes, but we manage. She's a good kid."

"Just a few more questions ..." she kept tapping her mouth while a little blush remained. "Did Arthur have any enemies at Marshall or elsewhere for that matter that you were aware of?"

"The elsewhere – absolutely not," he answered abruptly, "Arthur was just one of those guys that everyone just liked. At Marshall, Arthur was a corporate VP. Even nice guys don't get that far without stepping on some toes. Corporate politics at that level can be pretty cutthroat. Arthur could hold his own in the snake pit, but he never sank to their level. Are there people at Marshall who would have taken a shot at him politically? Sure, but no one would physically harm him."

"Can you describe Arthur's relationship with Jack O'Connor?" Detective Markus scanned her list.

Nicholas paused before answering, "they seemed to get along okay."

"Just okay? Can O'Connor be difficult to deal with?"

"Kerry, Jack's my boss now," Nicholas said slowly. "When I was a little boy in the backwoods of North Carolina, my grandmother owned a little country store. And, I just loved to hang out there. She had all these pithy little homespun sayings. One was, 'If you don't have something good to say about someone, don't say anything.' So let's just say I'm taking my grandmother's advice, so my answer is 'just okay.'"

"Alright, Nicholas." Kerry continued tapping, Nicholas noticed, with the crossing and uncrossing of her legs, Kerry was showing considerably more of her very shapely and very attractive lower thigh. He found himself not wanting the interview to end and searched for an excuse to stay in her presence. *She's a cop, you moron,* he thought to himself, as the green flecks dancing in her eyes mesmerized him. *Yes, she's a cop, but she's attractive, intelligent, and good company. Why not? Get a grip!*

"In the last week or so did you notice anything different; any change in Dr. Kronan?" Markus asked.

"I don't know, maybe it's hindsight, but I thought he seemed preoccupied and he did call in sick a couple of days before he died," Nicholas said.

"Preoccupied? How?" she asked.

"Well, he'd talked about stepping down sooner than planned, but didn't go into specifics. He just seemed to have something else on his mind. Oh, God, I almost forgot."

"What?"

"An email."

"An email, about what?" the detective in her stirred.

"The morning after or of Arthur's death, when I got in the office, there was an email from Arthur time stamped at 12:35 AM. You said he died at around 1:00 AM, right?"

"Yes, based on what Helen shared with us.

"What did it say?" she asked, scribbling notes on her pad.

"I can show you. I have a copy upstairs in my jacket pocket. I'll get it," Nicholas rose to go upstairs.

"Good. Can I use your restroom?

"Sure. I'll show you."

Showing Kerry to their downstairs bathroom, Harding went to his room to retrieve the first email he'd received from Arthur. After deliberating with himself, he decided not to show Kerry the others.

On his way back to the library, Kerry was ahead of him. Harding had an opportunity detective's figure from behind. *God,* he thought, *maybe Michael is right. I haven't had a relationship with a woman in so long I'm turning into a leach.*

"You have a beautiful home, Nicholas," Kerry said, returning to the library. "I've always loved Victorians, but most are old and require a lot of work. This one looks like an old Victorian from the outside, but it's actually almost new."

Resuming her questioning position with notepad and pen poised, legs crossed, Nicholas unfolded the single-paged email. It read: "I'm sorry Nicholas. I'll explain later."

"And, this means what to you Nicholas?" Detective Markus inquired.

"I don't know. I don't know what the 'I'm sorry' is referring to, but the 'I'll explain later,' certainly implies he planned to see me to explain. So this message, followed by a suicide thirty minutes later, I can't make sense of."

"Hum." *Tap, tap, tap.* "May I keep this?"

"Sure."

"Any other emails, phone messages, memos, any type of unusual communication from Arthur recently?"

"No," Nicholas lied. He decided since the other emails came after Arthur's death, obviously Arthur didn't send them. *Technically,* he reflected internally, *I answered the question honestly. I'm just not ready to share the other emails with Kerry Markus yet.*

"Oh, my," Markus looked at her watch and out the large window noting it was getting past dusk, "I've taken up much more of your time than I'd planned to. It's late." Smilingly, the detective caught Nicholas starring into her warm brown eyes.

Nicholas was desperate for her not to leave yet, but didn't know how to extend the moment. "Oh, I didn't mind," he said. "Actually, I've enjoyed talking with you – it's good to get this out."

Dorothy knocked at the library door.

"Are you going to interrogate him all night, Kerry?"

The detective blushed again and gathered her things. *Notepad, email and damn lucky pen*, Harding thought.

"Actually, we just finished, Mrs. Harding. I should be going," she said.

"Nonsense," Dorothy replied. "It's dinner time. You'll stay and join us."

"Oh, I couldn't, Mrs. Harding."

"That wasn't a request. You will stay and join us for dinner."

"I wouldn't argue with her if I were you," Nicholas said chidingly.

"Well, in that case, how could I refuse? I need to call the office and check out for the day."

"Good, you can make your calls in here and you know where the restroom is. Nicholas, can you help set the table?" As Dorothy and Nicholas walked towards the kitchen, she said, "you owe me one."

"What do you mean?" he asked.

"I see the way you're looking at her, and her at you, by the way. I'm not blind."

"But she's a cop!" he whispered.

"So what? You could do a lot worse," Dorothy said and ended the conversation.

Nicholas knew Dorothy had never liked Paula, but Dorothy had refused to ever say a bad word about Paula, then or now.

The dinner was enjoyable. Kerry and Andrea had hit it off with "Drea explaining the concept of teaching a cat commands in the Klingon language. She had also asked Kerry if she had a gun on now.

"Yes."

Had she ever killed anyone?

"No."

Had she ever shot anyone?

"No."

Disappointed, Andrea still wanted to know if she could take Detective Markus to school for 'show and tell'. Kerry answered in the affirmative, "yes."

Kerry thanked Harding's mom profusely for her dinner. "This was excellent, Mrs. Harding; I really enjoyed the meal and company," she smiled at Nicholas.

After coffee, Nicholas walked Kerry to her car.

"How much longer do you think the investigation will last?"

"Why do you ask?"

"Just curious."

"Actually, it's almost complete. It does appear to be a straight forward suicide. Sometimes, you never know why."

"It's just I can think of any number of people at Marshall, where this wouldn't surprise me. You know, wound a tad too tight? But not Arthur."

"I know. I know this has to be hard for you, Nicholas. I'll keep in touch." The green flecks were dancing again, "I may have more questions for you."

"I'd like that," Nicholas caught himself. "I mean I'd like to hear what's going on."

"Good night, Nicholas," Detective Markus extended her hand and they shook. Nicholas held contact for a moment too long.

"Night, Kerry," he said as she got into her car watching as she drove off.

God, thought Nicholas. Could things get any more bizarre? It's too much to think about now. Harding turned to go back indoors.

"She's very nice," Dorothy said when he entered the kitchen.

"Yes, she is."

"Attractive too."

"Yes, she is."

"Single, I noticed."

"Yes, she is."

"I'm surprised she didn't faint with that dazzling conversation of yours. Did you ask her out?"

"Of course not; she was here to interview or interrogate me about the death of my friend on police business."

"Um huh. Don't wait too long to give her a call."

"Thank you Dr. Phil" Nicholas went to his room to take another shower. "Good night Mom."

Before he went to bed, Harding called Helen. She said she was fine, but didn't sound well. He tried to get her to come back and spend more time with his family, but she refused. She said she had to get used to staying in the house alone, so she might as well do it now.

Nicholas said he'd see her at the memorial service the following day. He said good night and lay in bed while trying to shut off his mind.

22

Nicholas and Beverly

Helen had selected the local Episcopal church for the small non-denominational service. Most of the attendees were from Marshall, including all of Arthur's direct reports – now Nicholas' staff – Jack O'Connor and his wife. *What the hell did she do in a previous incarnation to deserve a life with that asshole?* Nicholas wondered. Sitting next to O'Connor and fidgeting was Grant Michner.

Roberta and Donna sat a few rows back; Roberta attended no doubt just to be nosey. At the very back of the service Karen sat alone, until Nicholas noticed Don Marshall slip in to sit next to her just before the service started. Dorothy sat next to Nicholas and a scattering of people he didn't know were here and there.

Helen designed the service to be very brief. Nicholas gave a ten minute eulogy touching on Arthur's parent's arriving from Europe at the turn of the century; he furthered with their relationship and love for each other; and then followed with Arthur and Helen's devotion to each other.

Arthur's remains were taken to be cremated after the memorial service and there was a brief awkward reception at Helen's house afterward.

"Nicholas," Helen said her voice soft and breaking. "I can't – can't do this. Can you please act as host and make my apologies to everyone? I'll be in my room." Helen disappeared up the old banister staircase.

"I'll take care of everything, Helen," he answered while watching her vanish.

Nicholas made an excuse for Helen and most guests didn't stay long when they learned she wasn't available. Jack, finding no one he could bully or terrorize, grabbed his wife and left as well.

If someone had to blow their brains out, why couldn't it be that turd? Nicholas thought to himself as he said goodbye to Jack and his tortured wife.

Soon only Nicholas, Dorothy and the caterers remained – the food having hardly been touched.

Nicholas went up and knocked on Helen's door.

"Come in, Nicholas," she answered.

"How did you know it was me?" he asked.

"Who else would come up here to deal with the batty old widow?"

"Everyone's gone. They all send their respect. The caterers are cleaning up. There's a ton of food left. What do you want them to do with it?"

"Whatever you decide, dear," she said.

"Okay, I'll have them leave enough for you and take the rest to the shelter," he responded.

Helen nodded in agreement.

"Helen, I'm leaving now, but I'm not going to let you sit here and waste away pining for Arthur. He's gone. At some point – soon – you're going to have to move on."

"I know. You're a dear boy, Nicky. Arthur must have seen a lot of himself in you. I'll be okay."

"I know you will," Nicholas said as he kissed her on the cheek and left.

Downstairs, he gave instructions to the caterers, and then after they left he and Dorothy drove home. On the way, Nicholas asked his mom, "can you check on her later today?"

"I'll go over this afternoon," Dorothy said. "I'll be such a pest; it'll take her mind off everything."

"Thanks, Mom," Nicholas said.

As he pulled into his driveway, he saw his limousine service car. He pulled his Lexus into the garage, quickly ran inside to pick up a small portfolio. He told his mom he'd be late and got into the waiting car for a short ride to Newark airport and an equally short flight into Reagan National Airport.

The new Reagan National airport was a monument to bureaucratic power. Situated on a small strip of land, planes were forced to approach and take off from very short runways and maneuver over the waters of the Potomac River. Dulles Airport could easily have taken on the flight load, but National's secret was its sinfully close proximity and convenience to the bureaucratic egos of Washington, be they in the Executive, Legislative or Judicial branch of the nation's government.

Nicholas had arranged to meet FDA agent Beverly Coston at the Willard Hotel in downtown D.C.

The Willard was steeped in history. This was where Abraham Lincoln and his family stayed on his first night in Washington after his election to the presidency. His Pinkerton (Alan Pinkerton himself) security agents had insisted the President-elect wear a disguise and sneak into the town at night.

Lincoln had been humiliated and vowed to never use such tactics again, regardless of the risk to him. The Willard was also where a victorious and famous General Ulysses S. Grant had stayed upon his arrival in the capital. And where, during the Civil War the term 'lobbyist' was coined, those trying to influence legislators at the Capitol awaited their turn in the Willard's spacious lobby.

The hotel was far too upscale for anyone to look for an FDA official here and out of the way of his usual DC haunts, although he had stayed at the Willard before. He took a taxi from the airport to the hotel, checked in under a different name, requesting a suite. Thirty minutes after he arrived his cell phone rang.

"Where are you?"

He provided Agent Coston with the hotel and room number. He had previously told her downtown. Another thirty minutes and there was a knock at the door. He looked through the peephole, saw Agent Coston and opened the door for her. B

He looked down the hall for any signs of other agents. "Are you alone?" Harding asked, closing and bolting the door behind them.

"Yes," she replied. "Nice room. You big drug company execs live well."

"Any wires – on you or in the room?" he inquired.

"Oh jeez, are we going through this again?" Coston stood arms out, legs akimbo. "Pat me down – I insist."

This time Nicholas took her up and gave her a thorough frisk, not quite sure what he was looking for and trying not to enjoy it.

"Okay," he said.

"And what about you?" She asked.

"What about me?"

"How do I know you're not wearing?" she asked.

"Why the hell would I wear a wire?" Nicholas asked, rather pissed she'd question his integrity.   "You're the investigator. You pat me down if it makes you happy."

"No thanks," she said. "I think that was more than enough 'patting' for the day."

"Where's your partner, deputy dog?" Nicholas asked.

"He's not my partner. I got stuck with him that day. He's been reassigned."

"Darn. I was looking forward to that massive intellect."

"By the way, I'm sorry about your boss, Dr. Kronan," Coston shared empathetically.

"Thanks, is Arthur's death part of this?"

"Don't know," Coston stretched out on the sofa. "Right now it looks like a straight up suicide – but who knows? Really … really … nice room!"

"So you mentioned you're so jealous of us evil drug execs, why don't you come over to the dark side and work for one of us? Look," Nicholas took a diet coke from the mini-bar and sat in the armchair next to the sofa. "You wanted me here – I'm here, now tell me what the hell's going on."

"May I?" she asked pointing to the mini-bar.

"Help yourself."

"Thanks," Coston removed and popped the top of an orange juice with ice.

"Okay," Nicholas pronounced, "so how do we do this?"

"Oh, that's easy, you tell me everything you know and I'll tell you some of what I know," the FDA agent smiled.

"You know," Nicholas rose from his chair, irritated. "Obviously I misjudged you. I get paid to work with assholes; I don't do it for free. If you stay after 6:00 PM, you have to pay for the room and the mini-bar is on your tab. Good day, Dr. Coston."

"Okay, okay, Harding. Sorry," Coston sat up and got serious. "I'll tell you what I can, but I can't tell you some things. First off, it's an active investigation. Second, you're still to some extent a suspect. And third, I'd be subject to federal prosecution myself if I told you what I shouldn't, okay?"

"Alright. So talk," Harding paced the room still thinking.

"Well, you must have figured out the two companies involved are Marshall in the U.S. and Tanaka in Japan."

"I figured that much since Tanaka's the only Japanese company I'm involved with. But what are they going to do and who's involved? What's my part in this?"

"We don't know for sure, but somehow it must involve MR-548, the new antiviral from Tanaka that Marshall is developing, which you're project lead on. This is where I need your help; I need you to learn what the hell is wrong with the drug" Emboldened by her statement, Coston hit the mini-bar again. This time she retrieved a little jar of macadamia nuts and bottled water.

"You don't get out much do you?" Nicholas asked as she fumbled with the nut jar.

"To a fancy place like this? Nope. Do you know what my daily travel allowance is?"

"No. Now ask me if I give a shit."

"Yeah, yeah. As for whom at Marshall is the baddest of the bad? That's probably not too hard either."

"That would be my boss – that fermented turd – Jack O'Connor."

"Bingo," she said while munching on the nuts. "God, these things are sinful. Want some?" Coston extended the jar toward Nicholas.

"No, who else besides Jack?"

"Don't know, but Jack's obviously the ring leader."

"So, why don't you go knocking on his door instead of mine?" Nicholas asked.

"Because, fermented turd he may be, he's not stupid and on paper, officially, he smells like a rose. This brings us to you. Dr. Harding, the official patsy poster boy. When all this goes down, it's going to look like you were in it up to your eyeballs: forged memos, reports, emails, and the works. At best, your career in the industry will be ruined."

"And, at worst?" Nicholas asked.

"At worst – you'll do time in a federal prison."

"So, what if I just walk away now – quit?" he asked.

"Too late, you'd still take the fall; O' Connor and friends have planned this for at least two years."

"Okay." Realizing the depth of shit he was in, Nicholas asked, "what about Tanaka? Do we know what's going on there?"

"Not much," she replied, looking disappointed her nuts were gone. "FDA doesn't have a lot of pull with the Kosaysho, that is, the Japanese Ministry of Health."

"My lawyer's theory is there's probably a Japanese version of me at Tanaka, patsy, and she suggests I should try to find them and see if we can work together."

"And, this lawyer would be?"

"Not important at this point, Agent Coston."

"Okay, but I don't know. The Japanese authorities are pretty picky and would not take kindly to an American pharmaceutical executive interfering in their affairs."

"Fuck them. So who's your contact in Marshall?"

"Uh, um, sorry – off limits," she replied.

"Then where do we go from here?"

"You try to find out what's up with MR-548. If we can figure that out, we might be able to stop their plan. I, on the other hand, have to try and figure out exactly what their plan is."

Nicholas looked at her in a hard stare. "That doesn't sound like much. No offense, but do you need some help on this?"

"I have access to all the federal resources I need, so no, I don't need help. And by the same token, don't you and this lawyer go and do something stupid."

"Agent Coston," Harding spoke slowly. "You may have observed I'm not the sort of chap who would thrive in a prison environment, so I'll do whatever the fuck I have to in order to avoid that eventuality, okay?"

"Okay," she replied.

"Are we done here Agent Coston?" Nicholas asked.

"Almost. Here." Costen stretched out her arm handing Harding a card with a telephone number. "You and I are the only two people on earth with this number; use it to reach me or to let me know how to reach you. We'll stay in touch."

"One more question. Yoshi Mikasi, was his death part of this?"

"We think so."

"And Arthur's wasn't?"

"I didn't say that, Dr. Harding. I said it looked like a straight-up suicide, but it still could have been part of this. So someone's playing hardball. Remember that and be careful."

"I will," Nicholas replied, moving towards the door.

"You mind if I?" Coston pointed to the mini-bar.

"Knock yourself out," Harding turned to exit the hotel, the bellman hailed a cab while only two blocks away within direct line of sight with his high-powered telephoto lens, U.S. Marshal Barry Keenan snapped a few pictures.

Nicholas' taxi drove off to the airport and 20 minutes later, Agent Beverly Coston left the hotel. She should have exited via underground, but she was tired.

Keenan snapped a few additional photos. He figured O'Connor would pay him enough for a big day at the track. He wondered if the drug company's "big shot nigger" had fucked Coston. She wasn't a bad looker. He'd made a move on her, but the bitch had shot him down. *Yeah, I bet she fucked that rich nigger,* he thought. He couldn't wait to get home and download the pictures. *We'll see who fucked who,* he thought as he drove through the heavy D.C. traffic.

Nicholas was able to catch an early flight and be home by 8:00 PM in time to hang out with Andrea. Afterward, he came down to talk to Dorothy. "Any word from Beth?"

"She called; she said we probably won't see her until the weekend, but her words, 'hunting's good.'"

Nicholas told his mom goodnight and wandered into his study to click on his computer. There it was; another message from Arthur.

From:	*Kronan, Arthur [MPC]*
Sent:	*5:30 PM*
To:	*Harding, Nicholas [MPC]*
Subject:	*Desert Fox*
Remember the Desert Fox.	

Great. Some asshole is sending me messages from Arthur's account and now he's making references to a World War II German tank commander – Rommel. And the whole world has gone fucking nuts!

After tossing and turning sleepless for a while, Nicholas went down to his library and sure enough found a book on Erwin Rommel, the Desert Fox. He took it upstairs, intending to read it, but fell asleep and all the cluttered issues on his mind haunted his sleep.

He dreamed of Kerry Markus, but she couldn't stop eating Macadamia nuts. And he saw Jack floating down a rapids looking like a log, no, a huge turd with fangs. He woke up at 2:30, tired and sweating and turned on a movie channel with a mindless comedy to lull him into a more restful sleep.

23

'Drea at Don's House

'Drea had been excited since she'd heard they were going to Don Marshall's mansion. The thought of someone she knew having their own private movie theatre in their home made quite an impression on the 11-year-old.

"What's his name?" Andrea asked, bouncing on Nicholas' bed.

"Who's   name?"

"Your friend with the movie theatre Dad, duh!"

"His name's Don Marshall. You can call him Mr. Marshall and haven't I told you not to 'duh' me?"

"I can 'duh' you if I want," she replied with a smug tone. "And, what movie are we going to see?"

"Something suitable for an 11-year-old, no doubt," he replied.

"I hope it's not some crappy Disney movie. I'm mature for my age, you know. Did you tell Mr. Marshall I'm mature?"

"When did you add 'crappy' to your vocabulary, missy?"

Ignoring the question, Andrea went on, "I could pass for 13 or 14, you know and I'm probably as mature as most 14-year-olds."

"I know I shouldn't ask this," Nicholas said, "but are you trying to make a point here?"

"Well, since you asked Dad," she was now standing on Nicholas' bed so she'd be eye-to-eye with him, (she knew all the tricks) "my preference would be an R-rated movie, but I realize you wouldn't understand."

As an only-child, 'Drea was comfortable conversing with adults, hence her style of speech did make her sound more mature than her age.

"However," she continued in a serious tone, "since I'm the equal of a 14-year-old in maturity, I should be able to watch PG-13 movies." Andrea folded her arms with a look of satisfaction for a job well done.

"Very good, 'Drea." Nicholas replied. "You should be a lawyer, but you forgot one small point."

"What?" she asked suspiciously.

"You're not 14!" He said loudly for emphasis. "Get dressed now, sweetheart."

"But Dad, I'll barf if I have to watch a G movie."

"Well, remind me to bring some anti-barf medicine. You know, maybe Don will have a nice *Barney* movie for us."

"Yuk! You're not funny," she said, going into her room to change and trying to figure out another angle to try next. Nicholas had arranged for Karen to meet them and then the three of them would drive to Don's house.

Karen arrived promptly as always.

"Good afternoon, Mrs. Harding," Karen focused on Dorothy, who greeted her at the door.

"Hi Karen," Andrea said coming down the stairs and noting her at the door.

"Ms. Harding, I almost didn't recognize you. You look so, ah, mature."

"See Dad," Andrea said to Nicholas. "Karen called me Ms. Harding. She thinks I'm mature."

Nicholas rolled his eyes, wondering how the two had planned this. "Give it a rest, 'Drea," he said. "Hi Karen."

"Hello Dr. Harding, thank you for inviting me."

"You're welcome. Oh, Karen, at least for tonight, can you try to call me Nicholas and 'Drea – Andrea, not Ms. Harding?"

"I shall try Dr. Harding – Nicholas," she said, correcting herself.

"Okay you three have fun," Dorothy said.

"You are not going to join us Mrs. Harding?" asked Karen.

"No, I'm not a movie buff like these two. Give me a good book and I'll make a movie in my mind."

Nicholas drove them to the Marshall estate and 'Drea was suitably impressed.

"Wow!" said 'Drea as they pulled up to the mansion. "Hey Dad, can we live someplace like this?"

"Sure, just as soon as you win the lotto."

When the car came to a stop under the front portico, once again a uniformed servant opened their car doors and showed them into the house. This time they were led into a large sitting room overlooking a vast garden topiary, which looked like a giant maze. Large bronze statues stood guard at the entrances to the maze.

"Mr. Marshall will join you shortly," the servant said before silently disappearing.

"Cool!" 'Drea exclaimed, looking out the large window-doors. "Look at the giant cat-bird statues."

"They're called griffins, Andrea. They are mythological figures with the head and wings of an eagle and the body of a lion, from ancient Greece. They were sort of like pets of the Greek gods."

"You mean like Zeus? He would have had a griffin for a pet?"

"Yes."

"Very cool."

Three different servants entered the room carrying two trays of canapés. One tray looked to be designed specifically to entice a mature 11-year-old. One servant took requests for drinks. Nicholas and Karen each requested a diet coke and 'Drea a Shirley Temple. Upon hearing the Shirley Temple request, Nicholas looked at the obviously genuine Oriental rug and prayed 'Drea would be careful.

Just before their drinks arrived, Don Marshall appeared through one of the three doors built into the wall that Nicholas loved so much.

"Well good afternoon, all," Don appeared his usual ebullient, carefree self. "I'm so glad you could come. Nicholas."

"Don."

"Karen, remember house rules, first names only," Don said, smiling.

"Don," Karen replied with a smile.

"And," he said addressing 'Drea. "You must be young Ms. Andrea Harding. I was not expecting such a mature young lady."

Andrea turned her head to Nicholas and mouthed "See!"

"Thank you," 'Drea replied sweetly to Don. "Can I get a tour of your house?"

"Why, of course Andrea, after we finish our refreshments here we can take a tour."

Don dutifully gave the three the grand tour of the mansion. Nicholas tagged along even though he'd seen the house a couple of weeks ago. Nicholas thought that Karen seemed a little bored.

"You okay, Karen?" he asked as they lagged behind, while Don and Andrea played a quick game of billiards in the Billiards Room (where else?).

"Oh, yes, Nicholas," she said with some difficulty.

"It's just after you've seen one huge multi-million dollar mansion you've seen them all," Karen retorted with an amusingly peculiar smile.

They concluded the tour at the library.

"And here we are at Nicholas' favorite room, my library." Don gave Nicholas a mischievous look and said, "Nicholas, would you do the honor and give the tour of the library?"

Nicholas, up to the challenge said, "of course Don," and, proceeded to give Andrea and Karen a detailed accounting of the library right down to the story about the roll top desk.

"Dad," 'Drea said. "We must get a house like this. I need an indoor swimming pool and a bowling alley and a movie theatre and a billiards room. And Rasputin and I could have connecting bedrooms," she said, eyes beaming.

"You *want*, not you *need*, dear. You'll learn the difference when you mature just a little more."

"I know the difference between need and want and I need!" she said defiantly.

"Very strong willed, I see," Don said, standing behind Nicholas.

"Now," Don announced, "time to select a movie." Looking at 'Drea, he said, "that we can all enjoy, I have a small selection of first run movies and I suggest we put ourselves in the capable hand of the women."

"Okay by me," Nicholas replied, figuring that Karen could exert some degree of control over Andrea's occasionally bizarre tastes.

"So Andrea, Karen, will you do the honors?"

"Of course," 'Drea replied for both. It was the first time Nicholas had seen Karen allow anyone to speak for her.

The three returned shortly and announced their selection: the latest *Star Trek* movie. "Your daughter's taste is quite mature, Nicholas," Karen said with an amused look.

"Tell me about it," Nicholas replied.

Don's in-home theatre could have comfortably seated a couple of dozen in wide, comfortably reclining movie seats. With an 8 x 20 foot high definition screen and surround sound Dolby system, who needed to go out to a movie? *So this was how the other half lives,* Nicholas thought.

Everyone enjoyed the movie, although Nicholas did sleep for a while. It gave Andrea a chance to show off and practice her linguistic skills in the Klingon language. Don and Karen were both exceedingly impressed that 'Drea not only spoke an extraterrestrial language, but had taught her cat commands in Klingon as well.

"I must meet this exceptional animal," Nicholas overheard Don tell Andrea. "Did I tell you about my pet porcupine? No one, but no one, messed with me when I had Petey, I'll tell you. But I never got stuck with a quill myself."

"You didn't have a pet porcupine," Andrea challenged.

"I'll send you a picture," Don replied. "In exchange for you teaching me a sentence in Klingon."

"Deal," she replied.

The two obviously hit it off. Nicholas and Karen tried to talk about things other than work. He'd learned that after going to public school in Germany and studying economics, at age 19, she'd accompanied her parents and her sister, who was three years younger, to America. Her parents had started a clothing store in Morristown. There was no man in her life now. She knew that half of the people at Marshall thought she was gay. She wasn't. And she also knew what the other half assumed about her and Nicholas. She seemed to take some delight in keeping her life private and keeping everyone guessing. But she said that she thoroughly enjoyed working with Nicholas and had been afraid that when he moved up to Arthur's job he wouldn't take her along.

"Not to worry Karen, I think we make a pretty good team."

"We do; a good team. Yes," she replied.

After the movie, Don served more refreshments, this time in the solarium which with its glass top you could now see the stars and crescent moon. A good time seems to have been had by all. Andrea was ready to move into the mansion and Don couldn't wait for his Klingon lesson. So Nicholas figured he'd have to invite Don over to reciprocate.

"Don, thanks for having us over," Nicholas said as they were about to leave. "I should have you over to our place, but I can't compete with these digs."

"I'd love to," replied Don, accepting the invitation before it could be further qualified or reneged. "Oh, I almost forgot, I have a small gift for each of you. Now, you can't open them until you're home. Promise?"

"Promise!" 'Drea said, speaking for the three.

"Good. I have found this evening most enjoyable," Don said as the silent servant appeared to escort them out.

Back at home, Nicholas invited Karen in, but she begged off. "No thank you, Nicholas," she said, looking at him with those luscious pools of blue. "But I must return home. On Monday, it will be Dr. Harding again, yes?"

"If that's what you want, Karen."

"It is what I want, yes. But it is not yet Monday," and she leaned over to kiss Nicholas on the cheek. "Thank you for inviting me," she whispered. "Good night, Andrea."

"Night, Karen. I'm going to go open my present," she said as she scurried off into the house.

When Karen arrived home – a three bedroom in the part of town struggling to remain affluent– her parents were waiting up for her as they usually did on the rare occasions she went out. She told them all about her evening, all about Don's mansion, and then she went to her room.

After changing for bed, she noticed the small wrapped box that Don had given her. She unwrapped the ribbon and opened the box to reveal two dazzling diamond earrings. She had a feeling they were unlikely to be cubic zirconium crystals. Karen smiled, turned out the light and went to sleep.

Andrea had opened her present as soon as she got into the house. Talking and opening at the same time in order to update Grandma on the really cool house, no mansion, she'd visited.

"Wow, cool! Look Dad. He really had one."

Nicholas saw that 'Drea was holding a 5 x 7 framed picture of a kid who looked to be around 12, but was obviously a young Don holding in his lap, what certainly appeared to be a porcupine. The picture was signed "To my new Friend Andrea – Don and Petey."

"Well, I'll be. I guess he actually had a pet porcupine," Nicholas said. "But don't you ever try to touch a porcupine 'Drea, they're dangerous."

"No duh, Dad! I'm not stupid. I'm going to show Rasputin and tell him about the movie," she said bounding out of the room.

"'No duh, Dad.' What would have happened if Michael and I had spoken to you and Dad like that?" Nicholas asked his mom.

"We probably would have slapped your little smart mouth across the room," she replied.

"That's child abuse."

"Not back then it wasn't. So what did you get?" she asked, pointing to the present Nicholas had under his arm.

"Hum, let me see." He unwrapped the package and tried not to let his surprise show.

"It's just a book. I'm sort of wiped out, so I'm going to head up to bed. Night, Mom."

"Good night, honey," she replied.

In his room Nicholas looked at the gift card. "From one student of history to another," then read the title of the book "Erwin Rommel – The Desert Fox."

No way was this a coincidence. He sat up and read the book and by the time he'd finished at 3:00 AM and gone to sleep, he'd solved at least one riddle from the emails. He knew what the Desert Fox referred to in this context. The new question now was Don Marshall sending the emails and if so, why?

24

Beth and Nicholas' Attack

Beth returned from New York early Sunday morning, claimed exhaustion and went to bed. It was a lazy spring morning in suburbia with everyone trying to catch their breath before starting the next frantic week.

Dorothy went to church as she did every Sunday. Nicholas got up and did a little work while watching the Sunday news talk shows, *Face the Nation*, *Meet the Press*, *Fox News Sunday*, and then read *The New York Times*. Andrea joined Nicholas in his study and played a puzzle game while he was reading the *Times*. The two enjoyed just being near each other even though they were both doing something different.

Around mid-afternoon Beth stirred, Dorothy returned from church and Nicholas and Andrea were getting restless. It was mutually agreed that no one wanted to cook, so they decided on an early dinner. Being an unusually warm day, a few of the braver restaurant owners in Morristown had put their sidewalk tables out. Selecting one of the outdoor tables, they had a slow leisurely meal, avoiding any discussion of the reason Beth was in town.

"So, what's with all the Revolutionary War mania around here?" Beth asked, looking at her menu with a picture of *Washington crossing the Delaware* on it.

"You don't know?" Nicholas asked.

"Ah, no. I'm from North Carolina, remember?"

"So am I and I knew before I came here," Dorothy piped in.

"Well, thank you Ms. School Teacher for making me feel stupid. I'm not talking to you two anymore," she said with mock severity. "Andrea, dear, could you please tell Beth what happened here during the Revolutionary War?"

Andrea sighed, rolled her eyes and said as though reciting for school, "George Washington headquartered his army here in the winter of 1780."

"Thank you dear," Beth said.

"His headquarters is only about a mile from here and remnants of some of the old forts are still here too," Dorothy said.

"Thank you, my curiosity is satisfied."

"So, do you get to New York often, Beth?" Nicholas asked.

"I usually make an annual shopping pilgrimage that I try to get my daughter to join. On the rare occasions when we're not at each other's throats, she joins me."

"How is Riva?" Beth asked.

"Oh, she's still just a dear," Beth replied with a fake smile.

Nicholas said, "Mom tells me she graduated Harvard Law. You must be very proud."

"Well, of course I'm proud, hon," she replied. "It's just that well, that degree from Harvard Law has put her little head so far up her little..." then Beth looked at Andrea and caught herself.

'Drea looked up from her Shirley Temple and said, "I know what you were going to say."

Beth laughed. "I'll just bet you do, sugar. I'll just bet you do."

After dinner when the waiter came to ask if anyone was interested in desert, Dorothy shooed him away. "We have apple pie and ice cream at home."

"Cool," said 'Drea.

"When did you make apple pie?" Nicholas asked.

"Yesterday, when you two were at Don Marshall's house."

"Sounds good to me. Besides, I need some private time with my client. Then I think we'll both need some desert."

On the way out of the restaurant, as he went through the door, Nicholas almost ran into Kerry Markus, looking decidedly off-duty in a hunter green flowing skirt with a silk tank top. The green top caught the flecks in her eyes, which immediately drew Nicholas in. He was, but shouldn't have been, surprised to see her accompanied by a man. Tall, mid-30s, that clean cut all-American look. After some awkward hellos in the doorway, each group went their separate way. Nicholas felt uncomfortable with himself for feeling uncomfortable about seeing Kerry Markus with a date.

She's a single, attractive woman, he thought to himself. Why shouldn't she be out with someone, and what the hell's with me anyway? I've only met her twice and I'm acting like some lovesick 12-year-old. Get over it. Besides." as being with Beth reminded him; He had bigger fish to fry.

Still, he thought as he looked back towards the restaurant and through the window he caught a glance of Kerry. "Now," Beth announced when they were back at the house, "Nicholas, why don't you and I make use of that beautiful study you have? We have a lot to go over. Let me go get my notes."

When she returned, Nicholas had poured two small glasses of sherry.

"You spoil me and I won't leave anytime soon," Beth said, taking a sip of the sherry.

"I don't want you to leave anytime soon," he replied. "What have you got?"

"Okay," she said, looking at her legal pad.

Nicholas had never quite figured out the thing with lawyers and legal pads. The incessant note taking, he could figure, but why they couldn't use the same size paper as everyone else? That one he couldn't get, even after being married to one for 13 years.

"First, the bug problem," she started. "I had my security boys check your house, car, phones, and office."

"And?"

"The good news is that your house, car and personal phones are okay, but I had them put scramblers on your phones and maskers that'll interfere with signals in the house anyway. What made me decide to do that was the fact that your office, your secretary's office and both your office phones lit up like Christmas trees. Someone's monitoring everything that goes on in your office."

"The feds?" Nicholas asked.

"We can't be positive, but I don't think so," she said. "Two reasons. First, unless it involves the highest level of national security, which for now let's assume this is not, even the Feds can't wiretap without court orders and leaving a paper trail a mile wide. There's no evidence of any such trail.

"Second," she went on, "the stuff we found in your office wasn't the top shelf stuff the feds would use. It wasn't bad either. Maybe second tier."

"Which means what?" Nicholas asked.

"Well, it could be top line private. While it is not state of the art Fed stuff, it's still top line for a private outfit. Another possibility is a rogue fed."

"What the hell is that?" Nicholas asked.

"A fed gone bad, on the take, doing someone else's dirty work. Someone at Marshall may have a fed in their pocket."

Nicholas thought about what he'd just heard. "A lot of maybe's. Do we rip them out, the ones at the office?"

"If you rip them out you tip your hand. I'd suggest leaving them in for the time being. Now your secretary, Karen Stemmer, you trust her?"

"Yes."

"Why?"

"I just do. Can't explain it."

"You screwing her?"

"No."

"You sure? I need to know."

"I think I'd know it if I were screwing Karen, and I'm not."

"You trust her enough to let her in on what's going on?"

"I don't know. I need to think about that one."

"Good answer. Now, this other woman you mentioned, Catherine Sullivan, same question: are you screwing her?"

"What's with you and screwing?" Nicholas asked defensively.

"Because sex complicates relationships and objectivity; so my question is 'are you screwing her?' and your answer is?"

After a pause, "yes. Ah, no. Well, we've had an on-again, off-again affair for the past two or three years."

"I see. So you were cheating on your wife?"

Nicholas was silent and went to the bar to switch from sherry to something stronger.

"Hey. I'm not passing judgment. I'm your lawyer, not your priest. So is this on-again, off-again affair, currently on or off?"

"Off. She moved to London about a year ago."

"Do you trust her?"

Another pause before Beth heard Nicholas soft response. "No."

"So other than Karen, is there anyone else in Marshall you trust enough to get them involved?"

"No, well, maybe Mark – a colleague."

"Is that a reflection on you or the state of industrial relationships?"

"Probably both," Nicholas concluded. "I do have someone of my staff, Glen Morgan, reviewing everything we have on the Tanaka drug to see if anything stands out. But he doesn't know why. I should hear something back next week. But we can get back to that. What else?"

"The dicks ran backgrounds on some key players to see if anything kicks up. Let's see," she said, flipping through her voluminous notes. "Jack O'Connor. He just smells bad, but he does a pretty good job of not getting his own fingers dirty. And, as expected, Ken Joseph is his hatchet man and Grant Michner's in his pocket. But we stumbled across something else. What was the name of that redneck U.S. Marshal who was with the FDA agent?"

"Barry Keenan." Just the thought of him pissed off Nicholas.

"Well, looks like old Barry has some expensive habits – ponies, gambling tables, hookers. He shows several large unexplained deposits over the last year. He may be in Jack's pocket also. Remember, we said that maybe there's a corrupt fed involved? This may be it, kiddo."

"Can we prove it? Submit the evidence to a federal judge or something?"

"Again, that would tip our hand. Timing is everything in these cases." Beth went on, "that FDA agent checks out okay and the local detective, what's her name?"

"Kerry Markus."

"Yeah, Markus. She looks okay. But from the way you were looking at her at the restaurant, I gather you think she looks okay too," Beth said with a chuckle.

"Ha, ha. What about Don Marshall?" Nicholas asked.

"Don's life story's pretty much an open book," she said.

"If this is some scheme to take control of Marshall, maybe it's Don trying to regain the control that his family lost."

"I don't know," Beth said. "He already controls 40%."

"But," continued Nicholas, "he only has one seat on the board of directors: his. So, he's a minority owner."

"But would he put his family's company in serious jeopardy to get it back? I don't see it," said Beth.

"I'm reasonably convinced he's involved. So he's either working with O'Connor, which the more I think about it the more it doesn't fit, or he's working against O'Connor. But here's today's big question: are O'Connor and Don both using yours truly to get what they want?"

"And what do you know that I don't dear?" she asked.

"The emails from Arthur?"

"Yes."

"Well, I believe that at least one, who knows maybe all, came from Don."

"Do go on. You've peaked my interest."

"The last message was, 'Remember the Desert Fox'."

"Yesterday," he went on, "'Drea, Karen and I went over to Don's mansion to see a movie in his private screening theatre, no less. After convincing 'Drea that she now needed a 50,000 square foot mansion, a good time was had by all. As we left, Don gave each of us a gift. He gave 'Drea a picture of him with a porcupine – don't ask. When I got home and opened mine, it was a biography of Erwin Rommel, 'The

Desert Fox.' I stayed up and read it and now I think I may know why Arthur committed suicide."

"Well, my God man!" Beth exclaimed. "Don't leave me here all hot bothered and wet – finish me off!"

"Are you sure you and my mother are friends?" he asked her.

"There's a side of her you don't know, sonny-boy."

"And let's leave it at that. Here's a free World War II piece of history trivia: Erwin Rommel was one of Nazi Germany's greatest fighting generals. A brilliant military strategist, he was mopping up the desert with the British in Northern Africa, until Patton showed up."

"Brass ones, that Patton," Beth said.

"Hum, I can see why you'd admire him. Anyway, Rommel was a national treasure. In fact, during the D-Day invasion, Patton's forces were used as a decoy to lure Rommel away from the Normandy beaches. If Rommel had commanded the German forces at Normandy, there's a good chance we'd be holding this conversation in German."

"By mid-1944 the German military leadership finally realized that being led by a psychotic, failed artist with one testicle was probably not going to work out. As 'Drea would say, 'No Duh!'

"The German military had made contact with the Allies and informally agreed to surrender Germany. There was only one thing in their way: the Füehrer himself, Adolph Hitler. Hell would freeze before he'd surrender. You know, O'Connor would have been happier than a pig in shit as a Nazi!"

"Timing's everything," Beth said, "speaking of which, more sherry, please."

Nicholas rose to get her more sherry from the small bar in his library and continued his story. "The German military knew that Hitler's way was going to lead to the complete destruction of Germany and its military. So, they decided to kill Hitler. There's a lot of debate about the extent of Rommel's involvement. He claimed he knew of the plot, but didn't actively participate. In any event, as one of Germany's highest ranking military leaders and a national icon at the very least, he had to give his okay that he wouldn't intervene. And he didn't."

"I remember this, I think," Beth joined in. "They tried to blow him up, didn't they?"

"Yep, July 20, 1944: a high-powered bomb was placed under a heavy oak conference table three feet from where the Füehrer stood. After it went off, four others in the room were dead, but from where Hitler was standing, the heavy oak table shielded him from most of the force of the blast. He had a few scratches and bruises and a ruptured ear drum – that's it."

"Damn shame," Beth murmured.

"Yeah. Now the Füehrer wasn't one to take such an affront kindly. He turned his SS pit bulls loose to find the conspirators. And they did. The show trials were brief and the sentences? Death. Hanging by piano wire; all filmed for the enjoyment of the Füehrer."

"Twisted little fuck, wasn't he? I guess when you've got only one nut it sort of warps you, don't you think?" Beth asked.

"I'd have to do some research on that one," Nicholas answered.

"Oh, sorry, Dr. Scientist."

"Now, one of the conspirators tried to buy his way out of Hitler's little macabre piano bar by giving up a big name. Hitler got the name, but reneged on the hanging. And the name was?" he asked, pointing to Beth.

"Field Marshall Erwin Rommel," She said.

"Bingo. But this presented Hitler with a problem. Even he couldn't drag Rommel, beloved national hero, through some sham trial and hang him."

"Sounds like time for a deal to me," Beth said.

"That's right. Rommel was home with his family waiting to see how this mess played out. Hitler offered him a deal. If Rommel would commit suicide, it would be announced to the world that he'd died in battle and he would receive the state funeral of a fallen hero. More importantly to Rommel, he received a guarantee – from a murdering sociopath, but that's the best he could do – that his family would retain their property and wealth and be unharmed. Under the circumstances, it was a good deal and he took it. The SS came to his home, he said goodbye to his wife and son and drove off with them. A few miles down the road, he took a cyanide capsule and died. And Hitler kept his end of the bargain. Rommel received a huge hero's burial and his family was safe. The end."

"Fascinating story, but what does intrigue amongst the Nazis have to do with you, Nicholas?" Beth asked.

"The Nazis: nothing; it's the story. This is all guessing at this point. But Arthur was somehow involved with O'Connor. Maybe he found out about whatever Jack's up to. Maybe he was involved all along and changed his mind, who knows. But somehow O'Connor had enough leverage over Arthur to make him commit suicide."

"That'll do as a working possibility for now, but *only* a possibility," Beth said. She sighed and stood up to walk around the library. "You love books don't you?" she asked.

"How'd you guess?"

She laughed. "Don't you think they'll ever be obsolete with all these new high tech electronic do-dads, Kindles, iPads and stuff?"

"Not as long as there're book nuts like me loose. And you're stalling. Why?"

"What I have to tell you next Nicholas is pretty rough. That's why I didn't want Dorothy or Michael here. In fact, I don't know if I should tell you at all. A lot of it's still just supposition."

"You're my attorney," Nicholas replied as he refilled his wineglass. "Don't you have to tell me?"

"No, at least not now."

"I'm a big boy, Beth, and as you've noticed I'm up to my neck in shit. Now," Nicholas said, looking directly into the steel gray eyes and speaking softly and slowly, "I've done nothing. This is all the result of some one's ones doing to me and frankly I don't like it one bit. So I need you to be straight with me. I'm trusting you. That's not an easy thing for me."

"All right Nicholas. I'll always be straight with you. I promise. The NY dicks did find a paper trail of the FDA – U.S. Marshall's office investigation of Marshall Pharm. It was an official request for information on all business relations between Marshall and Tanaka. It was received by Marshall in house legal thirteen months ago."

"So, O'Connor and Gerry Michael in Legal were lying through their teeth when they acted surprised by me being visited by investigators?"

"Yeah, I'd guess they knew all along. After it came in-house they shipped it to out their counsel, DCC. Since Marshall is a major client they gave it to one of their senior partners, who did what any good attorney would do for their client. They tied it up in red tape and formalities."

Nicholas began to get a tight feeling in the pit of his stomach. "Go on, Beth."

"Now, my NY boys have access to some things they shouldn't. I can't go into the how or why. But in a big firm like DCC, the master case file has to be logged everywhere it goes – chain of custody stuff. We saw the log and three weeks before she died, the Marshall/Tanaka investigation file was logged out by your wife, Paula."

"I see," was all Nicholas could say.

Taking a deep breath, Beth went on, "we also accessed Paula's scheduling diary, Nicholas," she said, looking at him. "A week before Paula died she had a two hour meeting with Gerry Michael and Jack O'Connor."

Nicholas stared at the floor. Had this evil reached this deeply into his home? Screwing someone in office politics was one thing, even illegal office politics, but involving someone's family? "What does this mean, Beth?" he asked quietly.

"I don't know," she said. "I called off my investigators. Normally the next step would be to investigate the next lead. In this case, the next lead is Paula."

"So, why don't you?" he asked coldly.

"Nicholas, look at me!" she shouted at him. "Give me some emotional feedback, God damn it! I just told you your wife, your *dead* wife, may have been involved in this mess and I get a response from you as if I told you it was going to rain tomorrow! What the fuck is wrong with you?"

"You sound like my goddamned shrink," he mumbled.

"Well, obviously she's got her fucking work cut out for her!" Beth glared at him. "Wait, wait, I shouldn't have said that. But you have to understand that if we investigate Paula you have to be prepared to deal with whatever the results might be. No matter how unpleasant. Some doors are best left closed, Nicholas. Once they're opened you can't take back what you see inside."

"I can't afford to leave any doors closed right now, Beth," he said. "Do it. We need all the information we can get. I'll figure out how to deal with it when the time comes. That's the best I can do. I compartmentalize and deal with what's on the plate in front of me."

"Okay – good, I think," she said. "I agree we need all the information we can get. I just hope I feel the same way after we get it."

"When will you have more info?" he asked.

"A week."

"Beth, these detectives, 'dicks', they sound pretty high-powered. How's a country lawyer like you have contacts like this?"

"It's a long story and one you don't need to hear right now."

"Okay, for now. I'm in London next week and I think I'll take an unscheduled swing by Japan on my way home."

"Whatever," Beth said, not picking up on the geographic reference. "Now, one last piece of business. The NY dicks have this – they say – cool new simulation modeling software. You feed in all the known variables of a crime and based on its known database from FBI, state, local and international agencies, it gives you a probability of what happened and who of the players most likely did what. We don't have enough details on your case yet, but in a week or so we should. We'll see what it spits out."

"I think we pretty much know the who," Nicholas said.

"Yeah, but without the details, we can't do much with that.

Hum. So, how are you handling all this, Nicholas? Are you okay? What's on your mind?"

After several moments of silence, Nicholas looked at her, then rose and turned on music, before returning to sit next to her on the sofa. "Are you relatively sure this room's not bugged?"

"Yes. But we'll sweep every few days," she answered.

"And everything I tell you is subject to attorney- client privilege?"

"Yes," she said, raising one eyebrow in curiosity.

"Everything?" he asked slowly, enunciating each syllable.

"Yes, Nicholas."

"Good." Nicholas moved his mouth close to almost touch Beth's left ear. "Beth, should the opportunity ever present itself, I intend to kill Jack O'Connor."

"You're not a killer, Nicholas," she returned the whisper in his ear. "You'll go to prison for that; maybe capital."

"I won't be caught. Once I decide to do something Beth, I do it well," he said softly and stood up. "Now, let's go try that pie and ice cream."

Nicholas opened the door to his study and was greeted by 'Drea running into his arms.

"Daddy!"

"'Drea-y!" He shouted squeezing her in a hug and swinging her around. When he stopped, he was still holding 'Drea, but looking directly into Beth's steel cold eyes.

"Dorothy honey," Beth droned, "your boy has plum wore me out with all his yammering and I seem to have misplaced my appetite. I think I'll just call it an early evening. Good night. Miss Andrea and Mr. Rasputin –good night to you both. Nicholas," she said and left the room.

"Dad," 'Drea said as Nicholas tucked her into bed under the watchful eye of Rasputin.

"Yes, munchkin?"

"I still dream about Mommy a lot. Do you?"

"Yes I do, honey."

"Tell me one?" she asked.

"Okay. It's one where you, your mom and I are up at the cabin."

"Dad, Mom hated the cabin!" 'Drea yelled.

"I know, but she always came didn't she?"

"Yeah."

"Yeah, well, you're right; she probably did hate the cabin, but I think she really enjoyed being there with you and me."

"Yeah, me too Dad."

"Well, me too – and it's time for you to go to sleep."

He kissed her on the forehead and rubbed the cat, which was lying next to her, purring. "Good night, hon. I love you."

"Love you too, Dad."

"Night Rasputin," he said, standing at the door for a moment wondering how it was possible to love anyone or thing as much as he loved 'Drea? She was a beautiful, bright, intelligent lovely child and the only thing in his world that he truly cared about.

In his bedroom, as he started to undress for bed, he'd replayed his conversation with Beth in his head. That threat to kill O'Connor – where the hell did that come from? This from a guy who hadn't been in a fight since the seventh grade. But if O'Connor's evil hand had touched as close to his home as he feared it had, he wasn't about to let it get any closer to 'Drea. And killing O'Connor to protect 'Drea was an easy decision.

He needed a shower to relax, when the phone rang. "Hello."

"Hello Nicholas, ah, Dr. Harding. It's Detective Markus – Kerry. I hope it's not too late," she said.

Nicholas felt his pulse race and his throat tighten. "No, not at all, how was your dinner?"

"Dinner? Oh, that's right; we've already seen each other today," she said. "Dinner was fine."

Nicholas took the cordless phone and sat in a chair in an alcove off his bedroom and started to visualize Kerry. – Those warm eyes with the green flecks and wondered if she was tapping a pen against her lower lip or better yet, if she was in a nightgown.

"I just wanted to tell you that the investigation into Dr. Kronan's death is nearly officially concluded. It's ruled as death by self-inflicted gunshot. Manner of death: suicide. I just told Mrs. Kronan and thought you'd want to know. I'm sorry Nicholas," She said as though she actually meant it. "But at least there's closure on this part."

Nicholas sat and thought about how enjoyable it was to hear her say his name, then remembered the reason for the call. "Thanks for calling to let me know, Kerry. That was very nice."

Some awkward silence, then Nicholas said, "I guess that means you don't have to question me any further?"

"I guess not. Was it that unpleasant? I've been told I have a relaxing interrogation style."

"Oh, no, that's not what I meant. I didn't find it unpleasant at all."

"Actually, Nicholas. I ah, sort of, ah," Kerry now started to stutter, "had another reason for calling." A brief pause, then "would you like to have dinner sometime?" she asked tentatively. Another pause, then Kerry added, "I hope I'm not out of line or anything."

"Oh no, Kerry, not at all. I'd like that. In fact, I was thinking of asking you out, but ah, your friend at the restaurant wouldn't mind?"

"My friend at the restaurant? Oh, you mean Dave? He's my brother, Nicholas. He was in town for a few days. I took him to the airport after dinner. I just got back, that's why I'm calling so late. Oh, I see. You thought he was my date? That's sweet."

"Well, yeah now that you mention it, I should have known – the family resemblance and all," Nicholas realized he was rambling.

"Oh, yeah. I'm adopted Nicholas," she said.

"Um, ah, Kerry could you hold on for a minute while I pull my foot out of my mouth?"

Kerry laughed with a deep boisterous laugh, not some effeminate giggle, and then Nicholas started to laugh as well. When they both finally stopped, Kerry said, "was this pathetic or what?"

"You know those smooth-talking debonair guys in the movies?" Nicholas asked.

"Yes," she replied sweetly.

"Well, I'm not one. Kerry, I wasn't very good at the dating game back when I was and I haven't since Paula died. But I really enjoy talking to you and yes, I'd love to have dinner with you. But, can I have a rain-check? There's a whole lot going on now and I'd just like to wait a bit. Is that okay?"

"Of course, we'll wait a bit, Nicholas. We'll talk soon."

"Good night Kerry."

Night Nicholas."

Nicholas had arranged to meet Glen Morgan at a diner in the Newark airport at 6:00 AM on Monday morning. He knew that the hour of the meeting wouldn't bother Glen, who worked odd hours anyway, and knowing Glen, he might even like the location. He didn't want to have this discussion about MR-548 at Marshall, where he knew at least his office to be bugged.

It hadn't yet been the two weeks that Nicholas had given Glen to review the MR-548 file. But he needed information now. Nicholas saw Glen sitting at a corner table near the back of the diner and joined him.

"My, my, Dr. Nicholas," Glen said by way of greeting. "Meetings at Newark airport. Is this how corporate VPs live? I must say I like it, but you're much too Armani for this, Nicholas."

"I'm on my way to London, and this was convenient for me," he added. "I know you haven't had time to complete the MR-548 file, but I need an update on where you stand."

"You need, you want. So demanding, Nicholas." Glen said as he ate his scrambled eggs and bacon.

"Nicholas ordered coffee and toast and as soon as the waitress left, said to Glen softly and quietly, requiring Glen to lean in to hear him, "You know Glen, I'm truly not in a mood to be fucked with!" pointedly through clenched teeth.

"Oh, I see. Reporting to O'Connor for what, four days now? It's put you in a foul mood," he said, finishing off his bacon. "You know there's a pool at work on how long you'll last under O'Connor. The shortest I saw was three months. Some people think that without Arthur around to protect you O'Connor will eat you for breakfast," he said, biting down on his toast for emphasis.

"And so say you, Glen?" Nicholas asked. "Where are you in the pool?"

"Me?" he laughed. "Old Glen's taking a different view. See, I tell all those other guys at the lab, 'that Nicky – he's not nearly the pussy he seems to be.'"

"I'll take that as a compliment," Nicholas said. "Now what do you have on MR-548?"

"It looks perfect," Morgan said leaning back in his seat now, satisfied.

"And?" Nicholas asked.

"And that's it. It looks perfect," he said with a smug smile.

"That's the best you can come up with? It's perfect?"

"You don't get it, man. It looks fucking perfect. How long have you been in the drug business? How many 'perfect' drug have you ever seen? None. They don't exist. They all have some warts; problems. But this stuff looks textbook."

"Too textbook?"

"Oh yeah, man." Glen went on, "the pharmacology dose-response curves? Beautiful. The toxicology profile? Gorgeous. They see minor toxicity at very high doses. The therapeutic index, the difference between the effective dose and the toxic dose."

"I know what a therapeutic index is, Glen," Nicholas said.

"Yeah, sorry. Well you want it to be wide, so there's a big difference between an effective dose and a toxic dose, right? Well this one you could sail the Queen Mary through. The absorption, metabolism, bioavailability, all textbook."

"What about the Phase I human clinical data that Tanaka generated?" Nicholas asked.

"Same thing: margins of safety like you wouldn't believe."

"So, what's your guess at this point?" asked Nicholas, drinking his coffee and ignoring his toast.

"Well, the first thought you jump to is someone's cooking the books."

"You mean the data's falsified?" Nicholas asked.

"Yeah, except in this case, I think this goes way beyond falsification. To falsify, you've got to start out with some real data."

"You don't think this data's real?"

"Nicholas, I don't know how the hell it could be done without a whole shit-load of folks being in on it, but I think someone just made up the whole fucking boatload of data."

Glen went on, "here's the other kicker. Through a little clever hacking I obtained a copy of the contract and license that Tanaka and Marshall signed. We can't conduct any tests on this compound. All nonclinical studies are run through Tanaka. The first time we run any tests on this drug will be a big 800 patient Phase IIb human trial. So, I'm doing a little work of my own on this side."

"What?" Nicholas wanted to know.

"You remember those predictive toxicology, pharmacokinetic and metabolism modeling software programs I've been bugging you about?"

"Yeah, they supposedly can predict toxicology, kinetics and metabolism based on molecular structure. But they're still in development and have some bugs in them, right?"

"Right, but we have some beta versions in house."

"And?"

"And, I ran MR-548 through a couple of the predictive modeling programs. And I didn't expect anything near a 1:1 correlation, because like you say, these programs are still under development. But I expect some correlation."

"What'd you get?" Nicholas asked.

"Almost none. This compound lit up warning flags like you wouldn't believe, Nicholas," he said leaning forward across the table. "If some of these projections are correct, when you guys go into your Phase IIb human clinical trials, at best you're going to permanently injure a lot of people."

"And, at worst?"

"You're going to have some dead human subjects on your hands. Man, it'll be the worst thing to hit the pharmaceutical industry ever."

"These predictions, anything you can hang your hat on?"

"No. Like you said, these programs are developmental, they haven't been validated. But," he said with a gleam in his eyes, "I've conned a friend of mine in Medicinal Chemistry to make a few grams of this stuff for me on the side and to keep his mouth shut. Then I plan to give it to a couple of dogs and see what we get. If the model projections are correct, we should see mortality. We can stand behind that."

"How long?"

"Well, that's the bad news. He needs two weeks," Glen said.

"See if he can do it faster."

"Will do, chief."

"Does he know any details?"

"Absolutely not. He doesn't' even know what it is," Glen answered.

"Have you discussed this with anyone else?"

"Of course not."

"Good. Don't. We don't know what the hell we're dealing with yet. But if it's half as bad as you say then someone pretty high up at Marshall must know about it. In other words – you can't trust anyone else at Marshall, Glen," Nicholas said.

"Yeah, I know."

"All right, I'll be back in a week. We'll touch base then."

"Good enough. You picking up the bill for this?" he asked, pointing to the remnants of breakfast.

"Yeah, Glen. I'll get it. And Glen," Nicholas said as they both got up to leave. "Be careful. Be very careful."

"You're scaring me, boss."

"I mean to."

"You got it, boss," and he walked away into the growing airport crowd.

Nicholas headed towards the United Club first class lounge to wait for his flight to be called. Could even Jack be this sick and twisted? And if so, how could Nicholas stop him and then how to stop him without all the blame falling on himself?

He picked a quiet corner in the lounge that overlooked the main concourse; the elites of the world overlooking every man. Only the current view from the top wasn't too good.

25

Katherine Sullivan

The flight from Newark to London's Gatwick airport landed at 7:30 PM, wingtips invisible in the thick fog. Although Gatwick was further away from London, he preferred it to the slightly closer but much busier and more crowded Heathrow. He quickly cleared Customs and hopped on the Gatwick Express for the thirty-minute train ride to Victoria Station in mid-town London. With most people leaving London after a day at work the train into London in the evening was almost empty. There was little of scenic note between Gatwick airport and Victoria Station. Rows of small countryside houses clustered together; rolling hills of pastures with a scattering of sheep.

Once at Victoria Station it was a short taxi ride to Charles Street in London's upscale Mayfair district. Catherine's office had made the arrangements, which would explain why Nicholas' hotel – the small, but luxurious Chesterfield Hotel – was only a short walk from Catherine's apartment on Corzon Street. Arriving at the hotel, Nicholas found that, as expected, Catherine's staff had spared no expense. They had reserved a small suite and there was a note from Catherine asking Nicholas to call as soon as he arrived. He knew the note would be waiting for him. And he knew that Catherine would be waiting for him; that was the concern that he'd given much thought to on the flight over.

Nicholas and Catherine had joined Marshall at about the same time; she on the Marketing side and Nicholas on the R&D side. They'd crossed paths occasionally over the years.

About three years ago, Catherine had been the Marketing Director for a new drug Marshall was about to launch.

Nicholas was on the product team as the Nonclinical Representative. He and Catherine had worked closely to position the product and craft the Package Insert – that little piece of paper with even smaller writing that came with each prescription sold in America. The Package Insert is part legal, part scientific and part marketing device. There had been much give and take with the FDA, so the two of them had spent a lot of time in Washington, actually Bethesda, Maryland.

Catherine was a beautiful woman, but as a strong business leader, could be intimidating to many men. Most men, not knowing how to relate to a woman they wanted to screw, but who was smarter than they were. Nicholas had no trouble relating to Catherine. He respected her professionally and while admiring her beauty it had simply never crossed his mind that Catherine had anything other than professional interest in him; the two had developed a casual professional friendship.

She was divorced. He was married to Paula, which provided its own set of personal problems. They were spending two to three days and nights a week, mostly in hotels in Maryland, playing a strategy waltz with FDA. The friendship simply evolved to fill a void in both their lives and became an affair. At first, it was mostly physical, just sex, but over time they both felt it becoming more. And when they felt their passion burning too hot into the emotional one or both would turn from the flame and move away.

This bizarre dance went on for more than two years. Rumors were starting to circulate through the company. And both Nicholas and Catherine, being career conscious, took note. Also, however bad Nicholas' relationship with Paula and however good his relationship with Catherine was, he'd come to the realization that he could never leave Andrea.

So a few months before Paula's death, Nicholas and Catherine had spent a passionate, painful, tearful three-day Bahamas adventure coming to the realization this was as far as the two of them could go together. They weren't sure whether it was love, but it had become a threat to both their careers and to Nicholas' marriage and thus to 'Drea – the most important thing in his world.

For three days in the penthouse suite, in a tropical paradise, they'd yelled, cried and made love. When they parted after these three days they were no longer lovers. The problem was Nicholas wasn't quite sure what they were. Then a few months later Paula had died and Nicholas had intentionally avoided Catherine, not wanting his feelings for her, whatever they were, to be complicated by his feelings or lack of for Paula.

The question that Nicholas had now and was uncomfortable with the answer. With all that was going on at Marshall – the investigation and MR-548 – was Catherine someone he could trust and count on as being on his side?

The uncomfortable answer was he didn't know. After all the time they'd spent laying in each other's arms, all the time he'd spent inside her, he still didn't know if he could trust Catherine Sullivan.

Nicholas showered, changed and walked the four blocks to Catherine's apartment building, which was unassuming and rather common looking on the outside. Nicholas went up the outer stairs and rang the bell. It was quickly answered by a uniformed servant.

"Dr. Harding, I presume?"

Nicholas chuckled and replied, "that's me."

"Excellent," the servant replied. Nicholas had the impression that the servant was one of those people whose parents and grandparents were also servants and had studied for years to master the profession. Leave it to the Brits, where everyone knew their station, unlike the Americans, where everyone, regardless of their puny IQ, wanted to be the boss. "Madam is expecting you. This way please."

"Madam," Nicholas thought. *Leave it to Catherine.* The interior of the four story apartment building was exquisite to say the least. It looked beyond the reaches of even the European Marketing Vice President of a major pharmaceutical house. Nicholas was shown into a small sitting room with a Victorian era decorating tone. He was looking out a window that overlooked a small park when he sensed her presence, then confirmed the sensation by a faint scent of the soft rosy perfume she favored.

"Madam," he said.

"Dr. Vice President," she replied.

He turned. The awkward moment of former lovers hung only briefly. Catherine Sullivan was a beautiful woman. She had the chiseled Nordic facial features of a fashion model, which she often joked that she would have been, had it not been for what was in her mind her one physical flaw: height. At 5'2", which she sought to correct with heels, modeling was never a serious alternative. Actually, Nicholas had considered her near-physical perfection to be her weakness. She was perfectly proportioned for her height, with perfectly coifed short blond hair.

Catherine was dressed in a floor length black straight skirt with heels and a slit that attracted the eye. The look gave her an illusion of height, but the beauty was no illusion.

She crossed the room towards him.

"The, ah, manservant?" he asked. "Perks of foreign lands?"

"He came with the apartment. He's a bit much, but I didn't want to hurt his feelings," she said.

Nicholas kissed her on the cheek.

She leaned closer and whispered, "I think we can do better than that."

Now in each other's arms they kissed passionately as lovers, tongues seeking and playfully caressing each other.

Nicholas was the first to break away. "Is this the official corporate greeting for VP's at Marshall," he asked.

"I think it should be for us," she said, still holding onto his hand. "That was good, Nicholas. You're still tasty as ever."

"You too, Cath," he replied. "But that was never the problem," he said, walking around and changing the subject. "So it looks like you're doing okay for yourself here."

"It'll do for now," she said. "How long are you here?"

"Just one day. I'm flying out tomorrow night."

"Back home?"

"Tokyo."

"You keep moving."

"Things are pretty hectic these days."

"I'm sorry about Arthur. Too bad it had to be this way, but you deserve the vice presidency, Nick," she said. "So, what're you going to do here for one day?"

"I just wanted to sit in on the European Marketing review of MR-548 to see how it's being received here. The marketing guys on the team are giving the presentation, which started today, right?"

"Right."

"How'd they go?"

"Not bad," she said, going to the bar to pour a drink. "Sherry?"

"Yes."

"So, you're only here for one night?"

"That's all I could swing this time," Nicholas replied.

"Too bad," she said handing him a small glass of sherry. "Cheers."

"Cheers," he said as they clinked glasses. "By the way Cath, you look lovely."

"Oh, you mean this little thing?" she ask, running her fingers provocatively, down her left thigh to that fascinating slit. "I thought you might like? And?"

"I like."

"Good. I'm disappointed, Nicholas," she said.

"How so?"

"I was hoping we would have some off time to discuss some, let's say non-work related issues."

"You mean something other than MR-548?" He asked.

"I don't give a fuck about MR-548," she replied. Most people were thrown off balance when they heard someone as petite and attractive as Catherine swear like a Marine.

"Hum, so tell me Cath, what do you give a fuck about these days?"

Cath had draped herself into a sofa with the slit leaving little to the imagination. Nicholas had taken a seat in a side chair to put some distance between him and Catherine.

"Us," she answered.

"Us? As in you and me?" Nicholas asked. "I didn't know there was an 'us,' Cath."

"There was once. Then things changed. Now, they've changed again. I'm sorry Paula died, Nicholas," she said. "But that does change things for us."

"That's strange, Cath," he said. "Because now that I think of it, I don't know if we were even an 'us.' Just two horny stressed-out people who couldn't stay out of each other's pants."

"We were an 'us,' Nicholas," she said confidently.

"Okay."

"And now I want to know if we can be again?" she said while brushing one finger down the slit-exposed thigh.

"You know Cath, I figured you would have hooked up with some European count or viscount or something. I'm old news."

"Tried it, didn't like it. I've decided and I want you. Why don't you sit here on the sofa, you'll be more comfortable," she said looking at him with those deep blue eyes.

Nicholas had always been and still was mightily attracted to Cath, but the relationship had always been an issue of power and Nicholas had managed not to get too close to the flame.

"I'm wounded, darling," she said with a small pout. "Do you doubt that my intentions are anything but pure towards you?"

"As I recall, my marriage wasn't only one reason the 'us' thing didn't work. The bigger issue was our careers at Marshall. The rumors about us were starting to go around, remember?"

"Yes."

"And it's not just that one of us was married, Cath," he said. "Let's be honest, you having an open relationship with a black executive or my having an open relationship with a white executive isn't going to help either of our careers. You know how conservative Marshall is."

"Fuck 'em!" she said. "I'm a board member now. You're a VP. If they hassle us because of this race shit it'd blow up in their faces. You know how image conscious they are. I don't think they want to see an article in *The New York Times* business section on how they discriminated against two single employees because one's white and one's black."

"Maybe. But why now Cath?"

"I just told you, dearest," she said with mock sweetness. "I've decided you're the one. I want you," she said slowly. "But if you'll look me in the eyes and say you don't want me then that's the end of it."

"That's not it, Cath," he said. "It's just that I don't know what I want right now. My life's rather complicated." Nicholas had moved to the end of the sofa, opposite of Cath now. She'd kicked off her shoes and was massaging/tickling Nicholas side with her toes.

"How so?"

"What do you know about current power plays at Marshall?" he asked.

"More specific?"

"Jack trying to take over Marshall," he said, feeling his attempts at distance failing.

"Jack's been trying to take over Marshall for years. So what else is new?"

"And you're not?"

Their eyes locked – knowing each other as old lovers do.

"At the moment I have other game in my sights." She quickly disentangled herself from Nicholas and stood up. "Hungry?"

"No."

"Good. You could have stayed here you know. Why didn't you?"

"I thought I might be safer a few blocks away."

"Silly boy," she said, leading him by the hand. "Let me give you a tour of the house."

She led him out of the sitting room, down a short hall to stairs, up the stairs into another room. She closed the door when they were in and turned to him.

"This is my bedroom. The rest isn't important," she said as she kissed him passionately. "I want you Nicholas. I want you inside me," she whispered in his ear.

"Not now Cath. Let's just lay here. Please."

"Okay, for now. There's always morning."

Nicholas awoke with a start, disoriented as to time and location. Then he slowly began to realize where he was. He glanced at a clock on the side table to see that it was 2:00 AM. Cath was sound asleep in a tangle of sheets next to him. With his biological clock being out of sync he was now wide awake and looking at Cath.

Once Cath was asleep, Nicholas knew she was pretty much down for the count and he was wide awake now, so he decided to take his own tour. He wandered through the old house. Most of the rooms were small and in his opinion, vastly over decorated.

He entered a room that appeared to be Cath's home office. Not being the neat freak that Nicholas was, the office was a bit of a mess. He didn't think he'd intended to pry, but found himself doing so. Cath's iPad was on her desk. He picked up the small device and keyed it open.

Hmm, not password protected, he thought. Now he knew what he was looking for: anything to link Cath to O'Connor.

Yep, there he was in her electronic address book, but no surprises. She and Jack were both on the Marshall Board. Then he saw something in her calendar. He quickly keyed in a calendar name search that would call up scheduled meetings/events linked to the keyed name. Cath had been spending a lot of phone time with O'Connor, including a teleconference that had occurred earlier today –7:00 AM

EST. She'd told him earlier that she'd been at the marketing meeting all day; no mention of O'Connor.

Closing the iPad and returning it to the clutter of her desk, Nicholas wasn't sure what it meant, but he did have an answer to his question: he now knew he couldn't trust Cath.

Nicholas returned to Cath's bedroom where she remained entwined in her sheets. He sat on the side of the bed and looked down on her. She remained lovely in sleep. Whereas in wake she strived for the illusion of height and power, in sleep she gave the illusion of innocence. He kissed her on the forehead, brushed her soft hair out of her face and whispered, "good bye, Cath."

At 3:00 AM the streets of Mayfair London were deserted but safe. They served to remind Nicholas of how alone he was in this mess. He walked the four blocks to his hotel.

"Good morning, Dr. Harding," the night clerk said, handing Nicholas his key, as if he'd just returned from an afternoon stroll.

Nicholas hadn't heard him. He took the old iron gated elevator up to his room and got into bed. Sleep came eventually.

He never saw Catherine Sullivan again.

26

On to Tokyo

"Jake, it's Nicholas, sorry to call you so early. I'm not going to make the Marketing Overview this morning. Can you cover it?"

Jake was the Marketing Director assigned to Nicholas' MR-548 team. And taking charge was something most marketing executives had no trouble with.

"No problem. Where are you?" Jake asked.

"In transit."

"Oh, travel problems?"

"Something like that. Thanks, Jake. We can touch base next week."

Just as Nicholas hung up the telephone in the United First-class Lounge at Heathrow, his flight to Tokyo was called.

The flight from London to Tokyo was about twelve hours long. Nicholas managed about six hours of sleep and devoted most of the remainder of the time to studying his problem. He'd decided to treat it like a chess game. O'Connor and others, possibly Catherine, certainly had some sort of game plan, so Nicholas needed one also. And to develop one he needed more information. He hoped he'd find more information in Tokyo.

Nicholas' plane landed at Narita, the large overcrowded Tokyo airport. Having traveled to Japan a few times before, he knew the routine. Narita was a large, bustling modern airport, much like a JFK, except when all the bustle was in Japanese it could be very intimidating to an American; much more so than when traveling in Europe.

He had the name and address of his hotel, the Hotel Tokyo Palace near the Royal Palace, written on a large notepad in Japanese. When he finally cleared customs he handed the pad to one of the white-gloved immaculate taxi drivers. He'd also brought along currency in Japanese yen. Nicholas usually kept some currency in British pounds and Japanese yen; the two countries he most frequented.

The drive from Narita to downtown Tokyo was almost 90 minutes in mid-morning traffic and, as Nicholas had learned previously, esthetically lacking in visual appeal. Take away the signs in Japanese and the scenery and you had the same drab look as any industrialized American city.

Old Tokyo, having been nearly fire-bombed to the ground by Doolittle's Raiders during World War II, was now a large cosmopolitan city with crawling traffic jams; a huge city of 13 million people. Comparable in size to New York, but in terms of cleanliness and politeness, it was far superior.

During his first trip to Japan, Nicholas had experienced some concerns regarding the racism a black American may experience in Japan; the Japanese being stereotyped as racist in America. He had been surprised to observe that he was treated no different from his white American colleagues.

The Japanese were equal opportunity superiorists. They were politely condescending to all Americans.

The staffs at the Hotel Tokyo Palace, like at all Americanized hotels, spoke excellent English and provided first class service. Nicholas checked in and went to his room for a few hours' sleep to try and minimize the damage to his internal clock.

When he awoke and showered it was early evening. He took a taxi to a part of town rarely visited by tourist or American businessmen. When he exited the cab, he saw row after row of brightly lit neon signs. He couldn't read the words, but the pictures left little to the imagination. This was Tokyo's upscale sex district. These were private sex clubs. Walking down the street alone, Nicholas felt uncomfortable and as a gijan, clearly stood out. He also knew that these were private clubs that would not take kindly to an American who didn't speak more than three words of Japanese trying to gain admittance. Many of these clubs were controlled by the Yakuza and if Nicholas stepped on the wrong toes here accidentally or intentionally, well, his problems with O'Connor and Marshall would certainly be over.

There were clusters of people in the entrance of the stairway to each club. In each cluster, several of these people were barely clad young women. These were no glassy-eyed burned out, used up street whores. These were some of the most beautiful women Nicholas had ever seen in person. Exotically beautiful women with flowing jet black hair. Nicholas knew that places like this existed, but not block after block, club after club.

Guess I don't get out enough, he thought.

He found the club he was looking for, the English name was House of Many Paradises or something like that. Looking at some of the women standing on the stairway, Nicholas thought it could probably live up to its name easily.

Nicholas approached the uniformed guard, a very large and muscular uniformed guard. Nicholas held a small envelope with a seal that he now noticed matched the seal of the club between the thumb and index finger of both his hands. As he approached the guard he bowed slightly, presented the envelope and spoke a phrase in Japanese that he'd been instructed to say.

"Good evening, honored sir. I come as an invited guest; my papers for your permission."

The envelope contained a letter of recommendation for admission, or so Nicholas hoped. The guard could have pummeled Nicholas to death with his little toe. He looked to be in his early 50s, but had the size and build of a small mountain. And, the toxicologist in Nicholas suspected, was no stranger to steroids. He took the envelope and looked Nicholas over head to toe like he was a fly that landed on his picnic food. He slowly and surprisingly gently opened the envelope and read the letter. He then as gently refolded the letter into its envelope shape and returned it to Nicholas, still looking at him like something he'd forgotten to scrape off the bottom of his shoe.

After what seemed like an hour of staring at Nicholas, the guard's frown turned to a smile, then a deep thunderous laugh.

"Did I frighten you?" he asked in surprisingly good English.

"Immensely," Nicholas replied.

"Good," he replied in a loud voice, still laughing. "Follow me."

The guard led Nicholas up the staircase past several of the young girls who looked Nicholas up and down. At the top of the staircase, they entered another alcove. The guard turned to tower over Nicholas and said, "good evening, Dr. Harding. We are not allowed to speak the names of our guests at the front entrance, lest spying ears hear too much. We value the privacy of our club and our guests very much. Do you understand?"

"Yes, very clearly," Nicholas replied, knowing a threat when he heard one.

"Very well, then," he replied. "I welcome you to the House of Many Paradises. Tonight, you are one of us – taking advantage of our many pleasures."

The mountain of a man opened a door that led to a dimly lit hallway. He pointed, "the second door on the left. Dr. Nomura is waiting for you." Then the guard turned and left, leaving Nicholas standing alone in the darkened hall.

Nicholas walked to the second door and, not knowing the etiquette of whether to knock or just enter, decided to knock.

"Enter," a soft female voice from within said.

Nicholas pushed the sliding door open and entered the room where he saw a beautiful woman blocking his way. She was wearing a peach colored translucent kimono which was leaving nothing to the imagination. Looking beyond her, Nicholas saw Asori Nomura on the opposite side of the small room with another young girl, similarly dressed who was pouring sake into cups. The two women in front of Nicholas made the girls downstairs look plain. They were almost painfully beautiful; they were physical perfection.

The girl before Nicholas said, "please allow me to remove your shoes," in perfect English.

Nicholas nodded agreement and she knelt to remove his shoes and socks and replace them with slippers. Only then did she stand aside, removing herself as an impediment to Nicholas' entrance to the room.

Asori Nomura rose and crossed the room to greet Nicholas.

"Dr. Harding, it's a pleasure to see you, even on such short notice," Asori, also clad in a kimono, but thankfully not translucent, was tall at six feet and very Western in mannerisms. A Wharton MBA and eight years in the U.S. in New York had insured this. Nicholas had heard that when Asori had been recalled to Japan he'd returned kicking and screaming.

"Dr. Nomura, please call me Nicholas and thank you for agreeing to see me."

"My pleasure; also, please call me Asori. What do you think of our little boy's club? I'll wager you don't have anything like this in Morristown, New Jersey," he said with a smile.

"You'd win – we don't. These are – uh legal?"

"Yes, they are, frowned upon, but legal, one of the few advantages of living here. We tend to take a more practical view on such things. These are places where a man can come to relax, relieve the pressures of the world, eat, drink and enjoy the pleasures of a woman. They are also very private and I know there are no other Tanaka people here as members – we may speak freely."

"Does your company pay for the membership?" Nicholas asked.

"We are enlightened, but not that much so. No, I must pay for my own, but it is an excellent investment. You must try our many services. After our discussions, you may try A or B," He said pointing to the two girls now standing side by side in the matching translucent kimonos. "A and B or we have much more to choose from. They are highly skilled in the art of pleasing a man."

Nicholas noticed that the two girls were twins. They were the same size and shape, same hair color, black with blonde streaks, and cut. He was fascinated to notice that even their pubic hair, which was also streaked, was cut in exactly the same pattern.

Asori led Nicholas to a small table in the center of the room. "We'll have a meal here and discuss our affairs, and then you can decide."

Nicholas was trying to decide how far to trust this guy as he sat at the small table. Was Asori a potential ally, foe or an indifferent horny Japanese businessman? Time was running out; he'd have to decide. The girls began to prepare for the meal.

Looking at the two girls, Nicholas turned to Asori and said, "Our conversation should be private."

"And, so it shall be Harding-sama. Clubs such as this have been in existence for over 500 years. Five hundred successful years because we have rules and traditions; rules and traditions that must be kept. And, in order for rules to be effective, there must be a cost associated with not keeping the rules. All involved are well aware of the rules here and the cost of violating the rules. And, believe me; those costs are swiftly and efficiently enforced. Believe me Harding-sama, privacy is not an issue here. This is not some strip joint where men come to get laid. It's an organization steeped in tradition, handed down from father to son, and mother to daughter in some instances, for generations.

"You make me want to start a charter branch in New Jersey, Nomura-sama," Nicholas replied.

"Believe me Harding-san, America is still too young and immature for such a tradition. I feel safer here than anywhere else on Earth."

"Then at Tanaka?" Nicholas asked, seizing the opening.

"I had the impression this may be a conversation you would want to have in a rather private setting, Nicholas," Asori said. "Was I incorrect?"

"No."

"You fly in on short notice. No one else at Tanaka knows you are here. You fly across the ocean to Tokyo like it's a short hop from New Jersey to Washington. You are only here for one night and wish to see no one else at Tanaka. You must be very dedicated to your work, Nicholas."

The girls, Nicholas still didn't know their names but apparently it wasn't important, began an elaborate serving presentation of sashimi: tuna, salmon, and lobster with various spices and sauces. They worked in tandem, one on each side of the small table; mirror images of each other.

"Ah, ladies, this is all very good and lovely and my apologies, but you must leave," Nicholas turned to his host. "Asori, my apologies, but there is much we must discuss, very little time and we must discuss this in private. Can you please ask them to leave?"

Asori spoke briefly to the two women in Japanese. They stood and again moving in unison, they bowed first to Nicholas, then to Asori. Appearing to float across the floor in their long kimonos, they gracefully exited the room.

"We can invite them back when we finish our discussions. They are mirror twins you know. One's right handed, one left. A has a mark on her left breast, B, the same mark on her right. But this is not what you wish to discuss, is it Harding-san?"

"MR-548," Nicholas said, letting the name of the drug hang between them.

"You are the project leader for Marshall. This important project must consume much of your time," Asori said as more of a question than a statement.

"And as the project leader for Tanaka, it must take up much of your time as well," Nicholas replied, willing to do the dance with Asori, but only for so long.

"Ah yes, but I am merely the window person for information exchange between our two companies. Since we have decided not develop MR-548, or TJ-955 as we refer to it, my role is much less so than yours, Harding-san. I forward information to Marshall and respond to your requests. I am the conduit and see all contacts," Asori locked eyes in a very un-Japanese manner with Nicholas with the last statement.

"All contacts?" Nicholas asked, taking the hint.

"Yes, all. For example Harding-sama, let's say someone were to attempt to electronically access our data-report files through the link we've supplied. I would be aware."

"Would many others be aware of this hypothetical access?"

"A few of our Information Management staff would see the contact. But they would come to me. If I say it's an appropriate contact, it quickly leaves their memory. If I say not, then consequences could escalate. But there is no need for that is there? Contrary to some of the rumors, I have much confidence in your skills."

Nicholas was wondering how long this game could go on and sensed that Asori was enjoying it.

"Okay what rumors?"

"Well, since you asked, Harding-sama," Asori began, while refilling both their sake cups. "There is always talking. Here it is about the arrogant Americans, as I am sure for you at home it's about the condescending Japanese."

Nicholas had to smile at the accuracy of that one. Asori continued, "there are rumblings, rumors only, nothing official, that Marshall is having difficulties with MR-548 and that it's because of the inexperience of the project lead – you. That there will be problems when you go into your clinical trials."

Nicholas was going to have to make a decision. He could either continue to play this dance with Asori to some unknown end and risk going home with nothing or push to get to the point. But he would have to decide whether he could trust Asori. Nicholas had always prided himself on being a good and quick judge of character. He was rarely off the mark, but much was at stake now.

Choosing to ignore the comments about himself for now and take some risk with Asori, Nicholas asked, "why did Tanaka stop development of MR-548?"

"Do you play poker, Nicholas?" Asori asked after sipping his sake. He rose from the low, small table. He wore a black silk kimono over his slacks, shirt and tie. The outer garment had an intricate design of a dragon fighting a warrior.

"No. I'm not much for gambling," Nicholas replied.

Asori walked around the room slowly and began to speak. "My ancestors, many generations ago, were Samurai. Warriors who fought and died and killed for what they believed in and valued. Your ancestors, Harding-sama, were brought to America bearing the shackles of the enslaved. What are we, Harding-sama? Would our ancestors be proud of us because of our successes, our wealth or material possessions? We are bureaucrats, Nicholas. We shuffle paper – oh, we do it electronically now, so technically we shuffle electrons – but we still shuffle paper. We do the bidding of others. We are pawns, Nicholas, and pawns are expendable. I have decided to trust you. I think you must have come from a type of Samurai stock."

He continued, "If I am wrong then I am expendable. You are here because there is something wrong with MR-548;wrong with Tanaka and Marshall. Let us compare notes, for I believe we are both being used as pawns and will be discarded by those others."

"The party line about not developing MR-548 yourself, why?"

"There is no backup, Nicholas. Well, not one that works. The so-called backups are useless. But the official position to Marshall and the rest of the world is that we have a superior backup."

"The nonclinical and Phase I clinical work on MR-548, it looks exceptionally clean; a therapeutic index a mile wide with no significant adverse effects. It looks almost too good to be true. Is it?" Nicholas asked.

"That's an excellent question, Nicholas. Again, there are rumors. Tanaka is a big company. The Pharma R&D group is more than 5,000 people. Obviously I don't know everyone, but I've been unable to find anyone who actually worked on this project."

"Meaning?"

"The rumors again, that it's a phantom; a ghost drug that does not exist. Tell me Nicholas, how is MR-548 perceived at Marshall?" Asori asked.

"The big brains, our Board of Directors, love it. They can't wait to get it into our Phase IIb trials that are set to go in six months."

"I spent many years in America, Nicholas. I loved it. Hated to come back. I learned to think like an American. I sense a 'but' here. What is the 'but' Nicholas?"

"You pick up on the term, 'there's something rotten in the state of Denmark'?"

"Ah, yes," Asori said with a smile.

"Well, that's where I stand with MR-548. I'm going to go way out on a limb here. The list of folks I can trust in Marshall is real short. We could all meet in a phone booth. But whatever is going on involves Tanaka too and I need someone I can trust in Tanaka. I'm betting the ranch that you're the right guy."

"And why is that Harding-sama?"

"Two reasons. Because I'm a good judge of character and my gauge is telling me you're an okay guy."

"And reason number two?"

"Because a patsy, a fall guy, is needed at each company to make whatever conspiracy is going on work. I figure I'm it at Marshall and I'm betting you're it at Tanaka. Am I wrong?"

"You and I, Harding-san, we could do much business together. I like you," he said laughing. "Yes, I have come to suspect that something is amiss at Tanaka. Things have not been the same since our Chairman, Yoshi Mikasi, died last winter. Our new Chairman, Akoni Konoru, has a keen interest in MR-548. Far too keen an interest, in my opinion, in a drug we out-licensed and have no interest in developing ourselves."

"So, Nomura-sama," Nicholas said, filling their sake cups and raising his in a toast. "I propose a partnership. You and I, we work together first to save ourselves and then to save our companies."

Asori paused in thought, looked Nicholas in the eyes, and then raised his cup to join in the toast.

"Yes, I accept your proposal, Harding-sama. Let us show the feudal lords what two descendants of warriors are capable of. Let us share all that we know tonight and come up with a plan. Then perhaps if there is time, A and B are still available."

"I'll tell you what, Asori, if we get out of this mess with our necks in one piece, we can party for a week with A and B," Nicholas said with a laugh.

"Agreed!"

Asori called for A and B to serve more food and tea, leaving plenty of sake. Then he and Nicholas spent the next five hours sharing all they knew about the Marshall-Tanaka plot.

Nicholas told Asori about the FDA investigation and his suspicions about Jack O'Connor. He spoke of Arthur's death and the strange email messages. He didn't discuss Beth Cowling's private investigations; only being capable of taking trust so far.

Asori spoke of the new Chairman, Akoni Konoru, who seemed to be a clone of O'Connor. He also informed Nicholas that he'd picked up Glen Morgan's entry into the Tanaka data system and kept it to himself. Nicholas shared what Glen had come up with so far: the near-perfect pharmacologic-toxicologic profile of MR-548 and a contract that bans Marshall from conducting tests prior to a big 800 patient Phase IIb trial. After some internal self-debate, Nicholas even told Asori of the predictive modeling work Glen was doing with MR-548 and the plan to synthesize a small amount for some toxicology work on the side.

They spoke of the suspected conspiracy to damage Marshall's credibility and make it susceptible to take over, but by whom they weren't sure. O'Connor and Konoru seemed the two most likely candidates, but neither seemed the type to share a kill.

After five hours, the two men had shared all or nearly all. Nicholas had kept a couple of aces up his sleeves and figured Asori had also. They agreed on how to communicate and their next steps.

"I feel the end drawing near, Harding-sama," Asori said as they rose from the table. "We will know the outcome soon, good or bad."

"But now we're going to have a say in that outcome, Asori. The battle has just begun."

"And, it shall be a glorious battle, Nicholas."

The two men left the room and walked down the hall towards the entrance.

"A car will return you to your hotel. Travel well, Harding-sama, my partner."

"I will, partner."

They shook hands and Nicholas went down the staircase that returned him to the entrance. Another uniformed guard, who could have been the mountainous brother of the guard he'd met earlier, met him. And Nicholas was escorted out of the House of Many Paradises.

It was not yet early morning. Back in his hotel room he noticed the several gift boxes on his dresser. Before he'd left for his meeting with Asori he'd asked the hotel Concierge to get him small gifts for 'Drea, Dorothy, Beth, and Karen.

Nicholas lay on the bed, trying to get a few hours' sleep before he left for the airport to fly to Newark. In his dreams versions of the twins A and B were feeding him sushi.

He tossed and turned for a couple of hours until first light at 5:30 AM and went out for a walk. His hotel was near the Imperial Palace grounds and he could walk through some of the public gardens. This part of the city was beautiful and colorful in contrast with the crowded, stark, gray bulk of Tokyo proper.

The return flight from Tokyo to Newark was long, boring and uneventful. Nicholas realized he'd spent most of the week in a plane, but he'd accomplished what he'd set out to do. He'd wanted to see where things stood with Catherine and what he'd come away with was where he listed those he could and could not trust Cath fell in the 'could not' column. It hurt to realize that, but not as much as he'd expected.

Perhaps it had all been based on the physical relationship. But he now suspected Catherine was somehow involved with O'Connor in this whole mess.

And he was satisfied with how the session with Asori had gone. He felt that he now had an ally in Tanaka; that or he'd signed his death warrant by trusting Asori. Now, he thought, it was time to gather his forces and mount his own offensive.

But for now, he had to rest. There would be much to do upon his return home.

When Nicholas entered his house through the back door, he found his mom and Beth sitting at the island in the large kitchen giggling and laughing like two teenagers. Then Nicholas saw the bottle of bourbon.

"Mom, what'd I tell you about having your rowdy friends over?" Nicholas asked teasingly.

"Very funny, Dr. Harding," Beth replied. "We're just catching up on old times."

"Old, old times," Dorothy chimed in.

"Well, at least offer me a drink," he said.

Then Nicholas first saw, then felt, a medium size blur, a.k.a. 'Drea, throw herself in his arms, accompanied by her partner in crime, Rasputin.

"Before anyone asks, yes, I have presents for all. Come on 'Drea, help me unpack and we'll find them. By the way, isn't it past your bed time?"

"Not in Japan," she said with a straight, serious face.

Dorothy and Beth almost fell off their stools howling.

"Don't be a smart-ass, kiddo, and pay no attention to those two."

27

Nicholas and Paula

His internal clock, unsure of its location and time, awoke Nicholas early Saturday morning and went down to make a cup of cappuccino.

"Make two of those, would you?"

He hadn't heard Beth enter the kitchen, she too still in her PJs and robe. "I didn't mean to startle you."

"I just didn't expect to see you this early, what with that bottle of bourbon you girls put away last night."

"Oh, I'm afraid your mom's out of her league, drinking with me."

"You're a piece of work, Beth Cowlings, aren't you? So, you make a point of catching me early before anyone else is up. You must have some news for me. Some results from your investigators. But you didn't mention anything last night when I came in. Must be bad news. In fact judging from your expression, it must be very bad news.

"How do you take your capp'?"

"Two sugars please; none of that fake stuff for me."

"Some good, some bad," he continued as he spooned steamed milk froth into the two cups. "And I suspect you learned a lot too. Obviously some bad, but I hope some good. But you know what Beth?" he asked as he turned and gave her the steaming cup of cappuccino.

"What?"

"Today's a cease fire. I call a halt to all battle activities today."

"Can you afford that Nicholas? Do you think your adversaries will do the same?"

"I don't know. Maybe they enjoy this stuff. Maybc I'm wired different from them. God, I hope so. But I can't afford not to take a break."

"This is good," She said, taking a few sips of the coffee.

"I'm hanging out with 'Drea today. So that's all I want today; to rest, get caught up on my mail and hang out with my daughter. Then tomorrow it's back to the battlefield. Okay Beth?"

"Okay boss. We'll have a lot to go over tomorrow."

"Get Michael here for tomorrow," he said, looking out the large bay kitchen window, out towards the pool and deck.

"You're sure? It may be rough."

"I'm sure."

"Okay. One question, but you can answer it tomorrow if you want; or now."

"Go ahead," he said.

"Tell me about Paula."

Nicholas was silent and continued to gaze out towards the pool. Beth finished her cappuccino and was about to leave when he said softly.

"Do you know 'Drea and I have been seeing a shrink since Paula's death?"

"Dorothy mentioned it."

"Dr. Loraine Coleman. She's supposed to be good with kids. She thought it'd be best if 'Drea and I had joint sessions. She also sees us one-on-one on occasions. We started a couple of months after Paula died."

"Has it helped?" Beth asked.

"'Drea seems okay, but she never went into a deep funk. Me? Who knows? You have to understand I rate shrinks about a half step above witch doctors and voodoo queens. Don't get me wrong. I'm sure they can help the mentally ill.

But will chatting with a stranger help us? I doubt it. You want another cappuccino? That was pretty good," he said.

"Sure," Beth replied, wanting to keep Nicholas talking, now that he seemed to be opening up.

"I'm sure that for people with real psycho-pathologies, shrinks can help. But for the average schmuck going through life – dealing with the ups and the horse shit of the downs – well, I just don't see much gain in paying a stranger $350 to talk to about your horse shit. Maybe I'm wrong, but that's what I think. Hell, get a dog. The advice is probably just as good and the dog will love you."

"You consider your wife's death just part of the 'horse shit'?" she asked, using her fingers to put 'horse shit' in quotations.

"Sounds a bit cold, doesn't it?" he asked.

"I'm not one to pass judgment."

"Bad things happen to good people, Beth. Some parts of life suck.

"Do you know I haven't cried for Paula? I didn't cry when I heard she was dead. I didn't cry when I identified her body at the morgue. The days before the funeral, at the funeral, since – dry as a bone. Nothing."

"Has Andrea cried for her mother?"

"Yes."

"Did you love her?"

"I think that's what Dr. Coleman is trying to find out. Pretty sad, huh?" he said with a detached laugh as he measured out a vanilla hazelnut coffee blend. "I have to pay a shrink to tell me whether I loved my dead wife."

"At least you want to know."

"Hum, could be just curiosity."

"You still haven't told me about Paula."

"You've seen the pictures around the house. She was beautiful. Tall, jet black hair, ebony eyes, body that wouldn't quit. But it's almost as if she never really knew how beautiful she was, or knew and didn't like it. She was much more proud of her brain and did like to flaunt her intelligence. Maybe that's what attracted me more at first, her wit and intelligence.

"We met at a party. A friend introduced us. I'd just watched one of those 'God's gift to women' guys make a move on her. She chewed him up and spit him out with that razor sharp wit of hers. She used words he'd probably never heard before to tell him to drop dead."

"The only way I'd go out with you is if I were an anthropologist studying primitive cultures," Paula said in a voice above a whisper that could be heard by a close few, before she walked away. Not wanting to be embarrassed by a brush-off and too stupid to know he was way out of his league, lover boy, who probably thought he was a young *Philadelphia* Denzel Washington look-alike didn't realize he'd run into that species his type most feared: a gorgeous woman with a huge brain and ego. He moved in front of her to block her path and continue his conquest.

"I can see I'm going to have to dial up the charm on you, baby. You might want to fasten your seatbelt and put your tray table in the full upright position," he gave her the smug look of a guy who was used to getting laid with these lines. Unfortunately, he was fishing in the wrong pond this night.

Nicholas had the perfect seating to observe all this interaction and loved it. He refilled his wineglass and watched round two. Paula looked at her Lothario acquaintance like he was a cockroach who'd dared to venture out into the light and began to laugh. Now more people in the apartment were starting to observe the exchange between Paula and lover-boy.

"Look pal, maybe I used a few words that were out of your vocabulary range, so let me try again. Crank back the testosterone dial and step back out of my space."

This time Paula's voice was loud enough to carry over most of the room. Much of the ideal chitchat conversations had ended and lover-boy realized he was now the center stage attraction.

Paula moved to get around him again. Lover-boy, not wanting to take the last blow and still unaware of just how far out of his league he was mumbled, "I guess you like the taste of women better, huh?"

The entire room was now dead silent. Paula asked the bartender for a glass of wine and slowly turned towards lover-boy. "Before I'd taste the likes of you? Yeah."

Several people in the room now openly howled at lover-boy. The host quickly grabbed his arm and pushed/pulled him out of the room.

"You know, I thought this would be a pretty boring party, but that wasn't half bad," Nicholas said to his friend. "Now, where's this irresistible goddess you said you'd introduce me to?"

"At the bar, getting a glass of wine."

"Vampira?"

"Yep."

"Hot damn!"

"Maybe now's not the best time, Nicholas," his friend said, fearing for Nicholas' life if he tangled with Paula.

"Hell, unless she shoots me, I can't do any worse than Casanova there."

The two approached Paula as she stood at the bar, sipping her wine, somehow managing to look casual, attractive and pissed all at the same time. Edgy – that was it. She looked edgy and Nicholas had a thing for edgy women.

"Paula Mason, Nicholas Harding," the mutual friend said, introducing the two. "I thought you two might like to meet, but I've been known to be wrong. I'm going to take cover now. Paula, please don't hurt him."

After shaking hands and a brief silence, Nicholas said, "I guess we're on our own now."

"I guess," she replied. Nicholas noticed that in heels she was slightly taller than he was. "So, you're the one Nancy's been trying to hook me up with the last two months."

"Yep," he said. "And you're the one she's been telling me about. Although I must say, your pre-billing doesn't do justice after having witnessed you in action."

"I don't like to be hit on, Nicholas. Especially by someone whose IQ is barely my shoe size," she, said fixing him with a less than warm stare.

"Yeah, me too," he said. "Would you like to see my MENSA membership card?"

"Ah, was that a smile?" he asked as Paula actually laughed.

Several others were looking at Nicholas and Paula, some probably expecting to see Nicholas go flying across the room.

"You probably think I'm one of those brainy ice bitches, don't you?"

"You probably think I'm one of those guys who's turned on by brainy ice bitches, don't you? People are watching us," he whispered. "I think they're waiting to see if you hit me with a wine bottle."

"Let's give them something to talk about for the rest of the evening," she whispered in his ear. "There's an all-night jazz club on South Street in Morristown. Follow me there. I hate parties anyway."

"We're leaving," they both said to Nancy and their host as they walked out, giving everyone something to talk about.

They met at the jazz club and got a table near the back where it wasn't too loud.

"So, Nicholas Harding," she said. "Nicholas is an interesting name. You don't hear it much anymore. Are you named after a relative?"

"Not really," he said, then ordering drinks. "My mom's a teacher and when she had me, she was reading a book about Czar Nicholas II, the last Czar of Imperial Russia."

"You're named after the Czar of Russia?" she laughed.

"The last Czar of Russia," he corrected. "And who the hell are you named after, Paula Abdul?" they both laughed.

"Touché. It's just that you don't think of black folks naming a kid after the Czar of Russia, even the last Czar of Russia."

"It gets weirder. Nicholas II's brother was named Michael. Mom named my younger brother Michael. It's sort of an inside joke in the family."

"Could have been worse, she could have been reading 'Snow White and the Seven Dwarfs.'" Paula said.

"So Paula Mason, what's a beautiful, but exceptionally brainy woman like you doing having her friends fix her up on blind dates?"

"I'm not. I hate blind dates. And by the way, this is not a blind date because, a) we were introduced at a party and b) it just isn't a blind date."

"What is it then, an interview for a date?" he asked with a smile.

"You know, Nicholas, you're not quite as funny as you think you are."

"So I've been told."

"To answer your question, I haven't had time for dates. Career, school, work, etc., etc."

"Um huh, ~~Princeton Law~~, new associate at DCC. Let me guess: over-achieving, only child of professional black parents."

"I see you've done your homework. Dr. Harding: over-achieving elder child of professional black parents. Are we two sides of the same coin or what?"

"You want to know why I blew off that asshole at the party?" she asked, changing the subject.

"Actually, yeah," he said, applauding as a set ended. "I want to make sure I never do whatever he did to piss you off."

"I hate that type," she said in a serious tone.

"What type?" Nicholas asked, thinking he knew the answer.

"That swaggering macho, black male stud routine. Any attractive woman is just the next lay. They think women are supposed to fall on the floor and spread their legs when they start strutting. When one of them looks at me, they don't see someone who finished in the top ten percent of her law school class, they just another piece of ass. That behavior is a remnant of slavery and there's no place for it today if we're to be taken seriously as a race. We're always whining about 'the white man this and the white man that' and how they don't respect us or take us seriously when we act like buffoons. I'm sorry, that behavior really pisses me off, Nicholas," she said.

Nicholas looked at her and asked, "and you know I'm not like that how?"

"I'm a reasonably good judge of character and if I thought you were like that for a second, we wouldn't be here."

"Ah ha!" exclaimed Nicholas. "So it *is* a date!"

"Okay. It's an almost date," she said with a sweet smile. "Are you really a MENSA member?"

"No. Are you really a brainy ice bitch?"

"Yes," then they both laughed.

She looked into his eyes and said, "I'm not looking for a relationship, Nicholas."

He turned to Beth, "and I'm not sure that we had one. It definitely wasn't one of those movie head-over-heels in love things. We were both wrapped up in our careers and we satisfied that small need for safe companionship. We had mutual interests in art, movies, and shows and enjoyed each other's company. After more than a year of this, we were living together; more convenient. Then we decided to take it to the next level and get married. We were comfortable, yeah, that's it, were very comfortable."

"But?" asked Beth.

"Sure you're not a shrink?" he asked her. "Over time each of our careers became more consuming. There was less and less left over. There was Paula and her career and Nicholas and his career. I'm not sure there was an 'us,' or at least that much of an 'us'. We probably would have drifted apart if it weren't for 'Drea."

"Paula wanted children?" Beth asked.

"Not at first. After we'd been married a couple of years, I raised the issue. Somehow, it had never really come up. She said absolutely not. It would interfere with her career – just not in her plans.”

“I thought about it for a few days and then told her I wanted kids and if she didn’t, I didn’t think the marriage would work. She went off and thought about it for a few days.”

“This is how you two fought?” Beth asked with an incredulous tone.

“Pretty much – few sparks good or bad.”

“Paula came back in a few days and said she’d give it a shot. So about a year later we had ‘Drea.”

“And Paula was a good mother?”

“Yeah.”

“But you and Paula?”

“The same – no, worse. I think after devoting time to our careers and to ‘Drea, there was nothing left over for us. So ‘we’ withered away and died. But maybe that’s what two-career 21st century marriages are these days: a business relationship.”

“Do you really believe that, Nicholas?”

“I believe it, but God, I hope I’m wrong.”

“So, did you love her?”

“I’ll let you know when Dr. Coleman finds out.”

Beth stood, leaned over and kissed him on the cheek. “Thanks for the coffee and enjoy your date with Andrea, Nicholas. We’ll talk tomorrow,” Beth then left Nicholas sitting at the kitchen island staring out the window.

Nicholas heard Andrea’s lithe, lyrical voice coming from her room. The door was closed, ‘Drea now insisting on her privacy. He assumed she was talking to Rasputin.

Odd, thought Nicholas. His mother had named him after the doomed Czar Nicholas II and he had his own Rasputin, albeit a furrier and more benign version, in his own house.

He was starting to feel more like the ill-fated last Czar with the problems at Marshall. The Czar's problems had not been resolved well, ending in his and his family's execution at the hands of Lenin's Bolsheviks. But Nicholas didn't' see himself in the image of his name-sake.

He knocked on 'Drea's bedroom door. "It's me hon. Can I come in?"

"Okay – wait a minute."

He heard drawers being opened and closed; obviously some minor cleaning occurring before the door opened. "Okay, you can come in now," she said.

Nicholas opened the door to see an acceptable level of mess and disorganization that he assumed to be normal for an 11-year-old. 'Drea was neither a neat-freak nor a slob, but somewhere in the middle. The dolls Nicholas had given her from his travels were neatly organized on shelves. She never actually played with them, but told Nicholas she enjoyed getting them and still wanted him to bring them.

There were a few clothes on the walk-in closet floor, but not too many. Her desk for school work was neat and organized, which impressed Nicholas. The full size bed, surrounded by a ceiling-floor length flowing golden, glimmery gauzy material, was unmade. The shimmering, flowing material surrounding the bed gave it the appearance of a large warm and inviting nest. The design of the bed was 'Drea's idea. She'd seen it in a movie and was able to describe it to Paula sufficiently to allow her to create it to 'Drea's satisfaction.

Inside the nest 'Drea sat in the middle of her rumpled bed with her faithful sidekick, Rasputin. Nicholas always marveled at how loyal the cat was to 'Drea.

"So, what are you two rascals up to?" Nicholas asked as he sat on the floor.

"I was showing Rasputin the book you brought me from Japan, Dad."

Nicholas had described to the hotel concierge what he wanted for 'Drea. It was an illustrated story about a little girl and her enchanted cat. The text was in both English and Japanese.

"Do you like it?" he asked her.

"Yep! So does Rasputin," she said. She was sitting cross-legged in the bed with Rasputin's rather large, fuzzy, tabby head in her lap, his eyes half-closed and purring. As was usually the case she was smiling and seemed happy, yet serious all at the same time.

"Good. I aim to please you both," he said and she giggled.

He always felt better in her presence and worried about her when they were apart. His love for 'Drea was absolute and strong. If O'Connor's plotting and scheming at Marshall threatened to imprison and take him away from 'Drea, that gave him strength of conviction and an almost animalistic fierceness to do anything to protect what he and 'Drea had.

"I'm sorry I've been away so much lately, 'Drea."

"That's okay, Dad. We understand it's because of your job. It's how you make money to support the family."

As an only child, her mannerisms, vocabulary and general persona were much more mature than her chronological age. She and Nicholas and Paula had tended to interact more like peers than parent-child. And now the two, Nicholas and 'Drea, were very close; "two peas in a pod," as his mother often said.

"So, what's up, Dad?" she asked with that adult-like tone.

"'What's up Dad?'" he repeated. "Can't I come in and visit my favorite kid?"

"Sure," she replied with her irresistible smile. "So, what's up?"

"I thought we'd go to Fosterfields today. There's a sheepdog trial."

"Cool!" 'Drea shouted.

Fosterfields was a 'living' historical farm in Morristown managed by the New Jersey Park Commission. It was operated as it had been in the late 19th century.

Harding wanted his daughter to learn how incredibly smart those little dogs were.

28

Jack-O

Nicholas was sitting at the kitchen island scanning the Sunday *NY Times*, most of which actually came on Saturday. He absentmindedly nibbled on a cinnamon bagel with a cup of cappuccino. Dorothy had gone to church and 'Drea was studying in her room.

"You know you could always get a job at Starbucks. Damn that smells good," Beth said, taking a seat next to Nicholas.

"Here, I made one for you," he responded while pushing a large mug topped with steamed cream and cinnamon to Beth.

She took a sip of the hot coffee. "Ah, bless you, child. Just what I needed."

"What time's Michael coming?"

"Around noon. He should be here in about an hour."

"Beth?"

"Yep?"

"What I said about Jack last week: I didn't mean that, at least I don't think I did. I just want my life back to be normal. And it's like O'Connor's trying to take it away. You know what, I can't figure out why. Is it something I did or didn't do to or for him? Is this my punishment? Or am I just convenient? I just need it to end, Beth."

"I know honey, I know," she said, gently putting her hand over his. "We'll figure it out."

"Thanks Beth," Harding smiled as he ventured to the bagels. "You want a bagel?"

"Nope, I'm still a country girl at heart – never picked up a taste for those things."

Michael's big black Audi SUV pulled into Nicholas' driveway, so Harding met him at the door.

"You know, why you don't just buy a school bus and paint it black is a wonder to me, Michael," he nudged his brother teasingly.

"You're just jealous of my big, black machine."

"Um huh."

"We're in my study. Want anything?" Nicholas asked.

"Coffee?"

"Cappuccino okay?"

"Oh yeah! I'm going to run up and say 'hi' to the munchkin before we get started," Michael spoke over his shoulder while heading to 'Drea's room. Her Uncle liked to spoil her mercilessly.

It was a cool, dark, and rainy Sunday. The kind young lovers should spend in bed, just being together. Looking out the large study window Nicholas, Michael and Beth could see the sheets of rain pouring down. Nicholas had the room lit only with lamps, adding to the gloomy effect.

"I'm staying the night and going in late tomorrow," Michael announced.

"Good." Nicholas drew comfort from his brother's presence. "So Beth, have you brought Michael up to speed?"

"Did it last week while you were flying all over the planet, Nick, so why don't you update us on the fruits of your adventures last week? Then I'll go over what's new on my end."

"Okay, right, last week. Let's see, first Newark airport."

"I meant the highlights, not the low points," Beth contorted chidingly in Harding's direction.

"You'll want to hear this; before I left for London, I met Glen Morgan at the airport. He's from my office, but before I go on, are we bug-free?"

"Yes Nick. Had everything swept again yesterday."

"Jesus! You guys are scaring the hell out of me!" Michael chimed in.

"Sorry, little brother. Anyway, Glen is one of my staff toxicologists. He's brilliant and eccentric, but he doesn't have a Ph.D. Technically he's better qualified than most of my Ph.D. staffers, but his people skills are, let's say less than optimal, so he reports directly to me and works on special projects to minimize interaction with other personnel. As the project lead for MR-548, I have an electronic hook-up with the Tanaka database on this program. I gave Glen access to it and asked him to note anything which looked odd."

"And?"

"Glen looked at the profile of MR-548 Tanaka gave us and he says it looks perfect – too perfect. His words." Nicholas went on, "you develop a drug to have a specific effect in people. The efficacious effect or desired pharmacologic effect, but science isn't exact. There's no such thing as a drug with only efficacious effects, so you have to take some bad along with the good. All drugs, no matter how good, have side effects or toxicities associated with them. The secret of our business is to find drugs with the desired efficacious effects and an acceptable side effect profile. It's hard; there are probably thousands of highly effective drugs sitting on our shelves because of unacceptable side effect profiles, and those side effects can range from headache to death."

"And, the side effect profile for this Tanaka drug looks good?" Michael asked. "Isn't that what you want?"

"No. It looks great," Nicholas replied.

"Is this all animal data or do they have real-people data?" Beth asked.

"Very good Beth, the 'unreal' animal data is what I do, but to answer your question: Tanaka has both. They've taken MR-548 through Phase I clinical trials. These are single and multiple dose studies in normal subjects. In toxicology, we continue to escalate the dose until we see side effects and then we study the exposure."

"Toxicity studies in people?" Michael asked.

"Sort of, but this is how drugs are developed. Most people don't have a clue about how complicated and risky the drug development process really is. It takes up to ten years and more than a billion dollars to bring a new drug to market today."

"So, what kind of effects did Tanaka get?"

"MR-548 was highly effective against viral titers at low doses and almost no side effects at very high doses. It looked almost perfect – textbook. According to Glen it looks too perfect. So he took his evaluation further. There are some new computerized, computational programs that look at the molecular structure of a compound and compare it to a known database. It then predicts pharmaceutical characteristics such as toxicity, absorption, bioavailability, pharmacokinetics, etc. We have some early beta versions of these tools and Glen ran MR-548 through some of them."

Nicholas got up to adjust the lighting in the room.

"Well, don't keep us in suspense," Beth said. "What'd he find?"

Nicholas continued walking over to the window, "these are new and un-validated tools. We're not yet sure how accurate they are, but you do expect some correlation between real data and the computer predictions. What Glen found was almost no correlation at all. It was like comparing two completely different drugs. The 'real' data says MR-548 is clean as a whistle; a huge difference between the therapeutic dose and the toxic dose.   We call that the therapeutic index. You want it wide; as wide as possible."

He went on, "the computer modeling data shows the opposite. In fact, the therapeutic dose and toxic dose overlap. If this is real this drug never should have made it this far."

He appeared to have the lighting where he wanted it. "And here's the kicker: the contract doesn't allow Marshall to run any test on this drug until the next series of clinical trials: multi-dose, multi-centered Phase IIb trials in about 800 patients."

"And now you have two opposite sets of information on how this drug will behave in these Phase II trials?" Michael stated.

"Exactly."

"If Tanaka's right, no problem. If this computer stuff's right?" Beth said, leaving the question open.

"If Glen's projections are right, we'll see severe side effects; clinical toxicities. Could be liver or kidney failure, could be death."

"Who else in Marshall knows of this?" Beth asked.

"Just Glen and I," Nicholas replied.

"Shit! What are you going to do?" Michael asked. "You can't let them start that study if you think people could be hurt."

"I know. And I won't," Nicholas answered. "The study's not scheduled to start for another month. We have a little time, but there's more. The contract with Tanaka also says we can't synthesize any of MR-548 ourselves. Glen, however, got another of his misfit friends in chemical development to make a small batch.

"He's going to run a small tox study in rats and dogs to see what happens. That's where we left it. I have to touch base with Glen next week to see where we stand.

"But skipping ahead to Tokyo, this fits in with what I heard from Asori Nomura. He's the project lead on the Tanaka side. Figuring that whoever is running this needs a fall guy on each side and I'm the likely it guy here. My guess is Asori is it for Tanaka. We both decided to trust each other and share information.

"And get this: Asori called MR-548 a 'phantom' drug. He's not sure it ever existed!"

"Okay," Beth said, starting to pace around the room. "Let's say you and Glen and Asori are all 100% correct. This MR-548 stuff is toxic as hell. Here's the $64,000 question: why? What possible motive could someone, particularly someone inside Marshall and Tanaka, have to do this?"

"That's easy, Beth," Michael said. "I don't work at Marshall, but I know the type and these guys are all wired the same: money and power. That's what gives them a hard-on."

"He's right," Nicholas said. "Let's say we ran the Phase II trial with MR-548 and the shit hit the fan. We'd seriously hurt a lot of people. Liver and kidney transplants would be needed; maybe even a few deaths. Federal investigations, lawsuits, and Marshall stock bottoms out. The bad boys buy at rock bottom and then, all of a sudden, they have a scapegoat: me.

"They do damage control, I'm indicted and go to jail, the new owners reinstate confidence and voilà: they own a major U.S. pharmaceutical company. In a year or so, the stock's back. Money and power, Beth. That's what makes the world go around."

"You left out London, bro. Did you find out anything useful?"

"Yeah."

After a long pause, Michael said, "and?"

"I think Catherine's part of whatever's going on with O'Connor."

"Jez. I'm sorry Nicholas," Michael said.

"That's okay. I always knew Catherine was no saint and for her, it's business. So that's what I have, guys," Nicholas said. "But I've decided I'm not going to sit back and wait to see what happens. We're going to end this and let the chips fall." He turned to Beth, "and what new information do you have?"

"Well, your office and office phones are still dirty. By the way, Karen has moved you down the hall into Arthur's office suite. The bugs moved with you, so someone's on top of things. House and car are clean. Want to see some show and tell?" she asked, reaching for a folder in front of her.

Nicholas subconsciously tensed.

Beth went on, "the CEO of a Fortune 500 company is like a mini President of the United States. There has to be a detailed log of where he's going, where he's been and whom he's with. The 'who' he's with part is easily falsified. The 'where' is harder, since he has to be accessible. My New York dicks have tapped into this information for Marshall."

"She has quite a little gutter mouth, doesn't she?" Michael laughed.

"Funny, Grant Michner was in New York for a week about a month ago for some sort of strategy session. They ran it at the Plaza Hotel on the Park. By the way," Beth shined a wicked grin. "Michner's 22-year-old secretary had a suite next to his, must be for those late night dictations."

"Man, what a way to live," Michael said.

"Well the Plaza, like all top rated hotels, is rather obsessed with security, cameras everywhere, most hidden from view, and in elevators, bars, ballrooms, entrances, and exits. Any time you set foot out of your room you're on *Candid Camera*. And since 9-11 there are open area cameras everywhere. Big Brother is definitely watching. And using nothing but the best electronics; it's all digital, that means it can be tapped into remotely. Do you catch my drift, boys?"

"Who the hell is this detective agency you use, the CIA or the fucking Mafia?" Michael asked.

"Let's just say they're damn good at what they do," she replied, looking into Nicholas' eyes.

She opened the folder and began to lay out 8 x 10 photos. "Here we have Grant Michner talking to his head of security, Ken Joseph; nothing unusual there."

She flipped to the next photo, "Here's Grant talking to Gerry Michel in legal. Looks normal enough."

Nicholas was sitting on the edge of his chair now.

Beth went on, "but what do we have here? Ken Joseph talking to Barry Keenan from the U.S. Marshal's office."

"Holly shit!" Michael exclaimed.

"Same time frame?" Nicholas asked quietly.

"Yep, and it gets better," she flipped over another photo. "Ken Joseph, Barry Keenan and Gerry Michael near a side exit. Looks like a heated argument. Then," she laid out yet another picture, "they're joined by Grant himself. They broke it up shortly after and Keenan left."

"My money," Beth said, "says Keenan's in their pocket; they bought him off.

"Oh, apparently there's a security camera in a tree outside Grant's suite that sweeps the area. Here's a good one of Grant showing his secretary the 'ins and outs' of business. Grant likes to 'exercise' with his drapes open."

Nicholas ignored the picture of Grant in bed with his secretary. "Bought off Keenan for what purpose?"

"'Why, the better to screw you my dear,' said the wolf to Little Red Riding Hood. Remember when I said the government can't fart without leaving a paper trail? Well, today it's electronic, so it's just easier to follow. Keenan filed a request with the Federal Prosecutor's office to open a formal investigation of you."

"For what?" Michael asked, incensed.

"Falsification of data and obstruction of justice," she replied. "It's just the first step to discredit you, so when the shit hits the fan they can drop it all on you. They probably figure you'll be so busy trying to stay out of a Federal prison that you'll be no threat to them."

"What about Jack?" Nicholas asked.

"He was there. We didn't see photos of him with Keenan. But we did see Jack and Catherine Sullivan. Did you know she was here a month ago?"

"No. So how do you and your dicks read this? Does their company have a real name by the way?"

"That's as much of their company name as you need to know. Our read is Jack is the head honcho bad guy. Grant's the figure head, but Jack's calling the shots. We suspect Catherine is on Jack's team but her role is unclear."

"Maybe her role was to deliver me or keep me occupied so I was distracted."

Nicholas was sitting on the sofa looking through the photos. Beth sat next to him. She took a deep breath and looked at Michael who nodded and then gently took Nicholas' hand into hers.

"Nicholas, honey," she purred in her sweet Southern accent. "I know that was difficult, but I don't think it was anything you didn't expect. But there's more and some of this I'm sure are things you didn't expect."

Nicholas looked at Beth, then at Michael. "She's told you?"

"Yes."

Nicholas was silent and had the look of a sad, lonely little boy. "Then, I think you should tell me Beth."

She removed another picture and turned it over for Nicholas to see.

"Oh God, no," Nicholas moaned.

The photo showed Grant, Ken Joseph, Gerry Michael and Barry Keenan along with Arthur Kronan. Nicholas recalled Arthur had gone into New York for a couple of days for the strategy session. But it was obvious from the photos the group, including Arthur, was in heated discussions.

"I'm sorry Nicholas," Beth said. "But it appears Arthur was somehow involved with the plot. Maybe he tried to get out – I don't know – but something must have gone wrong."

"I admired him, looked up to him, and probably loved him. Why would he do something like this?"

"Same as the rest: money," Michael answered.

"It doesn't make sense, Arthur was wealthy."

"No," Beth said. "Actually, his wife is rich; old New Jersey money. Arthur received pretty good compensation, but he made some bad investments. He'd lost most of his own money. All they had was his wife's. That can do weird things to a man."

"Okay, you've just told me my mentor was a felon, trying to frame me. What about the rest of it Beth? What about

Paula? Remember? You were going to have your guys dig for dirt in Paula's past. Let's have it. Come on, Beth, let's have it!" he shouted.

"No. Some other time."

"Wait, wait," he gently touched her arm. "Please. I'm okay. Please go on, Beth."

Beth looked at Michael, who nodded an okay.

She went on, "Okay Nicholas, this is what we've been able to piece together, but it's still a best guess. Paula stumbled across the Marshall Investigation file, probably by accident. As a partner, she had a right to review any active file so she requested it. She was probably shocked when she saw it involved a program you were involved with. We think she went to the senior partner at DCC, who referred her to O'Connor and Gerry Michael."

Michael added, "and, she couldn't discuss it with you because of lawyer-client confidentiality."

"So that's why she had the meeting with O'Connor and Michael?" Nicholas asked.

"It's gonna get rough from here, bro," Michael said as he sat next to Nicholas.

"Go ahead."

Beth took a breath and started, "Gerry didn't show up. Jack had Paula meet him in Grant's suite at the Plaza. We were able to pull some picture. Nicholas," she said after a pause. "It looks like he forced her to have sex with him, probably telling her it would buy your safety."

The only sound in the room now was of the rain now coming down in sheets and a dull, distant thunder.

"Show me the picture, Beth."

"Nicholas, it won't help or change anything."

"Show me the God damn picture!" he said slowly and softly.

A lone tear rolled out of Beth's left eye as she opened the folder and laid out three pictures. The first showed Paula standing and removing her bra with O'Connor sitting in a chair watching. She had a sad, distant look in her eyes. The second showed her in bed with O'Connor on top of her. Paula's head faced the window and the camera captured the tears rolling down her face. A third showed Paula exiting the hotel, crying and hailing a taxi.

Nicholas stared at the pictures and touched the image of Paula exiting the hotel.

"Excuse me. I don't feel well," Nicholas quickly left the room and almost ran into the bathroom down the hall. For a moment he'd felt like he would throw up, but it subsided as quickly as it came on. He splashed cold water on his face, toweled off and looked in the mirror at the sad, tired image of himself.

"I'm sorry," he said when he re-entered the study.

"Why don't we finish this later?" Beth asked.

"No, I want to do it now," Nicholas insisted.

"You okay Nick?" Michael asked.

"Probably not, but I need to do this now."

Beth resumed, "a lot's speculation. But we think Jack told Paula that if she slept with him you wouldn't be involved. Now – Oh God," she said with a sigh. "There's one more biggie we have to cover. I know Paula's death was ruled accidental; overworked, sleepy, overweight truck. But my guys suspect it may have been something else."

"Are you saying you suspect Paula may have been murdered?"

"Yes."

"And, the 'someone' behind this may have been Jack O'Connor?"

"Yes."

"Well, that's just great, just Goddamn fucking ass great!" Nicholas exploded.

"Nick," Michael said.

"No, let him," Beth said.

"Here I am trying to stay out of prison for doing what I forget – oh yeah, nothing! Just some schmuck trying to do their job and take care of his family. And, here's Jack Fucking O'Connor, breaking a couple dozen federal laws, getting ready to kill a few people in a sham clinical study and to top it off having my wife murdered, but not before he fucks her!"

He was standing now and staring out the window. "Give me one good reason I shouldn't walk into that son-of-a-bitch's office tomorrow and blow his goddamned head off!" Nicholas shouted.

"'Drea," Michael said without hesitation.

"You know what, Michael? That's the right answer; the only answer. Except, I'm not going to be much of a goddamn father to 'Drea when O'Connor's got me doing ten to twenty in Leavenworth!"

"We need a plan," Beth said to Nicholas. "You said you'd come up with a plan. A strategy is what we need. We have to have a plan and do it now or you're right, O'Connor will have you tied up in litigation and on your way to a federal prison."

"We can plan later," Nicholas said, opening one of the floor-ceiling window doors. "I'm going for a walk."

"It's pouring rain Nicholas," Beth said.

"I don't care."

"I'll come with you," Michael said.

Nicholas looked at Michael and started to say no, but said, "Okay." The two brothers went out onto the wraparound porch, through the back yard and onto the old wooded trails surrounding the house.

"Don't mind me. I'll just stay here and call 911 when you get struck by lightning," Beth said to herself.

The two brothers walked in silence. Michael a few steps behind Nicholas. The canopy of the woods softened the fall of the rain to a fine mist. It was after 6:00 PM and they'd been walking for almost an hour when Nicholas stopped and turned around.

"Michael, what the hell are you doing out here in the woods in the rain?"

"Just being here for my big brother."

"Thank you."

"Don't mention it. By the way, you look like a drowned rat in a cashmere sweater."

"Yeah, well you should check out a mirror, pal." They started laughing.

Nicholas sat on a large log from a fallen tree. "God, Michael, you were right. I should have left Marshall a long time ago. I'm out of my fucking league. O'Connor's the Goddamn Devil. I can't compete with evil on that level."

"You're a quick study; you don't have a choice now," Michael said, sitting next to Nicholas on the log.

"If it doesn't work out and I end up in prison or dead, since we know Jack's not above killing whatever gets in his way, will you raise 'Drea, Michael? Like she was?"

"You don't have to ask that, Nicholas. You know I would. But it's not going to come to that. We're going to come up with a plan to kick O'Connor's evil ass back to whatever ring of hell he came from. You hear me!"

"Yeah."

"Michael?"

"Yeah."

"You wet enough?"

"I was wet enough an hour ago."

"Let's go home."

When the two returned to the house, Dorothy and Beth were both furious.

"We thought you'd been eaten by wolves," Dorothy said.

"You mean the Jersey Devil; there are no wolves in New Jersey, Mom," Michael said.

"Whatever. You boys go upstairs and take hot showers and then come down for dinner," she said firmly.

"Yes ma'am," they said in unison.

"Mom, can you make a big pot of coffee? Beth, Michael and I have a lot of work to do after dinner."

"I'll make enough for all four of us. Now scoot you two!"

She turned to Beth and winked. "You just have to know how to handle them."

29

The Battle Begins

Before he went to bed Nicholas opened his laptop and logged into his Marshall email account. He scanned his inbox and saw the message from Arthur.

From: *Kronan, Arthur [MPC]*
Sent: *1:15 PM*
To: *Harding, Nicholas [MPC]*
Subject: *Good and Evil*
"Once to everyman and nation comes the moment to decide. In the strife of Truth with Falsehood; for the good or evil side." ~James Russell Lowell

---

Your moment draws near Nicholas.

Nicholas read the message over and over. How had he become drawn in a battle with evil? And did he have the wherewithal to prevail? Did he have the balls to go one-on-one with people who were willing to kill innocent people to get what they wanted, the likes of Jack O'Connor and Ken Joseph? Could he compete with evil on that scale? And if he could, what did that say about him? Was he any better than them? He didn't have the answers to any of this but he wasn't going to let them do any more harm without a fight.

He hit the Reply key and typed his message.

"The moment is now and I've made my decision. We must talk!"

Before hitting the Send key he highlighted Arthur's name, which was now in the To box, and deleted it. In its place he typed Don Marshall and then hit Send.

"Now we'll see," He said to himself as he logged off and went to bed.

Nicholas left his house at 6:00 AM while everyone else was still in bed. He arrived at Marshall before 6:30 and went to his old office knowing it would be empty. He walked into Karen's outer area and looked into his old office. It should have been a joyous moment, moving into the VP's office suite. But it felt like biting into a beautiful piece of fruit expecting sweetness but receiving a rotten, sour taste.

Furniture marks on the dirty carpet, paper clips, pens on the floor, phone and computer cables everywhere. Nicholas tried to draw up old feelings but nothing came. No feelings, so he turned off the light, closed the door and went down the hall to his new office suite.

The door was locked but Karen, in her usual supremely efficient manner had dropped a key off at his house over the weekend, when she also brought his important mail and reviewed his schedule with him.

He unlocked the door and turned on the lights. Karen had outdone herself. White was still the preferred paint color at Marshall. Karen's outer office, larger than before, was a vibrant peach and Nicholas' much larger space was a warm sand color. Everything looked new: furniture and computers with state of the art flat screen monitors, but not a cold machine-like new of an office building.

Nicholas sat at his desk in his new leather chair. Everything was arranged as he preferred. Pictures were hung; photos of 'Drea were placed where he could see them. A new mahogany conference table and chairs featured built-in videoconferencing capabilities. Karen might have broken a few corporate rules, but the place looked great.

But then Nicholas remembered the bugs. Electronic listening devices were in the room and any feeling of warmth and home left rapidly.

He heard someone enter the outer office and went to see who, half expecting to see Jack or one of his henchmen coming to off him in the early morning hours.

"Karen," he said when he saw her. "You're early."

"I thought I would beat you in, Dr. Harding, to make sure the new offices were in order. Apparently I have failed," she commented with no sign of humor in her voice.

"Well, in beating me in perhaps, but the new office looks great Karen. How'd you get anyone here to use something other than white? I can't wait for Roberta to see this; she'll have a cow!"

"I can be quite persuasive when I need to, Dr. Harding."

"No doubt. Well, since I'm here early I'll just catch up on email. Are the computer systems connected?"

"Yes. Everything checked out late Friday. I had to, ah, kick some butt in IT."

Nicholas looked up at Karen. "I can see that I've been a bad influence on you Karen," he said with a laugh and went into his office.

He logged onto his computer email account. Noticing the volume of messages, especially from his old department, he made a mental note that he'd have to fill that void quickly. No further emails from the ethereal Arthur, but there was one from Don Marshall.

From: Marshall, Donald [MPC]

Sent: 11:45 PM
To: Harding, Nicholas [MPC]
Subject: Good and Evil
Lunch – my house today. Tell no one.

Nicholas deleted the message and checked his calendar. It would be tight, but he could swing it.

"Karen," he said, heading out the door, "I'm going to touch base with Jack, since I haven't seen him in a while. And, I have to swing home for lunch to run some errands." Before he walked out he handed her a folded piece of paper. As he did, he looked at her and held his index finger to his lips.

Karen opened the note after he walked out.

I need to talk to you. It's urgent. Discuss this with no one and destroy the note. If you agree: 7:00 PM, my house. - Nicholas

Karen nodded and placed the note in the shredder under her desk and returned to work.

Nicholas went up to Jack's office past Roberta's desk, it being far too early for her to be in. He knocked, paused and opened Jack's door.

"Well, look what Airlines dragged in," he said with his mouth half-full of bagel and cream cheese. That and half a can of Coke in a coffee mug was Jack's usual breakfast. "So Harding, are you the new VP of Travel or Nonclinical Affairs?"

Nicholas took a seat. Being a foggy morning, there was no sun glare to avoid.

"Is there a problem, Jack? Do I need to clear my travel plans with you?"

O'Connor took a sip of Coke from his coffee mug to wash down the mouthful of bagel. "No, no. It's just I'd think you'd have your hands full moving into Arthur's old job."

"Um, well Jack, the division pretty much runs itself. The only big issue is to backfill my old position. I thought MR-548 needed my attention more last week."

"And, why is that?" he asked with his cold reptilian eyes bearing in on Nicholas. "Are there any problems?"

"Not that I'm aware of, Jack," Nicholas replied, returning the stare. "Anything on your end I should be aware of?"

"No, no. Look Nicholas, it's just being a division head is a big responsibility. That, plus the lead on a major project like MR-548, may be too much for anyone," he wiped remnants of cream cheese from his face and gave Nicholas the fake shark's smile he was famous for. It was the kind of stare which made you want to check to see if your wallet was missing.

"Do you want to pull me off MR-548?"

"No, no, certainly not now when we are about to go into Phase II; don't want to switch horses in mid-stream. Some good Phase II results ought to get Wall Street's panties all wet over us. Heh!   After, we'll see where things stand. How's that, Nick?"

One thing was certain: Jack O'Connor was no mind reader. If he was, at that moment sitting in front of Nicholas, Jack would probably have dialed 911 to get a SWAT team to protect him. But Nicholas had to admire himself. Here he was sitting in front of evil itself, who he'd truly like to see dead, and he gave no outward signs of anything being off.

"Sounds like a plan Jack," Nicholas said, getting up. "Anything else major on the plate?"

"Nope, I think the plate's pretty full, Nick, don't you?"

"Absolutely. I'll see you later, Jack," he said as he left.

O'Connor had already shifted his interest elsewhere.

When the door closed behind Nicholas, Jack picked up his phone. He dialed a special four digit prefix, heard a series of tones for five seconds, and then dialed a private telephone number. The prefix gave him access to a scrambled line.

"Yes?"

"He was just here."

"Who's 'he,' asshole? I'm not a fucking psychic."

"Nick Harding."

"And?"

"Are you sure he doesn't know anything?"

"He suspects generalities; he doesn't know shit."

"You're sure?"

"I've already answered the question. Do you want anything else?"

"No – no, I guess not."

Jack heard the click indicating the call had been terminated, in other words, Jack had been hung up on.

"Fucking bitch!" O'Connor said as he slammed down his receiver.

"Roberta," Nicholas said, seeing her as he exited Jack's office. "You have to drop by my new office and see what Karen's done with the place."

"Oh, I will," she said with a giggle. "You know how nosey I am."

As Nicholas walked down the hall he took some small satisfaction in knowing as soon as Roberta saw what Karen had done with his new office within two weeks she'd have her and Jack's lair re-painted any color but white. One had to take one's little pleasures where one could.

Nicholas headed back down to the third floor and went to Mark Steven's office. He knocked and entered. Mark looked up, saw Nicholas and stood, crossed a closed fist across his chest and said, "Hail Caesar!"

"Very funny. Got a minute?"

"Of course I do; you're my boss now. By the way, have I told you how immensely I've enjoyed working for you?"

"For all of two weeks?"

"Well, it's the thought that counts, Nick. I can still call you Nick, can't I? I can always call you Dr. Harding if you've got your head up your ass, but whatever works for you."

"What do you call O'Connor?"

"Let's not go there."

"Okay. Nick should do fine."

Nicholas took a seat across from Mark's desk. "So, Mark – what's up?"

"With what Nick?"

"Anything. What's the word on the street about me, Jack, MR-548?"

"Well my leader, there are some who wonder if you have the cojones to play in Jack O's sandbox. Do you want the unvarnished truth, Nick?"

"That's why I asked you, Mark."

"Okay. You've got a reputation of being good at what you do and of being a goody-two-shoe. And O'Connor has a reputation of being Satan's big brother. So people wonder how you're going to handle that."

"Arthur did."

"And God bless him. But you're right. Arthur was basically a good guy. Somehow he managed to handle Jack. Me? I'd rather try to roundup cobras before reporting to Jack.

I know I shouldn't say this but the man makes my skin crawl."

"I know what you mean Mark. What about MR-548?"

"Hey, you mean our new savior drug?"

"What do you mean 'savior drug'?"

"The last few days there have been a series of articles in the *New York Times*' Business Section about the potential for 548 to blow away everything else in class and become a mega-blockbuster. Wall Street's starting to notice."

"That must have been what Jack was referring to about Wall Street getting its 'panties wet' over us. That shouldn't have gone out without the team clearing it and I didn't clear shit," Nicholas said.

"I heard Jack cleared it personally. See what I mean, Nick?"

"Yeah, I see."

Nicholas rose to leave and handed Mark a note, then placed a finger to his lips. Mark read, "I need to talk to you. It's urgent. Discuss this with no one and destroy this note. If you agree – 7:00 PM, my house. -Nicholas."

He finished reading, looked up at Nicholas and nodded agreement and gave thumbs up sign.

Nicholas went back to his office.

"Karen, did you find Glen Morgan?"

"He called in sick today, Dr. Harding; said he had a bad case of the flu and may be out several days."

"Alright, I have to go out. I'll be back early this afternoon."

"Very well, Dr. Harding."

Nicholas left and drove towards Don Marshall's estate. He constantly checked his mirrors to see if he was being followed, unsure that he'd recognize if he was. It had started foggy and turned into a dreary cloudy day.

Nicholas pulled into the covered entry-way and was met by a servant who he recognized from one of his two previous visits. He was shown into the house.

"Mr. Marshall is in the library, sir. He asked you join him there."

Nicholas opened the double doors to the library and entered. The servant closed the doors behind him. Don was seated at the massive roll-top desk and was wearing English riding attire; tall boots and jodhpurs, a riding crop on the desk.

"I had planned to go riding this afternoon, Nicholas."

"Sorry to spoil your work," Nicholas said with condescension in his voice.

"Tell me Nicholas, what is on your mind that is so important?"

"Marshall Pharmaceutical."

"My apologies Nicholas, I don't have a Ph.D. like you, I'm afraid you'll have to be more specific, old boy."

"You know, Don, you don't get a degree at West Point and a Harvard M.B.A by being an airhead, so let's cut the crap. I'm tired of playing games and I'm very tired of being played with. I want to know everything you know about what the hell is going on and I want to know now!"

"So, the time has come. Sit down Nicholas. There is much to discuss."

Nicholas sat in a dark maroon leather Chesterfield sofa. He and Don starred at each other, the only sound the faint, rhythmic ticking of a clock. The two men silently sized each other up like feral dogs sniffing territory. Nicholas was the first to speak.

"The emails from Arthur – you sent them?"

"Yes. I wanted to keep you on your toes."

"We can get to the 'how' later. I'm more interested in the 'why'. Are you part of O'Connor's gang of thieves planning to take over Marshall?"

"You can't imagine how odd it is to have a multinational corporation that carries your family name," Don said, exhibiting his habit of shifting thoughts mid-conversation. "If I am," he said, going back to the original conversation, "you're pretty much screwed, aren't you, Nicholas?"

The two were still verbally circling each other. "Is that a yes or no, Don?"

"Of course not. Why would I want any part of that viper pit? Besides, you know what they think of me at Marshall. I'm a joke to them. But I know what they're up to and I intend to stop them."

"Out of the goodness of your heart, I suppose?" Nicholas asked.

"No, my reasons are completely selfish. I want my family's company back. I lost it and it's up to me to get it back."

"So what's with all the subterfuge with the emails from Arthur?"

"I had to be sure you weren't one of them."

Nicholas laughed. "Me? One of Jack O'Connor's boys? That's a laugh."

"Hum, you keep referring to Jack, Nicholas. You think he's running this operation?"

"Of course. It's certainly not that stooge Grant Michner."

"You're right: it's not Michner, but it's not Jack either. I know it looks like he is, but Jack's not calling the shots on this one. You really don't know, do you? Damn!" Don stood up and started pacing around the room. "That's funny!"

"Don't know what, Don? And you might have noticed that I'm not laughing."

"Why do you think I was leery of you? And thought you might be in on it yourself?" he asked. "Your girlfriend Nicholas!"

"What do you mean my 'girlfriend'?" Then after a moment, "Oh, my God – no."

"Oh yes! Your old girlfriend or whatever you two were, Catherine Sullivan."

"Cath's running this whole thing? I don't believe it."

"Believe it, old boy. She's head hog of the whole shooting match; has been from day one."

"I knew Cath was into power, but not something like this. If we take MR-548 into that large scale Phase IIb clinical trial we may kill people. I didn't think she'd go that far."

"Hey, a thirst for power does strange things to people. I knew that Catherine was calling the shots, even though it looks like Jack was. She was just using him and Akoni Konoru at Tanaka too. Since you were in bed with her I figured you were, well, in bed with her all the way and part of this too. My hunch, for what it's worth, is she intended to bring you in, but realized you were too much of a Boy Scout."

"And when they needed a fall guy; hey, who better than your personal Boy Scout? I knew Catherine was no saint, but Jesus!"

"You look like a man who needs a drink," Don said, opening a cabinet built into a wall. "What'll it be?"

"Sherry."

"Coming up."

"How the hell does Catherine control Jack?" Nicholas asked.

"Hey, she's a master at manipulating people."

"Tell me about it. Me, I can understand now. I was just a cat toy for Cath. But how the hell did you get into this mess

Don? Weren't you the Golden Child? Heir to the family fortune? West Point, Harvard? What the hell went wrong?"

"Ah, the question that everyone at Marshall is dying to know. How did old Donny boy screw up so big?"

"Well," said Nicholas, "seeing as how we're currently both in the same snake pit – yes, I'd like to know."

"Your daughter, Andrea, is a lovely child."

"What's 'Drea got to do with this?"

"She's an only-child, yes?"

"Yes."

"Um, be careful Nicholas. Only children tend to be different. Especially when affluent."

"Different how?"

"Too mature, too independent, more so than kids with siblings. I'm an only child, Nicholas."

"No shit," Nicholas said sarcastically.

"From the day I was born, my family, my father, and grandfather had my entire life laid out for me. All I had to do was follow the dance plan. If I'd been a girl it would have been different. But Dad got lucky and got the heir he needed on the first try. No need for more."

"What about the 'heir and a spare' theory of royalty?"

"Mother wasn't up to it. So Dad had to make do with one. I never had a childhood, Nicholas. I had a period of training, the right nannies, the right schools and boarding school, the right foreign trips. I'll show you."

Don pulled a small set of keys from a vest pocket and unlocked a glass paneled cabinet that appeared to be filled with ledgers. He pulled a small bound volume off a shelf and gently carried it over to Nicholas. The thin book was bound in dark blue rich leather.

"My father had this printed at my birth."

They had moved to a small reading table and taken seats. Nicholas opened the book to see listings of schools and accomplishments printed with handwritten notes. It started with Don's birth. Nicholas saw West Point, Harvard and took note of the last two entries:

Assume Chairmanship of Marshall Pharmaceutical.

Produce heir to Marshall family.

"As you can see," Don said as he gently replaced the book on its shelf, "it's incomplete."

"Do you want to complete it?" Nicholas asked.

"I do now. But for a long time I didn't."

"What happened? To throw you off track, I mean?"

"All I lived for as a child was to please my father. I kept my own copy of that damn book and religiously listed accomplishments."

"Why'd he want you to go to West Point?"

"What better way to develop into a disciplined man; a leader of men? He and my grandfather felt it would help me be in a position to lead Marshall in the future. So I went. Hated it with a passion. But by God, I got through it. Because my father wanted it and I wanted what he wanted. Then the required stint in the military. Not my cup of tea, by the by."

He went on. "Grandfather was gone by now. But Dad and the plan were still there. Then Harvard for the M.B.A. and the plan was ready. Dad brought me in as President to his CEO. Then a year later he died suddenly.

"I didn't know what to do. My entire life had been devoted to pleasing one man and he was gone. We controlled 78% of the stock then and had five positions on the Board of Directors. Most thought I wasn't prepared, but we weren't about to put a non-Marshall in as head of the company when

Mr. West Point/Harvard was at the ready. I was named CEO."

After a few moments of silence Nicholas said, "and?"

"And that was eleven years ago. CEO of a major pharmaceutical company at age 38. Everyone expected some brilliant West Point/Harvard strategy. I didn't have a clue what to do. You see, Nicholas, this wasn't part of the plan. It wasn't in the book. I wasn't prepared for my father's death.

"So, I just indulged myself. Started dating and screwing models and starlets. Do you have any idea how many beautiful women you can get when you're rich and powerful?" he asked with a sad tone.

"Can't say that I do."

"All you want. I started spending more and more time chasing women, partying, doing a little grass and coke and less time on Marshall. I looked weak and the wolves could smell blood. Then I announced a one year sabbatical as CEO to go on my around-the-world cruise.

"Well, that was all that was needed to start the feeding frenzy. My assorted family of cousins, aunts, uncles and sycophants dumped Marshall stock by the ton, leaving basically my 40% share. Then the snakes inside went to work. Everyone who'd had a reason to hate me because I was the boss's son and founder's grandson had their chance. The Board cut our family seats from five to one. I was fired as CEO and told not to hurry back from the cruise. All I had left was my seat on the Board and my 40% of the company stock."

"Forty percent of a $12 billion company," Nicholas pointed out. "I hope you don't expect a lot of sympathy."

"None," Don said as he sat on a bench in the large bay window. "Look, I don't expect or deserve pity. I'm still a billionaire. I'm sure the Board thought I'd just run off and piss away the rest of it. But I didn't. I stayed. Put up with all the jokes and waited for my moment. And this is it, Nicholas."

"Moment for what?" Nicholas asked, suspecting he knew the answer.

"For the past ten years, besides living well, I've studied the global pharmaceutical industry. Its trends and new technologies. I understand it. I've basically done nothing but study. So I'll be ready to lead Marshall when the moment comes. And it's come."

"Catherine and Jack have gone too far. In trying to gain control of Marshall in this manner, they put themselves at risk to lose what they have. And, I intend to capitalize on that."

"By controlling interest when they bottom out the stock with the MR-548 trials?" Nicholas asked.

"I'll be honest, Nicholas. I thought about it. That's certainly one way to do it. But no, that would harm Marshall Pharmaceutical and my family name, not to mention innocent people. I won't do that. And I won't let them do that either. I won't sit back and let them do that to Marshall Pharmaceutical; to my father's and grandfather's company. Somehow, hopefully with your help, I'll stop them. Expose them for what they are and throw them out. Then, I'll be in a position to lead Marshall."

"You want to finish your father's plan?"

"No Nicholas. It's my plan now. But yes, I intend to finish it."

"So, you're proposing that we work together?" Nicholas asked.

"Yes."

"Why?"

"Because, Nicholas, we need each other. We can't pull this off alone."

"Do you have a plan, Don?"

"To combine our forces. I know you have some contacts you trust, as do I." Don stood and walked over to Nicholas. Standing over Nicholas, he extended his hand, "partners?"

Nicholas stood, looked into Don's eyes and shook his extended hand. "Partners. I have some people I trust coming to my house tonight."

"Good. Come here instead. I'll have some of my people here. We don't have much time."

"Seven thirty?"

"Fine."

"Don," Nicholas said, looking out the bay window at the expanse of Marshall Estate. "What are the worst and best case scenarios in your mind?"

"Hum, worst: we can't stop the Phase II trial. People are hurt or killed. Marshall stock dives, the public loses confidence in us. You're blamed and indicted. I'd try to buy up as much of the stock as I could, but I'd be competing with Catherine and Jack's gang. I'd help you with your defense, but it would be a long, hard fight. Even if you stayed out of jail, you'd be debarred by FDA. Your career in the pharmaceutical industry would be over."

"I don't mean to sound selfish here, but it sounds like I have a little more at stake in that scenario," Nicholas said.

"No doubt you do. Best case: we stop the trial and expose Catherine, Jack et al. They're all out of Marshall and in prison. You're never indicted, so your reputation is intact. I gain majority control, get the CEO position, you have your choice of positions in Marshall and we all live happily ever after. Which do you prefer?"

"Guess I'll see you tonight at seven-thirty. I'll let myself out."

"Tonight, Nicholas."

On the way back to the lab, Nicholas stopped at a Quick Chek to make a call from a pay phone.

"Hello."

"It's Nicholas Harding. We need to talk tomorrow."

"The hotel again?"

"No, you can be followed. Is there somewhere else completely secure?"

"I'll call in sick tomorrow. Come to my house."

"I'll take the 8:00 AM flight. I should be there by 10:00. Give me your address and directions."

"You sound tense."

"I am. I'll see you tomorrow."

Nicholas then called Beth, brought her up to speed and asked her to join him at Don's tonight and to contact Michael, so he'd be there as well. He hung up then went back to Marshall where he was able to covertly convey the information to Karen and Mark to meet him at Don's at 7:30.

Restless in his office, he logged into email. A message from Catherine:

From:	Sullivan, Catherine [MPC]
Sent:	3:25 AM
To:	Harding, Nicholas [MPC]
Subject:	The meeting

Sorry our meeting broke off early. Thought it went well. Must reconvene to resume where we left off. We have unfinished business.

He opted not to reply and spent the afternoon clearing email and going through the motions of day-to-day business activities. Nicholas left the office early. He'd contacted Beth and Michael and they'd agreed to meet him at Don's. He'd then called Kerry and asked if she could meet him someplace where they could talk.

"I suppose. It's kind of slow here today. This sounds serious."

"It is."

"Okay, meet me at The Pub in Mendham. It won't be crowded this time of day."

"Okay. About half an hour?"

"See you there."

The Mendham Pub was only about a fifteen-minute drive from Morristown, deep in the Northern New Jersey wealth belt. Old money mixed with new. The Old resenting the New and the self-centered New oblivious to all. Nicholas arrived and turned his car over to the parking valet. He was about to ask the hostess if Kerry was there when he saw her sitting in a booth.

"Hey, thanks for coming with such short notice," then sat across from her.

"You said it was important; urgent. That certainly got my attention."

A waitress came over to ask for orders.

"Mineral water," said Kerry.

"Diet coke for me," then when the waitress left, "my call asking you to meet me here is something else entirely. I need your help."

"Is this about that rain-check?"

"Sort of."

"What is it Nicholas? I'm confused."

"I'm sorry. I need you to come with me someplace tonight."

"I'm listening," she said. "Where?"

"Don Marshall's house."

"Don Marshall, the eccentric billionaire?"

"Yes."

"Hum, is this a date?"

"It's a long story, Kerry."

Over diet cokes and mineral water and hot snacks, Nicholas told his story of Marshall Pharmaceutical intrigue. The detective in Kerry quickly kicked into overdrive, as he'd hoped it would, and she peppered him with questions.

"Who else will be at Don's on your side?"

"Karen Stemmer, my secretary, Mark Stevens, Beth my attorney and Michael."

"You trust them all?"

"Yes."

"Nicholas, why didn't you tell me any of this before?"

"This has all come about pretty quickly," he answered.

"Besides, I didn't know how much to trust you until recently."

"I don't recall any mention of this when I questioned you after Arthur's death. Did you withhold evidence?" she asked clearly and slowly.

"That's part of my problem Kerry," he replied. "I don't have any evidence. It's mostly supposition. Evidence is what I need."

"Hum," she said, tapping the straw from her mineral water against her lower lip. "I may have to interrogate you again."

"Really?"

"Yes. I think I was much too easy on you before."

"You were?"

"Um huh. I can see I'm going to have to be much firmer with you – more probing," she said with a wicked smile.

"I'm looking forward to it."

"So am I."

"So Nick, am I attending this evening as your cop-friend or something else?"

"As someone I trust," he said looking at his watch. "We need to get going."

Nicholas drove to Don's. Kerry turned towards Nick and said, "I've been trying to think about how I can help. Ken Joseph," she said.

Not seeing the link, Nicholas asked, "what about him?"

"Every conspiracy has a weak link. Ken Joseph could be theirs," she said. "He was thrown off the force before I got there, but I've heard a few rumors. He's not very bright and he's weak. We could work this to our advantage."

"How?"

"If he thinks he's about to be squeezed out he may break and turn on the rest. We may be able to manipulate him."

"Maybe, but he could be dangerous. I mean he did beat a prisoner to death and God knows what he's done for O'Connor. Be careful."

"I can take care of myself." She said with a smile.

The sun was starting to go down as they drove onto the Marshall Estate. Nicholas and Kerry had decided to arrive early to talk to Don.

"Detective Markus, my pleasure," Don said upon being introduced to Kerry.

Nicholas brought Don up to speed on his list of attendees. "Who're you bringing to the party?"

"Stephen Bernard – my attorney and Thomas Sinclair – my financial advisor."

"Jesus, you're not pulling any punches," said Kerry. "Or am I mistaken? Stephen Bernard, the former Secretary of Defense and Thomas Sinclair, former Secretary of the Treasury?"

"And, both close friends of my father, yes," replied Don. "They're in the sitting room and I've already briefed them."

Karen and Mark arrived at about the same time as Beth and Michael. Don and Nicholas made introductions all around. The group of nine met in a large sitting room with a wall of windows overlooking a well-lit, well-kept garden.

Nicholas observed, as Beth, dressed all in flowing white, went up to Stephen Bernard, a tall, distinguished looking gentleman. He looked slightly younger than the 65 years that Nicholas, the consummate news junky, knew his age to be.

"Stephen, you old dog!" she said. "Give me a hug, honey," to Nicholas' surprise the reserved Bernard smiled, eyes lit up and gave Beth a warm hug.

When Nicholas was able to pull Beth aside he asked incredulously. "You know Stephen Bernard?"

"You'd be surprised at whom and what I know, sweetie," she said.

"May I have everyone's attention please?" Don said, trying to get the group to quiet down.

"Excuse me, Don," Beth interrupted. Nicholas noticed that she was heavily pouring on the Southern charm. "I don't mean to be impolite, but I do have a question about ah-security or, more specifically, electronic surveillance."

"Ah, yes of course. Not to worry, Beth," he replied. "At your suggestion I had the house swept earlier today and," he said beaming, "I had this room made secure."

Nicholas and Kerry both stared at Beth. Nicholas whispered to Beth, "you're starting to frighten me."

Don resumed his talk, "I'd like to thank all of you for coming on such short notice. Such a response reflects, I think, the seriousness of the cause. I submit, ladies and gentlemen, that there is a war. In every war, there is good and evil. I leave it for others to decide whether we are good. But we are most assuredly not evil – but we know the face of evil. And it is our charge to triumph over this evil.

"The two of us in this room," he went on, "with the greatest stake in this war are myself and my friend Nicholas. My stake is my family name, reputation and fortune. Nicholas' stake is his name, reputation, career, family and possibly freedom. I submit that his is the greater need. But I am prepared to stand and fight side by side with him to the end. And I ask you all to join us in this fight. Nicholas," Don said with a flourish, "an overview for our colleagues in arms, if you please."

Don sat next to Michael, who whispered, "moving."

"Four years at West Point; it damn well better be," he whispered in reply with a wink.

Kerry squeezed Nicholas' arm before he stood and started, "thank you Don. And I also want to thank all of you for coming here. About a year ago Marshall Pharmaceutical signed a co-development licensing and acquisition deal with Tanaka Pharmaceutical in Japan. They get the rights to the drug in Asia and we get the Americas, Europe and the rest of the world. The rights are to MR-548, a potent antiviral agent."

Nicholas made a point of walking around the room and making eye contact with each person as he spoke.

"Shortly after the deal was signed Yoshi Mikasi, Chairman of Tanaka was murdered in what appeared to be a mugging in New York. Akoni Kororu succeeded him. I'm the project leader for MR-548 at Marshall and my counterpart at Tanaka is Asori Nomura. Asori and I have reason to believe that there are serious problems with MR-548."

He took a deep breath, looked at Kerry and continued. "About a month ago my boss at Marshall, Dr. Arthur Kronan, committed suicide. Shortly after, I started receiving cryptic email messages leading me to look into certain activities at Marshall."

"And the source of these messages, Nicholas?" Stephen Bernard queried in his deep and mellow lawyerly baritone voice.

"I," Don jumped in, "was the source Stephen; Unfortunately, I initially misled Nicholas to test his loyalties. But I supplied him with clues."

"Which led to my involvement as Nicholas' attorney," Beth volunteered.

"I wondered what brought a Southern belle like you this far north," Stephen said to Beth.

Beth replied with a wink to Stephen. "I'm a dear friend of Nicholas' mother. And based on my investigations, I can assure you there's evil afoot. But you go on, son, and tell us the story." She was in a Southern-charm overdrive.

"Well, our working hypothesis is that a small group in Marshall and Tanaka has a plan to create a crisis of confidence in Marshall that will crash the stock price, allowing them to buy up controlling interest."

At the mention of the plan to crash the stock price the internal antenna of Thomas Sinclair, former Secretary of the Treasury and current Wall Street God, perked up. "And just how does this cabal plan to crash the stock of a $12 billion company?"

"Failure of the Phase II clinical trials with MR-548," Nicholas answered.

Sinclair now bore in on Nicholas with a fierce intensity. "Well, I'm no expert in drug development like you son, but I do know one failed drug in development isn't going to cause a blip, much less a crash in the stock of a company the size of Marshall."

Don started to intervene but Nicholas, not wanting to back down from Sinclair's challenge broke in, "you're absolutely right, Secretary Sinclair," he replied, knowing how Sinclair preferred to be addressed. "But what if we kill or maim a third of the subjects in an 800 patient trial?"

Sinclair turned ashen. "Good Lord, man. How can that be? There must be safe guards in place."

"He's right, Nicholas," Mark added. "What about all the nonclinical animal work? The stuff we do and the Phase I and early Phase II clinical data? By the time you get to a Phase IIb 800 patient trial the safety's been pretty well established, right?"

"Supposedly, but in this case all the nonclinical work, the animal testing, was done by Tanaka. The Phase I and early Phase II work was also done by Tanaka. The first time Marshall does anything with this drug is the 800 patient Phase IIb trials."

"And what makes you suspect these may be a problem with this Phase IIb trial?" asked Stephen Bernard.

"As I mentioned, all the early development work was done by Tanaka."

"But you must have access to all their data?" challenged Sinclair.

"Yes. As the team leader I have an electronic link to the Tanaka database. But the contract forbids Marshall to conduct any test prior to the Phase II trial or to manufacture any material here. When I became suspicious, I asked one of my best scientists to review the Tanaka database."

"Glen Morgan?" Karen asked.

"Yes, Glen. He's a tad eccentric," Nicholas added for benefit of the others, "but he's brilliant. And I knew if there was anything to be found, he'd find it."

Michael whispered to Beth, "how do you think he's doing? This is a tough bunch."

"He's holding his own. They're pushing, but he's standing up to them. They respect him."

"What did Mr. Glen Morgan find?" Sinclair asked in his imposing Yankee Blue Blood tone.

"He found a perfect drug, sir," Nicholas replied.

"And, the problem with that is what, Dr. Harding?" Sinclair pushed back, as if in a cross-examination role.

Kerry was taking a decided dislike to Thomas Sinclair based on his accusatory tone with Nicholas. Beth saw her glaring at Sinclair and patted her hand. "It's okay; he knows what he's doing."

"Sinclair or Nicholas?" she asked.

"Both."

"The problem, Secretary Sinclair, is that there's no such thing," Nicholas responded. "Will you allow me to digress a bit on how drugs are developed?"

Sinclair nodded agreement.

"You see, drugs are designed to have a specific effect – the pharmacological effect. For example, a drug may bind to a specific receptor in the brain and have an effect on depression or block an enzyme needed for bacterial cell wall integrity and act as an antibacterial. But the science is imperfect and along with the desired pharmacological effects come undesired pharmacological effects. These are called toxicities or side effects. The goal is to have as wide a margin as possible between the dose that produces the desired effects and the dose that produces the toxic effects. If that margin is too narrow or overlaps you don't have a drug.

"And, believe me there are thousands of potent drugs with great desired therapeutic effects, but they're toxic, sitting on shelves in drug companies never to see the light of day because of unacceptable side effects."

"And if this MR-548 looks perfect, then what?" asked Bernard.

"Then that raises a flag sir. When Glen reviewed the data sent from Tanaka, he said it was text book clean. No significant toxicities picked up in animal studies and a huge margin between the estimated clinical dose and high doses where some minor toxicity was observed. It just looked too good. Too perfect."

"Maybe it's a fluke and it is perfect," asserted Sinclair.

"We don't think so, sir. There are powerful new computer tools such as predictive computational toxicology and pharmacokinetic modeling programs. These are massive databases taken from thousands of real drugs. Based upon what the system knows about the molecular structure and chemical properties of a compound and the toxicology/pharmacokinetic profile, it can predict with some degree of accuracy the toxicology/pharmacokinetic profile of an unknown compound with just the chemical structure. These tools are new and unproven, but very promising. We're evaluating some of these tools in my division at Marshall. In fact, that's Glen's primary role: new technology evaluation. Glen ran MR-548 through some of the simulation models," Nicholas stopped to pour a glass of water.

Sinclair raised his thin frame from his chair. "Here, let me do that. Don't tease me, son. I want to know what the hell happened," he said with a wink.

"Thank you sir."

"And you can cut the 'sir' and 'Mr. Secretary' crap," Stephen Bernard piped in. "I think we're all on a first name basis at this point. And if we're wrong, we damn well will be when some of us are sharing a jail cell."

That broke the ice and the group laughed and began to bond as a team with a common goal.

"Go on, Nicholas."

"As I said, these tools are experimental and you don't expect a 1:1 correlation between the computer predictions and your animal and human data. But you do expect some overlap. In this case there was none." Nicholas rose and started to pace the room. He knew that Karen, Mark, Kerry, Michael and Beth trusted him and believed in him, but he had to convince Bernard and Sinclair as they were the muscle he desperately needed.

"The Tanaka data showed a clean drug with few toxicities and a huge margin of safety. The computer predictions show an overlap between the effective dose and the toxic dose and a significant potential for hepatic and nephrotoxicity – that's liver and kidney damage. The simulations show if we go into Phase II trials at the doses we're planning to use, some patients will go into complete liver and kidney failure, requiring transplants and some may die."

Don now spoke up and turned to Sinclair, "and that, my friend, is how you crash the stock of a $12 billion company."

"But you still have no proof. An experimental computer program isn't proof," Bernard stated while playing with a leather cigar case.

"You're right, it's not," Nicholas agreed. "I pointed out earlier according to the contract we can't even manufacture MR-548 here to test. But Glen's very resourceful. He's getting a friend of his in the chemical synthesis group, another renegade geek type, to make a small batch that we can test in rats and dogs. If the simulations are anywhere near correct, that will be the proof."

"When?" Michael asked.

"Glen's been out since you left for London last week, Dr. Harding. He says he has the flu," said Karen.

"I'll track him down later this week. But there's more."

Bernard turned to Don and said, "you said this was good, but damn! I didn't expect anything like this!"

Nicholas went on. "I met with Asori Nomura last week. He's the MR-548 Project Lead for Tanaka; my counterpart. By the way the second part of my hypothesis is when the shit hits the fan after the Phase II study, yours truly gets the blame. I figured maybe there's a Tanaka fall guy too. Asori suspects something rotten at Tanaka and figures he's it there.

"He referred to MR-548 as a 'phantom' drug. Tanaka's official party line is they stopped their own development of MR-548 to focus on a better backup. But Asori says they never started development on MR-548 and he knows of no one who actually worked on the project."

"So what we're saying here," Beth concluded, "is Tanaka has this drug which they know to be toxic as hell and sold it to Marshall with a fictional database that's almost perfect. But why? What the hell's in it for them?"

"Probably a piece of Marshall," Don added. "A minority piece, but significant. The Japanese pharmaceutical houses have been unable to break into the U.S. hold on the industry. This would give Tanaka a foot up on their Japanese pharmaceutical competitors if they took a strong position in a major U.S. company. It would certainly be a first."

"And they want this bad enough to kill innocent Americans, Nicholas?" Mark asked.

"The 'they' in Tanaka is probably a small rogue group, just like here, Mark," Nicholas answered.

"And, the 'they' here are?"

Beth answered. "At this time we suspect 'they' include Grant Michner, President and CEO; Jack O'Connor, VP R&D; Catherine Sullivan, Executive VP European Sales and Marketing; Ken Joseph, VP Security; and Gary Michael VP Legal. We also think Arthur Kronan was involved."

"Jesus Christ, Don," Sinclair said as he too began to pace the room. "That's a who's who of the Marshall Executive team. If you're right, that's a frightening thought. If you're wrong, the slander suites will be un-ending."

The two former Cabinet members, men who probably did or still considered themselves of U.S. presidential timber, now paced the room like caged cats. All cylinders were firing and they were now fully engaged.

"Nicholas," Bernard rolled off his tongue. "You mentioned you were going to track down this Glen fellow later this week. Shouldn't you do that sooner rather than later since this could be hard evidence?"

"I agree that it's important sir -Stephen," he corrected himself.

"Just Stephen, son. I haven't been knighted." He added after a pause, "yet."

Nicholas continued, "but there's another complication."

"That's it, Don," Sinclair said. "I need a drink. Bar break. Take 20."

Don looked helpless to do anything as Sinclair and Bernard moved to the bar.

Beth, Kerry, Michael, Mark and Karen surrounded Nicholas like a prize fighter between rounds. "Can I get you anything, Dr. Harding?" Karen asked.

"Just more mineral water. Thanks Karen."

"You're doing great, bro," Michael added.

"You're swaying Bernard and Sinclair to your side," Beth added.

"I guess when Don calls in the artillery he goes right for the big siege guns," Nicholas said.

"You're going to need them in this pissing match, honey," Beth purred in that sweet Southern accent that gave off a strange sensation when she used vulgar language.

"Thanks guys," Nicholas said to the group. "It means a lot to me that you're here."

"You are most welcome Dr. Harding," Karen said with a smile, handing him his drink.

The group broke up as everyone headed to the bar, leaving Nicholas and Kerry.

"This is your chance to run for the hills," he said.

She took his hand. "I'm not going anywhere. We haven't even had a date yet."

"So Nicholas," Bernard's voice boomed from where he was playing bartender. "You were about to unravel yet another layer of the onion. Pray, proceed."

"The feds," Nicholas answered. "Even before Arthur died, the way I got tipped off there was something rotten in Denmark was about six or seven weeks ago when I get home and there was an FDA field investigator and deputy U.S. Marshal in my living room."

Sinclair added, "and I used to think scientists were all eggheads who lived boring lives. Obviously, I was wrong."

"Beverly Coston, the FDA investigator, told me of an ongoing investigation into something at Marshall. They smell something rotten with the Marshall-Tanaka connection, but haven't figured out what yet. They suspect Jack O'Connor as our head bad guy, and yours truly she referred to as 'the official patsy poster boy'.

"Gift wrapped with forged memos, reports, and emails, she thinks I'll be swimming upstream trying to stay out of a federal penitentiary."

"She's right," Beth added. "If this Phase II study goes as bad as we think, the public, fed by a rabid press, will want blood and O'Connor and all will serve you up as a sacrificial lamb."

"That helps, coming from my own lawyer," Nicholas said. He continued. "The feds think Yoshi Mikasi's death was part of this."

"And Dr. Kronan?" Kerry asked.

"What's the police finding?" Don asked.

"Death by self-inflicted gunshot; suicide," replied Kerry.

"The feds agree," Nicholas said.

"But we have an addendum to that theory," Beth added.

"I'd be interested in hearing that," Kerry said to Beth with an edge to her voice.

Beth replied, "suicide under coercion. We think O'Connor or someone had some leverage over Arthur and that's why he killed himself."

"So we're talking about people who've already killed and are planning to do so again on a larger scale," Bernard stated slowly and clearly for everyone to absorb.

"There's more," Nicholas said. "The U.S. Marshal I mentioned earlier: Barry Keenan. We suspect he's on the take and controlled by O'Connor.

"I'm meeting with Coston tomorrow in D.C. to see what she has new, and then I'll find Glen."

"*We're* meeting with Agent Coston," Beth added. "I don't want you meeting with any feds without me present. We're nearing the end game and things may get rough."

"I can call the Attorney General," Bernard added.

"No, it's too soon," said Sinclair.

"I agree; it's too early," Nicholas added. "Like you said before, circumstantial and supposition. We need evidence."

"I suppose you're right," Bernard sighed. "I just want to shut these people down. You've woven a powerful tale, Nicholas. I can't speak for my colleague, but you can consider me an ally in your fight."

Sinclair finally smiled. "I'll allow you to speak for me this once Thomas. You can count us both in. But we must be cautious. Our enemy is bold and fierce."

"I propose we meet here in one week to see where we stand," Don said. "If anything urgent comes up funnel it through me and I'll make sure the appropriate parties receive the information."

"Agreed," Nicholas replied. "Thank you, all of you."

The group began to break up. Bernard and Sinclair took their limos home, both living in wealthy northern New Jersey estates. Mark and Karen left and Beth left with Michael, reminding Nicholas of their early flight to D.C. tomorrow. That left Nicholas, Don and Kerry.

"I'll wait in another room and leave you two alone," said Kerry

"No, stay," Nicholas said, reaching out to her.

Don poured three small brandies and toasted. "Here's to the final battle."

"From what I saw tonight with Bernard and Sinclair, your style is more Grant than McClellan," Nicholas said. "Good."

"Four years of West Point wasn't wasted. Partner?" Don asked, extending his hand.

"Do I have a choice?"

"Not now."

"Partner," Nicholas said as the two men shook hands.

It was after 10:30 as Nicholas and Kerry drove to her house. "I'm sorry," Nicholas said.

"For what?"

"I should have told you about suspecting that Arthur's suicide was caused by O'Connor."

"Yes, you should have. But thank you for letting me in, Nicholas," she reached over to touch his hand.

As they drove into her driveway she asked, "Will you come in just for a little while?"

"Just a little while," he smiled.

He sat on her sofa, suddenly tired. She returned with a glass of mineral water.

"Are you afraid, Nicholas? God that was a stupid question."

"No it wasn't. Sort of. I'm mostly afraid of going to jail and losing 'Drea. But I'm not afraid of them. Right now my primary feeling is hatred and revenge. I want to hurt them, Kerry. I guess that makes me like them."

"No. Is there more you haven't told me?"

"Yes."

"Okay, when you're ready I'm here."

"Thanks Kerry. I have an early flight. I should go."

She watched him get in his car and drive off. The cop and woman in her feeling very protective of Nicholas. She wanted a relationship with a man, but wasn't sure if the time was right or if Nicholas was the right man. But realized some things were out of her control.

She'd also begun to think of how she could rattle Ken Joseph. No plan was perfect. Bad guys with big plans always made mistakes. But bad guys with the shakes made big mistakes. And she was about to give ex-cop, current executive thug, Ken Joseph a major case of the shakes.

"What the hell time is it?" Beth asked as Nicholas pushed a large cup of coffee under her nose.

"It's 5:30 and before you ask, our flight leaves at 8:00, which means we have to be at the airport by 7:00 and leave here by 6:00. Any questions?"

"Nicholas, honey," she purred with that sweet Southern accent. "If our plane leaves at 8:00, why the hell do we have to be there at 7:00?"

"Hey," said Dorothy. "I won't have that kind of language in my kitchen."

"What the he, ah, heck are you doing up at this God awful hour?" Beth asked.

"Where else would I be at 5:30?"

"In bed where all good souls are this time of day. You're all insane you know. And you," she said, pointing at Nicholas, "didn't answer my question."

"I don't like to rush, Beth."

"Well, I do."

"Let me guess, you're one of those people – Paula was one – who likes to get to the airport just before the plane's front wheels leave the ground?"

"You got it, pal."

"Well tough. You're traveling with me today. Perk up."

"So where are we meeting this FDA agent?"

"Her house."

"You trust her?"

"Mostly."

"You screwing her?"

"What is it with you? Why do you ask me that about every woman I know?"

"I'm curious too," Dorothy chimed in.

"Oh God!" Nicholas exclaimed.

"First off, as your attorney I need to ascertain your relationship with all the key parties.

"And second off, I'm a horny old broad who's got to get her kicks somehow!" Beth and Dorothy cracked up and high-fived each other.

"You know, maybe prison isn't so bad after all."

"By the way, Dr. Harding, as I recall this was a temporary gig until you found more competent counsel. Yeah, I know you didn't think much of this old bird at first, did you?" Beth asked with a twinkle in her eye.

"Beth," Nicholas said, looking at her and Dorothy. "I like my competent counsel – old bird that she is – just fine. Consider it a full time gig."

"Hot damn, then. Let's go."

"Speaking of birds of a younger variety," Beth started. "You and detective Markus seem to have hit it off."

"We're just friends. I'm kind of occupied right now, trying to keep out of prison and all.

"Okay our car's here; let's go. You get me out of this mess Beth and the first thing I'm going to do is find you a man. I pity him already."

"Deal! We are flying first class aren't we?"

"In your dreams."

They kept up the banter as they left the house. Dorothy felt confident that her son was in good hands.

30

Beth and Beverly

Nicholas and Beth went directly to the United Airlines President's Club lounge to check in. Nicholas traveled enough to belong to the club. Having quickly checked in, they sat in a secluded corner over glasses of orange juice.

Beth cleared her throat and said, "here's something you may not want to hear."

"That's always a reassuring opening statement from your lawyer."

"Remember, I told you the feds leave a trail of paper and electronic records?"

"Um huh."

"We know they've requested to open an investigation of you as it relates to the Marshall investigation. A next step could be nothing or it could be to move towards grand jury indictment."

"Indictment me? For what? I haven't done any God damn thing!" he said.

"We know that, but the feds don't."

"Which I don't quite understand Beth. Everything we've uncovered, why the hell couldn't the Feds get the same information?"

"They're not looking in the same places. But that's where I'm leading, sort of."

"I suppose this is the part I'm not going to want to hear, so let's hear it Beth."

"Okay, maybe, just maybe, we should think about going to the feds and negotiating an immunity deal."

After several moments of silence, Nicholas asked, "immunity from what?"

"From whatever the hell Jack O'Connor and friends are planning to shove up your ass, Nicholas! I know you haven't done anything wrong and I know you're thinking an immunity deal implies that you have. But Nicholas, I'm your lawyer and I have to make you aware of all our options; and that's one. It's just one card in the deck and we may have to play it at some point."

"Not now Beth, and you can consider me fully informed on that option, okay?"

"Fair enough."

At Reagan National airport, Nicholas and Beth were picked up by a limo service Beth called from the plane. They were picked up in a non-descript sedan with darkened rear windows, as she'd instructed. The car looked like any of dozens coming or going from Reagan at any time of the day. The driver drove into the basement parking garage of Beverly Coston's apartment building and used the electronic key access card that she'd sent to Nicholas. Unless they were being closely followed, it was unlikely anyone knew they were here.

Instructing the driver to wait, they took the elevator from the parking garage to the eighth floor of the non-distinct apartment building. The apartment was in a part of the district struggling to maintain an upper middle-class enclave against the rapidly expanding ghetto.

Nicholas rang the bell to Beverly's apartment. When she opened the door he quickly held up a large handwritten sign that said, "Don't say a word. We have to check for bugs!"

Beverly eyed Nicholas and then Beth warily, but stepped aside to allow them in. Beth quickly opened a compartment of her bag and removed what looked like a mid-sized hand held calculator. She quickly, but thoroughly, swept it past windows, electronic and phone sockets, telephones and electrical devices. A couple of times a red light panel lit up. Beth would point to an object and Nicholas would place a red sticky on it.

Nicholas wrote another note to Beverly, who was seated on a loveseat and not believing the whole scene.

"There are electronic listening devices in those items. Now we have to neutralize them."

They watched as Beth removed another device that looked like a miniature umbrella, stood it on a coffee table in the center of the room and set a timer to 30 seconds. She then scurried the three of them out into the hall. After a minute they reentered the apartment and Beth started the sweeping process again. After about fifteen minutes, she put most of the equipment away, but left one device on the table.

"Okay, we're clean."

"What the hell's going on and who the hell are you, lady? James Bond's sister?"

Nicholas made the introductions. "Beverly Coston, FDA investigator. Beth Cowlings, my attorney."

"You didn't say anything about your lawyer coming."

"My insistence, Ms Coston. My client's not going to talk to federal agents without counsel present."

"And the entire spook stuff?"

"I did an electronic sweep, looking for electronic receivers or broadcasters," Beth answered. "You can see from the red stickies that I found three. One in the phone, in the DVR and on the window. It captures vibrations of the glass produced by voices and broadcasts them."

"And that thing you set off?"

"A micro-EMR blast."

"Come again?" Beverly asked, now completely confused.

"EMR: electromagnetic radiation."

"Isn't that what you get with a nuclear blast?"

"Yep, but the device I used emits a micro-EMR pulse. It burns out electromagnetic transmitters. Anyone listening live now has a couple of ruptured ear drums."

"Just what kind of lawyer are you lady?"

"The kind you don't want to fuck with and who doesn't take kindly to having her client fucked with. Now, we don't have a lot of time. Whoever planted these will realize something's up. So who do you think would want to bug your home? By the way, your car, office and all phones are probably hot also."

"I don't know. I'm drawing a blank on who'd want to bug me," she answered, getting up and walking around her living room.

Beth following Beverly with her gaze, taking in her surroundings and noticed that although well lit, almost everything in the room was black or white; almost no color. "Who's your decorator, Gomez Adams?"

"Funny. You're real talented. I just moved in a few months ago and haven't had time to decorate. I've been busy trying to figure out whether your client is a felon."

"Barry Keenan," Nicholas interjected.

"What about Barry?" asked Coston.

"He bugged your apartment," Nicholas replied.

"You think, know or imagined?"

"We suspect that Barry bugged your apartment."

"I consider Barry a Neanderthal prick, but why would he want to bug my apartment? He's barely involved with this case anyway."

"You mean his motive?" Nicholas asked, looking at the knickknacks on Coston's shelves.

"Yes."

"You collect old medical devices? Quite a collection. Which of your parents was a physician?"

"My mother. You two are freaking me out. How the hell did you know that?"

"The initials R.C. on some of the instruments."

"Rebecca; she was an ob-gyn. And don't change the subject Dr. Harding."

"Oh, yes – why would Keenan bug your apartment? That's easy. He's on Jack O'Connor's payroll. He was paid to bug your apartment and probably keep tabs on the investigation and to guide it where O'Connor wants it go to."

"Dr. Harding, I don't care anymore for Barry Keenan than you do, but accusing a federal officer of taking bribes, planting illegal bugs and interfering with a federal investigation is not something you want to do lightly or you're going to find yourself in serious trouble."

"You know Agent Coston, even though we personally haven't hit it off, you seem to be an intelligent, competent woman. But I'm getting pretty sick of people telling me what I can and can't do while O'Connor and his gang, which includes one of your own, are busy trying to shove a telephone pole up my butt. So, here's the deal," Nicholas pulled one of his business cards from his pocket and wrote Don Marshall's address on it.

"Be at this address one week from yesterday at 7:00 PM. Come alone and come prepared to share all the information you have on the investigation."

"And you'll bring?"

"Evidence that will help you blow this investigation wide open and get the bad guys." Beth shot Nicholas a sharp glance that expressed 'What the hell are you doing?'.

"Real evidence?"

"Real evidence," Nicholas stood up preparing to leave. "Anything else, Counselor?"

"Nope. You've said it all," she said, moving towards the door.

Nicholas turned to face Beverly. "If you're there, we can work together to end this. If you're not, we won't be meeting again and I'll consider you my enemy."

"And, Barry?" she asked.

"We've told you what we know. You're on your own. Good bye, Beverly," he reached over to retrieve the small device Beth had placed on the table, and then said, "here, you keep it, you may need it." Then they left.

In the elevator, Beth hit the stop button and whirled to face him, furious. "I'm going to risk the elevator being clean. And what the hell was that? Evidence? Did I miss something or do you not have any fucking evidence?"

"Nope, so I guess that means we're going to be busy for the next week, doesn't it?"

"Look Nicholas, honey, I know how you feel."

"No, you do not!" he shouted and slammed his hand against the elevator wall, taking Beth by surprise. "I'm hanging on by a thread here Beth! My marriage was going down the drain, my wife died, maybe was killed, I'm trying to be a decent father to 'Drea, compete in that corporate snake pit, and in my spare time stay the hell out of prison. I am not okay and you don't have a fucking clue how I feel!"

Beth didn't back down one inch. She looked at her watch. "Thirty seconds," she said.

"What?"

"Thirty seconds of pitiful whining and that's all you get. You're right, I don't know how you feel. I'm your Goddamn lawyer, not your fucking shrink. It's not my job to know how you feel. It is my job to know what kind of fucking shit you're in and to help you get out of it. And that's exactly what I intend to do to the absolute best of my ability. And to do that you can't pull any more surprises like this evidence thing without consulting me. Do you understand?"

Nicholas leaned back, his head against the wall, looking up. "I'm tired, Beth. I don't know if I can do this. I feel like the fox in a fox hunt and the hounds are getting close."

"We can do it Nicholas! You're not alone; lean on us. You don't have to be strong all the time. And while your lawyer doesn't give a fuck how you feel, your friend does. So come here and give her a big hug, honey," she said, reaching out to him.

The two friends stood in the elevator hugging.

"You're a piece of work Beth."

"I'll assume that's a compliment, and it takes one to know one, by the way. Let's go home. We've got a lot of work to do in a week."

Beverly Coston arrived in her office around 1:00 PM. She opened her door to see Barry Keenan sitting in a chair reading *People Magazine*. She was startled and didn't know what to say at first after hearing what Nicholas had to say earlier about Keenan being on the take.

"Didn't mean to startle you Bev," he said with that smug smile of his. He'd come on to Beverly several times, but she'd made it clear she wasn't interested. But he still flirted with her whenever he had the chance.

"My office was locked," she said. "How'd you get in?" She crossed over to her desk, quickly looking to see if he'd moved anything.

"I guess the cleaning crew left it open. The secretary down the hall said you'd be in around 1:00, so I thought I'd wait. You're working half days now, huh?"

"I didn't feel well this morning, so I stayed home."

"Better now?"

"Yes, thank you."

"Woman problems?" he said with a wink.

"Excuse me?"

"You know, female stuff? Or maybe you had a visitor, an overnight guest, huh?"

"Can I help you with something, Barry, or do you just want to check up on my health?"

"How's the Marshall investigation going?"

"Why do you ask?"

"Hey, just curious. Big pharmaceutical company. It's exciting. Those pharmaceutical executives make a fortune and they still want more. That Harding, he probably makes four or five times what you make. I hear he likes the ladies too. Hey, maybe he's even tried to get in your pants. But no, you wouldn't do that. You know that boy's dirty and he's going down."

"Thanks for asking, but I have the Marshall investigation under control. If you don't mind, Barry, I have a lot of work to catch up on."

"Oh sure," he said, rising from his chair.

"If you need any help with the case, Bev, you just give old Barry a call, day or night." Beverly felt dirty and violated after Keenan left. She went through mail and messages for about half an hour, making sure that Barry was gone. She then locked her door and removed the small electronic device that Nicholas had given her from her purse. She tried to remember how to use it and pointed it at electronic devices in her office. The red light indicating the presence of electronic transmitting devices lit up at least four times. Beverly sat at her desk not knowing what to do. This type of thing happened in movies, not real life. The privacy of her home and office had been violated. She couldn't have a conversation without fear of it being overheard. But she did have an internal conversation with herself and came to a conclusion. She would meet Nicholas Harding in New Jersey next week.

But first there were some things she had to do. During her orientation as a field investigative agent a couple of years ago, an FBI agent had lectured her class about what to do if they thought there was an attempt to compromise an investigator or if they thought another agent had been compromised. She knew she'd have to be careful and was unsure of who she could trust, but she needed to start the wheels rolling to let someone of authority in the Federal Government know that Barry Keenan had been compromised.

31

Kerry Tangles with Ken

As one of four detectives assigned to the County Prosecutor's Office and the new sergeant in the group, Kerry rented an office in the Morris County Courthouse in Morristown. Her office was near those of the Assistant County Prosecutors. Her next big step towards becoming an Assistant Prosecutor herself was to pass the bar examination. Her timeline was one more year to pass the bar and one, no more than two, to make AP.

She called in one of the junior investigators and gave him instructions for a background search on Ken Joseph. Nothing that required a warrant, but a lot of detailed information. She tagged it to the Arthur Kronan case to make it look legitimate.

"I need that in two days."

"Yes ma'am, but-"

"But, what officer?" she asked, fixing him with a stone stare. Kerry was used to some male officers being hesitant to take orders from a woman and didn't tolerate it. "You have a problem with this order?"

"No ma'am, it's just that I know Ken Joseph is an ex-cop. This request is bound to get back to him."

"And?" she continued to stare down the officer.

"May I speak freely, ma'am?" the young officer said awkwardly.

"Have a seat. What is it?"

"Well ma'am, Ken Joseph, even though he's ex-cop, he doesn't have a lot of friends on the force. But he does have a few, so an inquiry like this will get back to him."

"So. It gets back to him. So what?" she asked.

"Like I said ma'am, he doesn't have a lot of friends around here. Most think he's a disgrace to the force. But he's got a reputation of being a real mean son-of-a-bitch, ma'am. I'm talking the sick kind of mean, ma'am."

"And, you're concerned I might not be able to handle a real mean son-of-a-bitch? Don't be. I want the report."

"Yes ma'am." he said, standing. "You'll have it in two days."

Kerry smiled as the young officer left.

Kerry and her brother had followed their father, Army General John Markus, all over the world. With Kerry the apple didn't fall far from the tree. She'd learned to deal with mean sons-of-bitches at an early age. She was counting on Joseph under estimating her as an adversary.

Kerry usually arrived at the office early to get a jump on the workday. The Prosecutor's Office was often nearly empty when she arrived a few days after she had put in her request. She'd gotten settled in at her desk when she sensed a presence and looked up to see Ken Joseph standing in her doorway. He loomed there, allowing his size and bulk to fill the doorframe – short graying hair, blood shot eyes.

"It's awfully deserted around here this time of day. I'm Ken Joseph," he said, moving forward with his hand extended.

"Kerry Markus," she said, standing to shake his hand. "Have a seat."

Joseph slowly looked Kerry over, his eyes lingering on her breasts.

"What can I do for you, Mr. Joseph?" she asked when both were seated.

"Actually, Miss Markus-"

"Sergeant Markus," she corrected him.

"Actually, Sergeant, I came to see what I could do for you. I'm sure you know I'm ex-force."

"I hope that's not all you came to tell me, Mr. Joseph. I knew that."

Joseph fancied himself a real man's man who didn't take shit from anyone, much less some affirmative action woman cop.

"Okay, let's get to the point, *Sergeant*," he said, practically spitting out the last word. "I hear you're asking a lot of questions about me. So I figure I'll make it easy for you; ask away."

"You seem a bit upset, Mr. Joseph. It's just part of an active investigation."

"What investigation?"

"The death of Arthur Kronan."

"That – it's closed. Old Art blew his brains out."

"It's almost closed. I still have a few loose ends to wrap up."

"Like what?"

"Well, since you're *ex*cop," she said, emphasizing the 'ex,' "I can't discuss an active investigation with you."

"I don't like to be fucked with, missy."

"Mr. Joseph, as a detective assigned to the County Prosecutor's Office, I'm an officer of the court. Threatening an officer of the court and a police officer are felonies. Do we have a problem here?"

"No, no problem," he glared at her, having lost interest in her chest and now just wanting to snap her neck.

"Good, you can leave now. Oh, one thing I did want to ask since you're here. Do you mind?"

"What?" he asked, standing near the door.

"Do you know a Mr. Barry Keenan?"

Joseph tried to show no reaction, but blushed slightly as he stared at Kerry and said, "no."

Before he reached the door, he turned towards Kerry looking at the empty workspaces and said smugly, "You know, hypothetically, it being all deserted up here, what's to stop someone from jumping across that desk and snapping you like a twig? Hypothetically?"

"Hum, I guess that would be the 9mm Berretta I'm pointing at you?"

Joseph noticed that Kerry's hands were out of sight under her desk. He smiled until he heard the distinctive sound of the bolt slide mechanism of the automatic weapon and heard Kerry say, "hypothetically. Now either do something stupid or get out."

Joseph left without a word.

Kerry brought the weapon out from under the desk and quickly dialed a two digit number on her phone.

"Security desk, Sergeant Jenkins speaking."

"Sergeant Jenkins, this is Detective Sergeant Markus in the Prosecutor's Office. A Ken Joseph, ex-cop, is in the building. Make sure he leaves and notify me when he's off premise. He just threatened an officer of the court."

"Yes ma'am, we're on it. Do you want him detained?"

"No, we'll handle it from the Prosecutor's Office. Thanks Sergeant."

There were signs all over the Prosecutor's Office that conversations could be taped. So even though she hadn't verbally informed Ken, he was legally informed. And Kerry now had him on tape threatening her and denying that he knew Barry Keenan. Ken Joseph had stepped into a major pile of shit by trying to intimidate Kerry. The threat was enough to get a warrant to tap his phones, search his car and home, and have him followed. Kerry had filled out the appropriate forms before Ken got there; figuring he'd be dumb enough to say something he shouldn't. Threatening to kill her was icing on the cake.

Kerry gathered the forms and removed the tape from the machine in her drawer and headed over to judges' chambers to get warrants to have Joseph watched and phone taps. She'd hold up on the search for now. She wanted to give him enough rope to hang himself and O'Connor. She figured he'd head straight to Jack's office. The mention of Barry Keenan almost made him wet his pants.

True to form, Ken Joseph headed straight to Jack O'Connor's office like a pit bull to his master.

"Sit down and shut up!" O'Connor said, going to his bar that he kept concealed in his credenza. He poured a large scotch and handed it to Joseph. "Here, this seems to be the only thing that can calm you down lately."

Ken Joseph took a big gulp of the single malt scotch. "She knows something, Jack." Ken was big but out of shape and was sweating profusely.

"She's yanking your dick and doing a good fucking job, you moron. She knows nothing. You said she and Harding are buddies, right? Barry was one of the investigators who visited Harding. He probably mentioned it to her. They don't know anything; it's compartmentalized. She's fishing; just trying to get you to trip up. And running in here after seeing her wasn't a good idea."

"The bitch pulled a gun on me!" he said, the alcohol making his face flush.

O'Connor was getting sick of Joseph. He'd used him like a trained dog, but he was stupid and Jack thought he was quickly outliving his usefulness.

"And what dumbass move did you make to get a police sergeant to pull a gun on you in her office, pray tell?"

"Hey, I was just trying to scare the little bitch. Let her know what someone like me can do to her. You know?"

"Yeah, I can tell you did an outstanding job of scaring her. That must be why you're about to wet your pants. Now, listen to me Ken, you stay the hell away from that detective. The last thing we need now is to have some cop nosing around. She's bluffing. Of course Harding suspects something. The feds are about to lock his black ass up!

"So, I don't want you messing around with that cop," Jack said as he looked out his window that gave him a sweeping view of the Marshall campus. "But maybe," he went on, "it's time to shake up Nicky boy. His little cop girlfriend may have balls, but Nicky's a pussy at heart. That's why I picked him. He won't fight back. So here's what I want you to do, Kenny boy. Go see the good Dr. Harding here at work, not his home."

Jack sat behind his desk and smiled. "Let him know that accidents happen. One could happen to that cute little girl of his." He leaned forward and looked directly into Joseph's red eyes. "Clean yourself up; you're a mess. And be subtle. Do you think you can handle that, Ken?"

"Yeah, sure Jack," he said standing and trying to make himself look presentable.

"Good. And from now on you don't make a move without clearing it with me first. You got that?"

"Okay Jack."

"Good, now go. This is the end run Kenny. Don't fuck it up."

Ken left Jack's office. "Goddamn moron," Jack muttered to himself. Jack thought that he'd have to find a way to eliminate Joseph when this was over.

Late that afternoon Ken entered Karen's office. "Is he in?" he asked, moving towards Nicholas' door, not bothering to stop for an answer.

"He's about to leave for the day, Mr. Joseph," Karen said, coming out from behind her desk.

"Don't you worry, honey," he said, his eyes lingering on her breasts. "I won't take up much of your boss's time. Why don't you just go on home now?"

Joseph entered Nicholas' office without knocking. Nicholas was packing some files to take home. He didn't look particularly surprised to see Joseph. "Ken, come on in, have a seat."

"Don't mind if I do, Nick – sorry, I mean, Dr. Harding."

"What can I do for you Ken? I don't think that I've ever seen you over here."

Ken ignored the question.

"This was Art Kronan's office wasn't it?" Ken sat across from Nicholas and slowly looked around the office.

"Yes, it was."

"Yeah, too bad about old Art," he said. "But hey, looks like you made out okay here, Nick, huh?"

"What do you want Ken? I have things to do."

"Yeah, yeah, you're a busy man aren't you Nick? An important man around here, Vice President and all. Gotta get home to that little girl of yours, huh? How old is she now Nick?"

"If you have a point get to it, if not, get out."

"No point Nick. Just wanted to drop by and make sure you're okay. I'm head of security, you know? What with what happened to old Art, we wouldn't want anything to happen to you, or someone you care for, would we, Nick? Because I don't have to tell you what with your dead wife and dead boss; sometimes shit just happens. And I'd hate to see anything bad happen to you, Nick, or say to your daughter. Hypothetically speaking, of course," he said with a crooked smile. Pleased he'd gotten to use his newest big word 'hypothetically' twice in one day.

But Ken didn't get the reaction he'd expected. Nicholas just sat back in his chair behind his desk and smiled.

"Have I said something you find amusing, Nick?" Ken asked, trying to regain the upper hand.

"Kenny, you don't mind if I call you Kenny, do you?" Joseph's face was starting to turn red.

"Kenny, everyone here knows that you're Jack O'Connor's house pet, incapable of putting together more than a two syllable thought on your own. So, assuming that's true – and I believe it to be so – then the next logical assumption is that everything you just said came from Jack. I also know, Kenny, that you like to get your rocks off hassling lower level women and minorities. Yeah, Kenny, I've heard about some of the shit you've done to some of the low-level black guys around here.

"Personally, I think it's directly related to the fact that you're ignorant poor white trash with a teeny weenie dick."

"I don't have to listen to this shit from you, boy!" Ken hissed.

"See? You're too predictable Kenny. But I want you to sit back and listen carefully to what I have to say. I'll speak slowly and use little words."

The two men exchanged looks of pure hatred.

"If you or Jack mistake me for one of those 'turn the other cheek Jesus boys' you're used to pushing around you're greatly mistaken. You see, Kenny, there are few things or people in the world that I truly care about. But my daughter is whom I most care for. And if anything were to happen to her now, I'll have to assume that you and Jack are behind it."

Without hesitation Nicholas said slowly and softly to Ken, "and Ken, do you know what I'll do then? I'll kill you, Kenny. I'll kill Jack. I'll kill your wife. I'll kill your kids. I'll kill your goldfish. I'll kill your dog and the goddamn fleas on your dog. That's a promise, Kenny. Now you get out of my office, you pile of shit."

Joseph was momentarily taken aback, but quickly regained his threatening posture and rose to loom over Nicholas' desk. Nicholas rose and said, "take the message back to your master. I'll write it down if you can't remember it." Ken, who had a good 80 pounds on Nicholas moved towards him, when Nicholas' door opened.

"Will there be anything else today, Dr. Harding?" Karen asked. Ken took a half-step back away from the desk.

"No thanks, Karen. Ken was just leaving. Goodbye, Ken."

"Yeah," Joseph said as he left the room, taking one more opportunity to ogle Karen's breasts.

"I thought you'd already left, Karen."

"I was worried Dr. Harding. Are you alright?"

"No. He threatened Andrea. Jesus, how bad can this get? I have to go and pick up 'Drea from school. I'll see you tomorrow Karen."

She moved towards him and put her hand on his arm and smiled. "It will work out, Dr. Harding. I believe in you."

"Thanks Karen."

When Nicholas left his office, Karen closed the door, removed a small electronic jamming device similar to the one that Beth used at the FDA agent's house. She activated it and called a number she knew well. She then informed the person at the other end of the call of what had just transpired between Nicholas and Ken Joseph.

When Nicholas and Andrea arrived home from school, Nicholas noticed a new black limousine, a black Suburban SUV, Kerry's car and Michael's Audi SUV. *Now what?* he thought. He'd rushed over to Charring Cross to pick up 'Drea taking Ken's threat seriously. He'd spent the drive home nervously glancing in his mirrors to see if he was being followed.

"Hi Grandma," Andrea said when she entered the kitchen.

"Hi honey, give me a hug," Dorothy said. Nicholas and his mother exchanged concerned glances as she hugged her grandchild.

"Is Uncle Michael here? Is that his car outside?"

"You bet, munchkin!" Michael said from the door to the family room.

"Uncle Michael!" 'Drea shouted as she ran to launch herself into his arms.

"Tell you what, hon, you go up and do your homework and I'll come up later. Okay?"

"Okay. Rasputin, *goS DaH!*" The large tabby scampered off a kitchen chair and followed 'Drea up the back staircase, leaving the three Harding adults in the kitchen.

"Michael," Nicholas said, putting his briefcase down.

"Nicholas," Michael replied.

"Mom," Nicholas said.

"Nicholas," she responded.

"Did someone forget to tell me about the party? Who's here?"

Michael answered. "Kerry, Don with a swarm of body guards, who look like they could take out a regiment, and Beth, along with a couple of her private dick security goons. I'm reasonably sure these guys have killed before; they have that look."

"Hum," Nicholas said as he walked into the family room. Dorothy and Michael followed. Kerry broke off her conversation to move to Nicholas' side.

"How'd you find out?" Nicholas asked.

Don spoke up. "Karen called me after your visit from Ken Joseph."

Beth spoke with the conviction of someone who shouldn't be fucked with. "We've come up with a solution."

"Then I guess I can just go to bed if you've all taken care of everything."

Kerry squeezed his arm and Beth said, "remember our conversation?"

"Okay, okay, I'm sorry. Let's hear your plan. And thanks guys."

"Well, it was mostly Don's idea, so he can explain."

"It's simple actually. One way or another, this is all coming to a conclusion in a matter of weeks. The Marshall estate is as close to a fortress as you can get to these days and I brought along some muscle. Although, it would appear Beth came prepared as well. I propose that all of you move into Marshall estate."

Nicholas was silent as he paced around the room. He stopped at the bar and poured himself a glass of wine. "Thanks Don," he said, slowly looking around the room. "I don't see as I have much choice. I don't want to take any chances with 'Drea's safety. I accept."

"Good. I thought you may give me a hard time."

Nicholas smiled. "I accept for 'Drea and my mother. I need more flexibility, so I'm staying here."

"Hah! Told you. Pay up, honey," Beth said to Kerry. Kerry reached into her bag, pulled out a one dollar bill and handed it over to Beth. "You, my dear, are so damn predictable," she said. "I knew you'd say that. So you and I'll stay here and coordinate the final battle."

"Count me in. I'm staying here too," Michael said.

"Me too," Kerry added.

Nicholas almost said something in opposition, and then said, "Okay, thanks guys." He looked into Kerry's eyes and smiled.

"Hot damn, it'll be like camp. I have a couple of my security boys from the firm – they'll stay also. I always carry protection," Beth said with a wink.

"And, I'll request regular police drive-bys," Kerry added.

"I'll call Charring Cross tomorrow and arrange to have all Andrea's school work sent to Mr. Marshall's house," Dorothy said.

"Please, call me Don."

"Okay, Don. I can dust off my old skills and teach Andrea for the next few weeks."

"Good." Nicholas added, "Don, the limo and Suburban, are they yours?"

"Yep. Driver's ex-British military. The boys in the Suburban are ex-South Korean Special Forces. The best of the best. The only way to make them any safer would be to move them into 1600 Pennsylvania Avenue," he said proudly.

Michael whistled. "Wow, I saw a special on South Korean Special Forces that trained for the Olympics. They mounted an assault on a terrorist position by walking down the side of a skyscraper and then kicking some major ass. Same bunch?"

"Same bunch," Don replied.

"I didn't realize you were so security conscious, Don."

"It's a long story. One day over drinks. Let's just say for now that I stepped on a few toes during my sabbatical."

"Okay," Nicholas replied. "I'll go and tell 'Drea she has to spend a few days at Don's house. I'm sure she'll be all shook up. Oh, Don, she doesn't go anywhere without her cat."

"Not to worry, Nicholas. Mr. Rasputin is most welcome. I'll have my chef prepare trout for him."

"You're going to have a hard time getting rid of them."

As everyone was making plans to act on the move, Nicholas managed to get Don off to the side. "Is there something you want to tell me about you and Karen, Don?"

Don laughed and said, "another long story Nicholas. Another long story."

'Drea had been upset about leaving home without Nicholas, but knowing that she'd be accompanied by her grandmother and the confidant Rasputin made up for it. But when she learned they'd be staying at Don Marshall's mansion she couldn't wait to leave.

"I'll see you in a few days hon," Nicholas said as Dorothy and 'Drea piled into Don's Mercedes limo. The long black car that Don had told him was bullet proof pulled out, followed by the Suburban security detail, and armed to the teeth. At least Nicholas thought he'd taken the concern of 'Drea's safety out of play. Now, it was him and O'Connor, each with their allies and forces in a battle over Marshall Pharmaceutical and Nicholas' future.

Beth was getting her two security guys settled in a spare room in the basement and getting them familiar with the house and its security system. Michael was settling into the room he used when he stayed over. That left Nicholas and Kerry alone in the large family room.

"Pinch me."

"What?" she asked.

"This has got to be some sort of nightmare. It seems I just keep sinking deeper and deeper into another layer of Hell."

"It has to end soon."

She looked at him and asked, "Nicholas, do you have a gun?"

"Sort of."

"Okay, how do you sort of have a gun?"

"I own a gun, but keep it at a gun club. I only use it for target shooting and didn't want it in the house."

"What kind?"

"Glock, 9mm."

"They must have big targets at your club. I think you should get it. Joseph's not stable. There's no telling what he may do."

"So, what exactly happened between you two this morning to set him off?"

"I wanted to rattle him, so I ran a background search on him, knowing that as a former cop word would get back to him. He came to my office and I casually let Barry Keenan's name drop."

"And did you rattle him?"

"Ah, yeah, enough for him to threaten to kill me."

"Jeez Kerry!"

"Not to worry," she said sweetly.

"What'd you do?"

"I pointed a gun at him under my desk and told him to either do something stupid or get out."

"And you would have shot him?"

"Yes. I'm a cop Nick, remember?"

"Yeah. I remember. I guess Kenny was a busy boy today."

"Busy and scared. He denied knowing Barry Keenan, but I could tell he was lying. His stupid move of threatening me, on tape I might add, allowed me get a warrant to tap his phone and have him followed. One guess where he went after our little meeting?"

"Jack O'Connor's office."

"Right-o. And Jack's got to be worried about Ken coming apart and whether we really know anything about Keenan. They're scared, Nick, and scared criminals make mistakes."

"Let's just hope those mistakes don't include killing one of us."

"Um, these NY private dicks that Beth has, what's the story with them?" Kerry asked.

"Don't know," Nicholas replied. "She keeps me and them at arm's length. This is the first time we've seen anyone and they seem to have some pretty high tech toys and access to confidential information. Why? What do you make?"

"If I had to guess I'd say ex-CIA or military intelligence. If I'm right, the next question is what's a small town North Carolina solo lawyer doing with connections like that?"

"Don't know. There's obviously a lot more to her than the homespun country hick image she tries to cultivate."

"Anyway, Dr. Harding, an important question. If I'm going to stay here, where will I sleep?" Kerry asked with a mischievous grin.

"Well, Detective Sergeant, if you're staying here to protect me you should probably stay close by. I'll setup a guest room for you."

"You're sure about that?"

"Don't tempt me."

Nicholas and Kerry decided to go by her house to get some things for her stay and stop by his gun club to retrieve his Glock and catch a late dinner. Beth and Michael passed, saying they didn't want to crowd the possibly budding lovebirds.

At the Bernardsville Gun Club, Nicholas and Kerry were able to quickly pickup Nicholas' Glock and some ammo. He put the gun, magazine and ammo in a lock box in the trunk of his car and drove towards Kerry's apartment. It was after 7:00 and dark. They were still on a small back road heading towards Morristown when Nicholas saw the flashing red and blue light of a patrol car in his rear view mirror.

"Shit," he said. "Was I speeding?"

"I don't think so," she answered.

He pulled over, rolled down his window and cut the ignition. The cop approached the driver's side, stopping behind the door, his flashlight shining into Nicholas' eyes and his right hand resting lightly on his gun.

"Let me see your driver's license, registration and insurance card now."

The officer's voice was brusque and to the point.

Nicholas, having grown up a black young male in the South knew exactly how to respond.

"My license is in my wallet, in my rear pants pocket. The registration and insurance card are in the glove compartment."

"Okay, get them," the voice said. The flashlight beam then moved from Nicholas to Kerry. "Are you alright, ma'am?" The beam moved back to Nicholas.

"I'm fine, Officer."

He slowly looked over the driver's license, registration and insurance card. "Nice car you have here."

"Thank you."

"Is she your wife?"

"No."

"Well, she sure ain't your sister. Girlfriend?" he asked smugly.

"Look is there some problem here, Officer?" Nicholas asked.

The cop took a half step back, hand now firmly on the still holstered gun. "Driver, slowly exit the vehicle now. Hands in the open."

"No!" Kerry shouted. "Don't do it.

"Officer!" she shouted. "I'm Detective Sergeant Kerry Markus, Morristown Police Department, County Prosecutor's Office. My badge is right here in my purse. Now, if you continue this line of action, you'll be unemployed tomorrow, I guarantee it."

The cop, now afraid said, "Driver, hands on the wheel. You just slowly put your left hand in that bag, Miss, and show me this ID."

Kerry did as she was told and produced the detective sergeant's shield along with her County Prosecutor's Office ID. The cop looked over the ID, mouthed 'fuck' to himself and handed them back. "My apologies ma'am, sir. I didn't mean any harm."

"I'm stepping out of the car," Kerry said. "Stand down now, Officer," she ordered.

"Yes ma'am."

Nicholas sat silent as a now furious Kerry exited and rounded the rear of the car to face the officer.

"Name and badge number, now!" she said. "You didn't mean any fucking harm? You apologize? Exactly what was the reason for this stop?"

"The car was speeding, ma'am," he muttered.

"Show me the radar reading," she quickly replied.

"It was a visual, ma'am."

"Horseshit! I was looking at the speedometer. Try again!"

"The car looked suspicious, ma'am!" he replied angrily.

"Oh, I see, 'suspicious'. You mean an expensive car being driven by a black man with a white woman in the car? That kind of suspicious?"

Silence.

"You have a problem with a white woman being with a black man?" she practically spit at the young officer.

"No ma'am," he answered slowly.

"You get off hassling Blacks, Officer?"

"No ma'am."

"I suppose you think I'd be better off with Neanderthal trash like you?"

"No ma'am."

The two angry police officers stared at each other.

"What's your duty officer's name?"

"Richard Harris, ma'am."

She handed him her card. "Be in my office 8:00 AM tomorrow morning. And bring your arrest and stop record for the last year. Now get out of my sight."

The officer mumbled, "good night ma'am," got in his car, turned off his strobes and drove off.

Kerry got back in the car. As soon as she was buckled in, Nicholas started the car and drove off towards Kerry's house.

"I'm sorry Nicholas," she said after a while. "Are you okay?"

"Leave me alone, Kerry," they drove the rest of the way in silence. At Kerry's, they both got out and went into her house.

"I won't be long," she said, going into the back to pack some things.

Nicholas went into the bathroom to splash cold water on his face. For a while he just starred at himself in the mirror. Then he went into Kerry's kitchen to get a bottle of mineral water. He was sitting in her living room in the dark drinking water when she came out. She pulled an ottoman in front of the sofa where he sat. She sat there in front of him. After about twenty minutes of silence, she said, "I'm willing to sit here as long as it takes for you to talk to me, Nick."

"I grew up in a small Southern redneck town. The kind of Norman Rockwell town where the Klan was proud to march down Main Street in their hoods in the 1960s. We all, my friends and I got our driver's licenses when we turned sixteen. And one of the first things we learned was how to behave when a cop stopped you. They always have their hand on their gun. You say 'yes sir' and 'no sir' and ask their permission to reach for your wallet or open the glove compartment. They knew how to make you feel like a little nigger boy. And you know what, Kerry? Today, today when I'm 38, a vice president in a Fortune 500 company, and a millionaire, all it takes is one asshole post pubescent white trash cop to make me feel like that 16-year-old little black boy."

"And I'm supposed to feel sorry for you because of this?" she asked.

"You wanted to talk, I talked. I don't give a shit what you feel."

"Oh, our first fight. At least you're not mad at that cop anymore," she said with a smile as she took his hand. "The world sucks, hon, we didn't make it suck. But we have to play the hand we're dealt. That's what my dad told me. So, I'm not going to feel sorry for a 38-year-old millionaire vice president," she said. "Ah, I saw that little smile. "And," she went on, "I'm sure having your friend who's a girl straighten out the mess didn't help things."

"My *white* friend who's a girl."

"Your white friend who's a girl. Are you okay with that?"

"Yes. My white friend who's a girl and a cop."

"Your white friend who's a girl and a cop. Are you okay with that? I need to know. We need to know."

"I'm okay with it Kerry, very."

"Good," she said, pinching and tickling him. "We'll make quite the couple, Dr. Harding."

"I know. Odd and odder."

"Instead of going to a restaurant, let's go back to your place and I'll make you dinner."

"You cook?"

"Of course I cook. Let me get the rest of my stuff."

Kerry came out with two bags. "Nicholas, I was just thinking about the note or emails you were getting from Arthur."

"But they were from Don."

"Not the first one. It went out before Arthur's death. So let's suppose Arthur actually sent it. Knowing that he was about to commit suicide. Maybe he was trying to tell you something. What did it say again?"

"'I'm sorry Nicholas. I'll explain later.'"

"Okay," she said, thinking like a cop. "Suppose Arthur knows what Jack's up to and how it'll impact you. He wants to help. How? Tell someone? Too risky. How about something you're to receive that will explain everything and include evidence?"

"Some evidence would be good right about now," Nicholas added.

"So, if you're Arthur, you're about to kill yourself. You have something that has to get to you, Nick, at some point in time. Who do you give it to?"

"Mail?"

"Maybe. What about his wife?"

"Helen?"

"Yep."

"So you think Helen has some evidence from Arthur?"

"Maybe. If so, she probably doesn't know what it is. Let's give her a call. Can't hurt."

"Thanks Kerry."

"You're welcome. Life's strange, Nicholas Harding. If all this hadn't happened, O'Connor trying to set you up, Arthur killing himself, we never would have met."

"Make the best of the hand you're dealt?"

"Um huh."

32

Helen's Secret

Helen agreed Nicholas and Kerry could come by. When they arrived, she had arranged a tea service. She kissed Nicholas on the cheek and shook hands with Kerry.

"Oh, yes," she said, leading them into the living room of the large old house. "You're that nice young police woman who helped me when Arthur died. Nicholas, how are you handling Arthur's old job?"

Nicholas felt uncomfortable. "It's okay, dear," she said. "He wanted you to have it, his job. That was his plan, not like this of course, but still he wanted you to have it. He'd be proud of you Nicholas."

Nicholas noticed that Helen now looked closer to her real age and sadder.

"How are you doing Helen, really?" he asked her.

She looked at him with a sad smile and said, "it's hard, very hard, Nicholas. I miss him so. He was more than a husband; he was my friend. I've gone from having my best friend with me to being alone. And I can't understand why. My counselor, psychologist actually," she said in a conspiratorial tone, "says it's a normal part of grief to be angry. But I'm not angry Nicholas. I'm confused. I can't understand why Arthur would do such a thing.

"I'm thinking of going away – at least for a while, but I can't decide where to go," she said in a barely audible small sad voice. Nicholas and Kerry noticed a tear roll down her cheek.

Helen reached into her pocket, pulled out a delicate small handkerchief like the one a grandmother would have and dabbed at her eyes.

"Must have lost a few pounds in tears these past few weeks," she said.

Kerry, sensing Nicholas' discomfort with asking Helen about Arthur, decided to start.

"Mrs. Kronan, if you don't mind, I just had a couple of more questions," she said.

"Why of course dear, but please call me Helen."

"Thank you Helen. Your husband sent Nicholas a message, an email, shortly before he died," Kerry said, deciding the direct approach might work best here. "It said, 'I'm sorry Nicholas. I'll explain later.' It was sent only 30 minutes before Dr. Kronan died. I know this is unpleasant for you Helen, but it could be important."

Nicholas watched as Kerry made eye contact with Helen and used her voice and body language to relax her. She did have a very relaxing interrogation style. Watching her, Nicholas knew she'd probably used this style to manipulate confessions out of criminals. Kerry went on, "we think that if your husband went to the trouble to send this message to Nicholas just before his death, perhaps he was trying to tell Nicholas something, guide him to something. Helen, in the days or weeks before he died, did Dr. Kronan give you anything for Nicholas or ask you to tell him anything or did he mention anything unusual to you?"

"Well," Helen said, turning to Nicholas, "Nicholas, you remember the last time you were here for dinner and as you were about to leave I asked you about Arthur?"

"Yes, I remember," he replied. "You said he wasn't sleeping well and had talked of retiring early."

"Um," she said returning her attention to Kerry. "I thought perhaps he was having an affair. You know, a younger woman. But I don't think that was it."

"What do you think was bothering him, Helen?" Kerry asked, looking into Helen's eyes.

"I don't know. But I suspect it involved work. Like Nicky, Art always hated the politics, but he could put up with it. But lately it seemed to have gotten worse. But he didn't confide in me about things at work. He said it was a dirty place and he wanted to keep me pure," she said smiling to herself. "He was quite the romantic, you know."

Kerry continued. "Did he seem to mention Nicholas or anyone else at work more frequently in the last few weeks or months?"

"Well," Helen said slowly. "I think he did mention Jack O'Connor a little more than usual. Art was never found of Jack and frankly neither was I. He was always looking down my top, even patted me on the behind a few times. He's really a very vulgar man."

"So I've heard," Kerry said, looking at Nicholas with a smile.

"Art said he could handle Jack, but things seemed to have gotten worse."

"Can you recall when things seemed to get worse between your husband and Jack?" Kerry asked.

"Oh, I guess five or six months ago," Helen replied.

"Okay, that's very helpful Helen. Now again, did your husband ask you to tell Nicholas anything or give you something to give him? It's very important."

"I know," she replied. "It must be. That Marshall security man, Mr. Joseph, asked the same thing."

Nicholas and Kerry now knew they were on to something. "When Helen, when, did Ken Joseph ask you this?" Nicholas asked.

"The day after the funeral. But you know what, I don't like him either. He came by with Jack O'Connor. Jack pretended to be concerned about me. But Jack's one of those people only concerned about themselves. Mr. Joseph asked if Art had given me any work-related files. I told him no. Then he mentioned you, Nicky, and asked if Art had given me anything to give you. I told him no to that as well. I've thought about it since, but Art never gave me anything to give you Nicky."

"I see," Kerry said. "Well, if you think of anything Helen, will you please call me or Nicholas?"

Helen didn't say anything for a while and looked off into space. Kerry and Nicholas assumed she was lost in thought about Arthur. She looked perplexed, and then returned her attention to them. "You know, there is one thing, but it's not work related. I don't think it's what you're looking for. I'd forgotten with all that's happened."

"Go on," Kerry said politely.

Nicholas was trying not to show his impatience.

"Well, a few weeks before he died. Killed himself, I should get used to saying that. Art came home with a present. He said he'd found the perfect birthday present for Nicholas. He made a point of showing it to me and where he put it. He said it was in case he forgot about it, since Nicky's birthday wasn't for several months. That did seem a little odd, since Art never forgot anything. He wouldn't tell me what it was, but just said don't forget it."

"Helen," Kerry said gently. "That could be what we're looking for. May we see it please?"

"Of course dear, I'll get it."

When she'd left the room Kerry turned to Nicholas and said, "this could be it, the break in evidence we need."

"Or," he replied. "It could be an early birthday present."

Helen returned with a gift wrapped box, the size of a shirt box and handed it to Nicholas. "I guess I should say happy birthday." She looked so sad.

Kerry reached for the box. "I'm sorry Helen," she said in a gentle but firm voice. "But I have to treat this as evidence. I'll take it and give you a receipt for it."

"Alright."

Kerry took the box and laid it on a waist high table. She pulled a pair of latex gloves out of her pocket along with a small pocketknife. Nicholas stood by her side and Helen a little back. Kerry slid the knife blade under the tape and sliced through it. The gold wrapping paper slide open to reveal a plain white shirt box. Kerry lifted the top of the box to reveal layers of white tissue paper. Nestled under the tissue paper was an 8 ½ x 10 ½ inch bound leather ledger with lined paper – 150 lined pages. She opened the ledger and saw neat meticulous handwriting on most pages.

"Is this Arthur's handwriting?" she asked.

"Yes," both Nicholas and Helen replied.

Kerry closed the book. "Okay. Helen, I'm going to log this in as evidence," she wrote out a receipt that both she and Helen signed.

"Will I see it again?" she asked.

"It depends on what's in it."

"He was in some sort of trouble, wasn't he?"

"Possibly, we don't know for sure, but this may help us. Thank you very much Mrs. Kronan. I'll be in touch. I'll wait by the door," she said, sensing that Nicholas wanted a moment alone with Helen.

Nicholas hugged Helen. "It'll take time, but it'll be okay Helen."

"When?"

"I wish I knew."

She looked up and smiled at him. "She's a keeper, Nicky."

"What?" he asked, surprised at her abrupt change of subject.

"You know what. I'm not that old. I like her. So don't let her get away. Or do I have to play match-maker?"

"Yes ma'am," he said.

"Will you let me know how all this turns out? No matter how painful you think it may be to me, promise Nicky?"

"Promise."

"Good. You take care, Nicholas." She kissed him good night.

"You too, Helen."

When they were both in the car, Nicholas asked, "did you get to read any?"

"Yep."

"Well?"

"I only skimmed it, but looks like Arthur was part of O'Connor's gang of thieves. But he kept a detailed journal of their activities."

"Is it proof?"

"Well, it's evidence, but it's not proof. It's still only one person's allegations. It doesn't prove anything, but it should be enough to get the feds to look into O'Connor."

"Hum..."

"'Hum' what?"

"Why would Art get involved with some hare-brained, not to mention criminal, scheme of Jack's?"

"First, it's not that hare-brained. Look how close they've come to pulling it off. As for motive —we know Jack's; he's just rotten to the core. Art — money, blackmail, women, drugs, who the hell knows; everyone has their price, Nicholas, everyone."

Nicholas had turned onto one of the deserted back roads that led to his house.

"Not that we don't have enough on our minds, but we're being followed," she said.

"How long?"

"Since we left Helen's house. They were staying back, but they're getting closer. Keep going to your house," she reached behind her and removed her gun from a rear holster, checked the clip and replaced the gun.

"An evening with you is never dull, is it?" he said.

"You know you like it," she said as she reached into her bag and removed her cell phone and dialed a number. "Hello Beth – it's Kerry. Are those security studs of yours still here? They any good?"

"Do bears bear, do bees be?"

"Good. Put the lead on the phone. Nick and I are on our way home and we have company." Kerry talked to the head of the security team and told him what she needed.

"Yes ma'am," he barked. "We'll be ready."

Yep, she thought, definitely ex-military spooks. Good, that means they're top shelf.

"Our fish still on the hook?" she asked, looking at the mirror.

"I think so. What's the plan?"

"We're going to reel him in and see what we've got. As soon as you get into your driveway, gun it and come around to face him, brights on. Got it? When you stop, get down and let us handle this. Okay?"

"You know this hiding behind you and your big gun thing is starting to get to me.

"Kerry – be careful, please."

"You're sweet."

Nicholas lived on a deserted tree-lined lane and was the only house at the end of a long drive. Seeing that their fish was still there, as soon as Nicholas turned into the long drive, he gunned the sporty Lexus, quickly moving ahead and turned to face the car behind him with his bright lights on. Nicholas saw a third car come out of nowhere behind the mystery car.

When Nicholas stopped the Lexus in front of the car the third car had blocked the mystery car from behind. Even before Nicholas came to a complete stop, he saw Kerry pull her gun, open her car door, yell, "get down!" to the driver, and then, taking cover behind the car door, take aim at the mystery car.. "Morristown Police!"

Not quite as intimidating as NYPD, Nicholas thought, *but should get the message across*, as he lowered himself below his dashboard out of the line of fire, in case there was one.

"Out of the car slowly. Let me see your hands empty – you're surrounded!" Kerry shouted.

She saw two empty hands come out of the driver's side window. "Hey don't shoot me," came a voice form the car. "I'm just looking for Nick Harding. I'm not armed. Don't shoot, damn it!"

Nicholas thought he recognized the voice and said, "Glen? Kerry, I think it's Glen Morgan."

"Name!" Kerry shouted at the car.

"Glen. Glen Morgan."

"It's okay – it's Glen," Nicholas said, starting to get up.

"Stay down!" she hissed at him. She then turned to face the mystery car. "Okay, slowly exit the car. Keep your hands in the open. No sudden moves. There are three guns on you now."

"Okay, okay man, I mean ma'am. I'm getting out. Just don't shoot me, damn it. I just need to talk to Dr. Harding." A trembling Glen slowly got out of his car, keeping his hands over his head. Kerry moved out from behind the Lexus door, but remaining in a shooter position with dead aim on Glen. The two security guys also moved out and quickly looked into the car to make sure it was empty. One moved to open the trunk while the other stepped to the side, gun – an automatic assault rifle-looking thing – pointed at the trunk. It was empty. Seeing that Kerry had Glen under control, the two security men quickly searched inside, under the car and under the hood and trunk and then announced the car safe.

Nicholas had come out. "He's okay. This is Glen Morgan. Glen – Detective Sergeant Kerry Markus Mor…"

"Yeah, Morristown PD. She introduced herself. This how they greet people in this neighborhood, man?"

"When they follow people in the middle of the night, maybe," Kerry replied, holstering her gun and obviously still pumped from the little adventure.

"Well you found me. Come on inside, Glen," Nicholas said.

"We'll take care of the cars, sir," one of the security guys said.

Kerry retrieved the ledger and gift box from Nicholas' car. She, Nicholas and Glen headed towards the house, Glen giving Kerry a wary look. Beth and Michael met them at the front door.

"You're spoiling me Nicholas, honey. Now, I'll never be able to go back to my boring little office in North Carolina. I may have to stay here," Beth said mischievously.

"Glen Morgan – my lawyer, Beth Cowling, my brother, Michael Harding."

"And, the lady Gestapo," he said, nodding towards Kerry. "I've met."

"Mr. Morgan," Beth cooed, turning on all her syrupy Southern charm. "We've heard so much about you. Do come in." She hooked her arm in his and led him inside the house.

Nicholas led the group into the family room. Glen said, "Almost getting shot has made me thirsty. Think I could get a drink?"

"What'll you have Glen?" Kerry asked.

Still wary and afraid of Kerry, Glen hesitated a moment before replying, "Scotch with rocks please, ma'am."

Kerry moved to the bar and poured Glen a scotch. He didn't take his eyes off her, perhaps afraid that having missed the opportunity to shoot him she may take this time to poison him. He took the drink she offered. "Thank you ma'am."

"Sure. I imagine that episode with all the guns outside must have been quite a shock, but would you mind telling us why you were following us Glen?" she asked in that disarming interrogator's tone she used.

Nicholas thought she'd missed her calling in the Diplomatic Corp.

"That's easy," Glen replied after taking a good sized slug of scotch. "I was scared; at least I thought I was until I met you."

Kerry just smiled sweetly. "Go on."

"That sicko Ken Joseph and some goon-types were hanging around my place asking questions. So I thought it best not to engage Mr. Joseph in conversation. I grabbed all my stuff and headed here. I called your office, Nicholas, and here. When I couldn't find you, I just headed out. I swung by Arthur's and saw your car, so I followed you here. I didn't expect a welcome parade, but then I didn't expect the 21 Gun Salute I got either."

"It's been a particularly bad day Glen. I apologize if I scared you," Kerry said while looking entirely, deceptively harmless. "But as you noted with Ken Joseph we're playing with some real bad guys here. We can't be too careful. You said you grabbed all your stuff, Glen. What stuff was that?"

Glen just stared at Kerry. "No offense lady, but who the hell are you anyway? Batwoman, Commissioner Gordon or what? I came here to see Nick, not you."

"No offense taken Glen," Kerry continued her eye contact with Glen.

"In addition to being with the Morristown Police Department, which you know, Kerry's also with the County Prosecutor's Office. She's investigating Arthur's death. She's also a very close friend who's trying to help me out of this little mess. So please answer her questions and treat any request from her as if it came from me. Okay?"

"Sure Nick," he replied, finishing his scotch. "But believe me, this is more than any 'little mess,' pal. This is a huge fucking pile of shit. My stuff's in my car. I need it."

"Is this it, honey?" Beth purred. "I had my boys bring it in."

"Yeah," Glen said looking around the room. "You people are creeping me out, man."

Nicholas refreshed Glen's scotch. "Okay Glen. I assume this has to do with you getting more information on MR-548. Tell us what you've got."

Glen took another swallow of scotch. "This is good stuff. Where'd you get it Nick?"

"Scotland."

"Oh, okay," he said. "You remember our conversation a few weeks ago about your new wonder drug MR-548?"

"Sure," Nicholas replied. "You said it looked too good to be true in terms of margin of safety. A wide therapeutic index, good bioavailability, and no significant toxicities. But when you ran it through the computer simulations, it set off the alarms. There was almost no correlation between the Tanaka database and the computational predictions. Tanaka's database shows a clean compound – no problems. The computer predictions suggest toxicities at the clinical dose. And the contract doesn't allow us to run any of our own tests prior to the Phase II clinical trial in a few weeks. We're completely dependent on the Tanaka dataset to start these trials," Nicholas summarized. "So what new information do you have, Glen?"

"Remember, I said I was going to get a friend in Chemical Synthesis to cook up a batch of MR-548? Well I did. And then I ran a quick toxicology study in rats and dogs. There's an advantage to being the lab wacko. No one pays a whole lot of attention to what you're doing. Here, let me get my notebook. The rest of you guys probably won't understand what we're talking about. Here it is.

"I made the material up in a simple saline solution; followed the Tanaka protocol to the letter. I dosed five dogs at ten times the estimated clinical dose set for the Phase II clinical trial and five more dogs at five times the clinical dose. Same for two groups of rats with all the appropriate controls. I dosed the animals daily for three days."

"And?" Michael asked, losing patience.

"Okay – rats first. The high dose wiped them all out. The low dose of five times the clinical dose had no deaths but marked weight loss, liver and renal enzyme markers for toxicity were all off the charts. I didn't do histopathology, because I didn't want to get too many folks involved, but

Mark gave me exposure – blood level support. I hope Mark's on our side."

"He is."

"Good. But I must have created enough of a ruckus to stir up Jack and Ken. Anyway, in rats the exposure looks good. Same for dogs. Similar effects: marked liver and kidney toxicity."

"Now, in English please, boys," Beth asked.

"Sure, it's simple," Glen said. "Based upon the computer predictions and this preliminary animal data, if Marshall gives MR-548 to people at these doses they're going to produce severe liver and kidney toxicity. Now, the liver and kidney are tough and resilient organs. They can take a licking and keep on ticking, but to get hit with a double-whammy, both organs at once, and the effect that appears to be this consistent. My guess is you may, just may, get lucky and not kill anyone. But at the least a few of these folks are going to be in critical care waiting for a liver and/or a kidney transplant. That's my best guess. Worst guess: use your imagination."

"My God," Michael said.

"Nah," Glen added. "I doubt God had a lot to do with this."

"And you have data to support what you just told us?" Kerry asked.

A cell phone rang and one of the security team called Beth into the kitchen. Nicholas and Michael exchanged worried looks.

"Yep. Got it all right here," Glen answered, pointing to the small box.

"Good, I'll take possession of it as evidence," Kerry said.

"Evidence for what?" Glen asked.

"Officially, as part of the investigation into Arthur's death."

Beth returned, looked at Nicholas and said, "we're going to need all the evidence we can get. I just spoke with the Federal Prosecutor's Office. I'm sorry, honey. But obviously Jack's been a busy boy. They've got a grand jury indictment of you Nicholas."

"For what?" Michael demanded to know.

"Conspiracy and obstruction of justice. Now, these are just the non-specific, catch-all terms they use when they're not sure what the hell to do."

"And what's next Beth?" Kerry asked, taking Nicholas' hand in hers.

"They want Nicholas to turn himself in."

"And, I hope you told them fuck no!" said a now seething Michael.

"Actually, I told them fuck yes. They said twenty-four hours. I said forty-eight and they agreed. So, we've got two days guys. My guess is the bad guys don't know what Glen has just told us."

"They also don't know about Arthur's journal," Kerry added.

Beth perked up like a cat smelling the scent of a mouse. "Journal? Arthur's journal? And, when exactly where you two going to share this information with me?"

"Things have been a bit hectic Beth," Kerry added. "But we got it from Helen earlier this evening."

Nicholas added, "Kerry figured out that the email I got from Arthur just before he died may have had a meaning. She was right."

The telephone rang, cutting the tension. Beth answered in her best down home Southern drawl. "Harding residence.

Why of course, just a minute," she mouthed to Nicholas. "It's Jack O'Connor, put it on speaker."

Nicholas nodded okay. "Hi Jack, what's up?"

"Sorry to bother you Nicky, but Gerry Michael's here also and we have some bad news. This FDA/U.S. Marshal's Office investigation thing; we don't know what the hell's going on Nick, but we just got word that the feds are going to announce an indictment tomorrow. I don't know how to say this Nick, but they're going to indict you, son."

After a moment's silence Nicholas asked, "Indict me for what?"

Gerry answered, "they said conspiracy and obstruction of justice. Something to do with the Tanaka deal. Sounds like a fishing expedition to me. We'll straighten it out Nicholas. But I suggest you hire your own counsel."

"I have to ask you this Nicky," O'Connor said, sounding distinguished. "Is there anything to this?"

"No Jack."

"I didn't think so, but I had to ask. Now don't you worry. We're family, Nick, and we take care of our own. We'll fix this. But in the meantime, I think it's best if you not come into the office. Officially, you're going to have to be suspended, with pay of course. But that's just the official party line, until we can fix this mess, Nick. Okay?"

"Sure Jack, whatever you say."

"Good. You hang in there, son. We'll be in touch. Good bye."

"Anyone else feel like they need a shower?" Beth asked.

"I'm glad I'm not a member of his family."

"You know," Beth added." Old Jack-O may have over played his hand. Tomorrow night; Don's house. Glen, you stay here where it's safe."

Without a word Nicholas left and went upstairs. Michael nodded for Kerry to go after him. She grabbed the two boxes of evidence and followed Nicholas.

"Glen," Michael said. "The security team will set you up down stairs. The third door on your left."

"Sure, thanks. Good night."

Michael turned to Beth, "you going up?"

"Not yet. I have some calls to make."

"Beth," he said before he left the room. "I know you enjoy this cloak and dagger stuff, but this isn't a game, don't play with my brother's life. Got it?"

"Got it, Michael. See you tomorrow."

"Oh God, did you hear that!" O'Connor said to Gerry, laughing uncontrollably. "I crack myself up. You know Gerry, that's one of my biggest strengths: the ability to sound compassionate while fucking someone up the ass. Get it?"

"I got it Jack. Let's just make sure we don't overdo it. Nicholas isn't stupid."

"No, he's not stupid, but you know what about old Nicky? He's just like his mentor, that pussy, Arthur. When push comes to shove? No balls. Have a drink with me, Gerry?" Jack asked.

Gerry looked at Jack like he was some sort of alien life form, "this isn't what I signed on for, Jack. Art's dead, Yoshi Mikasi from Tanaka dead, Nicholas is probably going to jail and we're talking about starting a clinical trial with a known toxin. We're supposed to be an 'ethical' pharmaceutical company. But I don't feel very ethical now."

Jack turned to face Gerry, his own face a furious red. "Now don't you go pussy on me too, Gerry. Yoshi Mikasi from Tanaka was stupid and Art was weak. And as for our clinical trial of MR-548, we're never going to put that crap in people. The feds are going to find out it's poison and the Tanaka data falsified. They'll think that Nicholas and that Asori guy at Tanaka were behind the whole thing. God knows we've got enough false data trails to lead them down that road. And as for what you signed on for, Mr. Lawyer boy, don't you go getting moral on me. You signed on for what everyone else did, boy. Good ole fashioned goddamned American money! I offered you the chance to be a fucking millionaire 50 times over and you took it. So if you want to cry in your milk, go do it some fucking place else.

"But you better make damn sure this goes as planned with Harding in a fucking federal prison and me as head of Marshall Pharmaceutical. Got it?"

"Yeah, good night Jack," Gerry said as he left Jack's office.

When they got into upstairs Kerry saw that her luggage had already been brought up and placed in the guest room next to Nicholas', but she joined him in his room. It was a large master bedroom with the sitting alcove off to the side. It had two large his-and-hers walk-in closets; the one that had been Paula's now empty. The bathroom had marble tiling and counters with his-and-her vanities, a large whirlpool tub and shower that easily fit three.

"Do you have someplace I can secure these files, Art's journal and Glen's notebook? They're evidence now," Kerry asked.

"Here," Nicholas replied, opening a door in the alcove to reveal a five-foot high replica of an old Wells Fargo gun safe. He turned the dial to unlock and opened the heavy door.

Kerry looked at the safe, then at Nicholas. "You're odd, you know."

"So I've been told."

"How the hell did you get that up here? It must weigh a ton."

"Fifteen hundred pounds actually, and the movers got it up here somehow after I had the floor re-enforced to bear the weight. Here's the combination."

"Thanks," she said, placing the two evidence files in the safe. Looking around the large room she asked, "so, this is your lair?"

"No, it's my bedroom," he answered. "My study, the library downstairs, which you've seen, is my lair. Make yourself at home."

Kerry sat in a leather chair in the alcove.

"I'm sorry Nick. Sometimes life sucks, right?"

Nicholas awoke at 2:30 AM. He went down to his study to make a call. The call lasted for almost an hour. Just as he ended the call, the door to his study opened and Beth came in dressed in a flowing white silk dressing gown.

"Don't you sleep?" he asked.

"I was about to ask you the same thing. The call?"

"Asori."

"Thought so," she said. So what's the story over there?"

"The shit's hit the fan over there. The U.S. Federal Prosecutor's Office has requested information from Tanaka to assist them in the Marshall investigation. The Koseysho –

their FDA – has impounded all data related to MR-548. Asori said he expects to be suspended indefinitely pending the outcome of the investigation."

"Hum," she said, sitting down across from Nicholas in a deep leather chair. "Tell me something I don't get."

"I thought you got everything, Beth."

"Almost, but I need a little help with this one."

"Okay, I'll try."

"Jack O'Connor. I understand what he's doing and I understand how, but I don't quite get the why. I mean I know he'll come out with control of Marshall, but there's got to be an easier way to gain control of Marshall or another pharmaceutical company or to gain wealth. Right?"

"Not really. He's already wealthy, so it's not just money for him. He could probably go elsewhere and maybe get a similar or slightly higher position, but it's unlikely he'd get a CEO slot elsewhere and here's the kicker; chances are he'd never get it at Marshall and that knowledge probably eats him alive. He looks at Grant and sees a dumb pretty-boy. Don, he sees a pampered spoiled rich brat. And he's jealous."

"But if he's so much brighter than Grant and everyone else why can't he get the CEO slot the old fashioned way?"

"Because he doesn't have something that Grant, Don and people like that have. Call it charm, people skills, charisma – whatever. To get a top slot like that you've got to have some degree of these traits. It's not enough to have the biggest brain. You've got to be able to get some really bright people to follow your lead. Jack has the personality of a rabid hyena. He'd have trouble getting people to follow him out of a burning building. He's gone as far as his talents can take him. So, bottom line, there's no way he'd ever be considered for the top job.

"But now, by putting the company in jeopardy and appearing to save it, he figures they'll have no choice, especially after the stock tanks and he and his cronies buy up enough interest to gain control of the board. It's a messy plan, but it can work."

"I wouldn't bet on it," Beth said.

"And who were you on the phone with?"

"Thomas Sinclair."

"At 2:30 in the morning? Why?"

"You'll see soon enough. Go to bed Nicholas," she said, rising from the deep leather chair. "The next few days are going to be rough. Besides, there's a lovely young woman upstairs who, from the way she looks at you, I think kind of likes you. Why are you down here talking to this old bird? What's going on with you two?"

"Don't know yet. And I have a fondness for old birds," He said as he kissed her on the cheek.

"Um huh, if I was twenty years younger honey," she said.

Nicholas went upstairs, slid into his bed, and fell asleep.

33

The Feds

Investigator Barry Keenan sat outside the Inspector General's Office, fidgeting nervously and anxious. Barry hadn't slept well. He'd received an anonymous email yesterday.

To:	bkeenan@usmar.gov
From:	?
Subject:	Future

Bend over Barry. Ken's about to fuck you up the ass!

Agent Beverly Coston had gone to the Inspector General's Office with her suspicions regarding Barry Keenan and the Marshall Pharmaceutical investigation. It wasn't much to go on, but the IG decided to question Keenan. Often just the intimidation factor of being called into the IG's Office for questioning was enough to get people to say more than they should. And Barry didn't let them down.

Barry wasn't the sharpest knife in the drawer or in the whole damn kitchen for that matter. The email plus being called to the IG's Office for questioning spooked him into a frenzy. It didn't take long before he was telling the Assistant IG everything he knew. The A-IG had to actually stop the questioning and inform Barry of his rights and tell him that he had the right to have an attorney present for any further questioning. But Barry was so frightened that he just kept babbling.

Unfortunately, Barry didn't have a lot of real information. He'd only dealt with Ken Joseph and only knew vaguely of Jack O'Connor. But having been convinced by the email that Ken was going to screw him, he tried his best to screw Ken by giving the A-IG as much dirt on Ken as possible.

Nicholas awoke early and showered. Kerry knocked and entered his room.

"And, where are you going so early, young man?" she asked.

"I have to go by the office."

"Nick," she said, "Jack told you to stay away from the office, remember?"

"I just have to pick up some things and see Karen. Then I have to run into New York for lunch. I'll be back mid-afternoon. Meet me here?"

"You're leaving now? And, what's in New York?"

"Not what, who. A friend of Paula's is a writer for the *Wall Street Journal*. I'm meeting her for an early lunch to see if this story interests her."

"You're digging deep in your little bag of tricks. Is she pretty?"

"As for my bag of tricks I'm at rock bottom. As for Leslie's looks, she's gorgeous."

"And, should I be jealous?" Kerry asked, now a tad beyond pissed.

"You already are and you're so cute when you're jealous."

She now blushed. "Puppies are cute. You didn't answer the question."

"Oh, yeah. Should you be jealous of Leslie? Ah, no. Yes, she's gorgeous and all, but truth be told, even though we still haven't had that date yet. I'm sort of hung up on you."

Kerry's blush turned into a smile.

"And, gorgeous though she may be, I'm just not her type. She's a lesbian. But she would love you."

"Nick?"

"Yeah hon?"

"Get what you need and get out. Don't play around with O'Connor and Joseph."

Downstairs, Nicholas grabbed a pear and expected to be out of the house before anyone saw him. He turned to go toward the garage door and ran into Beth, who was up, dressed and ready for anything.

"Don't you sleep?"

"You've already asked me that once this morning. And the answer is no. I'm pumped on adrenaline."

"Good for you," Nicholas said attempting to step around her.

"And you would be going where this fine morning, my dear?"

"Is white the only color you wear?" Nicholas asked, looking at Beth, who was in another white pantsuit with an Eisenhower waist-jacket.

"Yes. And don't change the subject. Your destination?"

"Is there a meaning to the white wardrobe? I have to drop by my office to pick up some things and see Karen. I won't be long," Nicholas replied, still attempting, rather unsuccessfully, to get by Beth.

"Let's save the discussion of my fashion style for some time when we need chit-chat. As for your going to your office, not a good idea. You'll recall that your boss, the Great Satan, told you that you were suspended and to stay away?"

"Fuck him."

"You know how much I hate it when you Ph.D. types use those big sophisticated terms." This got a slight smile out of Nicholas. "This isn't a good idea, honey" She added.

"I'll only be a few minutes – no trouble."

"Well, if you insist on going, then take one of the boys for protection."

"A bodyguard? I don't think so."

"Okay, then I'll go with you?"

"You're going to protect me?"

"The chances of them killing you in front of your lawyer are pretty slim. You choose: the muscle or me? But you're not going alone."

"Okay, if that's my choice. You. I figure you're better company. Let's go."

At the office, Nicholas explained the basics of what had happened to Karen. It was difficult, since they had to take turns writing questions and answers on a notepad for fear of electronic listening devices. Nicholas told Karen to take the rest of the week off and she agreed to meet him at Don's that night. Beth had gone into Nicholas' office and was sitting in a corner reading a book. Nicholas went through his desk and picked up a few items when he heard someone enter the outer office and looked up.

"You shouldn't be here. I thought we agreed you wouldn't come in. You're on suspension, remember?"

"Oh shit Gerry," Nicholas said sarcastically as Gerry Michael walked into his office. "You know, I'd forgotten all about that. I just have to pick up a few things. I won't be long."

"I'm sorry about all this Nicholas, but I think you need to leave now," as Gerry spoke very sincerely, he gently touched Nicholas' arm. It was the physical contact, not so much by Gerry, but by one of Jack's surrogates that infuriated Nicholas the most. Nicholas was always soft spoken at work, never yelled or lost his temper. Always in control. Gerry also had a couple of inches height on Nicholas. So, when Nicholas roughly removed Gerry's hand, put his own right hand solidly against Gerry's chest pushing him into a wall, then quickly slid his right hand up and took a firm grasp around Gerry's neck, Gerry's first reaction was shock and disbelief, then some fear. Gerry had yet to realize that a third person was in the room. Beth, all in white, was hidden by the glare of the sun. And at this point Gerry was concerned that Nicholas may actually physically harm him.

"Or what, Gerry?" Nicholas hissed, his hand firmly around Gerry's neck, squeezing, and his face inches from Gerry's. "What's going to happen if I don't leave now? You going to plant more evidence? You going to threaten my family again?"

"You're choking me! And I don't know what you're talking about!"

"You disappoint me Gerry," Nicholas went on. "I didn't expect any better from Jack. He's a fucking turd, but you, you know better, Gerry."

Nicholas released his grip on Gerry and he fell to the floor, gasping for air.

"You're fucking crazy, Harding! You're going to get exactly what's coming to you," he said, slowly getting to his feet and attempting to walk past Nicholas.

When Gerry was close enough, Nicholas pushed him hard with both hands in his center chest. The force of the push actually lifted Gerry slightly and forced him back into a bookshelf where he fell again. "Why don't you tell me Gerry, exactly what's coming to me? You must know. You and Jack have planned this whole thing."

The shove into the bookshelf and fall had hurt and Gerry was now furious. He rose with every intention of hitting Nicholas, when he heard a voice say, "I have to tell you, if you strike my client, that's assault and battery."

Gerry, thinking it was only the two men in the room, was momentarily startled. He looked towards the voice into the glare and saw Beth.

"Beth Cowling," she said. "Dr. Harding's attorney. Looks like he needs one right about now, just before you assault him."

Gerry glared at Beth and then at Nicholas, then said, "then I assume you saw him shove me across the fucking room, twice!"

"Um, afraid I missed that part, Gerry. I was reading my book. I'm at the part where I just can't put it down. But I assure you that you now have my undivided attention, so if you'd like to strike my client please proceed."

"Fuck both of you," he said heading towards the door. "If you're not out of here in ten minutes I'll have security throw you both out. And you just remember what I said, Harding."

When Gerry was gone Beth turned to Nicholas and said, "you boys and your testosterone. You see now why you needed a baby sitter?"

"Thanks Beth. Let's go." Nicholas turned off the light and looked back into his office, wondering if he'd see it again or if his next office would have bars.

They drove to the Morristown train station and purchased two roundtrip tickets on the mid-town direct train that would take them into Penn Station in Manhattan. They had about twenty minutes before the next train that would put them in

NY at 10:00 AM. The weather was nice and it wasn't too cool, so they waited outside on the platform, walking down away from the station office to be away from the crowds.

"So, who's this big city writer we're going to meet?" Beth asked after looking around to make sure no one was too close.

"Leslie George. She went to law school with Paula."

"She's a lawyer?"

"Yep, well, sort of. She finished Princeton, passed the bar and then got a job with *the Wall Street Journal*. Never practiced law a day. Actually she free lances, but writes mostly for the *Journal*.

"What kind of stuff does she write?"

"Investigative reporting type stuff; financial. You know, some big bad guy is fucking some innocent little guy up the ass – yada, yada, yada."

"Sounds familiar. You think she'll be interested in this story?"

"I know she will. I've been communicating with her for several weeks. And it was when I told her the part about Paula which sealed it. She wants Jack-O's balls on a platter almost as much as I do."

Beth stared at Nicholas.

"What?"

"You're full of surprises aren't you? Anything else you haven't told me?"

"Nothing comes to mind at the moment. Train's here."

Most of the rush hour commuters were gone and they had a one hour ride into the city. They found seats with no one near them as the train slowly moved towards New York.

"Beth," Nicholas said.

"Yes, honey?"

"You seem to know almost everything there is to know about me, but I don't know much about you."

"So, you're curious about the old bird? Ask away dear. But if you get too personal, I may have to smack you," she said with a smile.

"Did you ever re-marry? I mean, you were still young when your husband died."

"No. It never quite worked out. You see I was content, no, it may be hard to believe, but I was actually happy to just be his wife. But once he was gone I wanted more. I wanted to be me, not an extension of someone else. To go to law school, start my own practice. And I guess in the South most old boys didn't want me, they wanted a wife. But that part of me died when my husband died. Besides, you have to admit, I'd be a handful for a man, wouldn't I, honey?"

"You're still an attractive woman, Beth, and you're not old."

"You know, forget that twenty years younger thing, if you weren't my best friend's boy I'd take you on anyway. But I guess that would be too weird, huh?" she said with a chuckle.

"Yeah, too weird."

"Besides, I like Kerry. She's okay. Don't blow it."

"Yes ma'am. Judging from your New York buddies, all your connections aren't in the South. So what gives with the New York ex-military/ex-spy buds?"

"A girl's got to keep some secrets, Nicky," she said with a wink. "So, I've had a few lovers come and go. Some better than others. Some asked me to marry them. Fools. But no one I could be me with, you know?"

"Yeah. You don't talk about your daughter much," Nicholas said.

"So?"

"Well, I know she finished Harvard Law. You must be very proud of her."

"Hum, my only spawn, Riva."

"Pretty name. Where is she now?"

"She's with a prestigious law firm clawing her way to the top. My sympathy to whoever gets in her way. Riva is, let me see – how can I say this – a ruthless, heartless, cold bitch."

Nicholas looked at Beth. She returned his look, smiled and patted his hand. "It's okay honey. I've gotten used to it and I accept it. It's part of the price of being me. Everything has a price, Nicholas. Riva was sort of a lost soul after her daddy died. She was a daddy's girl, big time. She and I were never that close. And let's say the South and Riva were like oil and water. The week after her high school graduation she high-tailed it out of there and probably hasn't been back more than five or six times since. She did her undergraduate work at George Washington, then Harvard Law."

"Well, I can't say that I'm a big fan of the South either," Nicholas added.

"I know honey, but Riva's embarrassed by the fact that she's from the South and her 'good ole boy ma'ma' – well that was just too much.

"Nicholas," She went on. "Do you know that when most people hear a Southern accent, they unconsciously or consciously knock off ten to fifteen IQ points?"

"Um, and they add ten to fifteen if they hear a British accent," he said with a smile.

"Damn right," she said laughing. "So when they see this old white-haired gal all decked out in white, looking and sounding like Colonel Sanders' little sister, how serious do you think they take me?"

"Not very, Beth."

"That's right, sugar. And they let their guard down. And by the time they figure out I'm just a snake without rattles I've got my fangs about two inches in their jugular."

"I'm glad you're on my team. You and I we have a lot in common, Beth Cowling."

"So, where's this prestigious firm Riva's with?"

"Why, New York, darling. And no, I haven't seen her since I've been here. Riva and I get along best when we keep our distance."

"Maybe you're too much alike."

"Maybe, maybe," she said as she turned to look out at the New Jersey landscape as it rushed by.

Arriving at Penn Station at around 10:00 AM, they exited on 36th Street, got their orientation and headed uptown on foot. It was turning into a lovely late spring day, mid-50s and sunny. A nice day for a walk in Manhattan.

"I've always loved New York," Beth said looking up and soaking up the sun and atmosphere. "My husband first brought me here on our honeymoon. After that I had two loves, him and New York."

"So, why haven't you moved up here?" Nicholas asked, pulling out his dark sunglasses as they walked down the crowded street.

"I still like the South too. Felt at home there, but who knows? I was part-serious when I said I may stay after this is all over."

"Mom would like that," Nicholas said. "And so would I, Beth."

"We must make quite the picture," She said hooking her arm under his. "Me in my flowing white outfit and you all dapper as usual. Hey. You think people will think I'm some rich old New York broad and you're my kept young stud?"

Nicholas laughed. "God, you're something else Beth Cowling. We have got to find you a man."

"So, where are we meeting your writer friend?"

"Don't know."

"So, where are we going?"

Nicholas reached inside his jacket pocket and pulled out his cell phone. "I'm to call her and find out," he placed the call and spoke briefly. "Okay – the Grand Hyatt, room 1437. It's a few more blocks. You game for a walk?"

"Lead on honey," she said, taking his arm again.

They entered the large cavernous lobby of the Grand Hyatt on 43rd Street. An upscale hotel existing a block away from the homeless of Grand Central Station, it was a quick ride up the elevator to the 14th floor. Nicholas knocked and the door opened quickly. Expecting a small New York hotel room, they walked into the foyer of a spacious suite.

"Leslie," Nicholas said as he hugged the woman standing before them.

"Nicholas, it's good to see you again."

"Leslie George – Beth Cowling. Beth's my attorney that I told you about."

The two women shook hands, probably sizing each other up.

Leslie was fashion model beautiful. Tall, slim, face framed by long curly auburn hair. In fact, she had modeled just enough to make ends meet in college and law school. She probably could have done exceptionally well, but had no interest in a career based solely on transient physical attributes.

"Come on in and have a seat," she said as she led them into the suite to a sitting area.

"I see the *Journal* is treating you well," Nicholas said, removing his jacket.

"Not bad," Leslie said. "I had some snacks brought up if you're hungry. Nicholas, bring me up to speed on where you stand."

Nicholas spent the next hour telling Leslie everything that had occurred in the past few weeks, ending with the expected indictment.

"Good," she said nibbling on a carrot as he finished.

"Good? That's not quite the response I expected."

"Probably not," said Leslie. "But here's why. Based on what you gave me a few weeks ago Nicholas, I started digging myself. So far, I don't have enough to run a story on my own. The indictment would give me an angle to work with."

"Glad I could help," Nicholas said, sipping a bottle of mineral water.

"It's complicated, Nicholas," Leslie went on. "Whoever's behind this isn't stupid. They've covered their trails well. And if Jack O'Connor is the brain behind this, well, he's the wizard behind the curtain, because he's kept his hands clean in all this. If anything, what I dug up points to Grant Michner and Catherine Sullivan as ringleaders here. Takada's a harder nut to crack, and they're doing a good job of setting up your friend Asori, but it looks like the new CEO is in on it there."

"Ah, may I ask a question?" Beth said tentatively.

"Of course," Leslie replied.

"Well, I'm just a country lawyer and all, so I don't know how these big city newspaper things work. The question I have is when the indictment is public, will you publish an article and if so, what will be the tone of that article? If you don't mind my asking," Beth purred with the sweetest little smile.

Leslie smiled, and then quickly lost the smile. "You can drop the cornpone Barney Fife routine, Counselor. I've done my homework on you too. You're one of the sharpest, low key, legal minds around. And, someone who's argued successfully before the U.S. Supreme Court and worked with the National Security Agency knows exactly what's what. Okay?"

"You never told me you argued before the Supreme Court and the fucking NSA! What gives?" Nicholas half whispered.

"You never asked, dear," she replied. "And, Ms. George, your comments notwithstanding, my questions as to the existence and tone of your article is of immediate import to my client. Do I need to repeat it?" Beth was now done pouring on the Southern charm.

Nicholas looked at the two women. "If this is some girl lawyer-to-lawyer pissing match, can we save it for later? And can you two call each other Beth and Leslie and drop the 'Ms.' and 'counselor' shit? We are on the same team, aren't we?"

"Yes, we are Nicholas," Leslie replied. "And Beth, yes, I've gotten the go-ahead from my editor. There will be an article. It has to wait until after the indictment. The tone will be that although Nicholas has been indicted, things may not be what they seem. That this could be part of a larger scheme to gain control of a major U.S. Pharmaceutical house and there are international implications. I can't use names at this point. But that should deflect some of the heat off you, Nicholas, and onto others."

"Thanks Leslie," Nicholas said solemnly.

"Hey, I'm just going where the facts go. You mentioned new evidence that you've come up with in the last couple of days. Can you share it?"

Nicholas looked over at Beth, who nodded her agreement. "Don't use it without clearing it with us," she said.

"I deal only with Nicholas. No offense," Leslie replied.

"None taken. Do you agree?"

"Yes."

"We found a journal kept by Arthur Kronan. It details the whole plan and players."

"That's not evidence. It's his word against theirs."

"We know," Beth added. "But, it will give the investigators leads."

Nicholas added. "We also have some real hard scientific data that MR-548 isn't what it's purported to be."

"Both of these will be turned over to federal and local prosecutors as soon as the indictment officially drops," said Beth.

Nicholas rose and walked across the rose-colored carpet to look out the window. It was hard to see down to the street, but the sun had been obscured by clouds and everything appeared gray.

"So," he said. "Now it's a matter of who gets their story out first."

"That's a lot of it Nicholas," Leslie replied. "No doubt the indictment, vague though it may be, will hurt you. But if we can shift some of the focus back on the bad guys – that's in our favor. Especially if they're not expecting the focus. This is more than a one column article on page eight of the *Journal*. It'll get picked up by all the newswires and internet news services. I'm feeding it to a buddy of mine at *Fox Business News*. Once the indictment is issued, they'll expect all the attention to focus on you. They won't be expecting this type of attention on them. It'll scare them and they'll make mistakes. It'll also indirectly put pressures on the prosecutors to look beyond you."

"Think it'll work?" Nicholas asked.

"I don't know Nicholas," Leslie replied, "but it's all I can do."

"And, do you mind my asking you why?" Beth asked Leslie.

"Why what?"

"Why you're doing all this? Is it just the story?"

"You have to admit, it's a hell of a story. A small clique, including reps of a Japanese company, are trying to forcefully take control of a U.S. pharmaceutical house and do so illegally, breaking all sorts of federal laws, framing innocent people, maybe even murder. Hell yeah, it's a great story. But there are a lot of great stories out there.

"Paula was my friend in law school. Or as close as either of us let anyone come to being our friend. But we seemed to understand each other. If these people did anything to hurt her, they've made an enemy out of me. Reason enough?"

"Yep," Beth answered.

"Let's have lunch," Leslie said. "We can wrap-up while we eat. I'll order room service. Any requests?"

"Surprise us," Nicholas replied.

After a light lunch and discussion of a few odds and ends the three agreed to keep in touch. The trigger for the article would be the indictment. They parted unceremoniously and Nicholas and Beth walked back to Penn Station to catch a 3:00 mid-town direct return to Morristown.

On the ride back on an even more deserted early afternoon train, Beth commented to Nicholas, "she doesn't look like a lesbian."

"What?" he said, being pulled out of some distant thought.

"Leslie. You said she was a lesbian, but she doesn't look like one."

"You mean she doesn't look butch. What's your point?"

"No point. I'm just trying to make conversation, since you haven't said a word since we boarded the train. Penny for your thoughts?"

"Haven't you heard of inflation?" he said with a slight smile. "I was just thinking. I know this will sound weird, but this all seems a bit too easy."

"Easy? You lost me there kiddo."

"Well, Beth," he said turning towards her. "This whole conspiracy thing. We're supposed to just turn over everything we have to the feds and they'll say, 'Oh my God, we've made a huge mistake Dr. Harding. You're free to go and we'll just run right out and arrest Jack and his pals'. Is that how it's supposed to work? Jack's evil, not stupid!"

"Hell, I'd settle for that," she replied with a chuckle. "But I wouldn't bet on it going that way. You're right; Jack-O's not stupid. But I doubt they anticipated all the dirt we've dug up. Remember he pointed you to DCC for counsel. They'd recommend you plead out. It may not seem like much, but my boys in NY have dug up dirt on Jack that he probably didn't think possible."

"That's not what I meant Beth. I know all the work you've done and I appreciate it, really."

She patted his knee. "I know son. Believe me we're far from out of the woods yet. When we take all our information to the feds, here are the options I see.

"One: they say, 'nice try,' and indict you anyway.

"Two: they say, 'okay, we'll investigate others, but we'll indict you anyway.'

"Three: they say, 'hell, you're all lying, so we'll indict all of you and let the courts sort it out' (that's what I'd do by the way)."Or four: they'll hold up the indictment until they can investigate further – which is what I'll request."

"And what's your bet on which one they take?"

"I don't gamble honey. We'll see."

After a few moments silence, Beth asked Nicholas, "do you think he would have gone through with it?"

"Who?"

"Jack. Taking MR-548 into a Phase II clinical trial knowing it would hurt people. I mean we have enough information to block that now. But if we didn't, is Jack that ruthless?"

"The short answer is yes. But first off, we don't know exactly how much Jack's gang really knows about MR-548; how bad it really is. Also, yes Jack's that bad, but I don't know if he could have gotten the others to go that far. Lying, cheating and stealing are one thing, but maiming and killing people are another.

"Why?"

"Just sizing up the enemy," she replied.

They arrived in Morristown around 3:00 PM and drove back to Nicholas' house. It was looking crowded as cars belonging to Glen, Beth's security team and Beth were parked neatly to the side. Nicholas didn't see either Michael's car or Kerry's car.

When they entered the house, the security team lead gave them a status report. Michael had gone to his office and would return around 5:00. Sergeant Markus had also gone to her office and said she'd return at 4:00. Glen was downstairs involved with a computer.

"What time are we due at Don's?" Nicholas asked Beth.

"Oh sir," said one of the security agents. "Mr. Marshall called and suggested that you and your party come early, around 6:00 PM, for dinner. The meeting starts at 8:00 PM."

"Good. I'm going to go upstairs, shower and take a nap. I didn't get a lot of sheep last night," he said to Beth.

"Someone in the next room keep you up?" Beth asked mischievously.

"No. I just couldn't sleep, it being my first indictment and all. Smartass," he said as he went upstairs.

Nicholas showered, shaved, put on a robe, closed the drapes in his room, set his alarm for 5:00 PM and quickly fell asleep as soon as he lay down.

He dreamed about a woman who alternated between Paula and Catherine, then morphed into Kerry. In the dream, they were lying on a blanket under a giant tree by a lake in each other's arms.

Nicholas now awake, Kerry kissed him deeply as they rocked together as one.

"I thought this was a dream," he whispered.

"It is," she sighed into his ear. They made love passionately and gently and fucked roughly, alternating; reflecting all the passion from the past few days. Spent, they showered together, – went through Round Two of shower sex, and then lay in each other's arms in bed.

They came downstairs around 5:30 to see Beth and Michael in the family room.

"See," Michael said to Beth. "I told you they were still alive."

"I guess we should call off the search party," she replied.

"Chuckle, chuckle, chuckle, guys," Nicholas said, coming down the staircase.

Beth went on. "Well you two look all rested. I take it you napped and showered well?"

Kerry changed the subject. "What's the agenda for tonight?"

"Don's sending a limousine to take us to his house," Michael answered. "The car should be here soon."

"Who else will be at Don's?" Nicholas asked.

"Us, Glen and one of the dicks," Beth answered and went on, "then the same as before, Don, Karen, Mark, Thomas Sinclair and Stephen Bernard. We'll see if Beverly Coston shows up."

When Nicholas arrived at Don's mansion Andrea greeted him by jumping into his arms.

"Daddy!"

"'Drea bug!" he said hugging her tight. "God, I missed you."

"It's only been a few days, Dad," she said, putting it into perspective. Nicholas' entourage was shown into a parlor and informed by a uniformed servant that Mr. Marshall would be there shortly.

"Where's your Grandma?" he asked Andrea.

"Getting dressed for dinner. Come on, Dad, I'll show you my room," she said pulling him forward.

"I'll be back," he said to the others. Andrea had obviously made herself at home. She led him up a wide dark oak staircase down several long halls to her room. He saw a small suite, about four times the size of 'Drea's room at home, with a fifteen-foot ceiling and windows that overlooked the expansive manicured lawn and a lake. Nicholas saw Rasputin, who opened one eye upon seeing Nicholas, curled up on the bed purring.

"Grandma's next door," she explained. "I have a TV and computer with internet access. We decided to keep Rasputin here. If he had the run of the house, we'd never find him. Plus Don has a lot of antiques. But the chef cooks trout for Rasputin!"

"So, I guess you didn't miss me at all, huh?"

"Yes I did Dad. I love you," she said, not knowing how good it made Nicholas feel to hear that unsolicited comment. A side door opened and Dorothy entered the room.

"Hey Mom, am I going to have to drag you two out of here kicking and screaming when this is over?"

"Well, I must admit, Don has been awful nice to us, but we know where home is, Nicholas. Of course I can't speak for that pile of fur over there, now that he has a chef cooking for him," she said with a laugh.

The three of them stood in the middle of the huge room and hugged.

"Come on, let's go downstairs," Nicholas finally said.

34

Unconditional and Immediate Surrender

During a dinner light in consistency and conversation, Nicholas was pleased to see that 'Drea and Dorothy were adjusting well to their temporary forced exile to Don's estate. They heard, as others began to arrive for the meeting that Don had arranged to have all the participants gathered in a large parlor, which he had arranged as a conference room.

As the dinner broke up, Nicholas pulled Don aside. "Thanks Don."

"For?" he asked.

"Taking in 'Drea and my mother like this. I really appreciate it."

"Say no more. They've been a delight. We're nearing the end Nicholas. Are you ready?" Don asked, leading Nicholas into his library.

"Yes," Nicholas replied firmly.

"I have something to show you," he said, opening an embossed leather binder. Inside was an old sheet of note paper with the handwritten words:

No terms except an unconditional and immediate surrender can be accepted. I propose to move immediately upon your works.

> *Ulysses S. Grant*
> *Major General, U.S. Army*
> *To: General S.B. Buckner*
> *Fort Donelson*
> *February 16, 1862*

Don had moved to a small bar in the library and poured two small glasses of sherry that he now brought over to Nicholas.

"The time has come for us to take the offensive, Nicholas," Don said. "We must move upon their works. To our victory," he said, raising his glass.

"Our victory," Nicholas replied. Then they left to meet with their troops.

Nicholas and Don entered the room seeing the faces from the previous meeting. Nicholas noticed that Dorothy had decided to stick around and quickly scanned the room looking for Beverly Coston. He saw her nibbling on crudités.

"Beverly," he said when he reached her side. "I'm glad you made it."

"I could be fired for being here. In fact, officially, I'm not here. Why didn't you tell me this was Don Marshall's house, good God!"

"I was afraid you wouldn't come."

"Yeah, well if anything smells here, I'm out the door, got it?"

"Got it."

Don tapped his water glass for attention. "Can we all be seated?" He motioned for Nicholas to sit next to him. Don sat at the head of a massive oval mahogany conference table. Nicholas to his right, flanked by Beth, Michael and Kerry. Stephen Bernard and Thomas Sinclair sat to Don's left. Everyone sat and quickly became silent. There was room at the table for all. Each seat was a high back dark brown, deep soft leather executive swivel conference chair.

Don continued. "Good evening and thank you everyone for joining us. I see that our group has grown by three since our last soiree. We're joined by Mr. Glen Morgan of Marshall Pharmaceutical. Welcome, Glen. Ms. Beverly

Coston of the U.S. Food and Drug Administration Field Investigators' Office, who is here in an unofficial capacity. And Ms. Dorothy Harding, Nicholas' mother and advisor."

He went on, "if I may, let me read to you the quote from General Ulysses S. Grant I recently shared with Nicholas." He proceeded to read Grant's ultimatum to Buckner. "The end is in sight. But we must strike boldly and quickly. Counselor," he said turning to Beth, "can you please give us an update on your progress over the past week?"

"My pleasure Don," Beth replied. She chose to push back from the table and pace, her white floor-length dress coat flowing behind her. She turned to face her audience.

"Tomorrow morning at 10:00 AM, Dr. Nicholas Harding and I appear before the a federal prosecutor in Newark to receive an indictment against my client that was handed down two days ago by the federal grand jury for obstruction of justice and conspiracy as it related to the conduct of business at Marshall Pharmaceutical. To our best knowledge, there are no other indictments at this time. Unfortunately," she said, smiling sweetly at Bernard and Sinclair, "I'm unable to discuss my response to the indictment at this time. However–"

Sinclair interrupted in his usual gruff tone. "Unable or unwilling?"

Beth purred, "pick one, Thomas. Either way, I won't discuss my strategy with the grand jury here. You'll have to wait until tomorrow. As I was saying," she continued, "we have made several new and favorable discoveries this week. First, through Detective Markus' efforts we discovered a journal kept by Arthur Kronan that details specifics of the real conspirators: Jack O'Connor and friends. It's only supposition, but it's a first-hand accounting of a party to the crime."

Hearing Arthur described as a 'party to the crime' was disconcerting to Nicholas.

Beth continued. "Second, thanks to Mr. Glen Morgan," She nodded towards Glen, who blushed. "We now have documented evidence that this new drug, MR-548, is not what it's purported to be and in fact exhibits specific and potent toxicities. For the third discovery, Beverly perhaps you can share some of what you know with the group?" she said, turning to Beverly Coston. "For those of you who may not be aware, Ms. Coston is actually part of the investigation and therefore may not be able to share some things with us."

Beverly appeared a bit nervous at the prospect of speaking before a group that included two former U.S. Cabinet Members and a real live billionaire.

"Well," she began, "the investigation into Marshall actually began more than a year ago. We started to receive anonymous tips that there was something odd about the Tanaka deal. Over time, the allegations became more serious; that there were problems with MR-548. That data had been falsified and that a small group at Marshall and Tanaka were conspiring to tank Marshall stock so they could move in and buy up controlling interest. Then references began to come in mentioning Dr. Harding and raising questions about his actions and involvement and a Mr. Asori at Tanaka. We also received documents, emails, faxes, data records, etc. that implicated these men. All the information I collected as head of the investigation went directly to the Federal Prosecutor's Office. But something seemed odd, out of sync, that's when I went to see Dr. Harding several weeks ago."

"But Marshall had officially been informed of the investigation earlier?" Beth asked.

"Months ago. Actually shortly after the investigation opened, Grant Michner, CEO and Marshall's Chief Legal Counsel were informed."

"Which they kept from Nicholas and me," Don added.

"Agent Coston," Thomas Sinclair said, his well-bred Boston Brahman baritone immediately commanding everyone's attention. "Did you or do you know the source of all these 'tips'?"

"At first sir, we weren't sure. We thought it was someone inside Marshall. We questioned the validity and accuracy, but it all seemed accurate."

"This was our third discovery Thomas," Beth added. "Go on honey."

"A U.S. Marshal's office investigator was assigned to the case," Beverly explained. "Barry Keenan. I came to question some of Agent Keenan's actions and raised my concerns to the Inspector General's Office and an assistant in the I.G.'s Office called in Agent Keenan for questioning two days ago for routine follow-up questioning. We really had no specifics on Barry; it was just background. From what I hear, it was an interesting session. It appears that just prior to the I.G. session, Barry received an email implying that someone at Marshall was about to turn on him. So Barry, who by the way is no rocket scientist, decided he'd strike first. Before the Assistant Inspector General even started her questions Barry starts spilling his guts about his involvement in a conspiracy led by someone at Marshall."

"The source of this email?" Nicholas asked, looking at Don, although the question was directed to Beverly. Don raised one eyebrow, Spock-like.

Beverly replied, "we don't know. The I.G. gave Barry his rights and got him a lawyer. But he spilled it good. The problem is his tie back to Marshall was through someone that we think to be an intermediary. We don't think Keenan had any contact with the leaders of the conspiracy."

"Hum," Michael chimed in. "So, based on what you've told us so far, this mental midget Agent Keenan worked through someone other than the top dog, who's to say that Nicholas Harding isn't that top dog of the conspiracy in Marshall?"

"In case anyone doesn't know, that's my little brother, folks," said Nicholas. "Thanks Michael."

"The link back to Marshall?" Beth asked.

"Ken Joseph, Head of Security," Beverly answered.

"Number four," said Beth. "Take it away Kerry."

Nicholas looked at Kerry, somewhat perplexed, not knowing what to expect. Kerry had on a shimmery emerald green blouse, which shifted color and tone like the green flecks in her eyes. Nicholas suspected she'd worn it just to entice him. She also wore a long skirt with a just-respectable slit up one side, which Nicholas was reasonably sure she wore for him. Seated one chair down from Nicholas, with her legs crossed and slightly pushed back from the table, the allure of the slit was having its intended effect on Nicholas.

"For those of you who don't know," she began, "in addition to being on the Morristown Police Department, I'm also assigned to the County Prosecutor's Office. In addition, I'm the lead investigator on the Arthur Kronan case. Ancillary to the Kronan investigation, we started looking into Mr. Joseph. Based on some preliminary findings an Assistant County Prosecutor and I brought Mr. Joseph in for questioning this morning."

Nicholas looked and made eye contact with her. "Did you know about this?" he whispered to Beth.

"Of course I did."

Kerry continued. "There must be a rash of those emails going around. Ken Joseph, who brought his lawyer, mentioned receiving one threatening to put the blame for this on him. He admitted to paying off Barry Keenan, at his boss's request, to manipulate the investigation. He agreed to turn evidence against the conspirators in return for immunity. We worked out a deal with the feds late today. The good news is that Ken will say that he knows nothing of Nicholas being involved with this."

There were smiles and murmurs of congratulations.

"This calls for a drink. Bar break!" said Stephen Bernard. Everyone agreed. The mood and tone of the meeting had shifted for the positive.

"Does this mean I'm off the hook?" he asked Beth.

"We won't know until tomorrow, but this is a biggie – I mean a fucking biggie!"

"Can I see you for a minute?" Nicholas said, gently taking Kerry's arm and leading her to a balcony door. They went out into the cool night air, moved away from the window and he turned to her abruptly. "Two things. First, why didn't you tell me about this?"

"It all happened quickly and I didn't want to get your hopes up if nothing came of it. You have to admit it was quite the surprise, huh? Told you my interrogation skills were good!" she said quite pleased with herself.

"Quite."

"And, the second thing, sir?" she asked, leaning into him and wrapping her arms around his waist.

"Well," he said. "If you must know, I like your outfit."

"That was the plan," she said smilingly.

"You're a wicked woman."

"Think you two can stop flirting long enough to get things started in here?" Beth asked, sticking her head out the door.

"Kerry," Nicholas said as she turned to enter the room.

"Yes," she said facing him.

"Thank you."

"You're welcome Nicholas," she said with a serious look and smile.

Once everyone was re-seated, Kerry resumed.

"I said before that the good news is that Ken says he knows nothing of Nicholas being involved in this. Here's the not so good news. Ken implicates Grant Michner, Catherine Sullivan, Gerry Michel, Arthur Kronan and Akoni Konoru at Tanaka. He swears he knows nothing about Jack O'Connor being involved."

After a few moments of silence Beth asked, "You think he'll stick with that story?"

"If I had to guess, I'd say yeah."

"Why?" asked Don. "Why protect Jack?"

"Again, it's an educated guess," said Kerry. "But I think Ken Joseph is afraid of Jack. And Ken doesn't seem to be the type to scare easily. If that's the case, that Ken's afraid of Jack, than it doesn't bode well for getting anyone else to turn against him either."

"So," said Beth. "Even if we can't nail the captain now, we can sink his good ship lollypop?"

"I'd say yes," said Sullivan. "Should I tell them now?" he asked Don.

Don nodded agreement.

"I conferred with the Secretary of the Treasury, the Chairman of the Securities and Exchange Commission and the Chairman of the New York Stock Exchange yesterday. A halt to trading of Marshall stock will go into effect as soon as the Exchange opens tomorrow."

Don rose and for a moment said nothing, then, "thank you, all of you. Since the Civil War, the days of Ulysses S. Grant, the overarching United States military doctrine has been massive. Overwhelming military force brought to bear against an enemy. The few times we deviated from this doctrine, in Vietnam, Iraq and Afghanistan, the outcome was, let's say, suboptimal. What I've heard here tonight has been the massive and overwhelming force that we will bring against an enemy tomorrow. Nicholas, tomorrow, when you face the federal prosecutor in Beth's able hands I trust you shall prevail. Simultaneously I shall ask the Marshall Board of Directors tomorrow to terminate Catherine and Grant, name Stephen Bernard and Thomas Sullivan in their place and myself as Chairman and Chief Executive Officer. Jack I shall face and ask to resign. Tomorrow we fight the battle and the battle plan is good. Good night."

"Nicholas," Don said pulling him aside as the group dispersed. "I suggest that Andrea and Dorothy remain here for now. Jack remains a dangerous man."

"I agree," Nicholas replied. "Beth can I see you in private for a minute?"

He and Beth went into a small side room. "I don't care if Jack gets away with what he's done to Marshall. No one really got hurt."

"You did."

"I'll get over it. But what about Art and Paula? He has to answer for them."

"I know honey, but none of what I have is admissible."

"So, he gets away with murder?"

"We'll keep trying. But yes, he might Nick," she said, reaching for his hand. "Go home. You have a long day tomorrow."

They exchanged long, painful looks and then he left.

The next morning, Beth's two security boys drove her and Nicholas to the Federal Building in Newark in a black Chevy Suburban that had thick bullet resistant glass and Nicholas suspected was armored. They were admitted to a secure underground garage.

The previous evening Beth had gone over what to expect with Nicholas, Kerry, Michael and Dorothy. They'd all wanted to come, but Beth had vetoed it.

"Will I actually be arrested?" he asked.

"Possibly. But I can quickly arrange a bail hearing. It's going to be rough Nicholas, but you have to trust me. Can you do that?"

"I trust you Beth."

The office of the eastern district federal prosecutor was on the top 11th floor of the federal building. Beth had told Nicholas that it was unlikely he'd be dealing with the Federal Prosecutor himself, but likely a senior level Assistant Prosecutor. She'd also told him in no uncertain terms to let her do all the talking.

The meeting at which Nicholas was to turn himself over to the prosecutor and receive the indictment was scheduled for 10:00, but they'd arrived at 9:00. In the lobby, Beth said, "take a seat and not a word to anyone. I'll be back by 9:45."

To the security detail, she said, "no one gets near him. No one. Clear?"

"Yes ma'am."

"Beth?" Nicholas said.

Before Nicholas could ask where she was going, Beth said without turning around, "trust me honey."

Beth returned promptly at 9:45. "You ready?" she asked.

"I guess."

"Nervous?"

"I passed nervous about an hour ago. I think I'm about to pass out," he said with a weak smile.

"Okay, let's go."

The four of them took the elevator to the 11th floor. They had to get through two security zones, including a metal detector. At the metal detector, Beth turned to the security detail, which were armed to the teeth and said, "you'll have to wait here." The security guards were licensed to carry firearms, but wouldn't be allowed in the last parameter.

Beth and Nicholas were shown into a small conference room. Beth sat and removed files from her large briefcase and arranged them. Nicholas fidgeted. After about five minutes the door opened and three people entered.

It was easy to tell who was in charge. "Good morning Dr. Harding, Ms. Cowling. I'm Assistant U.S. Federal Prosecutor Linda Ellis." Pointing to the two people accompanying her, "this is my colleague Assistant Prosecutor Bill Preston and Lucy Thompson, Recorder." Everyone shook hands like it was just a friendly get together.

The first word that came to Nicholas' mind to describe Linda Ellis was 'severe'. She looked to be about 5'8" tall, dressed to hide the fact that she was a female, in a conservative pin-stripe dress suit, hair pulled taunt in a bun. She appeared to be early-mid thirties and had ambition written all over her. The second word that came to mind was 'ruthless'. Thwarting an attempt to take over a U.S. pharmaceutical house could be a career-making case and

Nicholas suspected that he was just a snack for Linda Ellis. This case was her ticket to the top. And the only thing Nicholas had to protect him from this barracuda was Beth Cowling. Now he'd see if she really had fangs.

Once everyone was seated, Linda Ellis nodded to the recorder who started keying the dictation recorder machine. "Let the record show that we started at 10:07 AM and in attendance are Dr. Nicholas Harding, Vice President, Marshall Pharmaceutical; Ms. Beth Cowling, attorney for Dr. Harding; Bill Preston, Assistant U.S. Federal Prosecutor; Lucy Thompson, Federal Prosecutor's Office and myself, Linda Ellis, Assistant U.S. Federal Prosecutor. Thank you Dr. Harding and Ms. Cowling for coming."

Nicholas hadn't been aware it was an invitation he could have declined.

"Now," she continued. "Let us began our business."

"If you don't mind, by the way, how should I address you?" Beth interrupted in her sweetest, syrupyest Southern drawl. "Is it Assistant Federal Prosecutor Ellis or Assistant United States Prosecutor Ellis or just Ms. Ellis?"

Linda looked at Beth like something she needed to scrape off her shoe bottom. "It's Assistant Prosecutor Ellis and I do mind the interruption, Counselor. Let's not began by playing games. The business at hand is most serious." Linda's last statement was directed at Nicholas. She spoke in an exaggeratedly slow, low tone, with overstated enunciation. The way high level professionals talk when they're pissed off but can't yell. Nicholas could tell that Linda Ellis wanted his head or something lower hanging on her trophy wall something bad.

"Oh," Beth continued, sensing that she was pushing Assistant Prosecutor Ellis' buttons. "I assure the Assistant Prosecutor that I'm not playing a game. I apologize if I've offended you or don't use the correct procedure. Not too many of my clients get indicted by the whole United States government you know?" she smiled at Ellis, whose face showed no emotion whatsoever.

"Then, let's get on with it Counselor," Ellis said slowly with exaggerated calm and politeness. "Now"

Beth interrupted again, "well."

"Listen," Ellis said barely above a whisper. "I don't know how you do things down in Opossumtown, Alabama or wherever you're from, but you need to shut up so we can proceed with your client turning himself over to this office for indictment."

"Well, honey," Beth drawled.

Ellis sat back in her chair and sighed.

"First off, I'm from Carrington, North Carolina, not Opossumtown. Although, I have been to Opossumtown in North Carolina, but that's for another day. And, second off," Beth said calmly as she smoothly slid a folder across the table to Assistant Federal Prosecutor Ellis. "I have here a writ from U.S. District Judge Norma Hollings, ordering the delay of the issuance of an indictment against my client, Dr. Nicholas Harding."

Harding could now practically see steam coming out of Ellis' ears. Now furious she grabbed the folder and opened it. "What the fuck is this shit?" she shouted. "No one told me about this." She looked at her assistant Bill Preston, obviously furious.

The recorder typed her comments.

"Don't type that, you fucking moron. Get out," she yelled at the recorder.

Beth stood. "The recorder leaves and this is no longer an official meeting, and we walk. Your call, Counselor. She stays and records or you can figure out just what that writ means on your own."

Nicholas now saw what Beth meant when she said, "by the time they realize I'm a snake without rattles, I've got my fangs two inches into their jugular."

Beth now had her fangs in Linda Ellis' jugular and was in the process of pumping in the venom. He couldn't help but notice the glee Linda Ellis' colleague, Bill Preston, seemed to be taking in her misery. Ellis was probably one of those over ambitious people who'd managed to piss off nearly everyone she came in contact with.

"Fine," Ellis hissed as she quickly read the writ. "Why wasn't I informed of this beforehand?" she asked to both Beth and Bill Preston.

"I just got it from Judge Hollings thirty minutes ago," Beth replied. "We can go across the hall to her chambers if you want."

"I know where the fuck her goddamn chambers are," Ellis replied having lost any semblance of calm.

"Ms. Ellis," Beth said, dropping the syrupy drawl. "We concede that there's been a conspiracy at Marshall Pharmaceutical. But my client was a victim of, not a part of, said conspiracy. Now, if the Federal Prosecutor's Office's goal is to solve this crime and prosecute those responsible, we can work together. If your goal is simply to fuck over my client, honey – you'll lose. I promise it. And, you'll lose in a very loud and very public forum."

There was silence in the conference room as the two adversaries glared at each other. Ellis, realizing that she'd grossly underestimated her opponent, quickly got over her wounded pride and refocused her energies on her career and how to use this to her advantage.

"The basis of the writ?" she asked.

"Your investigation is incomplete," Beth replied. "It's based largely on information created and provided by the conspirators to frame my client."

"If you're referring to Agent Barry Keenan's confession and statement, we're aware of that."

"And does Agent Keenan make any mention of my client being involved in a conspiracy?"

"No."

"And there is other evidence that your investigation is not aware of," Beth stated.

"Go on," Ellis said.

Beth continued. "We have a journal kept by a member of the conspiracy, Dr. Arthur Kronan. He committed suicide several weeks ago. It's very specific as to the 'who' and the 'what', and no mention of my client. It's evidence in the hands of the Morris County Prosecutor's Office. Here's a copy," she said sliding a large folder across the table.

"We also have the statement and confession of Mr. Ken Joseph of Marshall. Your office was involved in negotiating an immunity deal, so I'm sure you're aware that he confirms that there was no involvement of my client.

"And." Beth said, handing Ellis a CD-ROM disk, "an associate of Dr. Harding's was able to generate conclusive scientific data confirming that MR-548 is not safe to test in humans. The data was generated at Dr. Harding's request at great risk to himself, his family and his colleagues.

"And..."

"There's more?" Ellis asked.

"Yes. The SEC has halted trading of Marshall stock this morning. As we speak, Don Marshall has terminated obviously Ken Joseph, but also Gerry Michael, Chief Counsel; he's asked Catherine Sullivan to resign her position on the Board and Grant Michner to resign as CEO. He's asked Stephen Bernard, former Secretary of Defense and Thomas Sinclair, former Secretary of the Treasury to join the Marshall Board of Directors."

"My apologies and applause, Counselor," Ellis said. "I underestimated you. But you didn't mention Jack O'Connor."

"I'm not aware of evidence linking Jack to the conspiracy."

"Pity."

"Absolutely."

"You realize, Ms. Cowling, that this only delays an indictment against your client pending further investigations?"

"We're confident a thorough investigation will fully clear my client."

"My office will be in touch, Counselor," Ellis said, standing to signal the conclusion of the meeting. She extended her hand to Beth and they shook hands. Then she led the entourage out.

Nicholas turned to Beth. "Is that it? I can go?"

"That's it, kiddo."

"God Beth you're a genius!"

"I won't argue with that," she said as they hugged.

"How'd you get that writ?"

"Norma and I go way back. She's an Opossumtown gal too."

"Chances are that ice bitch Ellis probably would have indicted you anyway."

"And what are the chances she'll try it now?"

"Next to none. She'll never apologize. That type's never wrong. But I expect to receive a brief note in a few days that the indictment's been dropped. Come on," she said, packing her briefcase, "let's get the boys and go home."

The victors met again at Don's house. Glen had begged off, not being comfortable around so many big wigs, but very comfortable in the knowledge that he'd done well. Beverly Coston had gone back to Washington, but didn't expect to have much of a career with F.D.A. left. Don had offered to hire her at Marshall.

Nicholas and Don had spent the afternoon in consultation with Tanaka executives. Akoni Konoru, Chairman, had resigned in disgrace and he and his co-conspirators were about to be indicted. Nicholas and Asori agreed to meet soon for a victory celebration.

Don updated the group on his sessions with Grant and the others. "Grant and Gerry were both fired and escorted off site. Catherine has disappeared. The FBI and European agencies are looking for her."

"My money's on Cath; she's pretty resourceful," Nicholas said.

"You would know," Michael said sarcastically.

"And Jack?" Nicholas asked.

"Denies any involvement. But I told him the board's lost confidence. He steps down in two months."

"That's it?" Michael practically shouted. "Have I missed something here?"

Beth answered, "he's not stupid. There's no evidence to link him to the conspiracy, so unless someone testifies against him, you've got nothing. And it looks like Jack knows how to buy silence."

"Threats?" asked Kerry

"That'd be my guess."

"You trust that snake for two months?" Michael asked.

"No," Don replied. "I'll strip him of all power. He'll just have an office and Roberta."

"Now they deserve each other," Mark added.

"Don," Nicholas said, raising his glass in a toast. "To the new CEO of Marshall Pharmaceutical. Good luck, Don."

"Here, here."

"And, to all of my friends," he said, raising his glass to them.

"So Don," Nicholas said refilling his wineglass. "All the mysterious emails; you sent them, didn't you?"

"Actually, no."

"Yeah, right."

"No, really, I didn't send them.

"Then who did?"

"I did, Dr. Harding," Karen said.

"You?" Nicholas asked with surprise.

"Well, yes, at Don's request."

"How come he's Don and I'm still Dr. Harding?"

"Shall we tell them dear?" Don asked.

"Yes," she said, moving to his side.

"Well, this seems like the appropriate time and place and group," Don said. "Karen and I are engaged to be married."

"And, this has been going on for how long?" Nicholas asked.

"About six months," Don answered.

"Karen, you kept a secret from me," Nicholas said as he walked to her and hugged her. "Congratulations."

"Thank you, Dr. Harding."

"You know Karen, now that you're marrying my boss I think you can call me Nicholas," They all laughed.

"Congratulations, Don," the two men shook hands.

"But why the emails?"

"Well, Nicholas, I didn't know whether I could trust you. Remember, the early evidence suggested you were part of the bad guys."

"I told you he was good, yes?" Karen said.

"Yes, you did, dear," said Don.

"Thank you Karen. I'm glad someone around here had faith in me."

"So," Mark asked. "Who really was in charge of the conspiracy, Jack or Catherine?"

"Who knows?" said Beth. "They both probably thought they were and eventually would have turned on each other."

"Nicholas," Don said. "With Jack out of the picture, I'm going to need someone to take over R&D."

"I'll send the names of some top executive head hunters to your office."

"That's not what I had in mind. I want you to run R&D, Nicholas."

"You're kidding, right? Don – that's way over my head."

"I disagree, Nicholas, and I need people I can trust."

"I'll think about it."

"Fair enough. Well, I think I'm going to call it a day. There's room for everyone who wants to stay over and you're all invited."

Most decided to stay. Andrea and Dorothy were staying one more night.

Nicholas pulled Kerry aside. "Hey, wanna spend the night here?"

"No thanks. Can we go back to my place instead?"

"Sure, but why?"

"I want you all to myself tonight."

"I could look in your eyes forever," he said, watching the dance of the green flecks.

When they entered her townhouse that night, without turning any lights on, she took him by the hand and led him to her bedroom.

Nicholas awoke the next morning to an empty bed and after a moment realized where he was. He heard sounds in the kitchen and, making a toga out of a sheet, covered himself and went out.

"Hey, I'm making you breakfast in bed," she said upon seeing him enter the room. He hugged her from behind and nuzzled her ear.

"Check out the paper," she said.

The Wall Street Journal headlines blared, "Halt to Trading of Marshall Pharmaceutical stock, Corporate Intrigue and Conspiracy, Indictments Pending"

"Holly shit! Page one."

The article was by Leslie, who'd obviously been in touch with Beth and outlined the whole conspiracy and named names.

"How long do you think it'll take to straighten this out?" she asked.

"Months."

"Nicholas, Beth told me everything Jack's done. Are you going to be okay if he gets off?"

"As long as he's out of my life, I'll be fine."

"Why aren't you at work?" he asked.

"I took the day off, and your excuse?" she asked with a smile.

After breakfast, they showered and went back to bed, where they spent the rest of the day. Talking, holding each other in silence and making love. It was the best day Nicholas had in many months.

35

Nicholas and Jack

After two weeks everyone was slowly getting back to normal. 'Drea, Dorothy and Rasputin were home back in their routines.

"I got official word today from Ms. Ellis, Assistant Federal Prosecutor. The indictment against you has been dropped. It's over Nicholas," Beth said as they sat in Nicholas' study.

"Thanks Beth – for everything. What are you going to do now?"

"Well, a couple of days off for shopping in the Big City, then it's back to Opossumtown for the ole bird. But just temporary. I've decided to buy a place in New York or New Jersey. I have to wrap up some things down south and look for a place up here."

"You're always welcome here Beth, always."

"I know honey. What about you?"

"'Drea, Michael and I are going up to the lake cabin for a couple of weeks next week."

"Did you give Don an answer about the job, Jack's old job?"

"Yeah. I told him I'd take it for one year to help him get things straight and find a replacement, and then I'm out."

"You're leaving Marshall?"

"I'm leaving the industry period. I've made my point and proved everything I had to prove to myself."

"Good for you Nicholas. What'll you do?"

"Michael and I have talked about starting our own business, so here's our chance."

"You'll do fine. You do everything fine. Now, more important, what about you and the lovely Detective Sergeant Markus? "

"We'll see."

"Do you love her?"

"We'll see."

"Well, then don't wait too long to see, honey, or you'll lose it."

"Yes ma'am.

"Oh, by the way here," he said. "It came today. I heard from Cath."

"What?"

"I got a letter from Cath. Says she loves me and would have protected me. You know what; I wouldn't be surprised if they never found her."

"I'll send it to the feds. And, I think you're right."

Nicholas was acting as head of R&D, but Jack was physically still in his old office. Nicholas remained in his, or Art's old office, and Karen decided to stay with him through his remaining year, even though she was engaged to marry a billionaire – go figure.

Nicholas and Jack hadn't seen each other since everything had ended. Nicholas had been avoiding him, but Jack asked to see him early that morning. They'd agreed to meet in Jack's office at 7:00 AM; it was far too early for Roberta to be in.

In the past couple of weeks she'd been not too quietly trying to peddle her services to other executives and no one would touch her. She'd even approached Nicholas as acting head of R&D and he'd made it clear her staying on with him was not an option.

Nicholas knocked and entered Jack's inner office and closed the door behind him, then headed to the conference table. Jack joined him with his cup of Coke, sat down and sighed.

"Nicholas, Nicholas," he said, placing his hands on the back of his head, propping his feet up on his table and smiling. "What are we going to do? What the fuck are we going to do? Huh?"

The two men starred at each other. "How about you call the Federal Prosecutor and turn yourself in?" Nicholas said softly.

"Hum, let me think about that – fuck no!" he said, laughing loudly.

"If I go down, you go down boy! And, I do mean 'boy' in the most derogatory way, you God damn son-of-a-bitch. You think I still can't drag you down? Think again," he was fuming now.

"Three years. I planned this for three Goddamn years and you fucked it up. Some Goddamn coon fucked up my plan."

"Nice to finally see the real you, Jack. How do you know I'm not taping all this?" Nicholas asked calmly.

"Tape away, asshole," he replied. "You see that?" He said, pointing to an antennae-looking piece of abstract art. "That moron, Ken Joseph, hooked it up for me. One of the few things that idiot did right. Know what it is?"

Nicholas surmised Jack had started the morning with a couple of screwdrivers. All the better.

"It's an electromagnetic pulse generator. Any taping device, audio or video, picks up nothing but static, so I hope the hell you are wired, boy."

"So, it's just you and me huh, Jack? How does it feel to be brought down by a nigger?" Nicholas said, taunting Jack.

"You haven't done fuck, you dick!" he slurred. "And, if that asshole Don Marshall hadn't interfered, it would have worked. I would own Marshall Pharmaceutical. Every last bit of it and," he said with a twisted smile, "you'd be in jail. That last one I just might be able to still pull off.

"You know your Jew boy Kronan was going to sell you down the drain? But he chicken-shitted out and blew his Goddamn brains out. No great loss."

"So, you caused my friend to kill himself and almost sent me to prison," Nicholas said calmly. "Can I go now Jack? I have a new job now, you know."

Jack's complexion was flushed and clammy. "Go? Hell no, we haven't finished our little chat, boy. Let's not forget my fucking your wife and having her killed. Not much of a lay by the way," by now he could hardly control his laughing, which turned into a coughing fit. "And, you call yourself a man. You're a pathetic little nigger pussy boy, you know that!" he spat, then drinking more Coke to calm his coughing.

"So, why shouldn't I just go to the authorities and turn you in?" Nicholas asked, looking Jack in his now red eyes.

Jack smiled the smile of evil that was his true self. He spoke slowly in a hoarse voice. "Because if you do, I still have enough of the fake evidence to drag you down, maybe even get you some time in a federal penn. So then that little baby darkie girl of yours with her dead mammy will have to be raised by her old grand mammy while you rot in jail for nothing. You're a Goddamn pussy boy!" he said in a fit of coughing.

"Satori."

"What? What the fuck are you talking about?"

"Satori, Jack. It's a Japanese term. The moment of sudden enlightenment."

"And, what the fuck are you enlightened about, boy?"

"Not me, you, Jack. Are you okay, Jack?"

"I'm fine, fucker," he said, his speech slurred and his eyes now glazy.

Nicholas stood up and went to sit next to Jack. "Jack!" Nicholas now shook him. "Listen to me! Your breathing is getting more difficult and you'll be slightly paralyzed soon. Your heart is starting to palpitate. Try to relax. Don't fight it." Nicholas looked into Jack's cup to see it was almost empty.

"You p-poisoned me!" he coughed as he tried to reach for the phone, but couldn't lift his hand.

"You made my friend commit suicide, you raped my wife and had her killed, you tried to send me to prison and then, you sick fuck, you threatened my daughter! No Jack, I didn't poison you. I killed you, you prick!"

Jack made eye contact with Nicholas just as the pupils of his eyes started to dilate and he started to twitch and gag.

Nicholas pushed Jack's chair over, so he was lying on the floor. He kneeled over Jack and put his mouth to Jack's ear and said. "Are you enlightened now Jack? Rest in Hell!"

Nicholas then reached into his jacket pocket, pulled out a pair of latex gloves and put them on. He took Jack's cup of Coke and poured the remaining contents into the toilet in the office bathroom.

He then pulled a large heavy mesh polypropylene sac from another pocket and placed the cup in the bag. He wrapped the bag in a towel and stepped on it to break it into small pieces. He then double bagged the broken cup and put it in his pocket.

He took another clean cup off a shelf, returned to the now unconscious Jack and wrapped his hands around it to get his fingerprints all over it, put it to Jack's mouth to get his saliva on it and poured a small amount of Coke into the cup.

Nicholas thoroughly searched Jack's office for any other electronic devices using the scanner Beth had given him. Satisfied there were none, he then made sure everything was cleaned up and then walked to Jack's toilet and threw up.

After cleaning the bathroom again, he sat at the conference table and calmly did a crossword puzzle he had in his pocket for about 20 minutes. He checked Jack's pulse. He had none.

Taking a handkerchief, he covered Jack's mouth and forced air into his lungs vigorously and then performed CPR chest compressions on Jack until he heard a crack of a rib. Nicholas then called the internal Marshall emergency number to request help for Jack's apparent heart attack.

36

After the Storm

Nicholas, 'Drea and Michael had spent a week at a lake front cabin that Nicholas and Michael owned. The three Hardings bonded after the recent months of chaos in their lives.

One morning while 'Drea was sleeping in the two brothers sat on the porch watching the sunrise. "Something you want to ask me about Jack, Michael?"

"Nope."

"You're sure?"

"You know why we're so close, Nick?"

"Because we have the same parents?"

"Hell no, a lot of siblings aren't that close. It's because we accept each other for what we are, good, bad or indifferent. We don't criticize each other, pass judgment on each other. God knows there are enough folks out there to do that. We just accept, support and love each other, warts and all."

"Now I know a lot of folks think it's awfully convenient old Jack-O dropping dead of a heart attack like that right in front of you. And, some are saying that you being a toxicologist – a poison doc – maybe, just maybe you found a way to help old Jack exit this earth. You certainly had a motive."

Nicholas looked in his brother's eyes. "And, what does Michael say?"

He sat up and returned Nicholas' glaze. "Michael says whatever happened in that room is between you, Jack and your soul. Michael's okay with whatever happened."

"Thanks Michael."

"What now?"

"The full autopsy report – they ran a tox screen – will be available when we get back."

"And, it'll show? Do we need Beth back?"

"It'll show Jack O'Connor died of a sudden massive myocardial infarction, a heart attack. No more, no less. But that's not my concern. Jack's gone. It's the aftermath of all this." The cabin sat on the shore of a mid-sized silvery lake, all alone surrounded by woods. Nicholas rose and looked out over the lake. "'Drea seems okay, but I worry about her."

"She's a good, strong kid. She'll be fine. Maybe she's the only one who went through this mess and is."

"It's not fair she has to grow up without a mother, Mike. Whatever problems Paula and I had, she was a good mom to 'Drea."

"Kerry would make a good mom," Michael ventured.

"You think so, huh?"

"Yes. Do you love her?"

"Maybe."

"You think she loves you?"

"Don't know. Things are happening too fast."

"So?"

"I believe she thinks I killed Jack. No, she doesn't know whether I killed Jack and that's even worse."

"She said that?" Michael asked.

"No, but she avoided me before we came up here. Things were awkward. I don't know, Michael. Timing's everything and this may not be our time. Maybe we burned too hot, too fast. We'll see when I get back."

"And you and Mom?" Michael asked.

"Pretty obvious wasn't it? The way she avoided being in the same room with me. Mom's a righteous person. I do believe our mother thinks I'm a murderer."

"I know Beth talked to her before they left."

"Yeah, but Mom will decide for herself."

Michael rose to stand by Nicholas, looking over the lake. "It's been quite the spring, bro. It's going to take time to get over it all," he said, putting his arm around Nicholas.

"Do you think we ever will?" Nicholas asked. "Five years, ten years from now; how will we look back on this?"

"Another challenge for the Harding family that we met."

"You believe that?" Nicholas asked.

"No, but it sounds good, doesn't it?" Michael said smiling.

"There's a lot of evil out there, Michael. You were right. I should have packed up and gone to play somewhere else. I had to have that vice presidency, but I didn't know the cost."

"I know, but there's some good out there too. Try to hold onto some."

"I'm trying, bro, I'm trying."

"Hey, let's wake up the little bug and get in another day of fishing before we go home."

Nicholas and Kerry had made plans for a date at the Black Horse Inn in Mendham the evening of his return from the lake.

The Black Horse was originally an 18th century stagecoach and stable in George Washington's day. Now it was a very quaint and quiet, upscale northern New Jersey restaurant.

Dorothy had gone to North Carolina with Beth and hadn't returned.

He arrived at Kerry's house around 6:00 PM. She opened the door and his first response was, "Wow!"

Kerry stepped back and twirled around. She wore a green sweater that matched the green specs in her brown eyes with a tan leather mini-skirt. "You like?"

Nicholas stepped inside and she twirled into his arms. "I like a lot," he said as they kissed deeply. "God, I missed you. I feel like I've been off in the wilderness for a year and my woman's greeting me on my return."

She laughed softly. "You beast. Did you bring me the head of a moose or something?"

"Sorry, big game hunter, I'm not."

"That's okay. I missed you, Nicholas," she whispered in his ear.

When Nicholas and Kerry returned from Mendham and walked into her house, he took her in his arms and they danced cheek-to-cheek, as only new lovers can.

A while later they ended up in bed, where they made love and fell asleep in each other's arms.

After they'd showered and dressed the next morning, Nicholas helped Kerry clean up. They sat at the dining room table drinking orange juice, looking into each other's eyes.

"I think I love you, Kerry Markus."

"I know."

"We spent the entire evening together and didn't mention anything that's happened for the last three months."

"I know."

"We have to talk about it sometime."

"I know, Nicholas."

"Your conversational skills are amazing," he said with a slight smile.

She looked at him, took a deep breath and said, "The results of Jack O'Connor's autopsy report came back a couple of days ago." She stood and walked into the living room and curled up in a corner of the sofa like a cat.

"Really?" he said, sitting on the opposite end of the sofa. "Am I talking to my lover or a police sergeant? Do I need a lawyer?"

"I don't deserve that," she replied sharply. "You know I would never do anything to compromise or hurt you. I've stood by you through this whole mess, Nicholas."

"I'm sorry," he said. "The results?"

"Death by natural causes, a heart attack. Tox screen was clean."

"But? Do I hear a 'but'?"

"But nothing. Now it's over," she said.

"I sense not. Is there something you want to ask me Kerry?"

"No," she said firmly. "I would never do that."

"But Kerry," he said, reaching for her hand. "There's some piece of you that isn't sure whether I killed Jack O'Connor."

She pulled away and rose to go to another chair. "Damn it Nicholas! I don't know what to think. I do know you had every right to hate O'Connor and want him dead after what he did to you and to your family. Maybe it's not you, it's me." A tear rolled down her cheek.

He rose to come to her, but she said, "don't! Maybe, Nicholas, I'm afraid that if you did – and I don't think you did- but if you did that I'd still love you. And, what does that say about me, about who and what I am?

"I do love you, Nicholas," she said as others joined the first tear. "I love you so much, sweetheart. I never thought it possible to feel like this. All this week I didn't know how this would go – last night and today. I didn't know if I'd breakup with you or ask you to marry me. That's how much I love you Nicholas. It would make things a lot easier if you told me now that you don't love me," she said with a half-smile.

"I can't help you there Kerry," he knelt by Kerry and took her hand to his mouth and gently kissed it. "I love you Kerry. So, you're going to have to decide."

The two lovers, now secure in their love for each other, held each other and cried.

It was dark when Nicholas arrived home. He looked in on 'Drea. Sat in her room and watched her sleep, then softly kissed her. He went down to his study, poured a drink and still in the dark, opened the thick drapes to let in the stars and moonlight. He sat on the floor looking out into the night sky and softly cried.

"I thought you might come in here," he heard Dorothy say. She'd been sitting in one of the deep leather armchairs, unseen to Nicholas. He quickly wiped the tears from his eyes. She walked over to him, threw several pillows on the floor and said, "help me get down there."

She sat next to him and took a sip of his brandy. "Hum, the hard stuff."

They both sat in silence for a few moments.

"A man sitting in the dark crying after a big date usually isn't a good sign. What happened?"

"Oh, we decided to either get married or breakup. We broke up."

"I'm sorry, Nicholas. Kerry's a good woman."

"Yeah. We decided to give it some time and space. She's taking a leave of absence to study for the bar."

"Do you love each other?"

"Yeah."

"So why wait."

"The same reason you've been avoiding me lately."

"Oh – that."

"Yeah – that. Are you going to leave me too?"

"I don't know how to ask you this son." Nicholas could barely see in the shadows that his mother was crying.

"Well, we're a pathetic pair sitting here in the dark crying," he said. "You know there are some things a mother should probably never ask a child, Mom. Never."

"You sound like Beth. I don't know what to do, Nicholas."

"Do you love me Mom?"

"Yes."

"Would anything ever change that?"

"No."

"Then, why don't we leave it at that? Don't ask."

In the dark room looking out over the New Jersey woods as the trees swayed in the night breeze, creating shadows of moonlight, Nicholas and his mother sat starring out in to the night. He cried for Paula, the lost love and opportunity and what she did for him. He cried for Kerry, the love that could have been. But tonight when Nicholas Harding finally cried, he cried most of all for himself – for the part of Nicholas Harding that he'd killed when he killed Jack O'Connor.

But he knew that tomorrow the tears would be gone.

About the Author

Bill Powers worked in pharmaceutical R&D (Johnson & Johnson) for 26 years, rising to the position of Vice President of Global Preclinical Development. In various management roles, Bill led groups of scientists in the US, Europe and Asia; administered multi-million dollar budgets and was instrumental in the successful development of several marketed pharmaceutical products.

He has a Ph.D. in Toxicology and is a Diplomat of the American Board of Toxicology. He has published numerous abstracts, articles and book chapters on various topics in toxicology. Bill has traveled extensively in the US, Europe and Asia, leading research groups in Belgium and Mumbai, India. He is married, has one adult child and one brother.

Bill's love of words and books started in childhood, stimulated by parents who were both teachers. A voracious reader, he enjoys both fiction (R. Pearson, S. White, J. Patterson, H. Coben, D. Baldacci, S. Berry, etc.) and biographies (Lincoln, Grant, T. Roosevelt, J.P. Morgan, etc.). Now that he has moved away from his industrial career, he plans to aggressively pursue his passion of becoming a published fictional author.

Connect with Bill Powers

Social Media

Facebook: https://www.facebook.com/AuthorBillPowers

Twitter: http://www.twitter.com/AuthorBillPower

Blog and Websites

Wordpress Blog: http://authorbillpowers.wordpress.com

Website: http://www.bill-powers.org

Purchase Bill Powers title at:

DonnaInk Publications: http://www.donnaink.org.

Donnalnk Publications, L.L.C.
www.donnaink.org